Blood Runs Cold

Alex Barclay lives in County Cork, Ireland. She is the writer of two other bestselling thrillers, *Darkhouse* and *The Caller*.

For more information on Alex Barclay visit www.alexbarclay.co.uk

Also by Alex Barclay

ALEX BARCLAY

Blood Runs Cold

HARPER

Harper
An Imprint of HarperCollins*Publishers*
77–85 Fulham Palace Road,
Hammersmith, London W6 8JB

www.harpercollins.co.uk

This paperback edition 2008
2

First published in Great Britain by
HarperCollins 2008

Copyright © Alex Barclay 2008

Alex Barclay asserts the moral right to
be identified as the author of this work

A catalogue record for this book is
available from the British Library

ISBN: 978-0-00-726844-3

Set in Meridien by Palimpsest Book Production Limited,
Grangemouth, Stirlingshire

Printed and bound in Great Britain by
Clays Ltd, St Ives plc

Mixed Sources
Product group from well-managed
forests and other controlled sources
www.fsc.org Cert no. SW-COC-1806
© 1996 Forest Stewardship Council

FSC is a non-profit international organisation established
to promote the responsible management of the world's forests.
Products carrying the FSC label are independently certified
to assure consumers that they come from forests that are managed
to meet the social, economic and ecological needs
of present and future generations.

Find out more about HarperCollins and the environment at
www.harpercollins.co.uk/green

For Sue Booth-Forbes

Prologue

In the lights of the police cruisers, her face was a strobing image of pain and fear. But she was still, to the child in her arms, a haven. She ran as fast as her violated body would allow, pressing his head to her cheek, his hair soaking up their sweat, blood, spit, tears. A terrible, ruined stench rose from them in the damp heat.

She staggered on, flinching at the stones and branches underfoot, her shoes long lost, too beautiful for the night. The trees swayed toward them and away, and when they gave enough shelter, she stopped. She prised the tiny hands from around her neck, breaking the dead-man's grip of a seven-year-old boy. She tried to smile as she lowered him to the ground. Black pinpricks of gravel shone from her lips.

'Do not make a sound,' she said. 'Not a sound.' Her voice was edged in nicotine.

The boy quickly clamped his arms around her legs. She shoved him sharply backwards, away from her wounds. He fell hard. She watched without feeling. He got up and moved toward her again, tears streaming down his face.

'No,' she hissed, shaking her head. 'No.'

She crouched down. 'You have to hide, OK?' She pointed to the scrub close by. 'Go. I'll be right here.' She squeezed his hand as she released it.

He did as she said. She moved a few steps forward into a clearing, cracking the forest floor. Her face was in darkness. But in the faint glow of a flashlight, relief swept over her features; a picture, flashing like a warning.

The man walked from the trees. He looked at his wife – bloodied and soiled, her hand gripping her ripped-open blouse in what dignity she could find. She slumped against him, the sounds she made raw and disturbing.

The little boy watched.

> *As I was walking up the stair*
> *I met a man who wasn't there*
> *He wasn't there again today*
> *I wish, I wish he'd stay away*

'*Mira*, Domenica,' said the man. Look.

Domenica turned to where she had run from.

Beyond the trees, a fire raged and smoke filled the sky. She was transfixed.

'Hellfire,' she said.

But her eyes shone with something more than flames.

PART ONE

1

Rifle, Colorado

Jean Transom woke to the glow of her desk lamp and the feeling that someone had laid a trail of explosives under her world while she slept. Two work files lay in front of her – brown manila folders, the pages inside clean, neat and annotated. The top file held no photographs, but was open on a drawing – a basic floor plan, the benign geometry of rectangles and circles and squares coming together on a page to represent a space that had been so malignant. Jean inhaled deeply, but what followed was a broken breath. She pressed her hands on the desk and stood up.

She took a shower, rubbing a bar of soap briskly over her body under the hot jets. She dressed in a white shirt, tan tapered pants and soft leather shoes.

'Come here, baby,' she said, smiling as she walked

into the kitchen. She hunkered down and reached out a hand. 'Come here, McGraw, you sweet little boy.'

The shiny black cat stared her down.

'That's why it's called a catwalk, isn't it?' she said. 'You know how to move, don't you? And you know how to look at me like you are fabulous and I am not. But I can be fabulous, you'd be surprised to hear. Yes I can.' She laughed as he turned his back, raised his tail, and made his way slowly to his bed in the corner.

'Lazy, baby,' said Jean. 'I have a lazy man living in my house. And if you're not going to talk to me . . .' She reached over and turned on her old black stereo. For a few seconds, Jean Transom sang along to the music, gently and off-key.

She ate her breakfast – oatmeal, honey and fruit. She filled the dishwasher, wiped down the counters and folded the tea towel by the sink.

As she walked out of the kitchen, carrying a cup of decaf back to her office, pain and sorrow swelled again inside her. Everyone is born with places to hide secrets; mind, heart and body. A family can spread the burden along the branches of its trees; some shatter in the storm, others survive the most relentless assaults.

She sat down at her desk and stared at the diagram – years old, preserved in plastic, drawn in blues and greens by a child's determined hand. It was a diagram that Jean Transom could trust, a child she knew had screamed in the night with the visions. She put it in her work file and went into the hallway.

Her hand shook as she picked up her purse and pulled out her FBI creds. She snapped them on to the right inside breast pocket of her jacket and walked out the door.

Golden, Colorado

Ren Bryce woke to white porcelain and the feeling that someone had laid her free weights on her head while she slept. She reached a hand up to take them away, but her knuckles hit the underside of the toilet bowl. She opened her eyes wider and saw splashes of what had surged from her stomach at four a.m. Red wine. She rolled on to her back. Her blue dress, beautiful and complimented twelve hours earlier, was open to the waist, limp and stained. She turned her head slowly and saw her stockings in the corner by the toilet brush. She closed her eyes again.

She dragged herself slowly upright and was soon hanging over the bowl, heaving nothing, but hit with the smell of her previous efforts. She retched until silver stars burst before her eyes. She hauled herself standing and turned on the shower, spending ten minutes washing her hair and body with six different products.

From her bedroom, her iPod alarm exploded full volume with Dropkick Murphys.

Let's finish these drinks and be gone for the night
Cos I'm more than a handful you'll see
So kiss me, I'm shitfaced . . .

Ren jumped from the shower and ran naked to turn down the volume. She dried herself with a towel from the floor, then threw on pink lace boy shorts, a matching bra, a black fitted shirt, black bootleg pants and black heels. She walked past her dressing table, a wave of nausea sweeping over her at the thought of makeup. But she gave in. Her day was already going to be bad.

She grabbed a clip with one hand, twisted her wet hair with the other and pinned it up. She sat down at the mirror and moisturized in slow motion. Her face was a blank canvas; dark skin, pale green eyes, high cheekbones. Somewhere in her past, there was Iroquois blood. She dragged her makeup toward her and applied a calm surface to the choppy waters.

Vincent was downstairs on the sofa reading the paper.

'Hi,' said Ren.

'Appropriate song choice.' His voice was flat.

'Yes,' she said. 'Sorry about the volume.'

'The volume?' said Vincent, looking up.

Ren stared at him from across the room.

'Is that it?' he said.

'Is what it?' said Ren.

'Have you nothing to say for yourself?'

Ren kept walking into the kitchen. She poured a mug of black coffee.

Vincent came in behind her. 'Can you explain your behavior at least?'

'OK,' said Ren, turning around, 'you've just used three sentences – in a row – that my mom used to say to me when I was, like, seventeen.'

'Stop with the whole mom thing.'

'Yeah, well, it's true. That's what you sound like. I'm sick of listening to you treat me –'

'No, no, no. *I'm* sick. Of all of this.'

Ren opened her mouth.

'Listen to yourself,' said Vincent. 'You are thirty-six years old and you sound like a child.'

'Fuck you,' said Ren.

Vincent held up his finger. 'I can't do this any more,' he said. 'You were way out of line last night.'

Ren put her hands to her ears. 'Shut up. I don't want to know.'

He pulled her hands gently away. 'I know you don't. But you went ballistic.' He shook his head. 'I tried everything.'

Ren remembered the start of the evening, her nice dress, her perfect makeup, her pinned-back hair, Vincent's smile when he saw her walk down the stairs.

'Did you see a work file around here anywhere?' she said. 'Did you tidy anything away?'

'No, I didn't.'

'Shit.' She put her mug down and strode around the living room, opening drawers and lifting up cushions. 'Shit.'

'It's not there, OK? I cleaned the entire place this morning. Can we talk about last night?' He was close to grabbing her wrist.

Ren glanced at her watch. 'Shit. Sorry. I just don't have the time.'

'Tonight?' she called after her as she ran into the hall.

'No,' said Vincent, following her. 'No.'

'OK. What did I do last night?' she said, turning to him. 'Tell me.'

'It was more what you said.'

'I was drunk. It doesn't count.'

'Yes it does,' said Vincent.

'Jesus, why can't you just get that I say things I don't mean when I'm drunk?'

'Because it hurts, Ren. It fucking hurts, OK?'

'But if you know what I'm saying is not true, how can it hurt you? I mean, that's like me getting offended because you call me, I don't know . . . something I'm totally not.'

'Great, Ren. We've been over this before. You have a very simple way of looking at it. You think you can say what you like to me and I'll be fine. But what happens is you totally hook me into your bullshit. You are so convincing. The way you say everything, I believe you. It's like every time, you're having an epiphany.'

'Well, if you know it's every time, why don't you ignore it?'

'For Christ's sake, Ren, that's just not how it works. Do you even remember what you said to me last night?'

Ren said nothing.

'Well, at least I'm seeing the glow of pre-emptive shame,' said Vincent.

'That's mean.'

'Try this for mean: "Vincent, you're dull is your problem. You're conservative and stifling. You want me to be someone else. You can't accept who I am. You stand there, you righteous prick, and try and tell me what to do? Fuck you, Vince. Fuck you, because you have no idea how to live. None. You court the sameness of life because it is safe. And you like safe." All this, Ren, because I refused to buy the drunken lady here another vodka.'

Ren paused. 'Well, it's not like you are the most spontaneous guy in the world.'

'Oh my God,' said Vincent. 'See? This is what I mean! This is why I believe you! Because in all sobriety, however many hours later, even *you* find the truth in what you were saying. At the same time as trying to claim you were drunk and senseless.'

'I *was* senseless.'

'What, but now you see the merit in your ramblings? Oh God, how many times have I had this conversation with you? It is so fucking painful.' He stabbed a finger her way. '*This* is dull, Ren. This. You accuse me of being dull –'

'Get some perspective –'

'Me? Me? Jesus Christ. That's it. I've had it. I can*not* do this any more. I can't. I give up.'

'What do you mean, you give up?'

'Exactly that. I'm out of here. I've had too much of Ren Noir.'

She tried to smile. 'You like Ren Noir. She keeps things interesting.'

'Right now? I think she's a bitch.'

Tears welled in Ren's eyes.

'And,' said Vincent, 'I'm all out of sympathy.' He walked up to her and kissed her on the head. 'Look after yourself. I won't be here when you get home.'

Ren stared at his back as he walked away through the living room. *Fuck him.*

Her hand shook as she picked up her purse and pulled out her FBI creds. She snapped them on to the right inside breast pocket of her jacket and walked out the door.

2

Downstairs at Eric's was dark, packed and loud. The hallway was filled with kids in snow boots and giant parkas pounding pinball machines. By the entrance to the restaurant, two groups of schoolgirls stood hanging from each others' shoulders, waiting for a table. Half of them were Abercrombied, the other half Fitched. Inside, skinny blondes too old for braids leaned against the wall by the kitchen, flashing the restaurant logo on the backs of their T-shirts: *Downstairs at Eric's: Because Everywhere Else Just Sucks*.

Sheriff Bob Gage sat with a beer in one hand and a clean fork in the other.

'Damn, where is my pizza?'

'On a little yellow piece of paper,' said Mike Delaney.

'Hours from registering on my weighing scales.'

Mike rolled his eyes. 'Can forty-six-year-old men be body dysmorphic?'

'If I knew what that was, I'd love to tell you,' said Bob.

'You know – when you see yourself different to how everyone else sees you. Like *you*, for example, think you're fatter than you actually are.'

'Really? Are you kidding me?'

'No,' said Mike. 'You're a reasonably tall guy, Bob. You can carry a few extra pounds.'

Bob gave him a side-glance. Mike used to be a tanned, blond ski bum. Now, at thirty-eight, he was a tanned, blond, ski-bum Undersheriff, his eyes always a little red, his skin a little burnt, his lips pale from sunblock. Bob had choirboy styling – polished skin, neat side-parted brown hair, conservative clothes – but it couldn't quite hide the crazy. Most women were attracted to both of them, for different reasons.

The first night they worked together, they'd gone on a domestic violence call-out and the woman had told them she'd like to be 'wined and dined with you, Sheriff, so's you could laugh me right into bed with your pal, blondie, here.' Bob had looked at her and said, 'Didn't Blondie sing "I'm gonna getcha"? Yeah, well, gotcha! And probably gotcha for another twenty years for beating the shit out of that poor husband of yours.' She had looked at him and said, 'I would never lay a finger on you, cutie. Can you smell my breath?

It's Wintergreen. Winter in my mouth, but summer in my heart.'

Bob had shot a glance at Mike. 'What you have is Seasonal Affective Disorder,' he said, struggling to cuff her.

She made a grab for Mike's crotch, but he blocked it at the last minute.

'Yes,' Bob said, 'you're clearly very SAD.'

A waitress walked toward them, raising, then lowering Bob's hopes.

'I have not eaten since breakfast,' he said to Mike. 'I shouldn't feel bad about this.' He raised his cellphone, showing Mike a screen that told him Bob had fifteen missed calls or messages. 'Do you see this shit?' said Bob. 'Half an hour I want – of peace – after everything. Just thirty minutes.'

The Summit County Sheriff's Office shared a building with the jail and the courthouse. A riot had stolen his previous three hours.

'You need to keep some beef jerky in your drawer, some trail mix, anything,' said Mike.

'Gross,' said Bob.

Mike started to speak, but both their phones began to vibrate. The calls were from Dispatch.

'Look, let me take mine at least,' said Mike. 'Something is going on.' He pressed the Answer key and held the phone to his ear.

'Mike Delaney,' he said, then paused. Bob could hear a woman's voice talking quickly at the other end. Mike gestured to a waitress for her notepad. He scribbled across the page, nodding as he wrote. 'OK,' he said finally. 'Me and Bob will be along right away.' He hung up.

'No, no, no,' said Bob. 'Bob doesn't like "along".'

'Ooh,' said Mike, 'Bob is about to go up a mountain on the coldest January day Breckenridge has seen in about fifty years.'

'Oh, dear God, no,' said Bob, checking his watch. 'It's three fifteen. I'm almost home and dry. Why?'

'Search and Rescue got an anonymous tip-off. It all sounded a little bullshitty to them, but they checked it out and, sure enough, they found a body.'

'What?'

Mike nodded.

'Holy shit,' said Bob, his eyes wide. Mike turned around to where Bob was staring.

'It's my pizza!' Bob grabbed the waitress's arm. 'In a box, sweetheart. And I love you right now. You have no idea.'

Quandary Peak could breathe with the breath it stole from your lungs. Stony and chiseled, it could turn on you before you had the chance to conquer it. The sky overhead showered unpredictable snow and rain, beamed surprise sun. Two-hundred-year-old miners' cabins hid in the lodgepole pines that marked the timberline before the peak grew bare and rocky up to its full 14,265 feet.

On its south side, Blue Lakes Road stretched two and a half miles off Highway 9 to meet it. In winter, it was plowed halfway. A small group of Search and Rescue volunteers stood by the trailhead sign, like a spread from a North Face commercial. Others sat in their 4x4s, gunning their heating against the outside minus sixteen. They all had different day jobs, but came together every Wednesday night to train for Search and Rescue. They were twenty-two to sixty-two, high-energy, wired and bold.

An empty Ford 150 was the last vehicle in the line. It belonged to the Summit County Coroner, Denis Lasco, aka – depending on who you talked to – the Slowmobile, Heavy D, or Corpses Maximus.

'Can you believe the Slowmobile got here before we did?' said Bob.

'He was probably looking for a place to hibernate,' said Mike.

'With a mouthful of nuts,' said Bob.

'Lasco couldn't keep anything in his mouth without swallowing it.'

'That's pretty shitty,' said Bob. 'He's probably got a gladur thing.'

'It's glandular,' said Mike.

'No – gladur,' said Bob. 'Glad you're full, refrigerator, glad you're full.'

They cracked up.

'Right,' said Mike, 'we're going to have to step out of the vehicle.'

'Ugh,' said Bob. 'You first.'

One of the volunteers walked toward them as they got out of the Jeep.

'Hey, Sheriff, Undersheriff,' he said.

'Hello, Sonny,' said Bob. 'Mike, this is Sonny Bryant. His father, Harve, and me go way back. I've known Sonny nineteen years or, as the tired saying goes, since he was in diapers.'

'Yeah, I'm over them now,' said Sonny, smiling.

'They'll come back around,' said Bob. 'It's like fashion trends. I'm only a few seasons away from them myself.'

Sonny and Mike laughed.

'Good to meet you,' said Mike, shaking Sonny's hand.

'You too, sir,' said Sonny.

'What have we got?' said Bob.

'There's a body up there, all right,' said Sonny.

'Man, woman, child . . .?' said Bob.

'I don't think I'm allowed to say,' said Sonny. 'Mr Lasco . . .'

Bob rolled his eyes. 'Let me guess: wouldn't let you commit.'

Sonny smiled shyly. 'Yes.'

'He's some piece of work,' said Bob. 'Is he up there alone?'

Sonny nodded. 'Yes, he went up with a team of three and sent them back down once he knew where he was going. He said he hates people trampling his scenes.'

'That is too true,' said Bob. 'And too repeated. Soon, the day will come when Lasco won't even allow himself into a crime scene.'

Sonny laughed. 'OK, I'm going to take you up there,' he said. 'Are you both coming?'

'Sadly, yes,' said Bob.

'Should take about an hour,' said Sonny. 'We need to get going – that sun is starting to heat up.'

Denis Lasco was standing by the body with his back to them. He was dressed in a giant sapphire-blue parka and green ski pants. His head was bent over his digital camera. He half-glanced over his shoulder when he heard their footsteps in the snow.

'You all need to stand back,' he said, raising a hand.

'Jesus, Lasco, we're frickin' miles away,' said Bob.

'This accident slash murder could have *happened* miles away,' said Lasco.

'Hackles,' said Bob loudly, 'are the erectile hairs on the back of an animal's neck, particularly a dog. For the purposes of the moment, I am a dog. And it appears that, yes, I can confirm, my hackles are up.'

'Professionalism,' said Lasco loudly, 'is the art of performing one's job to the highest possible standards. For the purposes of this moment and all moments, I am a professional. And it appears that, yes, I can confirm, this is what makes me a grown-up and the sheriff a jealous baby.'

'America's Biggest Loser,' said Bob, loudly, 'is a –'

Lasco went rigid.

'All right, all right,' said Mike. 'That's enough of that. We can come closer, Denis, right?'

'Sure you can,' said Lasco. 'I've taken my wide shots from where you're standing, so just walk in my tracks.'

Bob muttered to Mike. 'Yeah, they're deep enough to leave a lasting impression on the landscape.'

3

Her face was masked in a layer of clear ice. Her warm, dying breath had melted the snow that covered her. The carbon dioxide she exhaled had no place to go except back into her lungs. She was wedged from the chest down into the snow. She was zipped into a maroon ski jacket with white stripes down the arms. A navy blue Quiksilver hat covered her head. The angle of her neck was not an angle for the living.

Lasco crouched down to the eerie eyes of the body, wide open, their frozen silver centers sparkling in the sun; a cruel trick of nature.

'Pupils fixed and dilated,' said Lasco. He stood up. 'I love saying that.'

'So,' said Bob, pointing, 'the glass-mask tells me she was buried alive, but how come her hat is still on? An avalanche would have ripped that right off her, right?' He turned to Mike.

'I guess so.'

'Depends,' said Lasco.

'You are a commitment-phobe,' said Bob.

'It's written into our contract,' said Lasco. 'Commitment comes back and bites you in the ass.'

Thirty feet back, Sonny Bryant stood beside the split stretcher he had assembled, ready to transport the body down to the trailhead. Lasco sent Bob and Mike over to join him and stayed with the body, taking the GPS co-ordinates and sketching a map of the crime scene.

'What do you think happened to her?' said Sonny, nodding in their direction.

'Wood poisoning?' said Bob. Wood poisoning was skier versus tree.

'Could there be some skis buried under there?' said Sonny.

'Who knows?' said Mike. 'I've given up speculating. I'm always wrong.'

'Come on, speculate,' said Bob. 'Make something up.'

Mike shifted from one foot to the other. 'Corpses Maximus said no guesses. It plants things in people's heads.'

'Nothing gets planted in this head,' said Bob. 'Nothing at all.'

Mike and Sonny laughed.

The wind rose, whipping around them, fighting

their balance. Mike and Bob had their back to it, buffering Sonny from the worst.

'Hey,' shouted Sonny, pointing to a figure higher up the peak.

Bob shook his head. 'Same idiots, different season. You could paper Breck with "Get off the mountain by midday or we will shoot to kill" and these people would still not get out of their beds in time to haul ass.'

Lasco didn't hear him and was waving from where he stood, holding something in the air, fighting to be heard over Bob and the wind.

'Oh, shit,' said Sonny. He lunged through the gap between Bob and Mike, lifting his spotting scope to his eye. He saw a man on back-country skis, moving east–west across a snowfield. Bob, Sonny and Mike stood mesmerized, a combined weight of fear suspending any motion. Above them, the wind had raked the promontories, packing snow into ravines and chutes, pressing it deep into every hollow. The skier didn't know what he was crossing; the difference between fallen and driven snow. He didn't know that the black rock beneath him was a magnet to the afternoon sun. He didn't know that the underside of the snow was heating up, turning to water, trickling downwards, weakening the platform beneath him.

Shooting cracks broke out under his feet, followed by the desperate sound of air rushing out of snow.

'Jesus Christ!' roared Bob. 'Avalanche!'
'Go right,' roared Mike, 'Go right.'

In seconds, a huge plume of white exploded into the sky as thousands of pounds of compacted snow shifted, plummeting toward them, four foot deep, warming as it moved, gaining the momentum to bury everything in its path, a deafening blast in the tranquil afternoon.

For seconds that felt longer, Mike was flying in an exhilarating powdered-snow rush. He was a snowboarder, busting a huge air, applause drowning out his proud cries. But somewhere inside, his instinct kicked in and he started to swim.

Bob felt like a rug had been pulled from under his feet, a rug he had been very happy with, the type that had protected him from the cold concrete underneath.

Lasco had descended barely four feet from the corpse when it was dislodged, hitting him hard in the back, forcing the wind from his lungs, sending them both plunging toward the ridge below.

Sonny became a centerpiece to the erupting snow, the height of its power, quickly descending to its crushing, savage depth.

In ten seconds, it was over. The snow had settled – twenty feet deep at the toe of the slide. Minutes passed before its powdery shower lifted, leaving in its wake a desolate white vacuum.

4

Mike Delaney knew that he wasn't driving this motion, he was at the mercy of it. There was no skill to the rotations of his body. The sound he was hearing was the avalanche's freight-train roar. If there was an audience that wasn't being swept up and deposited all around him, they would have seen a spectacular final display . . . but would have turned away for the crash landing that was strangely void of sound.

A waitress kept trying to serve Sonny Bryant cocktails. His hand shook as he took each one and dropped it to the ground.

'What is your *problem*?' she kept saying.

'You don't get it. I'm freezing,' he kept answering, again reaching out a shaking hand. 'I'm freezing. Is this hot?' He dropped the glass again.

'What is your *problem*?'

He jerked awake. 'I'm *freezing.'*

With the exception of one gloved hand, Sonny Bryant lay completely buried.

Denis Lasco was on his back, pinned beneath his charge, the pair taking the shape of a skewed cross on the snow. The corpse's vitreous mask had cracked open, leaving a pale cheek an inch from Lasco's lips. As he breathed frigid air through his nose, a slim strand of her hair was sucked against his nostrils. Lasco's head shook violently, struggling to exhale it away. But the rise of his chest was restricted. In his panic, his neck muscles went rigid, supporting him long enough to observe a contributory factor to the woman's death; a massive exit wound. A mash-up mix of reds and blacks had been ripped through the back of her snowsuit. It was the last thing Lasco saw before his breath exploded out of him and the picture went black.

When he was fourteen years old, Bob Gage had to dissect a cow's eyeball in biology class. He remembered how it flinched under his scalpel, how he fought to secure it, finally piercing what he expected would be soft, yielding flesh. But it crunched as the blade hit its center. What the butcher had given him was a frozen eyeball. And it had turned Bob's stomach more than cutting into the flesh of something that could have oozed.

Bob now stared at the heavy white world that surrounded him, possessed by the icy cold of his eyeballs, no less sickening now than a thirty-year-old memory. He knew nobody would be dissecting his eyeballs if he didn't make it out of this, but he knew a sharp blade would be coming into his dead world and it was more than he could take. You can't scream from the top of your lungs when they're searching for oxygen that isn't there. But Sheriff Bob Gage gave it his best shot.

For the second time that afternoon, an all-call went out and pagers across Summit County beeped, one of them under the snow of Quandary Peak. Twenty volunteers were called to a scene most of them were already at. The ones who hadn't made it first time around were paged again and told why, this time, they might want to show up.

Bob could see something blue sticking out of the snow. He turned on his side and rolled on to his knees. He crawled uphill toward it, staggering to his feet when he saw it was a gloved hand. He trampled a path to it, then fell down and started digging.

'We're going to get you out,' he said. 'Hang in there. Hang in there.' For a moment, he thought it might be the corpse. He pulled off the glove and felt a lukewarm hand and a weak pulse.

'Shit, come on,' he said, replacing the glove,

working harder to tunnel an airway to whoever lay beneath the surface.

'I'm getting there,' he said. 'I'm on my way.'

He could hear desperate, muffled groans. He looked around into the blank white.

'Help,' he shouted. 'Someone help.'

He kept going, scooping back snow, his arms trembling, his heart pumping hard. His body was on fire. He didn't stop. He couldn't. In his panic, he couldn't pin down the passing of time; did he still have a chance, or was it too late? Had he been there for wasted hours or just minutes? Finally, he heard a huge intake of breath.

'Thank God,' he said. 'Thank God. Jesus Christ. Who's down there?'

The voice was faint. 'Sonny.'

'OK, Sonny. You wait right there . . .' He paused. 'I mean, I'm going to get help. You're going to get out of there, OK?'

He heard a muffled reply. He sat back on the snow, his breath heaving. 'Jesus Christ.' He grabbed the radio from his belt and radioed down to the trailhead to call in Flight-for-Life, the medevac helicopter run out of Frisco, ten miles north of Breckenridge.

'I need to go check on Lasco,' he said to Sonny. 'I'm sure my buddy, Mountain Mike, is already back at the office.'

Further down the slope, by a small stand of trees, Denis Lasco lay on his back on top of the snow.

Bob dropped to his knees and checked him for a pulse. He found one. But he couldn't rouse Lasco.

The gentle snowfall quickly turned heavy.

'Lasco, you wake the fuck up by the time I'm back,' he said, hurrying up the slope to Sonny, slumping to the snow beside him. He pulled off one of his snow-shoes and used it to start digging. In ten minutes, Sonny's head and shoulders were exposed. But the rest of his body was compressed so tightly, Bob had to hide his fear.

'We need to keep you hydrated,' he said. He took a bottle of water from his jacket and held it to Sonny's mouth. Sonny's eyes started to close.

'No you don't,' said Bob. 'Wakey, wakey, OK? Jesus, I'm the one who's just done the physical exertion. If anyone gets to sleep here, it's me.' He wiped his sleeve across his forehead.

Sonny smiled a drunken smile, but opened his eyes wide. He sipped more water.

'Good,' said Bob. 'Keep looking at me. It's not easy, I know . . .'

Sonny blinked instead of smiling. Bob scanned the area for Mike, but found nothing. 'I've never been in an avalanche in my life,' said Bob. 'It's the scariest fucking shit . . .' He laughed through the panic rising in his chest. Sonny's skin was almost gray, his eyes shadowed and sunken, his lips pale and dry. Sonny was failing.

Bob's radio struck up. A calm voice said, 'Flights're on their way.'

'That's great,' said Bob. He looked up and down the slope. They were near the bottom, but there was no ground nearby at the right angle for a helicopter to land. And by the time the SAR team made it up to them from the trailhead, another half-hour would have gone by.

Sonny Bryant had got a perfect score in his EMT exams, so he knew exactly how he was going to die. He knew that the kind, smiling sheriff beside him knew how he was going to die. His limbs were crushed. As soon as the weight of the snow was taken away, toxins would rush to his bloodstream. His kidneys wouldn't take it. There were no IV fluids. There was only a half-liter of water that was almost gone. That was it. It wasn't enough. Bob Gage was holding his hand. Should he look him in the eye when they pulled him free? He didn't really want to leave Bob with an image that could haunt him for life. But he didn't want to stare into the blank white snow. Just in case wherever he was going was blank too.

5

The Summit County Medical Center stood on Highway 9 in Frisco. The Flight-for-Life helicopter hadn't moved from its hangar outside. Two hours after the avalanche hit, an ambulance had carried Denis Lasco and Mike Delaney from the trailhead. Lasco's deputy had arrived to take Sonny Bryant to the morgue in the van he used to call the Deathmobile.

Bob Gage stood by the window in Mike Delaney's hospital room. Mike was sitting on the edge of his bed, dressed in a navy sweatshirt and baggy track pants, pushing his feet into sneakers.

'We were pretty fucking lucky up there,' said Mike.

'No shit,' said Bob. 'No shit.' He shook his head. 'Christ Almighty, though, Sonny Bryant . . .'

'Poor kid.'

'Harve's a mess. He wanted to know every

detail. He was clinging to me, thanking me – for what, I don't know – then asking me to go through what happened over and over again. I was half-thinking of saying that Sonny said to tell them all he loved them. Then I thought that would be a shitty thing to do. Then I thought yeah, it would mean Sonny would have known he was going to die, which would mean that that would have been absolutely frightening –'

'Bob, Bob . . .' said Mike. 'Take a breath, OK? Take it easy. You did everything you could for Sonny, and I'm sure you'll do everything you can for Harve, if he needs you.'

Bob didn't say anything for a little while. When he finally spoke, his voice was showing cracks. 'I just . . . don't want to be elevated to some special status because I was the last person to see his son alive. Or he thinks I'm this great hero who tried to save him. I mean, there you were, Mike, with all your mountain experience; there's Lasco, a guy who knows all about the human body. So when you think about it, I am literally the last person who could have saved Sonny Bryant.'

'Bob, that's bullshit. None of us could have saved Sonny. Look, it makes no sense, but someone up there thought it was his time to go.'

'At nineteen,' said Bob.

'At nineteen.' Mike stood up. 'Life fucking sucks.'

Bob followed him to the door. They took the

elevator to the floor below. In a room at the end of the hallway, Denis Lasco lay sleeping.

'Damn that Heavy D,' said Bob, looking through the window. 'Here I am, giving a shit.'

'The laxative of concern,' said Mike.

'Where's my camera?' Lasco shouted, trying to struggle up from his bed.

Bob and Mike rushed into the room.

'Whoa,' said Bob. 'Lasco, lay back down for Christ's sake.'

Lasco collapsed on to the bed, freaking out when he saw the IV line, the hospital bed, the incongruity of worry in Bob and Mike's faces.

'Hey,' said Bob, putting a hand on Lasco's. 'You're all right, you're all right. Take it easy.'

'Don't cry on us,' said Mike, smiling.

Lasco squeezed his fingers to his eyes. 'Jesus. That was the worst . . . that . . .' He paused 'I've never . . .'

'Damn right it was,' said Bob. 'And here we all are, OK? We're good. We're living to tell the tale.'

'Have I been out long?' said Lasco.

'Not long enough,' said Bob.

'Where's my camera?'

'In a snowy grave,' said Bob.

'That was brand new,' said Lasco. 'Top of the range. And all the photos I took of the scene . . .'

Bob's phone rang. He held up a finger to Lasco and took the call.

'You have to be shitting me,' said Bob. He paused.

'Jesus Christ. Sit on this for now. I'll call you.'
He snapped his phone shut. 'Your camera's
the least of our problems,' said Bob. He stared
up at the ceiling. 'It turns out the body's gone
too.'

'What?' said Mike.

'Search and Rescue weren't able to locate it,'
said Bob. 'That's it. Swept away in the slide.'

'What?' said Lasco. 'What? It was on top of me!
How'd you get me out without pulling the body
off of me?'

'It wasn't there when I checked on you,' said
Bob. 'I guess you blacked out when it landed on
you. It probably slid right over your head, kept
on trucking.'

Lasco turned his head into the pillow, pressing
his hand to his stomach.

Mike turned to Bob. 'Are they going back up
there to get it?'

'Hell, no. They got us out. Hung around as long
as they had to. But it's way too unstable. They
won't risk anyone else.' He shrugged. 'Shit. No body.
We're going to have to have a press conference.'
He shook his head. 'So . . . let's get in agreement
about a few things. OK. Victim – female, aged
between thirty and forty –'

'Or male,' said Lasco.

'What do you mean "or male"?' said Bob.

'The body was wedged right in. We could only
see from the chest up, really.'

'So you're saying you didn't see tits and a va-jay-jay, so it could be a male? Give me a break. This noncommittal thing of yours is starting to get ridiculous.'

Lasco looked patiently at him. 'Well, I'm still not sure you're getting it,' he said. 'How many scenes have I been to where you guys have messed with shit before I show up? Pulling up people's pants, taking weapons and laying them on a night stand . . . You guys walk in and take a guess at what happened. What you need to do is go on exactly what is there in front of you. Not what you're adding to the picture. I could imagine all kinds of things happened to that body, but it doesn't mean I would be correct.'

Bob stared through him. 'FEMALE, aged thirty to forty, maroon jacket, white stripes down the arms. A navy blue wool hat?'

'Fleece,' said Lasco.

'Fleece,' said Bob. He was writing as he spoke. 'What about eye color?'

'Hard to say,' said Lasco. 'I wouldn't be happy making that call.'

'Hair?'

'Hat.'

'Nothing sticking out?'

'I don't recall.'

Bob looked patiently at Mike.

'Obviously, neither do you,' said Lasco.

'Yeah, 'cos you're so good about letting us get

close to the body.' He paused. 'So,' he said, 'in conclusion, we have . . . fuck all.'

'Oh,' said Lasco. 'Flashback: her hair went up my nose. Blonde.'

Bob sucked in a breath.

'Oh,' said Lasco. 'Gunshot wound. Massive exit wound through her back.'

'Holy shit,' said Bob. He paused. 'But why gunshot? You sure that wasn't a puncture wound, a tree branch . . .'

'No. It was a GSW,' said Lasco.

'You sure?' said Bob. 'It wasn't a hole made by some chopsticks, a broom handle? Let's keep one of those open minds here.'

'Ha. Ha,' said Lasco.

'Ha. Ha. Ha,' said Bob. He sat on the edge of the bed and closed his notebook. 'I'm not looking forward to this shitstorm,' he said. 'Not one bit.'

There was a knock on the door. Bob walked over and opened it a crack. 'Hey,' he said. 'How you doing?' He turned back to Lasco. 'It's a special visit from some Special Agents.'

The Summit County Sheriff's Office and the FBI were friends with benefits; one had local knowledge, the other had extra manpower, big budgets and technical resources. There were four hundred FBI resident agencies – RAs – across the United States, usually with one to three agents. The closest one to Breckenridge was in Glenwood Springs, one hundred miles west in Garfield County.

'We were on a call-out to Frisco,' said Tiny Gressett. 'We heard the report, thought we'd stop by, see how Mr Lasco is . . . see if there's anything we can do.'

There was no irony in Tiny Gressett's name – a hair cut would have put him under the FBI height requirement. He was in his fifties with the lined, papery face of a smoker and the wind-burn of a mountain man. He had wavy black hair and razor-shy sideburns.

'You enjoy the snow today?' he said to Lasco.

'Total blast,' said Lasco.

Todd Austerval stepped a shy foot toward the patient. He was tall, blond and in his early thirties, straight-nosed with sharp cheekbones. He should have been more handsome, but he had a snarly mouth and blue eyes two shades too pale to ever warm. He spent his life trying to soften his appearance with good humor. 'Heard you were snowcorpsing.'

'Nothing is sacred around here,' said Lasco.

'Sure isn't,' said Gressett.

There was another knock at the door.

'Let me get that,' said Gressett.

The door pushed open anyway and one of the new recruits from the Sheriff's Office walked in. He paused when he saw the two men in suits and looked, panicked, to Bob and Mike.

'Uh, we got an ID,' he said. 'One of the Search and Rescue guys found it. Where you were at,

Mr Lasco.' He turned to Gressett and Todd. 'I'm
sorry. Are you guys FBI?'

They nodded. 'Yes. From Glenwood.'

Lasco had an instant stab of memory – he had
held that ID in his hand. He had waved it at the
others: FBI creds.

6

Denver, Colorado

The Livestock Exchange Building was over one hundred years old with a history that had nothing to do with law enforcement. In skinny white type on the first-floor directory of offices, individual letters spelled out The Rocky Mountain Safe Streets Task Force, up there with the Colorado Brand Inspectors and Maverick Press. Behind the building was the Stockyard Inn and Saloon.

Gary Dettling sat in his office, reading an angry-wife email addressed to Stupid Stupid Asshole. After a while getting his breathing under control, he picked up the phone.

'Yeah, OK, I get it. Supervisory Special Agent: Stupid Stupid Asshole. Do I get a prize?'

His wife bitched about her being his prize, something about playing with the box. Gary rolled his eyes, then let them wander to the photo on the wall beside him. It was a group shot of the twenty-six agents he had trained, all of them with paper bags over their heads; the UCEs – Under Cover Employees. He wanted a paper bag for his wife. Or a plastic one.

'Gotta go,' he said. 'Something urgent is happening somewhere urgent. Urgently.'

'You asshole.'

'Stupid Stupid.'

She hung up. He loved her deeply, the crazy bitch. And he always fought for the things he loved. Gary was a violent crime expert and five years earlier had set this up – the FBI Rocky Mountain Safe Streets Task Force. He had fought the FBI, the chiefs of the local police departments – everyone who thought it was wrong to create a multi-agency task force and house it in a nine-dollars-a-square-foot non-federal building. The nine men and one woman who made up the unit were a mix of state troopers, local detectives, sheriff's department investigators and FBI agents, all sharing the old-school bullpen next to Gary's office. Egos were checked at the door and no one gave a shit who was from what agency. They worked robberies, kidnapping, sexual assault on children, serial killers, violent fugitives and crimes against persons in federal prisons, military bases, national parks and Indian reservations.

'Hey, where's our beloved Ren Bryce today?' said Robbie Truax, the youngest – twenty-nine,

toned, tanned and talky; Aurora PD's contribution
to Safe Streets. He was kneeling on a chair by the
window looking out at the fire escape. A hawk
was slicing back and forth through the entrails of
a dead pigeon like he was stitching up a wound.

'Nice work, buddy,' he said. He turned around.
'So where is she?'

'Stout Street?' said Cliff. Cliff James was fifty-
two years old and had spent twenty-five-years with
the Jefferson County Sheriff's Office. Stout Street
was the FBI federal building in downtown Denver,
a high-security, bulletproof-glass-fronted, charm-
less offensive.

Robbie shrugged. 'Maybe.'

'Where was she last night?' said Cliff.

'What do you mean?' said Robbie.

'Drinks at Gaffney's. She didn't show,' said Cliff.

'I wasn't there either,' said Robbie.

'Yeah? You weren't invited,' said Colin. Colin
Grabien was a short, dark-haired angry bulldog
who had transferred from the FBI's White Collar
Squad. He had a gift for numbers and for letting
people know he had a gift for numbers.

'Yeah, I was,' said Robbie.

'Yeah, I was,' whined Colin.

'Shut the hell up,' said Robbie, always dodging
the F-word. 'Anyway, she didn't say anything
about not showing today.'

'She's probably too busy fucking Vincent,' said
Colin.

'In fairness,' said Robbie, 'Vincent is never going to be the one doing the . . . you know.'

Cliff gave a gentleman's chuckle.

Robbie looked up and saw what Colin Grabien was about to do.

'Aw, screw you,' said Robbie, scrambling back to his desk. 'Screw you.'

Ren walked into the bullpen. Robbie hadn't made it as far as his desk. He was curled on the floor with his hands over his face. Red rubber bands bounced off him from Colin's desk. And Cliff's.

'Agent down, agent down,' said Cliff.

'You got my eye, dude,' said Robbie. 'My eye.'

'Here's Ren, she'll make it all better,' said Colin.

'Ren, you're coming out with us tonight,' said Robbie through his hands. 'I can't be alone with these freaks.'

'Hmm. I think I need to . . . go talk with Vincent,' said Ren.

'Get him to come in,' said Colin.

'You would love that,' said Ren. 'So you don't have to talk to me.'

'I don't have to talk to you anyway,' said Colin.

'Yeah, you'll be too busy with the sparkly tramp from Coasters,' said Ren.

'One night is all,' said Colin. 'It wasn't a prolonged attack on anyone's sensibilities like you are. Although, I did find glitter on my −'

'Don't,' said Ren, holding up her hand. 'Jesus.'

'And in my –'

'Shut up,' said Ren. She sat at her desk.

Robbie climbed up off the floor. 'I'm frickin' sweating here,' he said, shaking his shirt away from his body. 'Hey,' he said to Ren. 'What do you mean, you need to "go talk" to him? To Vincent? You live with him.'

'Hmm,' said Ren. 'Not since a week or so ago . . .'

'What?' said Robbie. 'Why?'

'Well, he walked out.'

'On you?' said Robbie.

Cliff and Colin were doing silent laughs behind his back.

'Yes, me,' said Ren. 'Can you *imagine*?'

'I seriously cannot,' said Robbie.

Ren smiled at him. Her mother would be thrilled if she brought Robbie Truax home. He was fit, clean and shiny. He wore perfect blue shirts and beige pants and polished shoes. He was probably a deviant.

Ren went to the bathroom with her makeup bag. One day she would put these trips on a résumé to signify her ambition; the mirror was distorted and the lights were fitted by a man who had never been in a bathroom with a woman. The guys got the famous Safe Streets walk-in urinal, a monster the size of a shower. Ren got horror-movie lighting and no shelf for her supplies. She leaned into her reflection and did a half-assed touch-up. She didn't ask the question, but she knew she wasn't the fairest of them all today.

'Coasters it is,' she said, walking back into the bullpen.

'What time is it?' said Cliff.

She pointed at him with her cellphone. 'Drinking time. Jalapeño poppers and beer all round.'

'How about we wait a little while and try eight p.m.?' said Cliff.

'Borrrring,' said Ren.

'I don't know if that's a good time,' said Colin, pointing a thumb toward Robbie. 'Hollywood here did his third piece to camera as the face of the FBI Rocky Mountain Safe Streets Task Force. It airs at eight.'

'Hey, I'm just *one* of the faces,' said Robbie.

'Ah, but the cutest,' said Ren. 'Apart from Cliff, obviously.' Women adored Cliff; big hands, big heart, bright-eyed and warm.

Robbie turned to Ren. 'You're next for the small screen.'

'Not unless I'm being wheeled from a shoot-out in a body bag.'

'Have you seen her near a camera?' said Cliff. 'She can make herself even smaller.'

'And you'd look good on television,' said Robbie.

Ren shook her head. 'Never gonna happen.'

'Well, anyway,' said Robbie, 'we can get Coasters to switch on the news . . .'

'You love it,' said Colin.

Gary walked in. They all stopped when they saw his expression.

'I've got some bad news. An agent from the Glenwood Springs RA – Jean Transom – has been found dead.'

'Oh my God,' said Ren.

Gary nodded. 'I just got a call from the Sheriff's Office in Breckenridge.'

'What happened?' said Robbie.

'Her body was found in the mountains. Up on Quandary Peak. GSW.'

'Holy moly,' said Robbie. 'When?'

'Just this afternoon,' said Gary.

'What the –?' said Ren.

'That's all we know,' said Gary. 'SAR responded to an anonymous tip – probably someone somewhere they weren't supposed to be. The Summit County Sheriff, Undersheriff, County Coroner were at the scene with one of the volunteers when some idiot triggered an avalanche, swept everything away. Including the body.'

'What?' said Ren.

Gary nodded. 'No body.'

'Jesus Christ,' said Cliff. 'Is that it? Are they still searching?'

'It's not safe up there, apparently,' said Gary.

'Wow,' said Robbie. 'Jean was so . . . I liked

Jean. I only met her once. She was, I mean . . . intense. But she was a good person.'

'Ren, we need to head up there now,' said Gary. 'The rest of you – stay with the bank surveillance tonight. Follow us to Breckenridge first thing tomorrow. Robbie, can you let the others know?' Four of the other task force members were on a job, two were on a training exercise.

'My car's in the shop,' said Ren.

'You can ride with me,' said Gary. He turned to the others. 'Ren's going to be the case agent on this one.'

Colin, Cliff and Robbie exchanged glances. Gary turned and left. Ren frowned and gave the others a not-my-fault look. She grabbed her purse. 'See you in Breck.'

Their faces all questioned her.

Two years earlier, Ren Bryce had transferred to Denver from the high-intensity of Washington DC. On her first day at Safe Streets she had almost changed from her suit to plaid shirt, jeans and boots by the time she made it from her car to the front door. She felt she was where she should have been from the moment she graduated.

She walked down the steps with Gary to a little blonde girl sitting on a Longhorn bull with a pink cowboy hat falling over her eyes. The child wore a wide tight smile for her parents' camera. The National Western Stock Show was in town. For two weeks in January, over seven hundred and fifty thousand visitors would come through the grounds where the Livestock Exchange Building stood.

'Shit,' said Ren. 'We're going to miss the rodeo tomorrow.' The Safe Streets office had seats for the matinee.

Gary looked at her. 'You were seen at the calf-roping earlier, so I don't feel all that bad for you.'

'I hate that – "you were seen". It's creepy. People who pass on information like that are creepy.'

'OK – I saw you. Does that make you feel any better?'

'Why didn't you just say that?'

He kept walking.

'And our seats were right by the bucking chutes,' said Ren.

'Yeah. I know.'

The cold air was spiked with barbecued pork. Ren glanced at Gary, but his head was down and his car keys were already swinging from his hand. A woman walked by with a deep-fried Twinkie on a stick.

'I'm starving,' said Ren.

'You're always starving,' said Gary without slowing. 'I've got an apple in the car.'

'An apple. I hate apples.'

He rolled his eyes.

'I'm not sure I can last until Breck,' said Ren.

'Yeah, yeah, you lose concentration if you don't eat,' said Gary.

'I do, though. You've seen me.'

'I've seen you trying to bullshit me about that.'

'It's true, though.'

'Jesus. Grab something from there.' He pointed at the closest stand – the last one on the way out of the grounds. 'Oh,' he said, 'that's just jars of caramel.'

Ren walked over with five dollars in her hand.

'You have cutlery, right?' she said, catching up with Gary.

'Christ, Ren.'

He opened the door of his Jeep and threw her a plastic fork. She turned it upside down. He put the keys in the ignition and drove up to the gate in the chain-link fence. He looked at Ren with her caramel fork, rolled his eyes and got out to be gate man.

As they drove west on I-70 for the eighty-mile trip to Breckenridge, he finally spoke. 'Do you want to tell me why I got a call from Paul Louderback asking me to make sure you head up this investigation?' Paul Louderback was Chief of the Violent Crime Section at Headquarters in DC.

'That's what happened?' said Ren. 'Are you for real?'

But Gary was almost always for real and he shot her a look to remind her. 'You sleeping with the guy?' he said.

'Jesus – straight to missiles. No,' said Ren and, more annoyed, 'No.'

Gary turned and hit her with his lie-detector stare. Ren hit back with open and honest eyes.

'Hey, the road,' she said, pointing him ahead.

'I got it,' he said. 'Look, I don't know if I can spare you.'

'I don't know if I want to be spared. But if Paul wants me to, I guess . . .'

Gary overtook the car in front of him, a small rush of anger in his driving. 'What's your connection with Louderback again?'

Ren had loved Paul Louderback from the moment she met him.

'He was my PT instructor at Quantico,' she said. 'And after that, my supervisor.' *And married with two kids. And ten years older than me. And handsome, kind and intelligent. And off limits.* On her second day in physical training, Paul Louderback praised her for not giving in easily to a man almost twice her weight. She had almost suffocated for the compliment.

'Ah. Responsible for your glowing reports?' said Gary.

'One of them, yes. And you left out the "much-deserved" part.'

She turned her attention to the passenger window and the cars speeding past. She wanted to count the white ones. Or the green or red ones. Any ones. Her heart was beating a little too fast. She was sure that a personal connection would not affect Paul Louderback's decision. He was a professional. But even she wasn't quite sure why he wanted her to head up the investigation.

Her phone beeped – text message. She read it, then put the phone back in her bag.

'Are we staying in Breck tonight?' she said.

'I was going to stay at the condo in Frisco. You're more than welcome.'

'Do you mind if I don't? I'd like to stay in Breck. At the, um . . . Firelight Inn.'

'Any particular reason?'

I just got a text from Paul Louderback recommending it. 'I'd like to be right in Breck. I'll have no car and if you get called away somewhere, at least that way I can walk to the sheriff's office if I have to.'

He glanced at her. 'I'm sure they can arrange a car.'

'And . . . I heard the Firelight Inn is a great place to stay.'

Ren didn't have a type; she had not-my-types – Truax's category. She also didn't do search and rescue for what she wanted in a guy. He either had it or he didn't. She always thought if a man senses what you're looking for, he will try to find it where it can't be found. And when he comes up empty, he'll fake it. Paul Louderback had no need to fake anything. He just had it. Yes, he was married, but once she realized that they could never take it further, she could relax into what they had; no real flirting, just a quiet, comfortable connection.

The exit for Golden flashed past. She thought about Vincent and their little house. She counted silver cars: America's most popular car color.

7

Sheriff Bob Gage's office was a neat, polished space. He had one notebook and one folder on his desk. His computer was on a table beside him. Behind him was a bank of file cabinets with family photos lined up across the top. Four smiling, dancing, sporting girls and boys.

His assistant led Ren and Gary in.

Bob stood up. 'Hey, Ren,' he said, giving her a light hug. 'Gary.' He shook his hand.

'You're back in action fairly quickly,' said Ren.

'Not much choice,' said Bob. 'Do you all know Tiny Gressett and Todd Austerval?'

'We've met,' said Gary, shaking their hands. 'That's very sad news about Jean.'

'Thank you,' said Gressett. 'Finding it hard to take it all in.'

'We said goodbye to her like she was just going on vacation,' said Todd. He paused, then turned to Ren, waiting for an introduction.

'Oh, hi,' she said. 'I'm Special Agent Ren Bryce with Safe Streets.'

'Good to meet you,' said Todd.

'Ren?' said Gressett. 'That mean you can sing?'

Ren smiled. It was awkward. 'Nothing you'd want to listen to.'

Gressett smiled and a remarkable amount of extra lines showed on his face.

'I wanted to say I really am very sorry that we're meeting under these circumstances,' said Ren.

Gressett paused. 'Well, thank you. Jean was an outstanding agent . . . and a friend.'

'I heard she was really something,' said Ren. 'I hadn't met her, I haven't been with Safe Streets that long –'

'But she's one of our best,' said Gary. 'Ren will be heading up the investigation here.'

'Oh,' said Gressett. 'Being that you're familiar with the area and all that.' He smiled and laughed alone.

'Nope, just being that I'm familiar with homicide investigation . . .' *And being patronized by men who aren't.*

'Well, good for you,' said Gressett.

'Yes, sir,' said Ren. *Now can we please stop this bullshit?*

'Right, everyone,' said Bob, 'Sit down, make yourselves comfortable. Coffee?'

Everyone nodded.

'Let me run through what we got,' he said. He placed a head-and-shoulders shot of Jean on the desk. 'Jean Transom, thirty-nine, single, worked in Glenwood, lived in Rifle, so far last seen by Todd and Gressett here, Friday, January 12th, five p.m. Body found on Quandary Peak, Tuesday, January twenty-third; possible GSW to the back or chest.'

Ren looked down at the photo. *There is something in your face that inspires trust.* A friend of Ren's called it a 'Can-I-get-you-a-Kleenex?' face.

'OK,' said Gary. 'Colin Grabien in Safe Streets will be running through phone records – he should have something back for us tomorrow.'

'I can go through Jean's desk at Glenwood, talk to Agent Gressett about what she was working on,' said Ren.

'Next of kin I have down as Patrick Transom, Jean's younger brother,' said Bob. 'We'll have to take care of the notification before this shit gets out. Ren, I'd be afraid to say it to another woman, but I'd like you to come with me for that feminine . . . presence.'

'Jesus. You have me down as feminine?' said Ren.

'There's a higher heel on your shoes,' said Bob.

'We've met Patrick,' said Gressett. 'Maybe Todd and I should . . .'

'Let's leave Bob and Ren to take care of it,'

said Gary. 'We don't want to all descend on him.'

Gressett slid forward on his seat. 'Todd and I could –'

'You're too close,' said Gary. Gary severed discussions; a quick, deep, cut – a special tone and a way of turning his head to focus on something else. 'Bob, can you show us where we can work out of?'

'Sure,' said Bob. 'We got an office cleared out there, computers set up, admin – you just let us know if there's anything else you need.'

'That's great,' said Gary.

'Thanks,' said Ren.

'How many of your guys are coming down later?' said Bob.

'Three more from Safe Streets to join Ren for the duration of the investigation,' said Gary. 'And a bunch of agents who will be sent to us from any offices that can spare them.'

'OK,' said Bob, getting to his feet.

They all moved out of the office into reception. Ren pulled on her jacket.

'Listen, go a little easy on people,' said Gary, lowering his voice, leaning into her.

'Like who?' said Ren.

'Gressett.'

'Sorry . . . but he was being an asshole.'

'Yeah, but we just got here.'

'I know, but –'

'You were the one who flagged the newbie thing,' said Gary.

'I know. It just came out. But, like he wasn't going to find out.'

Gary let out a breath. 'OK. Do you have everything you need for an overnight stay?'

'Will I be doing the walk of shame tomorrow? Yes, sir.'

Bob threw Ren his keys and told her to go ahead. Outside, powdery snow fell heavily. Ren walked quickly to the Explorer and got in the passenger side, slipping in the keys so she could listen to the radio. She skipped all the pre-tuned stations and tuned in her own.

What kind of crap do you listen to, Bob?

He came out five minutes later.

'What is that crap?' he said, turning off the radio. He started the engine. 'Right, we're taking a little detour to the hospital. You can meet Corpses Maximus, our County Coroner.'

Denis Lasco was sitting forward in his bed with his back against three giant pillows. He was freshly showered and watching a DVD on a portable player. He pulled the earphones out when he saw Bob and Ren.

'Lasco,' said Bob, 'I see your goddamn name in the paper every week, now this.' He threw the *Summit Daily News* on to Lasco's bed. 'This is what the townsfolk will be having with their breakfast tomorrow morning. This time you're not delivering the bad news, you *are* the bad news.'

'Right, so I'm bad news as the victim of an avalanche,' said Lasco. 'A near-fatal blunt force trauma.'

'This lovely lady is Special Agent Ren Bryce from the Rocky Mountain Safe Streets Task Force in Denver,' said Bob. 'And at least I don't have to say that every day. She'll be coming to talk to you – not right now, but I thought I'd have you guys meet.'

'Well, nice to meet you,' said Lasco.

'You too,' said Ren. 'How are you doing?'

Lasco shrugged, then winced. He picked up the paper.

'See the nice shit I said about you,' said Bob.

Lasco read through it. 'I see the *bull*shit you said about me. Blah, blah, blah . . . "we had to make a call. We knew we had a body and a possible crime scene. And Denis Lasco was committed to getting on up there to do his job. But that's what we've come to expect from Denis Lasco."' He glanced up at Bob. 'I like the ass-covering. Don't think for a second, people, that the Sheriff's Office marched him up the mountain.'

'Christ,' said Bob. 'Zero to whining . . . Listen, we're going to talk to Patrick Transom, the victim's brother. Is there anything you can give us?'

'What – to ease the blow? Like, she didn't suffer, or something?'

'I don't know. You're the coroner.'

'I'm sorry,' said Lasco. 'I'd love to be able to say something, but lying? Not so much.' He turned back to the paper. 'Ha,' he said, 'it's like you thought I wouldn't make it. It's like a frickin' obituary. "We love Lasco. We love Lasco. We are anticipating his demise."'

'You know you are, actually, a bitch,' said Bob. 'Next time a corpse slams into you, I'm going to tell the world you're a whiner. Who lives in his pajamas.'

'I'm in hospital.'

Bob rolled his eyes. 'I swear you go out of your way to piss me off.'

'It's why I couldn't die.'

'Yeah, well, maybe next time a real live person'll take you out. An elected official with the trust of the county.'

'*I'm* an elected official with the trust of the county.'

'All the better – you kill yourself, I don't have to get involved.'

Lasco let out a long breath. 'I think I need some quiet time.' He turned away.

'The drama,' said Bob. He pulled the paper

from under Lasco's fingers and walked to the door. 'Anyway, welcome back from the dead.'

'*To* the dead.'

'Your pals.'

'My income.' Lasco sighed. 'Good*bye*.'

8

Patrick Transom lived with his wife and four kids in a four-thousand-square-foot log home in Vail, thirty minutes from Breckenridge. Bob drove slowly up the steep curved drive and parked.

'Wow,' said Ren, getting out of the car. 'Nice.' She kept her face neutral in case anyone was looking out the window.

'But as my mother used to say – for all their money . . .'

'Yup,' said Ren. She buttoned the top of her jacket and stuck her hands in her pockets.

They walked up the steps and rang the bell. A man in a blue plaid shirt and jeans opened the door.

'Patrick Transom?' said Bob.

'Yes. What can I do for you?'

'I'm Sheriff Bob Gage, Summit County, and this is Ren Bryce with the FBI.'

Transom stared back and forth between the two of them. 'Okaay . . .'

'Can we come in?' said Bob.

'Sure, but . . . I'm sorry, what's this about? You can come in, but . . . you're making me nervous. Is everything all right?'

Bob put a gentle hand on the door and side-stepped Transom. Ren walked in after him.

'Why don't you take a seat?' said Bob.

Transom moved quickly to the sofa and sat down. His eyes were pleading; a sixth sense had taken over.

'You may have heard,' said Bob, pulling a chair out for Ren, taking the one beside her, 'that a body was found on Quandary Peak.'

Transom nodded. 'I did, yes.'

Bob looked him right in the eye. 'I'm so very sorry to have to tell you this, but we believe it was the body of your sister, Jean.'

'But . . . but the body is gone,' said Transom. 'I heard it on the news. There *is* no body.' He looked like he was about to stand up. A smile played at the corner of his mouth. 'There is no body.' He raised his hands like that was that – no body, no Jean, no grief, no heartbreak.

'Here,' he said, pulling his cellphone off his belt and flipping it open. 'Here.' He hit number two on his speed dial. He held the phone out to Bob. Bob's mouth opened, but didn't move. 'Here,' said Transom, holding the phone to Ren. She took it from him and saw Jean's name flashing on the screen. She closed it gently.

'I'm so sorry, Patrick, but it was Jean,' said Ren.
'The County Coroner, Denis Lasco, identified her
body before the avalanche hit. He found her FBI
credentials. The last time she was seen was ten
days ago. She had gone on vacation, as you probably know. That's all anybody knew. Following
the avalanche, Sheriff Gage, Undersheriff Mike
Delaney, and the coroner, Denis Lasco, went
through what they had seen of the body and the
clothing. They met with Jean's colleagues from
Glenwood Springs, they studied photos, and they
all agreed that it was Jean.'

Bob had shifted forward in his seat, but hung
there, mute. Transom was looking at him as if he
would disagree with Ren. Ren spoke to draw his
gaze back to her. 'I am so sorry,' she said. 'So sorry.
I wish I wasn't sitting here having to tell you this.'

Transom was rigid. His eyes were running everywhere. 'I'm sorry,' he said, looking back to them
both, 'I don't mean to be . . . I'm just wondering
. . . are you sure?'

The front door opened and four kids in ski suits
ran in, trailing snow behind them. The last one
slipped on the wet floor and slammed his head
into the side of the sofa. He burst out crying. Ren
was the first to make it to him, lifting him up
gently from the ground.

'You're OK, sweetheart,' she said. 'That silly
snow, making a mess on the floor.' He looked up
at her through his tears, wondering who she was

and why she was carrying him. Ren looked past him, waiting for his mother. An over-made-up brunette came in the door, leaning down, rubbing snow off a giant black Newfoundland.

Ren was already walking toward her with her crying son.

'Mrs Transom?' said Ren.

'Yes,' she said, reaching out and taking her child in her arms. She looked around the room at everyone. She gave Ren an extra up-and-down.

'Who are our guests, Patrick?' she said.

He turned to the kids. 'Hey, guys. Straight to bed, OK? You've had a late night. Take care of the little guy.'

The eldest girl went to her mom and took her little brother.

'This is my wife, Ellie,' said Patrick, when the kids had all left.

Bob stood up. 'Hello – Sheriff Bob Gage from Summit County.'

'And I'm Special Agent Ren Bryce with the FBI.'

'Oh,' said Ellie.

'Jean's dead,' said Patrick. His voice was flat.

Ellie looked at him like it was his abruptness that had caught her off guard, not what he was telling her.

'Your sister, Jean?'

'Of course it's my sister, Jean,' said Patrick. 'Who else would it be?'

'What the hell is wrong with you?' she snapped.

Ren stared at her. *What the hell is wrong with you?* 'He's in shock, Mrs Transom. Please, sit down.'

'I'm sorry. I've never . . . he's just not like that.'

A real Southern Belle. Manners over all. 'I'm sure he isn't,' said Ren.

Ellie walked around the back of the sofa and came in to sit beside her husband, putting her hand on top of his. It was an odd connection.

Ren sat down beside Bob.

'What happened?' said Ellie.

'We don't know yet,' said Ren. 'But her body was found on Quandary –'

'Oh my,' she said. 'The missing body? That one?'

'I wish I could tell you something else, but yes,' said Ren.

'Are you going to recover it?' she said. 'You *are* going to recover it.'

'Maybe not,' said Transom.

They all looked at him.

'I worked Ski Patrol,' he said. 'I know how it goes. If it's unstable up there, no one's going to go up, right? No point in risking real lives for a dead body. So you'll have to wait months until the snow melts. Am I right?'

Ren was happy to leave that one to Bob.

'Well, if you've worked Ski Patrol . . .' he said.

'So, OK, let me get this straight,' said Ellie. 'You have no body, but you're saying Jean is dead.'

'It's Jean, honey, OK?' said Transom. 'It is Jean. Do these people look like fools to you?'

Again, Ellie looked like she was listening to a complete stranger. She looked at Ren. 'My husband is not normally –'

'Mrs Transom, I'm sorry,' said Ren, 'but your husband is not normally told he has lost his only sister and her body may not be recovered for months.'

Ren could feel Bob's thigh clench beside her.

Ellie turned to her husband. 'Oh, honey. This is terrible news. This is just terrible. I'm so sorry, sweetheart.' She started to cry. She put her arms around him. He fell against her and it was only then that Ren saw how close they really were.

Bob and Ren gave their speech and their cards and left the Transoms alone. Ren looked at Bob with sad eyes. She leaned on his arm to walk down the icy steps.

'That was one hell of a lucky break, that he worked Ski Patrol,' said Bob.

'Can you imagine?' said Ren. 'I can't believe we got off so lightly.'

'Christ, though,' said Bob, 'we didn't even show him a photo, an ID, a scrap of clothing, nothing and he took our word.'

He opened Ren's door.

'I know. But,' she said, getting in, 'he's in total shock. He could come around and flip out. Or his wife could put pressure on him. Or on us. The media could get a hold of him –'

'I don't know,' said Bob, 'he seems a calm type of guy. Like that kind of outside influence wouldn't affect him.'

'But we only had two seconds with him before he realized something was wrong and started to react. I mean, what does two seconds tell you?'

'I just don't think he's the hysterical type . . .'

They drove in silence for a little while. Bob reached over and turned on the radio to Ren's least favorite – Seventies rock. She sat tight.

'Transom's what? Twenty-eight, twenty-nine?' said Ren. 'Their daughter must be seven. Is it me or are people who marry really young and have loads of kids trying to make up for a shitty childhood?'

'Spoken like the true single and childless.'

'Excuse me?' said Ren, smiling.

'How about,' said Bob, 'their childhood was so amazing that they wanted to continue the tradition?' said Bob.

'Hmm,' said Ren. 'I like your idea better.'

'There you go,' said Bob. 'Be sunny.'

9

The Firelight Inn stood at the cross-section of French Street and Wellington – a beautiful clapboard Victorian house in a muted blue-gray from the Breckenridge town palette. A picket fence ran around the garden. The snow had drifted up to the window sills.

'Good night,' said Bob. 'Sleep well. Seven fifteen at the office, OK?'

'Thanks,' said Ren, waving him off, pushing in the front door to the inn. The hallway was covered in thick mats and clumps of snow. Rows of snowboards and skis lined the wall. The Firelight was half-inn, half-hostel. Ren had a cozy suite on the top floor, with an entrance from the house and an external staircase. When she got to her room, she walked over to the window and stared out at the white night.

She took out her cellphone and dialed. 'I love it,' she said.

At the other end, Paul Louderback laughed. 'I knew you would.'

'When were you here?'

'Two summers ago. With Marianne and the kids. We took a suite –'

'Me too.'

'With the separate stairs up? Above the hot tub?'

'Yes. It's great.'

'I thought you might like it. Marianne wanted to stay in one of the condos . . .'

'I'd rather –'

'I know.'

'Condos are so the same everywhere,' said Ren.

'I know. Hey, don't forget to sign up for breakfast before you go to bed.'

'Do I call down?' she said, looking for a phone that wasn't there.

'Are you looking for a phone?' She could hear the smile in his voice.

'No, I'm not.'

'There's a list with a swinging pencil by the office,' said Paul. 'You go down and tick the box for whatever you want. It's all really good.'

'Is there a box for "the company of Paul Louderback"?'

Paul laughed. 'Yeah, for the crazies.'

'Exactly.'

'What was I thinking?'

Ren laughed, then sighed. 'So . . . Jean Transom.

I don't know what you know at this stage. Did you hear that Denis Lasco, the coroner, is OK?'

'No. And . . .?'

'All he would commit to was GSW. He didn't have long with the body.'

'Right.'

'He's going to be cautious. He blacked out, so he's doubting his memory – number one. And number two, this is a federal agent we're dealing with, a high-profile case. I doubt he wants to be the one making big statements, in case he's wrong. Or he derails the investigation. And? The body could show up in the morning and contradict anything he tells us.'

'Who found the body?'

'Anon,' said Ren. 'I would venture a back-country skier who was not supposed to be where he was. And with the FBI all over it, he won't be showing his face any time soon.'

'I see,' said Paul.

'Can I ask?' said Ren. 'Why me as case agent?'

'What do you mean?'

'I'm flattered, but why am I the chosen one?'

'Desperation is a word that comes to mind.'

'I was thinking . . .'

'You know why?' said Paul. 'No body . . . does it better.'

'Very funny.'

'Look, you're good at your job,' said Paul. 'There it is. The thing you can't believe in.'

'Well, thank you for your faith.'

'And thank you in advance for solving the crime.'

'And thank you for the pressure.'

'Any time.'

'Oh – you never answered me earlier. Did you know Jean?' said Ren.

'I didn't know her personally. But I taught her at the academy. She was quiet, kept to herself.'

'The poor woman.'

'I know. OK, I gotta go. Sleep well.'

'Thank you,' said Ren. 'You too.'

'And dream gently.'

She paused. 'I'll try.' *Damn you, Paul Louderback.*

The South Ridge Seafood Grill was the kind of place that sucked you under its awning and through its open doors. It was on a quiet strip on Ridge Street, but had taken most of the Tuesday-night diners in Breck. It was the right size with the right atmosphere and the right food. Ren walked in and moved in to order beside the two guys at the bar whose heads were not hung over their beer. They were both drunk, wind-burned and fit, dressed in green and navy fleeces, black pants and boots.

'Well, hello there,' said the tall one, leaning an elbow on the back of his bar stool to turn to her.

'Hi,' said Ren.

'What's a pretty girl like you doing in the personal space of the elderly?' he said.

'*How* elderly?' said Ren, raising an eyebrow.

'I'm sixty-two, he's seventy-two,' he said, pointing to his short friend.

'What?' said Ren. 'No way.'

They nodded.

'Why are we telling her our age so soon?' said the short guy.

'We could have been a contender,' said the tall one. 'So then, what's your name?'

'Ren.'

'That's a very pretty name,' he said.

'What's yours?' said Ren.

'Mauser here,' he said, shaking her hand.

'Mauser?' said Ren.

'Yes. Mauser. No first name. And this is Little Dick.'

Ren laughed. 'You let him away with that?'

Little Dick gave a shrug.

'You will join us for a glass of red wine,' said Mauser. He nodded at the barman. 'Put it on our tab.'

'Well, thank you very much,' said Ren. 'But I'm not really drinking. I'll just have water.'

'What?' said Little Dick. 'I don't know if we can let you do that. Can we?'

'It would be a first,' said Mauser.

'I've got an early start,' said Ren.

'What do you do?' said Mauser, handing her a glass of wine.

'Oh, OK,' she said. 'Thank you. What do I do? Mainly not talk about my job.'

'Little Dick here's a DDS,' said Mauser.

'A what?' said Ren.

'Doesn't Do Shit,' said Mauser. He reared back with a crazy, infectious laugh that made Ren laugh even harder. Little Dick gave what was obviously his trademark shrug.

'And what do you do, Mauser?' said Ren.

'I come from a distinguished line.'

'Of what?' said Ren.

'Of bullshit.'

'You are so funny,' said Ren.

'You mean it's not our bodies you're interested in?' said Mauser.

'Not if you keep calling him Little Dick,' said Ren.

'He'd need to do you three times to give you twelve inches,' said Mauser.

Ren laughed loud and hard. 'You guys . . .'

The barman walked their way with a tray.

'Oh God,' said Ren, 'what are these?'

'Mind Erasers,' said the barman, lining up six glasses filled with liquid in a shade of *wrong*.

'Six,' said Ren, deadpan. 'There are three of us.'

'Yeah, but you forget you've drunk the first one,' said Mauser.

'You sure do,' said Little Dick.

'They got twenty on their tab already,' said the barman, smiling. 'It's like, bam – Will Smith, *Men in Black*.'

Mauser smiled. 'This is what stranger danger is all about.'

Ren laughed. 'But I'm really not drinking,' she said, sliding her two toward her. She sucked each one up through a black straw. 'Wow.'

Mauser raised his. Little Dick followed. 'And we'll go again, sir,' said Mauser to the barman.

'Ooh,' said Ren.

An hour later, Mauser was leaning in to her. 'I'm not an advice column here, but this Vincent guy is insane. That's all I'll say.'

'Letting a pretty girl like you go,' said Little Dick.

'Aw, Vincent's a really good guy –' said Ren.

'Insane!' said Mauser.

'Insane!' said Little Dick.

'I'm the insane one,' said Ren.

'Really?' Mauser slapped the bar in front of them and looked at her with dancing eyes. 'Join the party, sweetheart.'

And she did, smiling a slow-spreading MindErasersmile.

10

Breckenridge was between busy holiday weekends – Martin Luther King Day had just passed and Presidents' Day was a month away. Kids were back at school. It was seven a.m. and skiers and snowboarders were heading to breakfast early before they hit slopes they were about to find out were quieter than they expected.

Bob Gage sat in Daylight Donuts spinning the playing card he was given when he placed his order. The ace of spades. He nodded his head to the beat. He was on his second coffee when a waitress walked by with the matching card and stepped back a few paces to his table to lay down her tray. She handed him a plate of bacon, egg, biscuits and gravy. His cellphone started to ring. He mouthed a thank you to her as he answered it.

'Sheriff Gage? It's Patrick Transom. I'm sorry. I tried to be understanding. I mean, I do understand. But I've had time to think about everything and . . . I want my sister. I need my sister back. I'm not going to wait months for warm weather to . . .' His voice caught. 'I . . . understand that Search and Rescue doesn't want to go back up there. But I do. I'm an –'

'Mr Transom, you're right. It's not safe up there. A snow assessment's being done this morning, but –'

'I don't care if it's not safe,' said Patrick. 'I want to –'

'We cannot let you do that,' said Bob. 'It's a crime scene up there as far as we're concerned. We can't let anyone in there. I'm sure you understand that. You probably haven't slept, and maybe this seems like the only solution right now . . .'

'If the snow report is good, if the conditions are stable enough, can I go?'

'No. But . . .' He paused. 'OK . . . if the snow report comes back good, we'll head on up there.' He pushed his plate away from him. 'I'll get in touch with Search and Rescue.'

Gary Dettling pulled up into the small driveway at the Firelight Inn. The street was quiet. He turned off the engine and waited. After five minutes, he texted Ren. He got no reply. He knocked at the door of the inn. The owner was on his way out with a snow shovel.

'Sorry to bother you,' said Gary. 'I'm looking for a woman checked in last night, Ren Bryce?'

'Oh, yes . . . I'm sure she's gone already.'

'What?'

'About twenty minutes ago.'

Gary shook his head slowly. 'Great. Thanks.'

Ren sat in Bob Gage's office holding a mug of coffee on her knee. She had started the day with Visine and extra foundation. A notebook lay on the low coffee table beside her and she was twisted in her chair to scribble on it. A night of drinking could take her to instant mental clarity or thick mental fog. Today, she was all-clear. *RenBryce OS-X*. She smiled to herself.

'Hey,' said Gary, walking in, nodding at Bob and Mike, Gressett and Todd.

'Wasn't I meant to pick you up?' he said to Ren.

'Oh. Didn't you get my text?' said Ren, pulling out her phone, about to show him the text that she now saw was pending in her Outbox.

'What were you doing, walking?' said Gary.

'I wanted to blast some cold air through my tiny mind.'

'You didn't think you were going to get enough up on Quandary?'

Gary had nearly been a lawyer. Ren was reminded of this with every question-after-question barrage. Gary Dettling couldn't stand the thought of being made a fool of with lies.

'Yeah and we're going *up* up,' said Bob, putting

down the phone. 'That was Search and Rescue. Patrick Transom called me an hour ago, insisting we go back up to try and retrieve the body. To be honest, I thought the snow assessment wouldn't be good, so I said we'd give it a go. Turns out there was no snowfall overnight, the winds were less than five miles an hour, so we're good to go.'

'Can we all go up?' said Ren.

'Sure,' said Bob. 'I know I'm really looking forward to it . . .'

Ren gave him a sad smile. 'You shouldn't go back up. We can take care of –'

'You know what?' said Bob. 'You're right.'

'Really?' said Ren.

'Yeah,' he said, placing his palms down on his desk. 'Take your digital cameras, video it, photograph it . . . and I'll be down at the base with clean underpants.'

Ren could see that Gary wasn't impressed. *Mr Action Hero.*

'Good for you,' said Ren to Bob.

'For whatever good it will do, going up there,' said Bob. 'We're not going to find her.'

'Probably not,' said Mike. 'But maybe Transom will feel better being part of the search.'

'Like all the families who look all over Breck for their father or brother or son or daughter who left a bar drunk in a blizzard and never made it back to the condo . . .'

Mike let out a breath. 'What else can we do?'

'Come up with some positive and hopeful sound bites to throw out to any reporters at the trailhead,' said Bob. 'And solemn, regretful ones for the way back down: "We did everything we could."' He turned to Gary. 'Are your guys on their way?'

'Yes,' said Gary. 'They'll meet us up there.'

'So by nine o'clock everyone'll know the FBI's in town,' said Bob.

Ren looked down at herself. 'I didn't think I was looking very FBI today. I'm wearing a little gray, some soft fabric . . .'

'It's an aura,' said Bob.

Ren smiled. 'It's the smell of fierce.'

'Don't fight the fierce,' said Bob.

'Shall we go?' said Gary. 'I think we're all ready.'

'Yes,' said Gressett. 'I think we are.'

'Oh, sure,' said Ren, standing up. 'Anyone seen my phone?'

'It's in your back pocket,' said Todd, too quickly.

The sky over Quandary Peak was one solid shade of promotional blue. Jeeps, vans and cars branded with the block-print logos of news channels, law enforcement and Search and Rescue stretched along Blue Lakes Road up to the trailhead. A large group had gathered from the Sheriff's Office, Search and Rescue and Safe Streets. A cadaver dog and handler had been drafted in, last-minute. 'The media loves a dog,' Bob had said, deadpan.

He stood at the head of the group and talked everyone through what happened the day before. When he was done, he laid out a map, showing where Jean Transom's body was when the avalanche hit, where Lasco had been found, and where the slide had ended.

Search and Rescue strapped on their packs and snow-shoes and started up the dark, steep path through the dense trees. Everyone making their way up behind them was used to hiking, skiing or snowboarding. Before Denver, Ren's main weekend workout had been wandering around a DC mall, but it wasn't long before her heart had warmed to the mountains. And even though her wardrobe now had a corner for Smart Wool and Marmot, she hadn't quite made the move to lining her hiking boots up beside her heels.

She stopped in the first clearing and let anyone who was behind her pass by. The view was spectacular – endless green acres of snowy lodgepole pines. For a few moments she was able to forget why she was there. Breckenridge was only an hour's drive from her house in Golden. There was no reason why she couldn't come here more often. As she was about to move on, she saw Robbie Truax and Colin Grabien walk up.

'Hey,' she said.

'Aw, hey, Ren,' said Robbie. He stopped.

'Hi, Ren,' said Colin. 'Bye, Ren – I'm going to keep on walking.'

'Did you hear about the robbery?' said Robbie.

'No,' said Ren.

'Yeah – that's why we only got here this morning. We were sitting on the wrong bank. Guys got away.'

'Who was it this time?'

'You'll love this. There was celebrity involvement . . .'

'What?' said Ren.

'They were all wearing masks made from celebrity mug shots.'

'No way.'

'I know – Nick Nolte.'

'That is hilarious,' said Ren. 'Who else?'

'They were all Nick Nolte,' said Robbie.

Ren laughed. 'That is just too funny.'

'Not if you're getting beaten around the head with the butt of an assault rifle by one of them.'

'True,' said Ren. She paused. 'You know, they're sending out a message: these are the only faces we'll give you for mug shots.'

Robbie let out a breath.

'Who did they assault?' said Ren.

'Everyone,' said Robbie.

'Everyone?'

Robbie nodded.

'They took the time to do that?' said Ren.

'While three of them were taking the money, two went crazy on the staff. So – no extra time wasted.'

'Hmm,' said Ren. 'So you didn't have the most productive night.'

'I was freezing my butt off out there. Sons-of-guns.'

'You should write a book: "When Bad Language Happens to Good People". Or "The F-word Diet".'

Robbie smiled. 'I couldn't write a book that you'd never read.'

Ren laughed. 'I'll swap you a copy of yours for a copy of mine: "On Alcohol, Coffee and Pre-marital Sex".'

Robbie was Mormon. He laughed.

'So what's going to happen with the robbery investigation while you guys are in Breckenridge?'

'The rest of the guys back at Safe Streets are going to keep working on the robberies that have happened so far, but if there are any new ones, it's business as usual for me, Colin and Cliff – we'll just have to head back to Denver. Which sucks. I mean, we're here to work on Jean's murder, obviously, but we can't shut everything else down completely.'

'I guess not,' said Ren. 'But it does suck.' She stopped to take a half-liter bottle of water from her pack. It was empty. *Shit.*

'Ren?' Mike called back to her.

She raised her head too quickly. 'Whoa.' She took a step back. Her legs went weak.

Mike jogged down to her. 'Are you OK?'

'My head.'

'You got a headache?' said Mike.

'Yes. Ow.' She pressed two hands to her fore-head. 'Shit, that's bad.' She turned to Robbie. 'You go ahead.'

'Are you sure you're OK?' said Robbie.

'Yes.'

'I've got it,' said Mike. He turned back to Ren. 'Did it come on all of a sudden?'

'Yeah,' said Ren. 'Let's just keep walking.'

Mike eyed her. 'OK, if you're sure.'

'Yeah. Come on.'

'Sounds like those teeth are gritted,' said Mike, taking her hand and pulling her up.

'I'm fine.'

They walked for another minute or two and Ren stopped again.

'Did you drink any water today?' said Mike.

'Em, no. Coffee.'

'And last night?'

'Em . . . alcohol.' *Which I probably reek of anyway.*

'Right, you're going back down,' said Mike.

'No way,' said Ren, taking a step forward, then swaying on her feet.

'You've got altitude sickness,' said Mike.

'No, I don't.'

'Oh, please. Yes, you do.'

Someone once described altitude sickness to Ren as your body trying to suck your brain down through your spinal column. She couldn't shake the image.

'It's not altitude sickness,' said Ren.

Mike rolled his eyes. 'Down,' he said. 'We'll meet you down there.'

'No,' said Ren. 'No. I need to see what's going on up there.'

'We'll have photos.'

'Yeah, but –'

Mike gave her the look that told her to stop. 'Will you be OK getting down?'

'Sure, I'll –'

'Whoa . . .' He reached out and she sank against him. He held her upright to stop her fall.

'Are you OK?' he said.

'I thought I was going to black out.'

'I'm waiting here, radioing ahead, and you are going to see a doctor –'

'No way. I'll feel like a loser going to a doctor for altitude sickness when I'm coming from Denver . . . and I'm –'

'What? An FBI agent? People expect FBI agents to be dumb.'

Ren smiled. 'Yeah, I'm still not going.'

'I have no idea how you forgot to keep drinking water when you arrived. Do you think your brain needs less oxygen that everyone else's?' He paused. 'Or just more alcohol?'

'Just the alcohol,' said Ren. 'Partying at altitude – cheap, but not so cheerful.'

'Right, here's the deal,' said Mike, 'go see Charlie Barger – on Ridge Street.'

'Is everything on Ridge Street?'

'It's a long street.'

'Charlie Barger sounds like a thief. The name, I mean. Like a Dickens thief.'

Mike stared at her. 'Now I think the altitude is really starting to work on your brain. Charlie is a retired doctor. And I can promise you he won't steal anything . . .'

Up on Quandary, the charge of the avalanche had been replaced by an unjust calm, like the smile of a man who had gotten away with murder. And the day before, Quandary Peak had, twice-over. The area looked untouched, except for the tree limbs – broken by the force of the slide – that protruded from the snow. The hole that Sonny Bryant had been pulled from was still there; his glove, with a light dusting of snow, lying beside it.

Search and Rescue moved in with probes. Anyone who had cameras took pictures. And the dog handler released her beautiful border collie to track the smell of death.

11

Charlie Barger lived in a three-story Victorian house, all peeling paint and haunted charm. The garden was an overgrowth on the pretty street – moments away from a council warning. Ren rang the doorbell. A redhead opened the door, dressed in pink thermals with tiny dogs on them. She was wearing frayed imitation Uggs.

'Hello,' said Ren.

'Yeah.'

'Mike Delaney from the Sheriff's Office sent me to see Dr Barger. I was up on –'

The woman was staring past her.

'I'm sorry. Is that OK?' said Ren.

The woman faked a smile. Her clothes made her look younger than she was. There was something worn about her face, the skin dry and loose.

'Yeah, come on in.' She had no interest. 'He's out back in his study. It's past the bathroom on the right.' She called out: 'Dad. It's for you.'

Ren walked into the hallway after her. Her sour air seemed to have tainted the entire place.

Ren knocked on Dr Barger's door. He opened it and from the grim hallway she was brought into a warm, old-fashioned study, a blend of academia and small-town, personalized medical attention. Leather, mahogany, walls of photos, ethnic artifacts, a thick bunch of laminated conference IDs on lanyards hanging from a nail in the wall. Lying on the floor along one wall were curving stacks of papers and files.

Ren pointed to them. 'Don't you worry they'll fall over?'

Dr Barger turned his drooping eyes to her and smiled. He was in his late sixties, early seventies, with a lined, but healthy face.

'I know most of what's in there,' he said. 'So you're Mike's friend?'

'Yes,' said Ren, 'we're working together.'

Barger nodded. 'I'm guessing it's the body on Quandary.'

'Yes.'

'And Mike was worried that, with your headache, you'd end up being another corpse.'

Ren smiled. 'Probably.'

Barger ran through all the checks and sat back on the edge of his desk. Ren eyed him with panic tugging at her chest. Every time she went to the doctor, she secretly expected him to tell her it was all over, that he had uncovered something terrible.

'Water, water, water,' said Barger. 'No alcohol. No coffee.'

I don't know which is worse. 'Really?'

'Yes,' he said. 'How can you function otherwise? You're dehydrating yourself. If you were at sea level, there'd be twenty-one per cent oxygen in the air. Up here, it's eleven. And there's a lot of tissue fighting for that. Your brain needs the most, so it's the first thing to go.' He tapped the side of his head. 'You could end up with the cognition of a small child . . .'

'I don't need oxygen deprivation for that.' Ren smiled.

Barger smiled back. 'You can't fool me.'

'I can't do no coffee, though,' said Ren. 'That would mess with my brain more.'

'Then just drink extra water.'

'OK. Thank you. And thanks for taking the time to see me.'

'Not a problem. Tell Mike I said hi.'

'I will . . .' She stood up. 'Um, what do I owe you?'

'Seventy dollars.'

Ren paused. 'Oh, OK.' *Thief.*

As Ren walked to the front door, Shannon Barger was ahead of her, walking into a room on the right-hand side. Ren couldn't help glancing in. She saw the muscular back of a man bending to pull on a pair of jeans. *Commando.* Shannon caught Ren looking as she turned back to close the door. Apparently the only real smile Shannon Barger had to offer was a smug one.

Casey Bonaventure, auburn-haired and full-lipped, stood in front of her cameraman at the base of Quandary Peak. Mike Delaney and Bob Gage stood a few feet away from her.

'That wardrobe choice must have slayed her this morning.' Mike's voice was low in Bob's ear. 'Serious, glamorous, outdoors. Crime scene, pretty mountain, viewers . . .'

Casey was dressed in a green ski jacket and matching pants. She sucked in an icy breath and started.

'A chill wind has blown through the picturesque resort town of Breckenridge . . .'

'Sweet Jesus,' said Bob quietly.

Casey went on. 'On the snow-white slopes of Quandary Peak, the discovery of the body of a dead female set in motion a chain of events that ended in a second tragedy when an avalanche claimed the life of a local volunteer rescuer. And a third tragedy when the body of the dead female was swept away in the slide. Sheriff Robert Gage and Undersheriff Mike Delaney, also at the scene, escaped with minor injuries. County Coroner Denis Lasco remains in a stable condition at Summit County Medical Center.

'In contrast to the sun you see shining here this afternoon, a dark cloud has descended on the quiet community of nearby Breckenridge as they awoke to a terrifying tale of high-altitude horror. Mystery surrounds both the death and the identity of the female, who has been described as "in her thirties or forties". A source close to the investigation has indicated that this was not a skiing accident, that this woman was the possible victim of a homicide.

'Law enforcement officers are working tirelessly to develop leads, their task made all the more difficult by the absence of the body. The FBI arrived early this morning, no doubt to offer up additional resources.' She paused. 'Let's hope, for all our sakes, this is one trail that will not run cold. I'm Casey Bonaventure –'

When she had finished signing off, she saw Bob to her left. He had turned at an angle to talk to Mike. 'No one can accuse the girl of not writing her own reports.'

'Shit. Here she comes,' said Mike, quickly stepping back to his right.

'One, two three,' said Casey, signaling to the cameraman. She paused. 'I'm here today with Sheriff Robert Gage of the Summit County Sheriff's Office. Hello, Sheriff Gage.'

'Hello, Casey.'

'How are you holding up?' she asked with a concerned face.

'I'm doing OK,' said Gage. 'My thoughts now are with the family of the brave young volunteer who lost his life.'

'As are all our thoughts,' said Casey, 'Is there anything else you can tell us about yesterday's events?'

'I think you got it all covered, Casey. I can confirm that the body of a woman in her thirties or forties was discovered yesterday afternoon on Quandary Peak. During our recovery of the body, an avalanche was triggered.'

'And the body?'

Bob paused. 'Was lost in the slide.'

'And this morning's search is to recover that body?'

'Yes, it is, Casey.'

She kept the microphone to his mouth. Bob was done.

She held her breath, then struck up again. 'And the volunteer rescuer? Do we have any more information on him or her?'

'Not until next of kin have been notified. No.'

'And the FBI presence here today? That would confirm reports of a homicide?'

'The FBI presence here today is a welcome addition to the team investigating yesterday's events.'

Casey held the microphone steady. Seconds went by before she nodded. 'Thank you, Sheriff Robert Gage.'

She turned back to the camera. 'We'll see you at the top of the hour with an update on the story unfolding here at Quandary Peak. Who knows where this particular trail will lead? I'm Casey Bonaventure . . .'

After sign-off, she turned back to Bob. 'Bob –'

'Casey, sweetheart? Don't come crying to me when your producers prematurely ejaculate all over a story. They send you out too early for anyone to make any sense of my crime scene, your story, the victim's ID, what in the hell happened – everything. Every time you show up, we tell you we have nothing yet. And every time, you stick that damn camera in my face and expect me to do the hard work. To do *your* job. I have my own job.'

'You know where I'm coming from,' said Casey.

'You're paid to talk,' said Bob. 'I'm not. But, if I have to, I'd rather have something to say.' He muttered as he walked away. 'How about a snowy cascade of suspects, a winter wonderland of weirdoes, an icicle of . . . something that begins with "i" . . .?'

12

Ren sat at her desk in the Sheriff's Office, a bigger, cheaper, shinier desk than the one she had at Safe Streets. She was thinking about self-sabotage – not for the first time. *Altitude sickness could happen to anyone.* But she had drunk a lot of contributory factors. There was a bottle of Fiji in front of her. And three more on the floor beside her. Robbie Truax, Colin Grabien and Cliff James walked in.

'Aw, look at her,' said Robbie.

Ren smiled patiently.

'The loser,' said Colin.

'Are you feeling better?' said Robbie.

Ren nodded. 'I am. I have drunk more water in four hours than –'

'Alcohol, hopefully,' said Colin.

Yeah, yeah, yeah. 'I actually wasn't drinking last night,' she said. 'I had just arrived here, as you know.' She turned to Cliff. 'So, what did I miss?'

'Not a lot, I'm afraid,' said Cliff. 'The cadaver

dog sat down, barked – his "alert" to show he
picked up a scent – but his handler said that could
have been from Sonny Bryant. Apparently the
smell of death kicks in the moment a person dies.
And we all smell the same dead, so it's not like
the dog can distinguish . . .'

'Do we?' said Robbie.

'Yup, apparently,' said Cliff.

'That's kind of depressing,' said Ren.

'Oh, you want to smell especially different when
you're dead?' said Colin.

'Shut the fuck up, Colin,' said Ren.

'So the dog was indicating there was a scent there,
but he didn't physically find anything,' said Cliff.

'So,' said Ren, 'what's the plan for going back up?'

'I don't know,' said Robbie. 'It was risky heading
up there to begin with. SAR's saying no way.'

Ren took another mouthful of water. 'Shit.'

'You want to look at the photos?' said Robbie.

'Sure. I love your photos. You really are very
good,' said Ren. 'You could have an exhibition –
Truax: Scenes from Scenes.' If the location was
interesting, Robbie shot landscapes from crime
scenes.

Ren reached out for the digital camera.

'Am I going to find any photographs of an inti-
mate nature here?' she said.

'Only the ones we took on Colin's desk that
night,' said Robbie.

Ren turned on the camera. The first series of

photos were exterior shots of a bank the task force had been surveiling. She ran through them quickly and got to the morning photos at the trailhead and up at the site. She reached for her bag and her USB cable and downloaded them into iPhoto.

She put her elbow on the desk, rested her chin on her hand, and started to go through the photos slowly. The guys took seats at different computers and started searching databases and making calls. When Ren reached the last of the photos, she went back to the start. She stopped at one, zoomed and leaned in close.

'Robbie? Did that cadaver dog get in there before you took these?'

Robbie shook his head. 'No. Jesus, why do I always get a hard time about contamination . . .'

'No, you don't, baby,' said Ren. 'No, it's just that, look – are those paw prints in the snow?'

Robbie came over to look. 'Paws? Are you sure?'

'Looks that way to me,' said Ren. 'But I'm not exactly Ren of the Mountains.'

'Could it have been an avalanche rescue dog?' said Robbie.

'There was none,' said Ren. 'It would have been too late. I went into everything with Bob: it was snowing when they were taking the bodies down, but there was no snowfall later that night. So, something was up there after the body was recovered, but before this morning.'

Colin and Cliff came over.

'I don't know,' said Colin. 'It's either shadows in the snow. Or it could or critters.'

'Yeah,' said Cliff.

'What do you think?' said Robbie, squeezing Ren's shoulders, looking over them.

'Could there have been a dog up there last night?' said Ren.

'And if there was?' said Colin.

Ren shrugged. 'I don't know, but it's interesting.'

'Why?' said Colin.

'Jesus. Did you drive your mama nuts when you were a kid?' said Ren. She ignored the smart-ass face she could see reflected in her laptop screen. 'And look,' she said, pointing again to the photo, 'right around here, there are other markings too, little disturbances in the surface.'

'It's just . . . I'm wondering why those paw prints – if that's what they are – would matter a damn,' said Colin. 'What – you think some other dog already found the body?'

'No,' said Ren. 'I mean, you looked all over that snow when you went back up, right? You would have noticed if something had been dug up, covered over. You couldn't hide that. You would have seen where a shovel had tamped down the snow. It would be harder. And there was no snow-fall to cover it up after.'

'Yeah,' said Colin. 'That's my point.'

'And *my* point is that paw prints up there are interesting,' said Ren.

'And possibly completely irrelevant,' said Colin, walking away. The others moved back to their desks.

Ren went to close iPhoto, but she hit a folder and sprung open a screen full of her and Vincent's smiling faces – alone or hanging out with their friends. They were holding up random objects, bending over furniture, pointing at things, flashing wide grins. She smiled. And felt miserable. She scrolled slowly through some more, but every one tried to draw emotions from places she had locked up.

'Where's Gary?' she said, closing her computer.

'With Bob and Mike,' said Colin. 'I think they just got back to Bob's office.'

Ren got up and went in to them, forcing herself to take a bottle of water with her.

Bob was alone on a phone call. He smiled at her and gave her the signal he was nearly done. She grabbed a Jolly Rancher from a bowl by the window and sat down. The television was on a shelf behind her, silent but tuned to the news. Bob finished up.

'So, how you doing?' he said.

'I'm fine. I'm fine,' said Ren.

'Good.'

'I believe we didn't get much up there today.'

'We got nothing.'

'I saw the photos,' she said. 'It looked like maybe a dog had been up there already.'

Bob gave her a big-deal shrug.

'Who knows?' she said. 'So . . . why do you think the body was left on Quandary Peak?'

'Because that's where she was killed,' said Bob, deadpan.

'Jurisdiction-wise, the Sheriff's Office has got the unincorporated parts of the county. Anything not in the township is yours, right?' said Ren.

'Right,' said Bob. He paused. 'Aha – you're saying this could be a killer who just wants *me* to take charge of the investigation, knowing that the case will never be solved . . .'

Ren laughed. 'Shame on you. But you know what I mean about Quandary Peak.'

He shrugged. 'It might have some significance. Or it might not.'

'I'd understand if they were going to throw the body down a mine shaft,' said Ren, 'it's a good place to dump a corpse. Not convenient, though. But leaving it just laying there . . .'

'We don't know where that body started out,' said Bob.

'Yeah, but it's not likely it was in a mine,' said Ren. 'The killer would have to be some mean weightlifting, skiing, Houdini.'

'It could have been opportunistic,' said Bob. 'Someone's up there, runs into her, kills her.'

'If I was hiding out in below freezing, I'd be too numb to pounce on anyone. I don't know, but I guess I'm imagining a struggle between two people in snowsuits, like inflatable Sumo wrestlers. It wouldn't be easy.'

'Not everyone wants easy. And not everyone kills in slim-fitting clothing.'

Ren smiled. 'And no body, no trace, no prints . . .'

'Yup. The lab is not going to be our friend on this one.'

'But time is,' said Ren, standing up. 'Can you get all your guys together?'

'Sure.'

'OK. I'll get Gary, we'll go talk to them. I'd like them to be *very visibly* all over town right away. Plagues of locusts. We have agents coming in from all over, but me, Colin, Cliff and Robbie will be working out of here for as long as we need to.'

'Is that so?' He smiled.

'If you'll have us . . .' she said, smiling back. 'Oh, and if your guys could report back to me directly, that would be great.'

Her cellphone rang. 'Excuse me for one second,' she said.

'Agent Bryce, hello – it's Patrick Transom here.'

'Oh, hello, Mr Transom.' She looked up at Bob and shrugged.

'I was speaking with Sheriff Gage and I know that Jean's body hasn't been found. He said the next step was just to wait. That's a very hard thing to do. Have you or does the FBI have a different view on that?'

'I'm afraid not,' said Ren. 'Nature isn't helping

any of us on this one. We went up as soon as we could, and that's all we can do right now.'

'OK,' said Patrick. 'OK. Uh . . . I was down at the trailhead and I saw you leave early. I didn't get a chance to go over and talk to you. I was just wondering if there was somewhere important you needed to be . . .'

What? 'I'm sorry, I . . .'

'Oh,' said Patrick, 'just that – were you called away from the scene to, I don't know, investigate a lead or something?'

Jesus Christ. 'No, I wasn't,' said Ren.

'OK. Then why –'

'My colleagues have given me a full report of their visit to Quandary Peak, Mr Transom. And I have another meeting to attend now, I'm afraid.'

'Sheriff Gage said that there was no trace evidence found.'

'Yes,' said Ren. 'I'm sure you can appreciate the massive disturbance of an avalanche. But despite what . . .' *you see on television* '. . . you might think, very few cases are solved because of trace evidence. It's usually down to good old-fashioned investigation. And as you know, we have the best resources possible at our disposal.'

'Yes, that's true. Well, I'll let you get to your meeting. Thank you for taking my call.'

'Any time,' said Ren. 'I'm sorry we were unable to recover Jean's body today, Mr Transom. I really am.'

'Me, too.'

'Take care.' Ren put the phone down. She looked at Bob. 'Wow. Intense.'

'"Good old-fashioned investigation",' said Bob. 'I liked that.'

'Shut up.'

'What was the "no, I wasn't" all about?'

'He spotted me leaving the trailhead early. It was a bit creepy.'

'That's not creepy. He was there, you were walking by. It's not like he's showing you grainy footage he took of you on his cellphone from your backyard.'

'That is true,' said Ren. 'I just don't like the feeling of being watched.'

'Gives you the feebie-jeebies?'

Ren smiled. 'I just hope he's not going to be on my back for this. He's a nice man, but . . .'

'Don't worry about that for now, Ren.'

'I know, I know. I overthink.'

'I underthink.'

'Yin–yang.'

'Dumb–dumber.'

13

Mike Delaney walked in to Bob's office with two large bottles of water and a giant, battered-looking bottle of Vitamin C tablets. He handed them to Ren.

'Hey,' he said. 'How you doing?'

'Much better, thank you. Dr Barger confirmed our findings . . .'

He smiled.

'Thanks for these,' said Ren. 'You're very kind. Now, what I also need is a list of people who regularly go up Quandary Peak.'

Bob and Mike shot glances at each other.

'Undersheriff Delaney,' said Bob, 'could you call in the three thousand residents and, let me see, five thousand tourons currently spending time in Breckenridge. Rustle up some sandwiches and soup, keep them talky.'

'Tourons?' said Ren.

'Tourist plus moron,' said Bob.

Ren smiled. 'What I meant,' she said, 'was, you know, people who have a reason to be up there –'

'I repeat,' said Bob, 'Undersheriff Delaney . . .'

Ren laughed. 'For example, Search and Rescue, Forest Services, the groomers, gondola people . . .'

'People *employed* to be up there,' said Bob. 'Does it matter? Employed, up there to ski, up there to snowboard, up there for the holy hell of it . . .'

'Just go with me,' said Ren. 'Please. I have to start somewhere and I might as well have a list that doesn't run into the – as you may have mentioned a few times – thousands.'

Bob smiled. 'OK, we'll put that together, but it'll still be a long list.'

'That's fine,' said Ren. 'With the kind help of your team, we should be able to get through it quickly enough. And, Bob . . .? You should move your desk. It's bad Feng Shui to have your back to the door. Something about being stabbed in the back.'

Bob smiled.

'Anyway, thanks again,' said Ren.

'I'll call if I need any more decorating help,' said Bob.

'I'll draw you up some plans . . .' said Ren. 'OK, I'm going to head over to Glenwood. And when I get back, I'll be just three doors down from you with the other Safe Streeters. Please thank whoever had to vacate that nice office for us.'

'Yeah,' said Bob. 'Your desk's the one facing away from the door.'

Conoco was Ren's last landmark when she drove off I-70. She took the next left and swung into the small parking lot of the Glenwood Springs RA. She looked up at the building: three stories, pale yellow brick, normal. No history like the Livestock Exchange Building – not a place to harbor a giant urinal. She walked into the quiet foyer and took the elevator to the third floor. The door was jammed open. She rang the bell and walked in.

'Hello? Agent Gressett? Agent Austerval?'

'Hello,' she heard back. 'Be right with you.'

Tiny Gressett came out with one hand on his belt. 'Oh . . . Ren. It's nice to see you again.'

'You too.'

They both looked at each other as if they were thinking the same thing; the number of sentences in life that were assigned to bullshit.

'Follow me,' he said.

They walked a short hallway into the office.

Gressett gestured around the room. 'This is . . . was Jean's desk right here.'

'It's terrible what happened to her, so unfair.'

'What's fair?' said Gressett with an explosive snap.

Jesus Christ.

'What's fair?' he said again. 'Have you any idea?

Do you know something none of the rest of us don't?'

'I'm . . . I just meant I'm sorry.'

Gressett paused and let out a breath. He pointed to the wall beside Jean's desk. There were plaques, certificates and framed awards. Ren leaned in. She had most of them herself and a few others.

'Very impressive,' said Ren.

'I'd take Jean Transom as my right-hand man any day of the week.'

Ren nodded and moved toward Jean's seat. 'I'm just going to have a look through her desk and files, see if there's anything . . .'

'Go ahead,' said Gressett. His tone said *you're not going to find anything.* 'Can I get you a coffee?'

'Thanks, that would be great.'

She sat down and pulled the files on the desktop toward her. They were a mix of cases: drugs, bank fraud and embezzlement, child abuse, one crime aboard an aircraft, domestic abuse, theft from interstate shipments, robbery, unlawful flight to avoid prosecution. There was a folder called 'RUTH'. Inside were photocopies of child sexual assault files. There were eight files – each marked with colored, numbered tabs – twelve different girls and the abuse they had suffered. It spanned almost thirty years of offences, including indecent exposure, fondling, attempted abduction, and rape, carried out across Summit and Garfield Counties.

Ren casually started re-arranging the files in

date order. She could see Gressett almost climbing over his desk to look at what she was doing.

'Was Jean working this file alone?' said Ren, holding it up. 'The little girls and the perverts. These appear to be photocopies of original files whose numbers I'm guessing are the references here on these little tabs.'

Gressett came over from his desk and looked at the file. He leaned in and closed the cover. 'RUTH – yes, I've seen this on Jean's desk. She handled any of the child sexual abuse cases here in the RA.' He opened it again. 'These are all different girls.'

'Yes,' said Ren.

'Oh,' said Gressett. 'I had assumed it was just one girl called Ruth Something.'

Ren went through the photocopies. 'OK – there is *one* girl here called Ruth. But the file doesn't have a tab on it. Actually, it seems to be the only one that doesn't have a tab . . . or a photo . . . or a last name . . . or a location . . . or a date. So I'm wondering,' said Ren, 'what it's doing here.'

'Well, I can't help you with *any* of that,' said Gressett going back to his desk.

'I guess Jean must have figured all these cases were linked.'

Gressett nodded. 'I guess so.'

The two most recent assaults were on top of the pile and had happened within the previous twelve months. Ren cross-referenced the numbers and pulled out the files. The assaults – indecent exposure and attempted abduction – had originally been reported to Frisco PD and Silverthorne PD. Jean had then interviewed the little girls and typed up the transcripts.

Ren read through them. *Impressive.* Jean had clearly developed a way of interviewing children that elicited a lot more information than a traumatized child would normally volunteer.

'I guess it *is* just one of *many* files Jean was working on,' said Gressett.

Subtle.

'Besides,' he said, 'it wasn't exactly occupying her time any time recently. The latest incident was in October last year – that much I do know, because it was at Hallowe'en.'

Ren nodded. 'Had Jean any leads?'

'Just lists of known sex offenders and no evidence to link them to anything.' He shrugged. 'They are real clever in the children they choose and how they cover their tracks . . .'

Gressett nodded and went back to his computer.

No editorializing with Tiny Gressett.

14

Ren pulled another slim pile of print-outs from the back of Jean's desk.

What the hell?

At the same time, she tipped over the mug of coffee Gressett had left on her desk.

'Shit.' She shouted louder than she wanted to. She jumped to her feet, scooping up a phone charger before it got wet. She found some napkins in Jean's drawer and slapped them down on the desk. 'Oops,' she said, looking over at Gressett's impassive face. She wrapped the phone charger in a napkin and put it in a dry corner. 'Did Jean use a Motorola?'

'Yes,' said Gressett.

Ren sat quietly staring down at the print-outs, dabbing at pools of coffee where she noticed them. She had been too late to stop the coffee soaking into the edges of most of the files.

'Gressett, sorry to bother you again, but do you

know what Jean was doing with these print-outs on Domenica Val Pando?'

He paused. 'I have no idea.'

I'm fucking here to go through Jean's things to help the investigation, you dickhead.

'I mean,' said Ren, 'I don't even know why –'

'That is some woman, Domenica Val Pando,' said Gressett, sitting up. 'Seven shades of crazy.' He reached out his hand. 'Give me a look at those.'

Why don't you come get them yourself? Ren got up and handed them over to him.

'Domenica Bin Killin,' he said.

Not funny.

'Now, this is where there is no justice in the world,' said Gressett. 'You have Domenica Val Pando, an amoral, psychopathic – female! – spends years holed up in New Mexico, killing and maiming and drug-running and all the rest of it, sending other people to kill and maim and . . . avoids arrest. And now, she's probably lying on some beach somewhere in Aruba. And then you have Jean Transom, a wonderful person, a helpful person, an excellent agent . . . and she's the one who . . .' He hit the back of his hand off the pages. 'It was a damn shame she didn't get finished off back then.'

For a moment, Ren thought he was talking about Jean. 'Oh. Val Pando . . .'

'For one of the most successful undercover jobs the FBI ever worked on . . .' said Gressett.

He shook his head. 'Todd Austerval started Gary Dettling's Undercover Program, but he didn't make the grade. He said that on day one Dettling scared the living daylights out of the trainees with the Val Pando case. He held it up as the gold standard of undercover work: one agent, under deep cover with Val Pando for a whole year, absolutely undetected. And still, *still*, after all that, it was screwed up at the end. So that was the big lesson from Gary Dettling at the start of the course – this is what you should aspire to. And here's how it can go wrong. Do you know how it went wrong in the end?'

A man would never ask another man a question like that. The I-know-something-you-don't-know tone.

'It would be very interesting to hear your take on that,' said Ren.

'Agent safety,' said Gressett. 'That was it. Pull one agent out instead of bringing a whole organized crime operation down. And that *is* Bureau policy. That's what has to be done.'

'Yup,' said Ren. 'It sucks that the Bureau can't recruit suicide agents.'

'I don't mean that,' said Gressett. 'It's just . . . it all seemed like a waste.'

Don't even think of criticizing Gary Dettling to me. 'Agent safety is what it is,' said Ren. 'The same reason SAR doesn't always go back up mountains to recover bodies. You just can't risk lives like that.'

'To a point, to a point,' said Gressett.

'To what point?' said Ren. *As you sit here in your comfortable out-of-the-firing-line office.*

Gressett was obviously not used to having his opinions questioned. Todd was either too dumb or too used to tuning him out.

'Well, to the point that you achieve your goal,' said Gressett.

'Tell that to a dead agent's wife and family,' said Ren. 'Todd is a lucky man he didn't make the grade.'

Gressett opened his mouth and closed it again. Todd stood in the doorway, sweating, straight from the gym.

Shit.

He pulled headphones out of his ears.

'Hey,' he said. 'Hey, Ren. I'm just . . .' he gestured out the door. 'Let me go take a shower.'

Gressett was smiling a smile that told Ren she was on her own and that he was glad there was a little black mark against her funny little name.

None of the drawers threw up anything interesting. None of the undersides had anything taped to them, there were no secret compartments, there was no note saying: *If you are reading this, then you know I am dead.* There was nothing other than what Ren would have expected from the contradiction that was Jean Transom. *A private, open book.*

*   *   *

Jean had lived in a two-bedroom ranch house in Rifle, a town of six thousand, twenty-seven miles west of Glenwood Springs, where the cost of living was not so high. Ren wanted to visit the house alone so she could go through it in silence, without a backing track of shouting, wisecracks or sports scores.

Jean's was a house of neat rows. In the living room: DVDs, CDs, candles, cushions. In the kitchen: mugs, ceramics, spice jars. In the bedroom: bears, dolls, pillows, books. In the bathroom: soap, super-market shampoo, conditioner and moisturizer.

Ren stood in Jean's lavender-and-white bed-room, quaint and warm, even without the lamps and candles that looked as though they burned every night. On the shelf above the bed, there were romance novels, perfectly preserved Care Bears, a Strawberry Shortcake doll and a Cabbage Patch Kid. Ren couldn't resist taking it down. *After all these years, you're still creepy.* Ren had the Garbage Pail Kids – collectible cards with grotesque draw-ings: interpretations of Cabbage Patch Kids with missing teeth, eyes, limbs and green slime spewing from their noses and mouths.

Ren went to the chest of drawers under the window. She pulled out the top one. It had a handful of pastel cotton multi-pack panties. Ren smiled. One of her friends called them darkroom panties; things would only develop if the lights were out. Every woman had a couple, but they didn't make up their entire underwear collection.

The next drawer down had bras – big, plain and seamless sporties or minimizers. *My head would fit in one cup. You go, girl.* The rest of the drawers were filled with neatly folded T-shirts and shirts from Gap and J. Crew.

Jean's office was like a preserved room on a historic tour, but without the human touches of a cup or a pair of folded glasses or a diagonal pen. Everything was laid straight. There was no sense of interruption. Her laptop had already been taken away, so there were no files to go through, except the paper ones, organized perfectly in the cabinets behind the desk. A phone charger was plugged in with the lead wrapped around it.

All over the house, there was sad, unfinished business: leftovers of salad wrapped on a shelf in the refrigerator, sticks of carrots and celery, a hand-washed sweater lying flat on a dryer, a pile of photographs. Ren flicked through them – they were from inside the house. She looked around and could see everything in the photographs, wide shots, macros, with flash, without. Jean Transom was testing a new camera and a new printer. A house and its contents suspended, waiting to strike up again when the right person came through the door.

Ren looked at the family photos on the wall; Jean and Patrick Transom, his wife, their children. *And no shadows in the background.*

15

'Hey,' said Ren, walking toward the next-door garden. An older woman was backing down the path, bent forward, dragging a rug, giving it an emergency shake-out. She was wearing red oversized pajamas and giant silver snow boots. A cigarette was gripped tightly in her mouth at a ninety-degree angle.

She turned to Ren and rolled her eyes. Ren looked down at the rug.

'Ooh, sick dog,' said Ren.

The woman nodded, stood up and pulled out the cigarette. 'Why do you think I've got this under my nose. Whooo.' She batted her hand in front of her face. 'Stay back,' she said. 'This shit is some age-old curse coming back to wreak vengeance on the world.'

Ren laughed. And stayed back, watching the woman from Jean's drive. People underestimated how much neighbors noticed. They had quiet, familiar eyes. Depending on what they thought of you, they could store a massive amount of accurate details about you, or they could process it all through a filter of distorting emotions – dislike, bitterness, jealousy, lust, love, hatred, mistrust. One person's hot neighbor was another person's freak. Or to a third person – both. Ren talked to neighbors from the neck up, distracting them from the hand she was shoving through their belly to wrench out their gut for inspection. There was no face value with neighbors.

'Seriously,' said the woman, pulling a black garbage bag from the waistband of her pants, 'let me wrap this up tight and I'm all yours. I presume you're with the FBI.'

'Yes, ma'am. My name is Ren Bryce.'

'Well, I'm Margaret Shaw and I clean up more shit than you ever will.' She laughed and pushed the cigarette back between her lips. 'OK,' she said. 'I'm done.' She had washed her hands under an icy outside tap.

'Margaret, I'm investigating Jean Transom's death,' said Ren. 'And I'd just like to talk to you a little about her.'

'Go ahead.'

'What was Jean like?'

Margaret shrugged. 'That's a good question.' She nodded her appreciation.

'Right . . . is it a question you'd like to answer?'

'Ha. Sure. "I don't know," is the answer.'

'OK,' said Ren. 'Why is that?'

'She's the stereotypical quiet neighbor you hear talked about on the news. I'm wondering should we all be noisy so we won't get killed?'

'You could be on to something,' said Ren.

'I didn't even know Jean was an FBI agent 'til I saw it on the news. I thought she was a forest ranger with her clear skin and those tan pants of hers.' She looked Ren up and down. 'You don't look like one either. You could be . . .'

Don't say anything that will scar me.

'. . . well, you have those eyes, so . . .'

Don't say squaw.

'. . . one of those *Disney on Ice* people.'

Original.

'My son used to be the letter D in Disneyland Paris,' said Margaret. 'The ones that dance in the parade. He was dating Y . . .' Margaret's face said she wasn't impressed with Y.

'Hmm,' said Ren. 'Interesting that Y picked one of the only letters there were two of. And don't tell me – one day she made the mistake of going with the wrong D.'

'Or *did* she? *Did* she make a mistake – that's what I said to him.'

'But the . . . suit,' said Ren. 'Didn't that . . . like, didn't she notice, after the suit came off?'

'He said they didn't always take them off . . . sometimes they worked around them.'

Ren was stilled with mental images.

'Anyway,' said Margaret. 'He's Pinocchio now.' She paused. 'My guess is he'll need to do a lot of lying to keep that Y bitch happy.'

'And I thought it was the truth that hurts.'

Margaret slapped Ren's forearm and let out a dirty, smoky laugh. 'Good for you,' she said. 'I like your style. I've decided not to bullshit you about Jean now.' She laughed more.

'Well, I appreciate it,' said Ren. 'So, back to business . . .'

'OK. Lowdown is as follows: Jean was private. Hello, goodbye, good weather, bad. I had no keys to her house. None of the neighbors did. She was quiet and a subdued kind of friendly. She ran in the morning . . . like she was being chased by the devil. She went to work early, she came home six, seven, seven thirty . . . I could hear the TV at night. She looked after her cat.' Margaret paused. 'I guess she was one of the millions of women in the world who do exactly the same.'

Ren was nodding her head without raising it from her notebook.

'Now, that's how come I'm telling you all this,' said Margaret, 'so the scene is set.'

Ren looked up, frowning. 'OK . . .'

'Well – and this could be absolutely nothing – in the last few months, she had a visitor, a very attractive woman, must have been in her mid-to-late twenties.'

'Was she . . . a friend, a relative?'

'I have no idea.'

'Did Jean mention her name to you, or did you see them greeting each other, saying goodbye at the door, the car, anything like that?'

'I saw her arrive, this young woman, with maybe a bag of something from the store. And I would only see her getting back into her car alone. She had flowers once, quite a small bunch; I thought they were kind of measly.'

'What did she look like?

'Like I said, attractive, tall, brown hair, healthy looking, dressed normal, nothing too fancy, nothing too sporty.'

'Did you notice, or did Jean tell you, anything about dating? Was she dating anyone?'

Margaret paused. 'Oh, I see where you're going with this . . .'

Ren paused. 'I'm not going anywhere . . . I'm just wondering about other visitors.'

Margaret shook her head. 'I saw her brother – I've met him; nice man – but that was it. I wish I could tell you something to help you find who did this to her. And I'm guessing already that I can't.'

'We don't know that. Can you tell me what car the woman who came to see her was driving?'

'A red one.'

Ren's pen hovered.

'I don't know the first thing about cars,' said Margaret.

'OK. Anything else I need to know about Jean? Anything that might have stood out?'

'Nothing stood out about her,' said Margaret. 'And I really don't mean that in a bad way.'

'No, I understand. Would you remember – did you see her on Friday, January 12th?' said Ren.

Margaret thought about it. She nodded. 'I saw her when she came back from work, around seven o'clock.'

'And after that?'

'No, I did not,' said Margaret. 'But I was in bed by ten thirty.'

'And what about Saturday morning?'

'Her car was gone by the time I got up. So she could have been there all night, or she could have stayed somewhere else.'

'OK, Margaret. Thank you so much for your time,' said Ren.

'A pleasure. And here's where I get your card in case my memory springs back to life with a vital clue and I save the day.'

Ren smiled and handed her a card. 'Now, don't let Pinocchio get his hands on that . . .' She walked down the path to her car. 'Hey,' she called back, 'where's the cat?'

'McGraw?' said Margaret. 'He's not in the house?'

Ren shook her head. 'No.'

'Oh dear,' said Margaret.

'What's he look like?'

'Evil. Tabby.'

'Is he Quick Draw? Or Phil?'

'Tim,' said Margaret. 'Tim McGraw. *My* cat's called Faith Hill.'

'Really?'

'Don't be ridiculous. Cats? No way. They don't give a damn about anyone.'

'And clearly your dog gives a big shit about you.'

Margaret let out a laugh, almost slipped on an icy patch and let out another laugh. Ren waved goodbye.

Poor McGraw. Please don't be out in the snow.

16

I-70 was a slow-moving stress-fest. Ren checked her watch. It was four p.m. *Shit.* Skiers and snowboarders had started to make their way down off Vail Pass. Ren gripped the steering wheel, swapped her old gum for new gum, changed the temperature settings, rubbed moisturizer into her hands. One minute passed. *Shit.* She punched through her phone contacts until she got to H.

'Hey, Helen. It's Ren. Can you talk?'

'Sure. How are you doing?'

'I'm OK. Oh, hold on.' She braked, slamming her hand on the horn. 'You idiot! Fuck you, too, mister. Asshole. I'm sorry, Helen.'

'Are you OK?'

'Yes. I am. How are you?'

'Well, I'm fine. You under pressure?'

'Not really, I . . .' She leaned out the window. 'I do not believe this shit. Another rollover. Another idiot lady driver in an SUV without chains. I am going to be so late.' She closed the window.

'Ren,' said Helen.

'Sorry,' said Ren. 'I got this new case – the agent who died in Breck.'

'Ah.'

'I'm lead investigator.'

'Will you be in Breck for the next while?' said Helen.

'Yup.'

'Is there any hope of seeing you?'

'I . . .' Ren rolled down the window again and stuck her head out. 'This is a nightmare. Why today? When I need to get back for a briefing and I am in charge of –'

'Ren, what I'm getting is you calling me on your way to and from meetings. I'm on speaker phone, you're in the mountains, your signal's going . . . it's not great.'

'I know. I'm sorry –'

'There's no need to be sorry. Just, why don't you come to Denver?'

'I can't. I'm sorry. If I drove to Denver, I'd lose half a day.'

'You might lose half a day, but do you think you might gain something?'

'I didn't mean it like that. I just –'

'It's been a while.'

'I know,' said Ren. 'I really want to. But for now, the phone's the best I can do.'

'I guess it's better than nothing.'

'I gotta go. It's moving a little. I'll call you.'

Helen paused. 'Sure.'

The conference room at the Sheriff's Office was full. Ren was three-quarters of an hour late by the time she arrived.

'OK, everyone,' she said as she stood at the desk, staring out at the assembled team. *Get your shit together.*

'You're lucky we can confirm the MVA on I-70,' said Bob.

Ren stared at him. *Not in front of the children.*

'OK,' said Ren. 'The last known sighting of Jean Transom was at the Glenwood RA on Friday, January 12th by her colleagues, Tiny Gressett and Todd Austerval. Our White Collar Squad is going through the financial records. What we got so far are recent transactions. So we know that that evening she went to the nine p.m. showing of a chick flick at Rifle Creek movie theater. We're waiting for an ID on her there. The movie was over at eleven p.m. If she went straight home, earliest she would have made it was eleven thirty. I've just come back from speaking with her neighbor, Margaret Shaw. She saw her walk into her house at seven p.m. and didn't see her later on that evening. Mrs Shaw herself had gone to bed by ten thirty.'

Ren looked through the notes that had been

left for her by the Sheriff's Office detectives and the Safe Streets guys. 'On Saturday morning, January 13th, Jean paid for breakfast at Mort's Diner in Rifle at nine a.m. She went to the outlet mall in Silverthorne. She bought a shirt in J Crew, a necklace in Zales and a grill pan in Le Creuset. They were still in bags in her house. She then went to the Open Book in Frisco. The owner called here after she saw the news. She remembered Jean, says she was polite, they talked briefly about the weather, that was it.'

You can go through a day, a week, a month, a year without ever thinking that someone will end up retracing your steps because you've never come home.

'Colin Grabien over there,' said Ren, 'is our phone expert in Safe Streets. He's waiting for Verizon to get back to him. So we should have cellphone and office phone records by tomorrow morning. I visited Jean's office and her home. There was a phone charger in each location, but they were not for the same phone – there was a Motorola charger in her office, which Tiny Gressett confirmed was her regular work phone. And in her home, she had a Virgin charger.' Ren flicked through her notes. 'I haven't seen any references yet to the corresponding phone.

'I've taken away her work files from the Glenwood office – she had forty open cases. I'm going to split them between you all, so we can check for possible links to her murder.

'Lists of people with priors in town are currently being checked out by the detectives here at the Sheriff's Office.

'This evening and tonight, I need people pounding pavements.' She paused. 'Thank you for your time.'

Everyone left and moved back to their offices. Ren gathered up her notes and was walking toward Bob's office when she heard Tiny Gressett's voice around the corner. Something made Ren stop: *her* name and *his* tone.

'. . . Bu Babe who probably has Safe Streets wrapped around her little finger.'

Bureau Babe. Nice. There was a brief silence. Ren wondered had they heard her.

'Uh. Do you think?' said Todd. 'She doesn't seem the type . . .'

'Really?' said Gressett. 'You don't think she goes in there and –'

He made a noise – Ren wasn't sure what it was supposed to represent.

'I've never seen her do that,' said Todd. His tone was 'wrap it up'.

'Well, look at you . . .' said Gressett.

'She's not my type,' said Todd. 'Have you ever seen me with a brunette? What about you, Gressett? You pulling her pigtails, is that what this is about?'

Gressett snorted. 'Sure. Yeah. Sure.'

Ren held her cellphone to her ear and spoke – loud and cheery. 'Not a problem, I'll do that. You bet.' She had turned the corner by the time she pretended to hang up. 'Hey, guys. What's up?'

'Not a thing,' said Gressett.

17

Ren walked into Bob's office with a face to match her feelings about Tiny Gressett.

'Is everything OK?'

'Yes, sir,' said Ren. 'Are you ready?'

Bob nodded and got up, grabbing his jacket from the back of his chair.

Mike Delaney walked in. 'Hey, a call just came in from Reign on Main. Hal Rautts says Jean had supper in there on the Monday night – January 15th.'

'Hal Rautts is the owner,' said Bob to Ren.

'OK, you want to swing by there, check it out?' said Ren.

'Yeah,' said Bob.

'See you later,' said Mike.

'Where are you going to go?' said Ren.

'Me and your friend Robbie Truax are going to hit the bars on Main Street, starting out at the north end – Big Mountain Brewery.'

* * *

On quiet sidewalks covered with snow, Breckenridge still had warmth. It was a mining town that had ridden the boom and bust rollercoaster and come out on top; a resort town that managed to keep its charm.

Ren looked out the window of the Explorer at the thousands of tiny white fairy lights that lit up the trees along Main Street.

'Here's how I see it,' she said. 'Aspen is the beautiful, aloof sister. Breck is the cute one who everyone really wants to be with. And Vail is the one who's had all the plastic surgery to try to be like the other two.'

'Interesting,' said Bob.

'Even their names sound that way,' said Ren.

'You've put a lot of thought into this.'

'I have.'

'Doesn't mean people are going to agree with you,' said Bob.

'It's not about that. It's about me working out how I feel about things through the use of analogies.'

Bob smiled. 'I like it here.'

'I love it.'

They drove past the Prospector, a little diner on Main Street.

'A parking space is the gold dust around here,' said Bob. He drove up Main Street for the second time and took a left on to Jefferson Avenue. 'Round and round we go . . .'

'It's cool,' said Ren. 'I've –'

'Do not say you've just said one of those parking-space prayers,' said Bob, turning to her.

'They work.' She pointed to a space on the opposite side of the street.

'Sure,' said Bob, looking over. 'Let's park in front of a doctor's entrance.'

'Oh . . .'

'Yeah – oh. We'll keep on moving.'

'Just do the church car park and we'll walk.'

Bob drove around the block. 'One more shot,' he said. 'Hey. Look at that. One right there. Right outside.'

Ren smiled.

People resorted to Reign on Main. It was where they went when every other restaurant was full. Every table had a folded coaster under one leg, every waxed tablecloth had a knife wound.

'Hey, Hal,' said Bob.

'Hey, Bob. Thanks for coming in.'

'Thank you for calling.'

'I saw the photo.'

Bob nodded. 'Tragedy, tragedy. Hal, this is Ren Bryce with the FBI.'

'Nice to meet you,' said Hal. 'Can I get you guys something to eat?'

'No thanks,' said Bob.

'N . . .' said Ren.

They waited.

'Actually, would you mind?' she said.

'Not a problem,' said Hal. 'What can I get you?'

'A cheeseburger is fine,' said Ren.

They sat down at a table in the back corner.

'So – Jean Transom,' said Bob.

'Yes,' said Hal. 'She came in, took a table,' he pointed to the window, 'she ordered and she split under an hour later. She left cash. I can get you the till receipt, so you can have the exact time.'

'Anything stand out about her?' said Ren.

'No. Just, she had a formal way about her. Most people in here are more chilled.'

Stoned. 'And Jean was . . .?' said Ren.

He shrugged. 'Just – she didn't match the place, that's all.'

'Did she seem anxious or anything?' said Bob.

'Maybe, like, focused?' said Hal.

'On anything in particular?' said Ren.

He shrugged.

Ren felt a flash of irritation.

The cheeseburger arrived with the lid off and a dull pool of grease on top of the meat. Ren's stomach tightened. Even the ketchup paused. Ren smiled at Hal. 'Thanks. This looks great.' She had never eaten a mouthful of food quite like it.

'Oh. I'm vibrating,' she said, standing up. 'Excuse me.' She walked outside and rang Bob. 'Don't say my name. And don't look out the window. It's me. Ren. I'll give you ten dollars to start eating that burger.'

Bob nodded as she talked. 'I'm afraid that's not possible right now. But if you can make it in to me some time soon, I can look at an alternative. And we can discuss payment at a later date.' He put the phone down and apologized to Hal. Ren waited two minutes and came back in. Bob stood up to let her past and put a finger with just enough pressure on the edge of the plate.

'Oh. I *am* sorry,' he said. The burger fell to the floor, followed by a shower of fries.

Hal stood up. 'Let me go order you –'

'Really,' said Ren, putting a hand on his forearm. 'It's fine. I . . . I'm good. We don't really have the time. Maybe we could just move tables?'

'If you're sure,' said Hal.

'Positive.'

They took a small table in the corner of the diner.

'Is there anything else you can think of?' said Ren. 'Was Jean checking her watch? Did she look like she was waiting to meet someone?'

Hal paused. 'Hmm. I can't be sure, but I wouldn't say so. And she didn't seem to leave in a real big hurry.' He shrugged. 'It all seems kind of lame now. I mean, you guys came all the way in here, and now I feel, like . . . whatever.'

Ren shook her head. 'We got to talk to one of

the last people who saw our victim alive. That's really important.'

'Thanks,' said Hal. 'I kind of hope I remember more, like something will come back to me when you're gone.'

This is not a movie. 'Well, if it does, you can call either of us.'

They both handed over their cards. *Even though it feels like a movie some times.*

As they got up to leave, a group of tourists stood staring through the window, dressed for a nicer restaurant they clearly couldn't get a table at. None of them looked as if they wanted to be the one to say no and keep the group walking the streets in the snow to find another place that could be full. *Do it. Go, go, go. Don't ruin your night.*

'Jesus Christ,' said Bob when they got out on to the street, 'was the burger really all that bad?'

Ren paused. 'It was the kind of meat that brought you on a journey from hairy abattoirs to small-town processing plants where workers play games like Kick the Cows' Balls into the Grinder.'

'Bulls' balls.'

'Yeah, OK. Because that makes it better.'

'Why didn't you just leave it?' said Bob.

'I didn't want to offend the guy.'

'Politeness could kill you some day,' said Bob. ' "Please sir, would you mind not firing that gun into my temple? And really, you are squeezing

my waist a little too tight. But I must say, the
tattoo on your forearm is beautifully drawn."'

'It's more I don't like hurting people's feelings,'
said Ren.

'Jesus, you'll go right up the ranks of the FBI
with that stony attitude,' said Bob. 'Hey, do you
think Jean Transom actually ate her meal?'

'If she did?' said Ren. 'That's cause of death
locked off.'

18

Ren loved the sound, the resistance, the effort of walking through snow. She made her way down Washington Avenue toward Main Street, looking out at the mountains across the lightening, early-morning sky. Four peaks from the Tenmile Range – seven through ten – made up the Breckenridge ski area and were the draw that boosted the population from three thousand to twenty-seven thousand at peak season.

The Breckenridge Welcome Center was at the corner of the Blue River Plaza on Main Street. Ren walked through the small foyer into the first room of the exhibition on gold and silver mining in the area – eight thousand six hundred acres of shiny economy. And when it all dried up, the only thing that rescued Breck from ghost-town status was the fight put up by the residents.

Main Street used to be dance halls and saloons, and the merchants had Ridge Street. Now Ridge

Street was lined with restaurants, offices, inns and homes. Ren studied a photo montage of the change – the same building and its different roles, different smiling people standing outside each time.

She went upstairs to find the display on Quandary Peak. It was the highest peak in the Tenmile Range. Jean Transom's body had been found off the East Ridge trail, which was a recently carved route – less than ten years old. Ren pulled her camera out of her jacket pocket and took photos of the display.

She ran into Colin Grabien on her way out the door.

'Having a tourism moment?' said Colin.

'I'm actually researching,' said Ren.

'Researching is great,' said Colin. 'Everything is covered. Do you use coffee as a fuel expense?'

'I'm getting to know Breck, the . . .' *This sounds dumb.*

'You think Jean was killed by the ghost of an old prospector? Or maybe, like the Brown, a dead madam rose up for revenge against the right-minded.'

Ren frowned. 'What?'

'You haven't been to the Brown Hotel? A madam was shot dead on the attic stairs. She was going to turn the place into "a house of ill-repute".' *Air quotes.* 'The owner vanished,' said Colin. 'You should go – weird shit happens in the ladies toilets.'

They both paused.

'And can I ask?' said Ren, 'while you're giving me a hard time, what that has to do with solving this case?'

'I'm not giving you a hard time,' said Colin. 'Who said that?'

'Yeah, like those people who say, "I'm not criticizing you, but . . ."' *Why am I having this conversation?*

'I was meeting the owner,' said Colin. 'I thought if Jean had paid the place a visit, he could have something for us.'

'I'm not feeling the whole Jean-in-brothel vibe,' said Ren.

'But you're feelin*g* the whole Jean-in-historic-Breckenridge *vibe* . . .'

'I'm feeling the need to keep on working here. Gotta go.'

'Dinner later with the guys at Kenosha. Six thirty.'

'Great.' *I'll be back at the inn, sticking hot needles in my eyes.* She looked at her watch. 'I'm giving a briefing shortly. So I'll see you back at the Sheriff's Office then, anyway.'

He looked at her. She smiled.

'In Bob's office?' said Colin.

'Like we're all going to fit in Bob's office,' said Ren. 'The Sheriff's Office I refer to is the entire building. It covers all the offices, including Bob's and the one that has been loaned out to us. Bob's office is *Bob's office*. We'll be meeting in the conference room.'

'Thanks for clearing that up so slowly,' said Colin.

'Aw,' said Ren. 'Thanks for listening so loudly.'

Ren was walking the hallway to her office when she heard Mike saying, 'Oh, good God, she's a train wreck.'

His voice was coming from Bob's office. Ren knocked on the open door and walked in.

'Are you talking about me?' she said.

Mike turned and smiled. He pointed at the television screen in the corner.

'Bob, turn that up,' he said.

Bob grabbed the remote control and the voice of Casey Bonaventure filled the room.

'. . . disappearance in February last year of twenty-eight-year-old Mark Allen Wilson, whose body has never been found. Wilson was last seen at the Brockton Filly, a bar five miles outside Breckenridge at the base of Quandary Peak – a mountain that in the past year has cast a shadow over the lives of two families –'

Bob shook his head. 'Jesus, Casey is something else. I told her to go off and do some research, and she comes back with this non-story again.' He turned down the television.

'Hey,' said Ren. 'That could have been interesting.'

'Seriously, it's not,' said Bob. 'Missing guy from out-of-town, drinking all evening at the Filly, gets loaded, gets into a brawl, wanders out in the snow, goes to relieve himself in the trees, falls over, hits his head, gets hypothermia, dies. No body, but, hey, that's the story of our lives around here.'

'That's it?' said Ren. 'No trace of him?'

'Nope,' said Bob. 'Last person he was seen hanging out with in the bar was a guy called Terrence Haggart. And when I say "hanging out with", I mean "getting badly beaten by". Next thing, Wilson's reported missing. And never shows up again. So, there you have it.'

'I see,' said Ren. 'Has the family given you guys a hard time?'

'He was an alcoholic they had no time for,' said Bob.

'That's very sad,' said Ren. 'An illness that seems too recreational for people to do anything about until it's too late.'

'Whatever,' said Mike.

'Has anyone seen Tiny Gressett?' said Ren.

'Last time I saw him,' said Mike, 'he was in the kitchen down the hall.'

'Thanks, see you later.'

Gressett was on his way out of the kitchen with a coffee.

'Tiny?' said Ren.

He stopped, but didn't turn around. 'Yes?'

She walked around him to face him. 'I know you probably didn't have that kind of relationship with her, and that women can be tricky to read at the best of times, right? But can I ask you about Jean's personal life?'

Gressett nodded. 'For what it's worth.'

'Did she talk about boyfriends or dating? Did anyone ever come pick her up from work, or meet her for lunch?'

He frowned. 'Not that I can think of.'

'She never went to lunch with anyone else?'

'She ate at the office a lot . . . or we went together.'

God help her.

'I don't know after that,' said Gressett. 'She could have. I've seen her in Sacred Grounds a couple times with a magazine. It's a coffee shop in Glenwood.'

'So, alone?'

He nodded. 'Yes. Always.'

'Did she seem interested in dating?'

'In dating? Well, she kept to herself. Maybe she liked it that way.'

Ren nodded. 'Did you ever get the feeling, maybe, that . . .'

'That what? She didn't like dating?'

'Do you think there's any possibility that Jean could have been gay?'

'I would say absolutely not.' He almost recoiled.

You asshole.

'Nothing wrong with it, if she was,' said Ren.

He looked at Ren sideways, then tried to recover. 'I . . . I know that . . . It's just . . . she wasn't.'

'Maybe it was something she kept hidden,' said Ren. *Because of your biased ass.* 'So, just as far as *you* know, she didn't go on any dates, that you were aware of, while she worked with you.'

'*Our* relationship was strictly professional, if that's what you mean.'

No, that's not what I meant, but knock yourself out.

'So she wouldn't have talked to you about her personal life?' said Ren.

'No. No, she would not.'

'And to Todd?'

He snorted. 'Does he look like someone you'd confide in?'

Tiny Gressett, your mask is slipping.

19

Ren stood at the top of the conference room, waiting for everyone to make their way in. After ten minutes, her patience had taken a turn for the worse.

'Hi,' she said. 'I don't have time to wait for everyone, so I'm just going to start. Thank you, first of all, for the information that's been coming through. We have Jean's phone records from her home and office, so we'll be working through them to see what we come up with. We have yet to locate the second cellphone.

'From the detectives here at the Sheriff's Office, we have a list of people in Breckenridge with priors, and we're following those up.

'We got a positive ID from several of the staff members at the Rifle Creek movie theater. And Jean was alone that night.

'We also found out that she had been to Breckenridge, Wednesday, January third and had shopped at Wardwell's, an outdoor clothing store on Main Street, owned by Malcolm Wardwell, run by him and his son, Jason. I looked into them both, and it appears Malcolm Wardwell was locked up briefly for child pornography in the seventies. Does anyone from the Sheriff's Office here have any more details?'

Mike and Bob shook their heads.

'Has there been any trouble since?' said Ren.

'No,' said Bob. 'Model citizen . . .' He shrugged.

'And do people know about him?' said Ren.

'It's not like people are stoning the store,' said Mike. 'Some of the locals know, but obviously there's always new people drifting in and out, people moving away. And I think he was living in Frisco at the time, so that bit of distance helped him out.'

'OK,' said Ren. 'Jean was working on some child abuse cases – the most recent in Silverthorne and Dillon. Nothing in Breck, nothing in the last three months, and nothing to do with Wardwell – right?'

'That's correct,' said Gressett.

'OK,' said Ren. 'What we don't have: there was no cellphone found at the scene. It's unlikely the unsub left either of them with her, if she was carrying them. And even if he did, the phone was probably lost in the slide. We don't have Jean's vehicle – a silver Subaru Forester – but we do have someone who came forward to say, among other things, that he may have seen it in the parking lot at a bar called the Brockton Filly. His name is Salem Swade – a Vietnam vet who lives in an old miner's cabin up on Quandary.

'The Brockton Filly is right near the base of Quandary and is run by Jean's one-three-seven – confidential informant. His name is Billy Waites. Gary Dettling from Safe Streets has more on Waites' background.'

'OK,' said Gary, 'In the late Nineties, Billy Waites was part of a narcotics operation, run by an ex-Navy Seal, ex-SAS guy, and a German communications expert. And then their distribution network. They were bringing drugs in from Colombia. The drugs would come in on a tugboat to whatever port; the guys who ran the operation would have already rented some luxury home in the area. They'd set up their communications, whatever they needed to do. And they'd go from there.'

'How were they caught?' said Cliff.

'One of the shipments was intercepted by the coastguard and some of the guys turned. They were allowed to complete the drop – this particular time it was in Atlanta. The subordinates were all using throwaway phones so we couldn't trace them back to anyone. Eventually, OCDEF convinced a judge they had probable cause. They did a Title III, the place was bugged. They had guys sitting on the wires every day who couldn't get shit. The gang were using codes, talking about their families every couple of minutes – they knew the drill. And that's where Billy Waites came in. Waites is smart. He was the codes guy. But the code was finally cracked and we were able to take them down. And Waites turned.'

'Was Waites a user?' said Ren.

Gary nodded. 'He was working as a prep chef in a restaurant. There was a lot of blow going around. That's when he got caught up with the gang. One of the distributors brings in meth, Billy tries it, gets hooked. After a year, he packs himself off to a cabin in the mountains for two months to detox. And he did it. But came right back into the business.'

'So he cleans up, comes out of his cabin rehab, and throws himself back into the whole scene?' said Ren. She paused. 'Will power.'

Gary gave her his patient look. He kept talking: 'He was dealing again, but not using, according to Jean, who would recount her meetings with Billy Waites to her colleague, Todd Austerval.'

'But how did she know he wasn't still using?'

'She'd know. Jean didn't have a problem with him. He was relieved to co-operate. He was very grateful –'

'Aren't they all?' said Colin. 'Grateful . . . and manipulative.'

'The head guy in the gang was insane,' said Gary. 'By the end, Waites had had enough.'

'So . . . Waites and Jean,' said Ren.

'We have no record of her calling Waites that night, but if this Salem guy is correct, she did pay him a visit around the time she disappeared.'

'I'll go talk to him tonight,' said Ren.

'OK,' said Gary. 'I'll pass his file over to you. Maybe you could go with Todd Austerval.'

'Sure,' said Ren. 'I just need to go home, pick up my Jeep.'

20

Ren needed a ride back to her house in Golden –
an hour's drive east on I-70 toward Denver – to
pick up her newly repaired Jeep and some supplies.
Robbie offered to take her. She wasn't feeling
sociable enough for him, but she said yes. She
threw him one-word answers, but he had enough
questions to keep it going indefinitely. It had been
a while since she rode with him.

'So – big case,' said Robbie.

Ren glanced at him. 'Yes.'

'Murder of a federal agent.'

'Yes.'

'And you're heading it up.'

'Yes.'

'I wasn't going to say anything, but . . .'

Uh-oh.

'Well,' he said, 'Colin thinks you and Paul
Louderback . . . you know . . .'

'That's so weird,' said Ren. 'When Gary got

Colin to head up whatever, I thought he and Gary . . . you know . . .'

Robbie glanced at her. 'I was just saying what I heard.'

'Who else was in on this conversation?' said Ren.

'A few of the others.'

'You're like a bunch of old ladies in a hair salon. Christ. Paul Louderback and I did not . . . you know.'

'Really?'

'Really.'

'So, how's Vincent?' said Robbie.

'I don't know,' said Ren. She paused. 'I might be about to find out.'

'He'll be home?'

'I don't know.'

'Why don't you call him?'

'Why? It doesn't matter if he's home or not. I'm just going in, picking up clothes and leaving.'

'Are you sure? I'm not going to sit out in the car like a loser while you have some big, emotional reunion.'

Robbie's cellphone rang. He answered. 'Really? Sure. OK. Not a problem.'

'Slight detour here,' said Robbie. 'There's a body in the cooler I need to check out.'

'Here?'

He nodded.

'Did it come in from Summit County?' said Ren.

Robbie shook his head. 'No – Clear Creek.'

*   *   *

The Jefferson County Coroner's Office was in a government complex ten minutes from Main Street, Golden. Dr Tolman was an on-call pathologist for sixteen counties, including Summit County and Clear Creek County.

'Male, late forties,' said Tolman as he let them in. 'He was found in the Clear Creek River. Some numb-nut deputy coroner brought him here, didn't call anyone, didn't quite pick up on the fact that this was a gunshot wound. The water had washed all the blood away.'

'Even so . . .' said Ren.

'I know,' said Tolman.

They walked in to where the body was laid out on the stainless steel.

Denis Lasco stood by the scales.

'Hello again,' said Ren.

'Hello, there,' said Lasco.

'Back on the job already?'

'With a heavy heart,' he said, holding up what he had just taken from the chest cavity.

Ren smiled.

'When I realized the only thing to jump my bones recently was a corpse, I knew I had to get back out in the world.'

'I'm sure that's not true,' said Ren. She gestured to Robbie. 'This is my colleague, Robbie Truax.'

'I was thinking of easing my way back into the job,' said Lasco, 'start with some paperwork, come down here, bring some notes to the doc. And here I am, suited up, today's head sawer-offer and chest cracker.' He looked at them. 'His assistant called in sick. Next thing two bodies require attention. We had a DWPA,' said Lasco. 'And then this.'

Ren was nodding when she realized she had no idea what he meant. 'What's a DWPA?'

Lasco smiled. 'Death With Paramedic Assistance.'

'Ooh,' said Ren, smiling back. Robbie cracked up.

'He was an old guy, heart attack,' said Lasco. 'I'm sorry, but these flatlander doctors run all these health checks at sea level, then give people the all-clear to go up two miles on vacation. It's crazy. It's sad. I just hate seeing those wives when their husbands are lying dead of a heart attack. Unless those wives are under thirty. Then I'm wondering whose idea was it to take a high-altitude holiday? "Honey, come on up where your heart is going to have to work harder. And maybe in a couple days, my bank balance won't."'

'Grim,' said Ren.

'Totally,' said Lasco. 'And, natural causes, ski accidents, ODs – it's unbelievable how mercenary the families are. *They're* the ones with the death grip, know what I mean? I have pried credit cards and jewelry out of their hands. Can you imagine? Now I photocopy every single personal belonging that comes in with the body. It's disgusting. It really is disgusting. I'm laying out wallets and ski passes and drivers' licenses and frickin' Chapstick on my photocopier . . .' He shook his head.

'Karma will get them,' said Ren. 'I really believe that. You can't live a greedy life like that without it coming back and biting you in the ass . . .'

Robbie nodded.

'I hope so,' said Lasco. He pointed to a shelf unit by the wall. 'OK – suits and masks are over there.'

Ren and Robbie put them on. When they were done, they looked around for a box of booties. Ren noticed that Tolman's stylish leather shoes were uncovered. Lasco caught her.

He spoke quietly. 'I know,' he said. 'He doesn't wear them. And I'm sorry, these are mine. I've no extras.'

Ren looked down at her two-hundred-dollar lace-up hiking boots.

'What's the worst that can happen?'

'I've done the chest already,' said Lasco, when they were standing at the body.

'So,' said Tolman, 'GSW to the back of the head. Exit wound here in the lower jaw . . . Denis, help me out here.'

He and Lasco turned the body over. Ren couldn't take her eyes off it. She didn't notice the liquid draining from the chest cavity on to the floor. The men stepped back in time. Ren's boots took a hit.

'Aw, shit,' she said.

Lasco ran and got her some paper towels, coming

back to hand them to her with a face that said they both knew it wouldn't make much difference.

'Shit,' she said again. But she barely drew her eyes away from the body.

'Do you want to go take them off some place?' said Tolman, pointing to her boots.

She shook her head, motioned for him to continue.

'Anyway, what I was showing you was this,' said Tolman, drawing his finger down the spine. 'The victim's cachectic, so you can –'

'He's what?' said Robbie.

'Look at him,' said Ren, pointing to the body. 'What do you think it means?'

Robbie glanced at her. So did Tolman. Ren would have blushed if she was able.

'Skinny?' said Robbie.

'Basically,' said Dr Tolman.

Ren was staring at the body. 'He's . . . got scoliosis.'

> *There was a crooked man*
> *And he walked a crooked mile*

'Yes,' said Tolman. 'Yes. That's what I was going to show you – how clearly you can see the curvature of the spine.'

Robbie elbowed Ren. 'Ren . . . are you there?'

'What?' said Ren. 'Yes, sorry. OK – so this dirtbag was found in the Clear Creek River . . .'

'Yes,' said Tolman. 'In a foot of water. Hadn't gone too far, no injuries from rocks and not there very long.' He looked at them. There was hope in his expression. 'I guess I was on high alert because of your colleague on Quandary. I don't know any details, I'll be waiting for Denis here's report, but anything suspicious . . .' He was talking faster to get it over with in case he was wrong. ''Cos of where this guy was found, I was thinking maybe he was on the back way out of Summit County. It could mean something.' He shrugged.

'It does,' said Ren.

They all looked at her.

'But my guess is he wasn't on his way *out* of Summit County. He was leaving Denver on his way *to* Summit County, until he heard the news that the FBI and God-knows-who-else would be heading along I-70 that way too. Instead, he and his buddies went through the Canyon and something this guy did pissed off the posse.'

'Specific,' said Robbie.

'A hunch,' said Ren.

21

Robbie dropped Ren at her house in Golden.

'I won't park in the driveway,' said Robbie. 'In case . . .'

'In case what?'

'Vincent might think . . . you and me . . .'

'He knows me better than that,' said Ren, too quickly. 'What I mean is . . . he knows I wouldn't run from him directly into the arms of another – albeit handsome – younger man.'

'Your Jeep is looking very nice and shiny,' said Robbie.

'It is,' said Ren. 'I better head in. You can come with me if you like.'

He glanced at her. She was half-smiling.

'I don't think there'll be any reunion,' said Ren.

'I really like Vincent,' said Robbie. 'I approved of Vincent.'

Ren smiled and patted him on the leg. 'Thanks

for the ride. See you back in Breck. I won't be long.'

Vincent came to the door barefoot and dressed in sweats. He had a bottle of Bud in his hand.

'Hi,' said Ren.

'Hi.'

'You're drinking early.'

'Well, it's later than when I started . . .'

'And when was that?' said Ren.

Vincent shrugged, slowly.

'I . . . just dropped by for the Jeep and to pick up some stuff. Did you know it is almost impossible to find any nice underwear in Breckenridge?'

'I did not,' said Vincent.

'Yes.' She paused. 'It looks like I'll be staying in Breck for the next while – which might make things a little easier.'

'How do you figure that?'

'Come on,' she said. 'Give me a break.' Her tone was gentle.

'Why should I?' said Vincent.

'I'm not here for long, OK? I don't want to get into anything.'

'What's going on?'

'We've got a dead agent up there.'

'I meant with us. But shit – who?'

'Jean Transom. She worked out of Glenwood.

Nice woman, according to everyone; great agent. No one knows what happened.'

'Was it homicide?'

'Yup. And the body's gone.'

'What?'

'In that avalanche.'

'I saw it on the news.'

Ren nodded. 'So, it's all snowstorms and shit-storms. And I'm leading the case.'

'Good for you.'

'Thanks.'

She looked past him. 'Can I come in?'

'Sure. Sorry.' He stepped back.

Ren walked past the kitchen and saw a pile of empty beer bottles on the floor and a bumper bottle of Advil, cap off, on the counter above them. *What have I done to poor Vincent?* She couldn't look at him. She went quickly upstairs, gathered more than she needed, packed it into one of his nice suitcases and dragged it down to the hallway. Vincent was knocking back his beer and smiling sadly at her.

'You know, some day, Ren? All those negative emotions you run away from will pick up the pace and they'll catch up.'

Ren shrugged. 'If they haven't yet . . .'

'They will. I shouldn't care, but I do.'

'Look, I'm about to work an important –'

'You need to work on yourself.'

Ren rolled her eyes. 'I'm fine.'

'Christ, how can you take responsibility in work like that and, like, absolutely none in your personal life?'

'That's not true and you know it. It just feels true to you right now.'

'It *is* true.'

'Whatever. You love holding things over me, don't you? *You're* all stable and reliable, and *I'm* on the run from shit.'

'You're the only person I know who says "whatever" and then keeps on defending themselves. Most people say "whatever" and they mean "whatever". They mean "whatever you think", so they don't bother saying any more.'

'Jesus, you are anal. You try to shut me up based on linguistics? You think that's going to work?'

'Oh Lord, no. Nothing works with you. Nothing.'

Ren stared at him, her eyes alight.

'So, do you think you're better off without me?' said Vincent.

'What do you want me to say to that?' said Ren. 'No answer is good. I'm fine, OK?'

'I know I shouldn't, and I don't really want to, actually, but I care about you, Ren. So much.' He touched a hand to her cheek.

She looked into his eyes and could feel hers well up too. 'Shit,' she said. 'Shit.'

'Hey, at least you're having an emotion,' said Vincent.

*   *   *

Salem Swade looked like he'd just stepped out of a wind tunnel he had no recollection of going into; it was in the angles of his thin gray hair, the speed of his blinks, how he spun on his heels.

He stood, dressed in a giant green parka, gray cotton pants and leg-warmers, with the smoking attorneys outside the Sheriff's Office. He had watercolor-blue eyes that should have been called striking or beautiful, but on a disheveled old man, talking and walking alone down Main Street, people looked at them like they were stolen.

'You dudes are slaves,' said Salem, smiling.

The attorneys laughed. 'Yes, sir,' said one of them.

Salem tipped him with his elbow. 'You get any lucky breaks today?'

'We're still here,' said the attorney, deadpan.

'As a witness to potentially suspicious activity,' said Salem, 'I might be giving Sheriff Gage a lucky break myself.'

'Good for you. You want a cigarette?'

'I do second-hand smoke,' he said.

'Glad to be of service,' said the guys.

Salem nodded. 'You boys behave.' He nodded again. 'I'm going in.' He slapped his thigh and a scruffy black-and-white border collie uncurled from her spot under the bench behind them. Mike Delaney met them in the foyer to take them through security.

'How you doing, Salem?' said Mike. 'Thanks for coming in so late.'

'I'm doing good.'

Mike brought him through to reception.

'Let me tie Misty here to your flagpole,' said Salem.

'Sure, go ahead.'

They left Misty and went down the hallway to Bob's office. They walked past a board with the FBI's Most Wanted on it. Salem pointed to a man with a handsome face, fair hair and sharp cheekbones. 'Now, him I've seen. That guy.'

'Uh-huh?' said Mike. 'Really? That'd make you the first since he disappeared.'

Salem smiled wide. 'Really?' he said. 'First is good. Damn right. I never come first.'

'Well, today's your lucky day, then. What was he doing, this guy?'

'Wearing a mask.'

'Right. This happen at Hallowe'en time?'

'Couldabeen. It was a couple weeks back, right in December there, but couldabeen.'

'Right. So this mask covered his face?'

Salem nodded, holding his hand over his mouth.

'And behind this mask, you saw this guy right here?' He smiled as he pointed at the poster.

'It was clear. Exactly,' said Salem. 'You're a smart kid.'

Mike laughed. 'Not as smart as you, buddy. You got vision like nothing I've ever seen. It's like superhero X-ray shit. ' He laughed.

'Mike, give the guy a break,' said Bob, walking into the hallway. 'Come in, Salem.' He shook his hand. 'We'll have an extra pair of hands here today. A lady called Ren Bryce. She'll be along in a little while. She's an FBI Agent. You'll like her.'

Salem nodded. 'I'll do my best.'

22

Ren placed each foot down carefully on the icy steps up to the Sheriff's Office. She held her arm out for balance. When she was nearly there, her right leg shot out and she landed hard on her left side. Her hand scraped down the edge of the concrete.

'Ow, you fuckers,' she said.

The attorneys flicked away their cigarettes and ran to her.

'Are you OK?'

'Ow,' she said, sitting up. 'I have no idea.'

'Here,' said one of them, taking her gently under the elbow, 'let's get you standing, see what the damage is.'

'Oh, I'm scarred for life,' said Ren. 'It's these boots,' she said, kicking a foot out.

'Ah, they were the fuckers. We thought it was us.'

She laughed. 'No. I don't know you well enough

to work that out. No, these boots – already today – have been covered in bodily fluids . . .' She paused to push her hair back behind her ear. They were staring at her. 'At an autopsy!' she said. 'Jesus, guys.'

They laughed.

'New boots for you, then,' said one of them.

'My most extreme excuse for a shopping trip yet,' said Ren. 'Thanks for your help.'

'Any time.'

She gave them a small wave as she disappeared into the building.

Misty lay by the flagpole in the Sheriff's Office reception, but stood up when Ren walked in.

'Aw, hello, there,' said Ren, 'How cute are *you*?'

She walked over to her. Misty sat down and started barking.

'Whoa,' said Ren. 'Not liking me very much.'

She took another step toward her. 'Come on,' she said. 'I'm not all bad.' She reached out under her collar to look for an ID, but she found nothing 'And who might you be?' Misty barked a few more times.

Bob strolled through reception. He looked down at Ren. 'Are you causing a disturbance?'

'Who's the dawg?'

'That is Misty, canine companion of Salem Swade, the Vietnam vet – our guy in the cabin. Hmm – she doesn't seem to be a fan of yours.'

He reached out his hand to pull Ren up.

'I'm a little hurt by that, actually,' said Ren. 'Dogs don't usually bark at me.'

'You'll get over it,' said Bob.

'I think she's looking for treats,' said Ren.

'She's come to the wrong place,' said Bob.

'So,' said Ren. 'Fill me in on Salem Swade. I only had a short note on him for the briefing.'

'Yeah, that was from me. Sorry about that. It's just we're used to him here. Basically, he showed up a couple days ago with tales of people up in the woods, wearing masks, some shit like that.'

'Okaay.'

'Yeah, I know.'

'But, obviously, we can't ignore the fact he saw Jean's lesbo-mobile at the Brockton Filly the Monday after she finished up work.'

'Sheriff Robert Gage, I would expect better from you,' said Ren.

'My sister calls it that herself,' said Bob. 'Give me a break.'

'How did Mr Swade know it was Jean's?' She paused. 'Don't tell me – from the description in the paper.'

Bob smiled. 'Why, yes.'

'So, you're used to him – meaning he shows up with revelations on every case you handle? Or just you're used to him about the place?'

'In fairness to Salem, he's not a crank that way. But he does try to help us with things –'

'Like, if he reads about them in the paper, for example?'

'Well, we haven't issued him with a police radio . . .'

Ren smiled.

'. . . Miss Smarty Pants. And how else do concerned citizens know what the Sheriff's Office needs?'

'Pillow talk?' said Ren.

Bob shook his head slowly. 'What you're seeing right now is a look known as "wistful".'

'Aw.'

'Why don't you come say hi to Mr Swade?'

'Sure.'

Bob looked at the torn skin across her hand. 'What happened to you?'

'Dead people's insides. Icy patch. Dumb boots. I'm going shopping later.'

'My wife blames clothes for things too.'

Ren glanced down at him. 'Does she blame *your* clothes . . . for that little problem you're having?'

Mike was still giving Salem a hard time about identifying people through masks.

'Damn right,' Salem continued, nodding at Ren when he walked in. 'Nothing wrong with these.' He pointed two index fingers at his eyes.

'Salem, meet Special Agent Ren Bryce.'

'Hi, Salem.' Ren shook his hand. 'Nice to meet you.'

'Hello,' said Salem, 'a pleasure to meet you.' He turned back to Mike. 'Super vision. That's what you tell me, buddy.'

'That's what I tell you,' said Mike.

'And you all are the sheriffs,' said Salem. 'You know shit.' He pointed at Ren. *She knows everybody. From Mohammed Ali to teachin' Bruce Lee how to do karate.*

Ren laughed, then finished for him: *'I can lead a parade while puttin' on shades in my Maserati.'*

Bob and Mike looked at each other and back at Ren and Salem.

She turned to them. 'It's John Prine. Genius. "She Is My Everything". Go to iTunes. Anyone who can write "Jesus, The Missing Years" . . .'

'Got my music here, anyone wants a listen,' said Salem. He rooted around in his pocket and pulled out a pink iPod Shuffle and clipped it to his coat. He hung the headphones around his neck.

'Well, fuck me,' said Mike. 'Where'd you get your hands on that? Where do you even charge it? You got a laptop in your other pants?'

Salem patted his pockets. 'Can't say that I do. The pod is from the kids work at the resort. Good kids. Take it in, charge it, load it, give it back to me at the Gold Pan.'

Bob laughed. 'Well, why the hell not?'

'Damn right,' said Salem. 'Beats that silence up in my cabin any day. That mountain silence. Sometimes it's just got the wind to keep it company.'

'Take a seat, Salem. What do you need to tell us?'

Salem shook off his parka. He was slight and wiry.

'I hear stuff at night,' he said, sitting down.

Behind his back, Mike stood with his hands on his hips, shaking his head. Bob glanced up at him.

'Go on,' said Ren. 'What do you hear?'

'Voices.'

Mike gazed at the ceiling.

'What kind of voices?' said Bob.

'Quiet ones.'

'Do you have your headphones on when this happens, Salem?' said Mike.

Salem turned around to him. 'Now you tell me how I could hear a damn thing with headphones in my ears?'

'Go ahead,' said Ren.

'I saw people with masks on,' said Salem. 'Some of them were in funny suits. And I'm not talking aliens,' he said, turning back to Mike. 'They were regular people.'

'What were they doing?' said Bob.

'They were walking around, then they headed out, maybe to one of the other cabins.' He shrugged. 'It was hard to tell what the point of this was.'

'What kind of masks?' said Ren.

'These kind,' said Salem, slapping a hand over his mouth.

'Not Hallowe'en masks,' said Mike.

'I told you – no,' said Salem. 'But it was dark.'

'OK,' said Ren. 'And you came in because you saw the posters up.'

'Exactly,' said Salem. 'If you see something strange . . . Lord knows what it's linked into. There's a lot of links in the background of things, people need to trace.'

'You're right,' said Ren. 'Now, can you tell me about the car?'

'Yes,' said Salem. 'I read about her missing car. A silver Subaru Forester. I recall seeing it in the parking lot of the Brockton Filly.'

'When was that?' said Ren.

'It was a Monday night. The weekend after it said she went missing.'

'Does January twelfth sound right to you?' said Ren.

Salem nodded.

'Had you seen her car there before?'

'Might have,' said Salem. 'But I know I did that night.'

'Did you see the missing woman, Jean Transom?' said Ren. 'If it helps, I can show you a photo of her.'

'I saw the photo in the newspaper, but I'll take another look.'

Ren laid it on the desk in front of him.

He shook his head. 'Damn. I don't know. I can't say that I've seen that lady anywhere. But you just don't know the links going on places.'

'We're keeping an eye out for them,' said Ren. 'Is there anything else you can think of?'

Salem shook his head and started standing up and putting on his coat. 'I'm fairly medicated right now I've got to tell you. Thirteen meds last time I checked. I don't know if they make me sharper. I can still get a little angry. But not so much.'

Ren shook his hand. 'Well, you look after yourself, Salem, OK? And you know where to find us. And is there anywhere we can find you?'

'My cabin – there's no number on the door.'

Everyone waited for a laugh that didn't come.

'Bob, do you have a map of Quandary there?' said Ren.

'I do,' he said, going to a file, searching through it and pulling one out.

Do you ever keep anything on top of your desk?

'OK,' said Ren to Salem, 'would you mind marking round about where your cabin is on this map?'

Sure,' he said, taking a red Sharpie she was holding out, marking the spot.

'And what's the best route to it?' said Ren. 'Like, the easiest.'

'Right here,' he said, moving his finger along it. 'You want, I can mark it in.'

'Yes. Please.'

She studied it. 'OK. That's great. Thank you, Salem.'

'Thanks, Salem,' said Bob.

He turned his pale eyes toward Ren. 'You gonna come up and see me some time?'

'I would really like that,' said Ren. 'Do you need a ride home?'

'Yeah,' said Mike. 'Why don't I take you and Misty back to the cabin?'

'Thank you,' said Salem. 'It was a pleasure, ma'am, all of you.'

'You too,' said Bob.

Mike walked Salem down the hallway.

Ren turned to Bob. 'Bless him,' she said, her hand held to her heart.

Bob smiled. 'Yeah? Well, whatever you do, don't look at his file. Whoa. That's some sick shit.'

Ren's eyes widened. 'What?!'

'I'm kidding. Little lamby.'

23

Ren pressed the cellphone to her ear with an icy hand as she walked down Main Street.

'Putrescine and perverts combined with shoe-shopping,' she said. 'What a start to my day. Never have business and pleasure collided so well.'

'I'm laughing, and I'm not sure why,' said Paul Louderback.

'OK – my nice boots got ruined with chest-cavity juice yesterday. And I'm going to buy a new pair in a store Jean Transom visited a few weeks back, owned by a man who was arrested for child porn thirty years ago.'

'Well, you never know,' said Paul.

'Exactly.'

'Anything else you want to tell me?'

'Let me see – weird paw prints in the snow that probably mean absolutely nothing. Spoke to the guy who served Jean supper on Monday, January fifteenth – not a lot there . . . I've gone through

Jean's case files and nothing jumped out at me. Jean's neighbor saw a lady visitor at the house a few times – no ID on her yet. I'm about to check out the pervert I mentioned. And I'm going to go talk to Jean's one-three-seven tonight.'

'Sorry,' said Paul. 'Gotta go.'

'OK,' said Ren. 'I'll keep you posted.'

'Yup. Next week on *Clues and Shoes* . . .'

Wardwell's was a basement store with dummies in the window that were meant to be life-like but weren't quite hitting the mark. Inside, every inch of floor space was taken up with rails of tops and tables of folded jeans and sweatshirts. A young, handsome guy was standing impressively still beside a messed-up pile of T-shirts. Ren got him straightaway: *I'm tall, thin, beautiful, my jeans are too big, they're belted below the band of my boxers, I rock.*

'Hey, what's up?' he said. He had come alive. *Like Mannequin.* 'I'm doing good,' said Ren. 'How are you this morning?'

'Well, I'm good too, as a matter of fact.' He beamed a genuine smile.

Ren gave him a break. 'That's great,' she said. 'That cold out there is something else.'

'It sure is.'

'But we're in here all over-cheery and polite.'

He laughed. 'Well, we've got to fight it some way. Is there anything I can help you with today?'

'I've shopped before,' said Ren.

He paused, then smiled. 'Well, I'm here if you need me.'

'I appreciate it.'

'You bet.'

She wandered up a few steps to the back of the store, where she spotted the man who had to be Malcolm Wardwell. She knew he was seventy-one years old. Any years he could have dropped with his muscular frame were added back by rheumy eyes and slack skin.

'Hello,' said Ren. 'Are you Malcolm Wardwell?'

'Yes.'

'I'm Ren Bryce with the FBI. We're investigating the death of Special Agent Jean Transom.'

'Oh, yes. Hello.'

'If I showed you a photo of her, would you be able to tell me if she came into your store?'

'If it was a day I was here, I hope so.'

Ren handed him the photograph.

He nodded. 'Yes, she was in here. I remember her. She was with her daughter – a little blonde girl.'

Niece, probably. 'And when was that?' said Ren.

'It was a couple of weeks back. And I know it was a Wednesday and it was before lunchtime, because we were clearing floor space for a delivery, so we were all trying not to get in the way.'

'OK.'

'It was right after New Year, in fact,' he said. 'That same week.'

I know that.

'I'm sorry to hear about her death,' said Wardwell. 'I remember thinking she was a nice lady.'

'She was,' said Ren. 'Was there anything you noticed that you think might help the investigation?'

He paused, then shook his head. 'Nothing out of the ordinary.'

'OK. Thank you for your time.'

Ren walked through security at the Sheriff's Office and grabbed her purse as it slid out of the X-ray machine. She searched through it for her cell-phone.

'Pardon me, Agent . . . Bryce?'

Ren turned around. It was one of the attorneys who'd caught her when she fell up the steps.

'Oh, hi,' she said. 'Did I look like I was about to fall again?'

He smiled. 'No, you were doing OK. You're with the FBI, right?'

'Yes. And you're . . .?'

'Ollie Haggart. Oliver Haggart. I'm a defense attorney.' He gestured back toward the court-rooms.

Ren tried to hide any recognition when she heard the last name. 'Nice to meet you.'

'Could I have a word with you?' he said.

'Sure. Go ahead,' said Ren.

'I guess you've seen the news report about the guy who went missing last year? Mark Wilson?'

'Yes.' She looked at him.

'My brother is Terrence Haggart. He was the last person to be seen with Mark.'

'Ah. OK . . .'

'And I don't think he had anything to do with Mark going missing.'

'OK.'

'I know he was always getting into trouble, but he just wouldn't have done something to someone like that . . . He's my brother, I'd know.'

'OK,' said Ren.

'I know, I've just come up to you with this. But . . . I'm having a hard time with it all. So are my parents. And Terrence leaving town did not help. He looks guilty.' He shrugged.

'Do people around here really believe he did something to Mark Wilson?'

'He was mentioned in all the news reports,' said Haggart. 'This is a small town. You've seen the *Summit Daily News* is everywhere. It kind of kept it in people's psyches.'

'I can see how that might happen.'

'Terrence would not have done anything bad like that. He just wasn't from that kind of family . . . we're not that kind of family.'

Ren smiled at him kindly.

'I know,' said Haggart. 'Probably everyone says that.'

'In your line of work, you know that.'

Haggart nodded. 'Yes. But just seeing that news report was kind of bam – there it was in full-color widescreen, all dragged up again. I mean, sure, old reports are on the internet, if anyone wanted to look . . . But it's all resurfaced and the name . . . my name is up there. It doesn't look good for me, for what I do.'

Something about how he said it made her empathy shift back a gear.

'I'm sure that's very difficult,' said Ren.

'I'm talking to you about it because I . . . can't really approach the Sheriff because it would be weird. Or the Breck PD, because they were like Terrence's personal chauffeurs and it got to pissing them off. I mean, he was a funny guy, people liked him, so he got away with a lot, but when this all came up, people were looking at him a different way.'

Ren nodded.

'But you're not from here,' said Ollie, 'and I was wondering if you could look at the file to see if it makes sense to you.'

'Did you look at it?'

'Conflict of interest.'

'I don't know if it's appropriate for me to look at it either. I'm here to investigate Jean Transom's death . . .'

'I know – on Quandary. Wilson's disappearance was a year ago, but it was the only other recent alleged crime out that way. Wouldn't that make it at least worth a look?'

Ren paused. 'OK, I'll read through it. That's the best I can do.'

'Thank you,' said Haggart. 'I appreciate it. My mom's been very upset the past few days.'

And at the last fence, Ren saw a little spark of humanity in his eyes. And she promised herself she would remember that a side effect of Ollie Haggart's job was having to keep that part of himself hidden.

24

Bob rolled his eyes with spectacular dramatics. Ren smiled at him, but stood her ground while she had him at his desk and could temporarily tower over him.

'We get people coming in all the time – look at this, look at that, re-open this, re-open that,' he said. 'You know the drill – they think by wishing someone was a good person, that's enough. If they believe their husband couldn't rape and murder women, then that is so. "Please look at this again. I just cannot believe XYZ is capable of murder. You've got the wrong man/woman/teen psychopath . . ."'

'Oh, come on – this is different,' says Ren. 'It's not a confirmed murder. I mean, there's no body.' She paused. 'Hey – maybe Quandary Peak feeds on dead bodies. Maybe we're in a Stephen King novel.'

'Yeah – *Misery*,' said Bob.

Ren smiled.

'Think about the guy who came to you,' said Bob. 'Ollie Haggart is twenty-nine years old, a new defense attorney.' He pointed in the direction of the courthouse. 'This is all about him. And his last name.'

'That's a little harsh,' said Ren. 'If it was one of *my* brothers . . .'

'Older, I bet,' said Bob.

'Yes they are. How did you know that?'

'Women are different if they have older brothers. They don't take any shit from men. Sadly, my wife has older brothers . . .'

'But, luckily, she has a very nice husband.'

Bob looked at her.

'What are you looking at me like that for? I mean it.'

'Well, that's very nice, thank you.'

Ren smiled as Bob shuffled some papers around his desk.

'Anyway,' he said. 'Terrence Haggart was known around town for being a troublemaker – by the older people anyway. We've taken him in a few times. Breck PD knows him well. So the ski-pole of suspicion was pointed his way. Do you like that? My Casey Bonaventure? Anyway, people here didn't give a shit about Mark Wilson disappearing – Christ, his own family barely gave a shit – but they didn't want their own kids to get sucked in by Haggart. Terrence Haggart's a loser, but a charming one

– the guy who has the party house that everyone wants to go back to . . .'

'Like your place,' said Ren.

'Exactly,' said Bob. 'And I'll stress he's charming – *if* he's been drinking the right kind of alcohol. Throw some hard liquor into the mix and anything can happen. He doesn't do it a lot, but when he does, it can get ugly. The next day, he's all remorseful, so people give him a break.'

'So . . . where's he now?'

'He moved away. He got too much grief on this one. Either way, Ollie should know better than to pay attention to the media. If something happens around here, they bring up three cases – the 1982 case about the two murdered hitch-hikers, the Quandary disappearance, and the Scoop Daniels missing attorney case.'

'Right now, I'm having a Quandary quandary,' said Ren.

'It was inevitable,' said Bob. 'One of us was going to crack and say that . . . I'm just glad it wasn't me.'

'The word has three syllables, Bob. It was never going to be you.'

Gressett broke up their laughter. 'That Haggart guy is being an arrogant prick if he thinks his job is going to be compromised because of his last name. That's his problem.'

'And it's a problem he wants us to solve,' said Bob.

Gressett stared at Ren. 'You're being taken for a ride . . . Haggart sees a woman –'

Bob could see the fire flash in Ren's eyes. He tried to put it out with the calm in his.

'Yes,' said Ren, turning to Gressett. 'You're right. He said a dick was the last thing he needed to deal with.' She turned back to Bob. 'Look, it's in Haggart's interest if his brother is *cleared* of any association. But if this case is re-examined in the middle of a media circus and it is discovered that his brother *is* a murderer, Ollie Haggart is grabbing a big huge spotlight and shining it down on his family again. Why would he risk all that? He has to believe that something else happened.'

'Back to my point,' said Gressett; 'the family always believe something else happened.'

Stay calm. Stay calm.

'Like what, though?' Gressett continued. 'In the course of investigating Jean's homicide, we'll trip over Wilson's frozen body covered in Big Foot's massive frozen footprints?'

Ren didn't like people who had no sense of humor. But they were always more welcome in her life than people who had a bad one. Especially the smart-mouthed, unfunny crap that came out of Tiny Gressett.

She beamed angry eyes and a matching smile. 'Let's just agree to disagree.' *You overbearing shit.*

Gressett was a smiler too. He stood up and left the room, his hand hovering over his belt.

Ren turned to Bob. 'Why does he do that? Start opening his belt on his way out the door to go to the men's room?'

'Maybe he feels he has such a long length of cable to unroll, he needs a head start.'

'Oh, Jesus Christ,' said Ren. 'What's this? Bring-a-Hideous-Mental-Picture-to-Work Day?'

Bob laughed.

'One thing that's interesting,' said Ren, 'is that the Brockton Filly where he was last drinking is also the place where Jean Transom may have been last seen.'

'Hmm,' said Bob. 'You know what's funny?' he said. 'You don't seem to do anything for Gressett.'

Ren laughed. 'What? Yeah. Him and millions of other men.'

'I don't know,' said Bob. 'I'm kind of used to seeing guys get a little, you know, weird around you.'

'What? Are you high?'

'I'd like to be.'

'What could have happened that night to poor, drunk, beaten-down Mark Allen Wilson?' said Ren.

'S.E.P.,' said Bob. 'Someone. Else's. Problem.'

25

The Brockton Filly leaned left in pitch country blackness. The skeletal trees that ran around it were wrapped at their base in hard, dirty white snow. The bar was named after an Irish madam who was run out of Boston and came west in the mid-1800s for lonely miners and their gold.

Todd pulled into the oversized side lot that might have been packed with wagons a hundred years ago, but was scattered with few trucks tonight. Ren zipped her jacket to the chin and pulled on a fleece hat for the short walk. Todd started to get out.

'Would you mind?' Ren shrugged the request, looking toward his open door.

Todd paused. 'What, waiting out here?' His eyes flashed with the anticipation of diminishment.

Ren nodded. 'It's just, Jean came here alone. And I'm thinking there was a reason for that. Waites might just respond better to women. And maybe not to intimidating blond men.' She smiled. Todd didn't.

'Sure,' he said. 'Whatever you think. I'll be here. Intimidating the bears.'

'Thanks, Todd. I appreciate it.'

Ren walked to the door, pushing on it three times, finally shouldering it open. Inside, the boxy hallway was peeling wallpaper, flaking paint, creaky floorboards and photos of long-dead alcoholics with their arms around other long-dead alcoholics. And a few recent ones of gummy regulars; a sparse bunch. The most prominent black-and-white photograph told Ren that the Brockton Filly was named more for her teeth than her spirit. The Brockton Beauty had a better ring to it, but could have had her driven out of Colorado for false representation.

Ren moved into the bar. She liked to tag people in two adjectives or less, not all of the words traceable to an FBI handbook or an English dictionary. Tonight she had pockmarked john, fat sleaze, married skank. She had seen Billy Waites' mug shot – bearded, rough and stoned. She continued scanning the room. Porn freak. Meth face. Hairy biker. Hot, fit barman. She had gone over her adjective allowance and included the word hot. *Not good.* He caught her eye and nodded. Without the beard, with a short hair cut and clear eyes, Billy Waites was a completely different food group. Ren looked away.

In the corner by the men's room, she saw a woman slumped on a stool with both hands wrapped around a dying pitcher. Ren knew the type – hand-jobs and blow-jobs for beer. When God was handing out good looks, this lady was in line at the bar. And the all-you-can-eat buffet. And the makeup counter. She was wearing the type of short skirt that you'd never want to see a woman like her uncross her legs in. A low-cut black top maxed-out on Lycra did its best for her breasts. But for backup, a pretty silver pendant pointed its way to the wide valley in between.

Somewhere you had a family, somewhere you lost people dear to you, and somewhere along the way, you gave up.

'Hey,' said Ren. 'How're you doing?'

'I'm doing great,' said the woman, cheerier than expected. 'Just great. What's an expensive lady like you doing in a dive like the Filly?'

Ren laughed. 'Not expensive enough that I didn't come here for the cheap beer.'

'Have a seat, then. Jo's my name.' She pointed to the stool opposite.

'Rachel's mine,' said Ren, sitting down. 'Can I buy you a drink?'

Jo shook her head. 'No, thank you.'

'Are you sure?' *It might keep your knees from the cold tiles in the men's room.*

Jo nodded. 'Positive. But you can give me a few quarters for the jukebox.'

'Sure,' said Ren, opening her wallet.

Jo heaved herself up and walked over to the jukebox, her eyes struggling with the swimming print. 'Any preferences, Billy boy?' she called out.

'Ladies' choice,' he said, taking a clean towel from under the bar.

Jo put her money in and the music cranked up. Nothing Ren knew started to play.

'What can I get you?' he said to Ren.

'Let me see,' she said, getting up and walking toward him. 'Uh, bottle of Coors . . . Coke . . . Coors. Yeah, Coors. Thanks.'

'I'm a friend of Jean's. Jean –'

'I guessed,' said Billy. He turned his back to her and grabbed the beer from the fridge. He handed it to her and glanced over toward Jo. The last trace of her was a slight swing to the men's room door.

'Why don't you take a seat over there,' said Billy, pointing the opposite way.

Ren took her beer and a seat in a far corner of the bar. Billy showed up five minutes later and stood by the table.

'Hi. I'm Ren Bryce. Not Rachel.' She smiled.

'Hi,' he said. 'I'm Billy Waites.'

'You heard about Jean?'

He nodded.

Ren waited for condolences or something to replace the indifference. Nothing.

'I'm investigating her murder,' said Ren.

Billy nodded. She could see his boredom gauge like a thermometer and the mercury was rising. A few more sentences and the bulb would blow.

26

Billy Waites was staring at the wall, his brow furrowed, his lips almost pouting. Ren studied his arms. They were tanned, well worked out. She looked at his hands – strangely long-fingered with clean, buffed nails. On his right wrist was a tattoo – two words and what looked like a date. He turned back to her. Her breath caught.

'I'd like to know if there's anything you could tell me that might help the investigation,' she said.

He shot her a bemused look. 'What would I know?'

'When was the last time she came in to you?'

'January fifteenth,' said Billy. 'It was a Monday night.'

'What time?'

He thought about it. 'Six thirty.'

'She came in here?'

'Yes.'

'Well, that makes you – for now – the last person to see her alive,' said Ren.

Billy let out an angry breath, shook his head, rolled his eyes. 'Fuck that.'

'What's your problem?'

'You know what? I was cool doing whatever for her, OK? A quiet little visit every couple weeks, no harm done, no big interference in my life, my chance to pay back whatever debt you guys will hold me to for life, probably. I'm a lot less cool about being here with you and knowing that Breckenridge is crawling with law enforcement. I know how you guys work. I know how desperately you will want to take a cop killer off the streets, or how desperately you want to take at least someone who can look like one in a mug shot . . . How do you like this?' He opened his eyes wide and bared his teeth.

'Look, this is not about you, OK?' said Ren. 'This is about the murder of one of my colleagues. I couldn't give a fucking shit about Billy fucking Waites, OK?'

'Nice.'

'I just want all the information that's out there on all the cases Jean was working on and all the people she came in contact with in the last few whatever – months, years, whatever it takes. You may be able to help me with that. What was she coming to you for?'

He shrugged. 'Hard to tell. She comes in, asks

me questions, I answer them or tell her what shit I've heard. I have no idea what she's doing with that information after.'

'And what had you heard recently?'

'Not a lot.'

'Look, this is fairly easy, OK? What. Did. She. Want. You. To . . .'

'Right there,' said Billy, 'right there is how you're going to charm me.'

'Listen to me, you fu—'

'We're done,' said Billy.

'No,' said Ren. 'No, we're not. You owe *Jean*.'

Billy tilted his head. 'Were you two close?'

Ren paused. 'She was a brilliant, talented agent –'

'Oh, say can that star-spangled banner . . .' He spoke the words.

Ren stared through him.

'I'm not surprised you weren't close,' said Billy.

'What makes you say that?' said Ren.

'Why are you all defensive?' said Billy.

'I'm just wondering,' said Ren.

'You care now what Billy fucking Waites says?'

Ren sighed and got up. 'This is bullshit.'

'Damn right it is.'

'Billy,' shouted one of the old guys at the bar, waving a drunken arm around, 'keep your mind on the job. People need beers.'

Billy smiled tightly and pushed himself upright. 'People need beers,' he said.

'They always do,' said Ren. She followed him back to the bar. He looked at her like she was nuts.

'OK,' said Billy. 'Was I the last person to see her alive? Maybe the last you know of. Maybe the ninth last you know of. You know the killer is the last. And I, at least, know that's not me. You'll get there, though.'

'You think so?' said Ren.

'You look smart enough,' he said. 'Sheriff Gage's a good guy. Between you – who knows?'

'You have got to give me more,' said Ren.

'I can give you my view of Jean Transom. Brisk –'

'Do you mean brusque?' said Ren.

Billy stared at her. 'If you see a major difference between the two words . . .'

She looked at him. 'You have a point, there.'

'Thank you. OK, Jean, from my point of view, was business-like: no small talk, ordered a Diet Coke, asked me what she needed to ask me, sometimes came in with that blond dork, but I think trusted me enough not to have him there all the time. Leave him home to go brush his big teeth.'

Ren tried not to smile.

'When she was alone, did she ever talk to anyone else while she was here?'

He shook his head. 'No.'

'Did you always just meet here?'

'Yes.'

'Why?'

'Because no one bothers me here.'

Ren glanced out toward the customers. The lights above her head were tilted backward, the customers were shielded by darkness, like she was on the stage and they were the audience.

'I'm it,' said Billy. 'I'm not the boss, but I'm like the boss. And I couldn't give a shit what any of those losers out there think. Same as they couldn't give a shit about me. I'm the man who gives them beer.'

'Oh – do you ever get a guy in here called Salem Swade?'

'Yes.'

'What's he like?'

'Gets a little out of hand if he drinks too much, but he's a good guy. He's always welcome here. Makes me laugh.'

'Is he in here a lot?'

'It's the closest bar to his cabin, so he comes in quite a bit.' He shrugged. He was eager to turn away.

Ren smiled extra-wide. 'Thanks for your time.'

'Sure. Whatever.' His sneer unsettled her. But he held her gaze. And he didn't give her the eye-fuck . . . which most guys in a power play do. Even if they have no weapons, they'll always have the eye-fuck.

But then, maybe Billy Waites has an arsenal.

27

It was early enough that everything seemed wrong – the color of the sky, the silence, the sharpness of the trees and the leaves. Ren was hit with the sensation of walking through a bright airport after a long-haul flight; weighed-down, cold, disorientated.

The first time she woke in the middle of the night to study, she was seventeen years old and motivated by fear. The alarm went off and she wanted to stay in her bed and have the whole world disappear around her. But she got up and realized that, once the coffee kicked in, her brain had a strange alertness she could use. So for years, around exam times, she would get up, sick and dry-eyed at six a.m., and take her textbooks down to the sofa while her family slept. She needed to find the quickest way to process the information so that the answers would be right. She never imagined her interrupted sleep would take her, twenty years later, on to the snow-covered streets of a Colorado morning with the same plan.

Her skin felt tight. Vincent used to tell her how her face could transform depending on her mood, that when she was angry she looked like a different person – an ugliness came out. Ren hated when he said it, and could never see it herself, but she knew that every time he said it, she felt the same as she did this morning. She didn't want to eat. Her breakfast would be coffee and case notes.

When she got into the office, there was a message at reception for her to call Margaret Shaw, Jean Transom's neighbor. Ren sat at her desk and dialed the number.

'Hello, Margaret? It's Ren Bryce here. You left a message for me.'

'Yes, I did. I didn't want to call your cellphone. I thought that might be too personal.'

'Oh, you can call that any time,' said Ren. 'How's your dog?'

'He's getting there. I'm just not quite sure where "there" is . . .'

Ren laughed. She pulled a Post-It pad toward her and grabbed a pen. 'Now, what can I do you for?'

'I feel dirty,' said Margaret. 'I'm an old hippy. And here I am helping the Feds.' She paused. 'I took down someone's car registration last night. For you. Can you imagine? It was the lady I told you about, the one who visited Jean.'

'Really? That's great, Margaret. Shoot.'

Margaret called it out. 'Now, I only saw her leave. I was nervous enough about my carpets with the dog. The spying nearly killed me.'

'Well, the FBI – your favorite – thanks you very much.'

'I would say it was a pleasure, but it was really terrible,' said Margaret. 'I couldn't do what you do.'

Colin Grabien sat at his borrowed desk, scrolling rapidly through a screen of numbers. On the wall beside him, the regular owner of the desk had created a beautiful world of kittens hanging out of buckets, tugging on balls of wool, hanging off tables, licking ice-creams.

Ren walked up to him. 'Hey, P. asterisk asterisk asterisk asterisk Magnet.'

Colin looked up at her. 'What?'

'I can't use bad language in front of Robbie.'

Colin paused, then laughed. Cliff joined in. Robbie was not so sure.

'How can people look at that shit all day?' said Ren. 'Sorry, Robbie.'

'Same way I can sit opposite you in Safe Streets,' said Colin.

Gary Dettling walked into the room. 'Listen up. I just got a call from Denver PD. There was a robbery at Washington Mutual on Colfax one hour ago. Same freaks with the celebrity mug shots . . .'

'Who was it this time?' said Colin.

'Paris Hilton,' said Gary.

Yesss. 'Were they violent?' said Ren.

'Along with their guns, they had some nice big sharp knives,' said Gary.

'Jesus,' said Ren. 'What happened?'

'Two of the tellers are seriously ill from knife wounds, massive blood loss, etc., but at least it looks like they're going to pull through.'

Ren let out a breath. 'They know enough that they're not going so far as to kill.'

'I'm heading back to Denver,' said Gary, 'to hook up with Denver PD. Is everyone OK here?'

They nodded. Gary left the room.

'I'm *very* OK,' said Ren, pulling out her notebook. 'Right – Colin, you said Robert Downey Jr.; Cliff, you had Larry King – hello? showing your age. Robbie, you had Lindsay Lohan. And I, gentlemen, had Paris Hilton. Five dollars from each of you, thank you very much.'

'Paris Hilton was way too obvious,' said Colin.

'Exactly,' said Ren. 'Double bluff . . . or jeopardy . . . or whatever. Are you guys sticking with the same choices?'

'I'm going to change mine,' said Cliff.

'Hallelujah,' said Ren. 'Larry King . . .'

'To Dudley Moore,' said Cliff.

'Who?' said Robbie.

'Are you for real?' said Ren.

'I am,' said Cliff.

'You're like the anti-better,' said Ren. 'It's not even, like, you go for the underdog. It's like you go for a completely different animal from a different galaxy where betting doesn't exist.'

She sat down at her computer and ran the license plate that Margaret Shaw had given her. Caroline Quaintance, twenty-seven years old, a radiologist with an address in Silt. Ren grabbed her bag and her jacket and left. Outside, Ollie Haggart, the ADA, stood in the porch, smoking, kicking at a wedge of ice.

Shit. 'Hi, Oliver.'

'Oh, hi.' He had an expectant look in his eyes.

Deflect. Ren glanced at the steps. 'You can relax. I'm not planning on slipping today.'

'So, no bodily fluids on your boots this morning.'

'No,' she smiled. 'I'm sorry – I haven't had a chance to take a look at that for you. You can understand, with the investigation . . .'

He nodded. 'I know. I just . . . you know the way you can't help thinking about something . . .'

Silt was a two-hour drive west of Breckenridge. Working in Colorado meant driving . . . a lot. 'Go check a map,' Ren would say to East Coast agents asking her to follow up on a lead in Colorado that they thought she could take care of in an hour.

Ren pulled up outside a pale green stuccoed house on a quiet avenue in a nice neighborhood. She rang the doorbell, but by the time Caroline

Quaintance came to the door, Ren was already halfway down the path to the Jeep.

'Oh,' she said, turning around when she heard the porch door open.

The woman standing there was tall and thin, with light-brown shoulder-length hair. She was dressed in tan pants, brown hiking boots and a navy blue zip-up fleece.

'Hello,' said Ren. 'Are you Caroline Quaintance?'

'Yes.'

Ren walked up to her and flashed her creds. 'My name is Ren Bryce. I'm with the FBI. I'm here to ask you about Jean Transom.'

'Oh.'

'Can I come in?' said Ren.

'Sure.'

She showed Ren into the living room, a tidy room – one sofa with a Native American throw, one battered chair, a tiny television, a guitar, a chest. Ren badly wanted the sofa, but she took the chair.

'How did you know Jean Transom?' said Ren.

'We worked at the same animal shelter in Rifle – Homeward Friends.'

'When did you first meet?'

'She started volunteering about a year ago. I had already been there about a year before that. We've been friends ever since.'

'How often would you see each other?'

'Every two weeks or so, on weekends at the shelter.'

'And did you spend time in her home?'

Caroline paused. 'Yes.'

'How often?' said Ren.

'Maybe once a month, something like that.'

'When did you find out about her death?' said Ren.

'I guess, a few days ago.'

'So last night, you visited her home because . . .'

Caroline looked at her. 'Last night? I . . .'

Ren nodded. 'Don't worry – I'd just like to know why that was.'

Caroline opened her mouth, but paused. 'Here's where I sound nuts.'

'Go ahead,' said Ren.

'Jean had a cat, McGraw, that she really cared about.'

Ren nodded. 'I heard about McGraw.'

Caroline smiled. 'I went to Jean's house to check if he was OK. If a family member hadn't taken him, I was going to take him in or take him to the shelter, make sure he was being looked after. I didn't go into the house or anything. I mean, how would I?'

Ren nodded. 'That doesn't sound too nuts to me.'

'I guess it's because I feel I'm better with animals than I am with humans.'

Nuts.

'Am I going to get in a lot of trouble for this?' said Caroline.

'For looking for a cat?' said Ren. 'No. We're not

in the business of putting resources into attempted cat rescue . . . we're too busy monitoring civilian cellphone calls and emails.'

Caroline smiled. It lit up her face.

'When was the last time you saw Jean?' said Ren.

Caroline let out a breath. 'It was a Saturday, at the shelter. It would have been . . . January sixth.'

'And how was she doing?'

'She was good,' said Caroline. 'A dog she had been looking after had made great progress. He'd been abandoned, but could do lots of tricks. It was weird because his owner, obviously, had put a lot of effort into the dog and he was –' She paused. 'Oh. I'm sorry. I'm going off on a tangent . . .'

'Not a problem,' said Ren, 'but I'm afraid I do have to make tracks.' She stood up. 'Thank you for your time, Caroline.'

'That's OK. I wish I could be more help.'

Ren handed her a card. 'Who knows? Maybe you can.'

Maybe if you decide to tell me some of those things you are hiding behind those pretty brown eyes.

28

Ren went back to the office and sat at her desk. She quickly typed as much as she could of her conversation with Caroline Quaintance. Paul Louderback wasn't just her PT instructor. He had given her advice across the board. He always said to write everything down verbatim. Skim over what an interviewee is telling you and you miss vital verbal clues. 'Put something into your own words,' he said, 'and you put yourself into the frame. Never forget that you're supposed to be the one looking at the picture.'

Ren thought of Terrence Haggart being put in the frame of a missing person's case and, by association, Oliver Haggart. Maybe her first encounter with Oliver Haggart had influenced her empathy; a man who had come to her rescue after her icy fall. *That was a weird day.* And gradually, something about it started to tug at her. *Crooked man. Bodily fluid. Boots. Misty the dog . . .*

* * *

Salem Swade sat on a stool at the bar of the Brockton Filly, looking like there was nothing in the world that could ever trouble him. Ren wondered what medication he took. *And where can I get some?* Misty lay quietly beside Salem, her leash tied around the base of the stool.

Ren walked over and put a hand on his forearm. 'Hello, Salem,' she said. 'Do you remember me? I'm –'

He gave her a broad smile. 'My John Prine buddy.'

'Yes, sir. Would you mind if I talked to you a minute?'

'Sure, go ahead.'

She nodded toward a booth. 'You can take Misty with you.'

He untied Misty and they went to sit down.

'No barking at me today, Misty,' said Ren, smiling, rubbing the dog's silky head, massaging her back. 'Salem, how long have you had Misty?'

'I want to say five years. Maybe more?'

'Where did you find her?'

'I got her from the shelter.'

'Was it by any chance from Homeward Friends in Rifle?'

'No. It was a shelter out in Frisco. That I do know.'

'Oh,' said Ren. 'OK.'

'She was in great shape, I'll tell you that much. She wasn't a scraggy thing.'

There was something in the lines in his face, the brightness in his eyes when he spoke. There was a lost boy inside Salem Swade who Ren wanted to wrap her arms around.

'I think Misty's got a special talent,' she said.

'She sure does,' said Salem.

'Well, even more than what you think,' said Ren. 'I think your little pal there is a very well trained dog.'

Salem's eyes shone. 'Well, how about that, girl?' He ruffled Misty's coat, pulling her gently toward him, hugging her tight.

Ren's gaze was drawn to a man who stood up from a booth in the corner and walked up to the bar. He was heavily built on top, his neck and shoulders broad, his biceps pushing his arms wide of his body, his legs short. He was wearing a white vest with baggy green and pink work-out pants and white sneakers. His hair was pulled back tight into a thimble-sized pony-tail. He brought a bottle of Bud down to his booth with the stiffness of a man whose muscles wanted to pay him back.

Ren turned to Salem again.

'Do you remember the day the FBI agent's body was found on Quandary?' said Ren.

Salem nodded. 'I do. Same day I hitched a ride to Fairplay.'

'Did you come home that night?'

'Nope – the next morning. Cop cars everywhere. I had to go the back way to the cabin.'

'What back way?' said Ren.

'The way that meant I didn't have to go through the trailhead.'

'You'll have to show me. Was Misty with you?'

'I left her in the cabin. Not a lot of people want to take you with a dog.'

'Was she chained up?'

'Yes, ma'am. I left her food and water, too.'

'Of course you did. She's a very loved little lady. And when you came home, was she where you left her?'

Salem nodded.

'OK,' said Ren. 'Thanks for that.'

'No, thank you, ma'am.'

She placed a hand on his and squeezed it. 'You take care.'

'Hey,' he called, 'what do you think she's trained in?'

Finding dead people.

Ren smiled. 'Karate.'

Ren walked up to the bar and took a stool. She thought about Robbie's beautiful, arctic photo and the possibility that they were Misty's paw prints across the snow. Had Misty gotten free of her chains that night and someone had tied her up again? Had Salem? Had he forgotten? Had he deliberately lied? Or had someone else taken Misty, untied her and brought her out into the snow to find a dead body?

Officers were at the trailhead that night, but because of the avalanche threat, no one was right up at what had been the scene. And Salem had said there was another easy route up to his cabin . . .

Ren watched the guy with the ponytail in the mirror behind the bar. She waited for Billy to come over and ordered a Coke.

'Hi,' said Ren.

'Hi,' said Billy.

'Who's this guy behind me?'

'Which one?' said Billy, not taking his eyes off her. *Amazing eyes.*

'The opposite-of-a-Minotaur guy.'

Billy paused, then laughed when he realized who she was talking about. 'Head of a man, body of a bull?'

Ren smiled and nodded. 'That's the one.' She felt bad that she thought he might not have known.

'I don't know. He's Mexican, doesn't speak a lot of English.'

'Does he come in here a lot?'

'Once or twice a week.'

'Anything I need to know?'

'Jo and him seem to take toilet breaks at the same time . . .'

Ren glanced over at Jo, who had her bare right foot up on her left knee, dirty sole out.

She was bent low, running a fingernail under each toenail. *Jesus Christ.* Ren watched the guy in the mirror behind the bar. He had the look of a man who was not choosy. Which made her smile when she caught his eyes on her ass. His gaze then slid over in Jo's direction, a slow, heavy-lidded leer. A shiver ran up Ren's neck. *This guy is wrong.* He smiled with his mouth closed, his chin raised and a slight nod. Soon he was back staring at Ren's ass. *Jesus Christ. There's a mirror, idiot.* She looked back at Billy. He was looking at her. He quickly looked away. Her heart flipped. *Oh, no.*

'Do you know what he drives?' said Ren.

'The green truck out front.'

Behind her, Salem had taken Misty by the leash and walked to the window.

'I feel like we're in a snow globe,' he said, tracing a finger in circles like the snow falling outside.

'Snow globes are pretty,' said Billy. 'People want to look at what's inside.'

Aw.

The sleazy guy got up behind them, zipped up a light ski jacket and gestured to Salem that he would give him a ride.

Ren glanced over at the corner. 'I'm amazed he didn't take Jo . . .'

'No go for Jo da Ho,' said Billy.

Ren laughed. 'OK, Billy at da Filly. I'm done here. Thank you.'

'Any time,' he said.

Two magnetic men walk into a bar . . . one repelling her, the other drawing her in. *There is no punchline. This is not funny.*

29

Colin and Robbie were in the office, quietly working at their computers. Ren walked in and dropped her bag at the desk. 'I have a shaggy dog story.'

Colin didn't look up. 'If it is relevant to Jean Transom's murder, I'd love to hear it. If it's a sidebar from the CNN website –'

'Don't be a dick,' said Ren.

'Tell me your story,' said Robbie. 'I don't care.'

'I *will* admit,' said Ren, 'that it may be as irrelevant as a human interest story, but anyway . . . Remember the day I came back here after the autopsy in Golden? And there was shit on my boots from the autopsy? Salem Swade, the vet up the mountain – his dog sat down and started barking at me when I walked into reception. But she didn't react that way to anyone else –'

Colin raised an eyebrow.

Ren rolled her eyes. 'Anyway, I thought about

it. And thought, hold on a second, cadaver dogs are trained to react to putrescine – eau de mort.'

'Oh de what?' said Colin.

'Do you always have to be irritated by things you haven't come across before?' said Ren.

Colin said nothing.

'Eau de mort – I made it up, OK?' said Ren. 'Anyway, I remember Cliff saying the cadaver dog that day on the mountain sat down and barked to show he'd picked up the smell. I called his handler and she filled me in – said that was something a lot of cadaver dogs do. Then the handler rewards them with a treat. Which I didn't do, obviously, with poor Misty, so she kept barking. She stopped eventually, but when I came out again, there she was . . .'

'Love the sound effects,' said Robbie.

'Thank you,' said Ren. 'Anyway, Misty was normal last night when I met her with my new boots on. So there you go.'

'OK,' said Robbie. 'But –'

'What is the point?' said Ren, 'I know.'

'The point is – guess what? It's all about Ren,' said Colin.

'You know what?' said Ren. 'You're really going to have to go fuck yourself at some stage.'

''Cos you won't be doing it with *her*,' said Robbie, pointing to Ren.

'We don't all want to fuck Ren Bryce,' said Colin. 'That's your special fantasy, Truax.'

'Leave him alone,' said Ren. 'That's not true.'

'Yeah,' said Robbie. 'And unlike you, Colin, I would know how to treat a lady.'

'Oh, I know how to treat a lady,' said Colin. 'Treat 'em mean, keep 'em –'

'Repulsed,' said Ren. 'Back to the matter at hand – remember the paw prints up on Quandary that were in your photos, Robbie? I think someone who knew about Misty's little gift took her from Salem Swade's cabin – he wasn't there that night – and brought her out to look for the body. Which Misty may or may not have found.'

Colin nodded. 'OK, that's interesting.'

'Is it now?' said Ren.

'But who could know that about the dog?' said Colin.

Ren shrugged. 'That? I don't know.'

'And who knows the dog well enough to be able to get her away from the cabin like that?'

'Strikes me that the whole town knows Misty,' said Ren. 'And she is one very friendly dog. Especially considering what her secret talent is. And she is a food whore. All the restaurants feed her. A nice steak would have her out in the snow right away. And snow is hard to sniff a corpse out in.'

'My photos rock,' said Robbie.

'Update number two is on Caroline Quaintance,' said Ren. 'Turns out she was a friend of Jean's from the animal shelter Jean worked at as a weekend volunteer. Caroline was seen outside Jean's house last night. She told me she was looking for Jean's cat in case he was still there or wandering the neighborhood or whatever. I think she was telling the truth about that. She said Jean and her had been friends for about a year. The animal shelter is in Rifle. It's called Homeward Friends. I have one of the detectives here getting a list of the employees, so between us we can go talk to them all. And hopefully I can get to the bottom of what it is that Caroline Quaintance is lying to me about.'

She walked out into the hallway and saw Todd Austerval up ahead. She called out to him. He stopped.

'Hi,' said Ren, 'I just wanted to say. I don't know if you heard Gressett and me talking . . . that time in Glenwood when you came in from your run.'

'I did hear,' said Todd. 'And what I was guessing was that Gressett was telling you I didn't make it through the undercover program?'

'Yes,' said Ren. 'But –'

Todd shrugged. 'He loves telling people that, for some reason. I guess it makes him feel –'

'Not so Tiny?'

Todd smiled. 'And you were right. I *am* lucky I didn't make it.'

'You do have a touch of the White Supremacist about you, though. You could have pulled it off . . .'

Todd laughed. 'Anyway, don't worry, you didn't say anything to offend me.'

'Thanks.'

'I'm not that sensitive.' He smiled. 'Hey, I put up with that prick all day.'

When Ren got back to the inn that night, the lights were dimmed and the fire was dying. She went in through the main door and lay back on the sofa in the living room. She pulled a cushion to her side. She expected more people to be up, but then she remembered they would be heading to the slopes early. She closed her eyes. The front door banged shut. She opened her eyes. But whoever it was went straight upstairs. She thought of Billy Waites. What was his story? How did he end up where he was? *How did any of us?*

Her eyes closed again. Her body struggled to keep her awake. But for a while, in the darkness of her mind, she was somewhere she did not want to be; she lay on dried earth. A boot was pressing hard on her jaw. Before her, several faces, swelled by humidity, seemed to change expressions like the images on a one-armed bandit. Their eyes bore into her. She didn't know what configuration of ugly, haunting looks would take shape. She wanted to wipe the dirt from her lips, but she couldn't move. Saliva leaked slowly from her mouth, the skin on her neck was tight with heat. Her heart pumped harder.

Ren jerked awake. She breathed in and out slowly, slowly. Through the window, she could see snow falling hard. She forced her feet on to the floor. Everything ached. She checked the time – eleven thirty p.m. She wondered had anyone come in and seen her. She wondered had she cried out. She wondered if she could ever dream gently.

30

Ren went into the office the next day and asked Bob for the Mark Allen Wilson file. She could not admit she considered the possibility of a link to both crimes. He would think she was nuts.

'Indulging Ollie Haggart?' said Bob.

'Maybe,' said Ren. 'I just want to take a look, at least.'

'Why?'

'Look, I understand where you're coming from about Ollie Haggart's motivation. But you know when something's at the back of your mind? It's bound to put a little pressure on the front. So if I can get rid of it . . .' She shrugged. 'It'll take me a half-hour.'

'Don't waste your time.'

'I can spare a half-hour,' she said. 'I'll take it out of lunch.'

'I haven't seen you eat once since you've been here,' said Bob.

'Excuse me? I had one of your Jolly Ranchers.'

'Knock yourself out. Talk to Mike, he'll get you the file,' said Bob. 'You looking to distract yourself from something?'

Ren stood up. 'Miaow.'

Ren drove to Main Street, parked and walked a few blocks to the Crown. It was one of her favorite places in Breck – a café up a short flight of steps in a strip of red-brick stores. The eighties entrance led into a totally different world – frescoes, chandeliers, antique wall lights and comfortable chairs.

The seat by the fire was free. Ren rushed to the counter to order. It was the same every time: the Cinnamonster, like a Cinnabon. It was cinnamon, it was monstrous, it was a cake covered in something she could never find the words to describe. She grabbed a black coffee, got the waitress to throw two espresso shots in it and made it back to the fireside chair before anyone had taken it.

She opened the Missing Persons file on Mark Wilson:

Case Initiated

At 4 p.m. on February 12th, I, Undersheriff Mike Delaney, received a call from Hal Rautts at Reign on Main reporting that Mark Wilson did not attend a job interview that they had scheduled the previous week. He failed to reach Mark Wilson on his cellphone. On hearing that

Mark Wilson had been in an altercation with Terrence Haggart the previous Saturday and had been last seen badly beaten, Rautts called to the Cheapshot Inn on Ridge Street where Wilson had been staying. Wilson had not been seen there since the day before the altercation with Haggart. Rautts then called the Sheriff's Office to report Mark Wilson as a missing person.

Case Investigation

I interviewed Terrence Haggart who acknowledged the incident, which had happened at the Brockton Filly on Saturday, February 10th at 11 p.m. They had been arguing about money. Haggart said Wilson owed him two thousand dollars. Terrence Haggart said that the last time he saw Mark Wilson, it was in the parking lot of the Brockton Filly. Haggart admitted that Wilson was very badly beaten by him, but was standing when Haggart left him to go back into the bar. It was confirmed by Billy Waites, bar manager at the Brockton Filly, that this was correct. He also confirmed that Mark Wilson had been drinking steadily from 4 p.m. that day.

Terrence Haggart left the Brockton Filly at 1 a.m. to drive home. Mark Wilson had not re-entered the bar since the altercation outside. Wilson had hitch-hiked to the bar

that afternoon. He did not have a vehicle to
drive back to Breckenridge in.

Ren skimmed through the rest of the file – all the
obvious parts, the witness statements that added
nothing to the overall picture. Every time Billy
Waites' name appeared, she got a sensation she
couldn't quite pinpoint.

She stopped skimming to get a sense of who
Mark Wilson was.

Social History:
On February 14th, I spoke on the telephone
with Mark Wilson's mother, Diane Wilson.
She confirmed she had not heard from her
son, but stated that she 'never' heard from
him. He grew up in Iowa and had developed a drug and alcohol problem in his late
teens. His family made several attempts to
rehabilitate him, all of which failed. He had
been estranged from his family since he was
twenty-three years old, but had made inter-
mittent contact over the years, according
to his mother, 'looking for money or
sympathy'.

Wilson had worked different jobs since he
left home, mainly in factories, on farms and in
manufacturing. He had moved to Breckenridge
one month before his disappearance . . .

Ren slumped back in her chair. It was amazing what people would commit to in a legal document, what awful words they would allow to be attributed to them. Mark Wilson – a tragic man, a troubled drunk, did not deserve to have his disappearance described, she read, by his family as 'another pathetic stunt'.

31

The windscreen wipers did little to help the visibility. Ren drove a thin line between patience and urgency. Adrenaline and a can of Red Bull were pumping through her. Main Street was like the ghost town it had never become. The lights twinkled brief joy before the dark roads ahead. She passed a handful of cars on the way to the Filly. She pulled in behind the green, filthy truck she was hoping she would find there. The reverse-Minotaur guy. She glanced in the window and saw a mess of papers, coffee cups, a box of NoDoz, some hair gel. She moved on.

He wasn't there when she walked in. But he walked out of the men's room not long after Jo.

'Another pitcher, please, Billy,' Jo called out across the bar. 'Hey,' she said, waving to Ren. 'How've you been?'

'Good,' said Ren. 'Good. How you doing?'

'Super.'

Ren went to the bar. Billy was sitting behind it reading a book.

'Working hard?' she said, smiling.

He smiled back. He put the book down. 'I have to be here to take care of the kegs that have just come in. And I have not sat down all evening until about five minutes before you came in.'

'Oh, OK, then,' said Ren.

'I actually love my job,' said Billy.

'Do you?' said Ren.

'Yes, I do. Do you?'

'Yes,' said Ren. 'I did different things when I was younger that didn't suit me, but now, I know I'm in the right job.'

'Yup, because you have no life,' said Billy.

'I . . . do have a life,' she said. 'I'm just wondering exactly where it is.'

Billy smiled. 'I'm sorry. That wasn't very nice.'

'No,' she said. 'So, what are you reading?'

The Man Who Fell in Love with the Moon.'

'That is one of my favorite books.'

He nodded. 'Me too. It's just so strange. And so beautifully written.'

'Show it to me.'

He frowned. 'OK.'

He walked toward her and lay the book on the bar. Ren leaned in to look at it, but whispered to him: 'Could you take our friend's beer bottle, so I can run his prints?'

'Sure,' said Billy. 'Now?'

'Well not, like, right now, no.' She smiled. 'But yes – tonight.'

'Sure.'

After finishing his beer, the guy finally left. Billy waited a while, then went to his table. He put a napkin around the top of the bottle and took it into the back room behind the bar. He stayed back there a while. Ren started flicking through the book. When she turned around, she realized the bar was empty. She could hear Billy rolling kegs of beer somewhere. She caught a glimpse of him through the doorway. The last confidential informant she'd dealt with had been an ever-moaning man – five-foot nothing and fought the world to gain a few more inches in height.

'Are you OK out there?' Billy shouted.

'Yes. I'm fine.'

'I'll be out in a little while,' he said.

Why am I still here? 'OK.'

She wandered around the bar, looking at the photos on the wall, the madam's 'girls' dressed up to look older and primmer than they may have been. She started to read the yellowed newspaper cuttings about them being run out of Boston to Denver and finally settling in their famed out-of-town spot by Quandary Peak. Billy came down to join her when he was done.

'Can I ask you about Mark Allen Wilson – the missing guy?' said Ren.

Billy frowned. 'Sure.'

'What happened the Saturday night between him and Terrence Haggart?'

'Wilson came in here in the afternoon and started drinking. A couple of hours later, Terrence Haggart came in – he was a regular.'

'What was he like?'

'Terrence Haggart thought the world owed him a living. He'd get aggressive with lottery tickets that didn't have the right numbers printed on them.'

Ren smiled.

'He was always disagreeing with people about sports or work or women. He would just pick the opposing view of whoever he was talking to. I'd see it played out in front of me every time. I used to hope he'd meet someone who would take him from his bar stool to a booth, so I wouldn't have to listen to his bullshit. He was ignorant.'

'Can I guess that you served him hard liquor?' said Ren.

'What – as opposed to soda?'

'No. I just heard he was charming, depending what kind of alcohol was coursing through his veins.'

Billy rolled his eyes. 'Sure, whatever. I guess in the early stages of an evening, yes. But it was the later stages that left the lasting impression on me. I mean, he had a party guy rep, but he's not the kind of guy I'd want to party with.'

'And what was Mark Wilson like?'

'A heavy drinker, but a harmless one, from what I saw. He'd only been here once or twice before the night he disappeared.'

'So what happened that night?'

'I got the impression they knew each other. So it was all friendly until Haggart had one of his lottery-ticket meltdowns. Wilson started laughing at him. Haggart went ballistic and said if Wilson hadn't owed him so much money, he wouldn't have been in such a desperate need of a lottery win.'

Ren rolled her eyes. 'God, alcohol sucks people into the most petty bullshit.'

'Tell me about it,' said Billy. 'Anyway, they start punching the crap out of each other. I try and get between them. I break it up for a little while. Then Wilson starts calling him Terrence Jackpot Haggart. Haggart loses it, pushes him out into the parking lot, kicks the shit out of him and leaves him there. He comes back in for a few drinks. And a couple days later, we hear Wilson's disappeared.'

'How come you let Wilson leave alone when he was clearly so drunk, he had been beaten up, and it was a freezing cold night?' said Ren.

'Have you ever worked in a bar?'

'Yes . . . when I was in college.'

'Well, was it a nicer bar than this?'

She smiled. 'It was in a five-star hotel. But . . . all bars serve alcohol. And last time I checked, alcohol has a pretty similar effect on people with pockets full of cash and people with pockets full of unobliging lottery tickets.'

Billy smiled. 'OK. But at least you will acknowledge it was a bar, not a day-care center.'

'I will.'

'And no matter what, the pretty girl serving the drinks on a tray doesn't have to subdue the drunks,' said Billy.

'Ah, but I worked the door,' said Ren.

'What?' said Billy.

She nodded. 'So maybe you could have done with me that night.'

'Maybe I could have,' he said. 'So, are you working the Wilson case?'

'No,' said Ren. 'I said I'd look into it as a favor. I'm keeping track of my man-hours, so if it goes over a particular number, I will stop.'

'How many hours?'

'About one point five.'

He smiled.

'Five,' said Ren. 'So that's one lunch hour a day, one working week.'

'I bet you don't even do lunch.'

'But I do delusion pretty well.'

She went over to the window. The snow was falling relentlessly.

'Holy shit,' she said. 'How did that happen?'

'What?' said Billy.

'It's dumped, like, seven inches out there.'

'Uh-oh,' said Billy.

'Shit.'

He came over beside her and looked out. 'They might have closed McCullough Gulch Road.'

'What?' said Ren.

He nodded. 'There've been too many accidents there.'

'No way.'

He nodded. 'Let me go call Traffic Watch.'

He came back with bad news. 'Looks like we might be stuck here.'

32

'This is a disaster,' said Ren. She rubbed an arm across the window and looked out on to a black-and-white night. 'Screw this.' She turned around to him. 'Did you listen to the forecast this morning?'

'Oh, this is my fault?' He was smiling. 'I don't want to be here either. I want to close up.'

'You are closed up.'

'I want to go home to my own bed, instead of . . .' He threw a glance back behind the bar.

'What's back there?'

'It's not five star.' He looked embarrassed.

'Do you stay there a lot?'

'No. Jesus. In the back of a shitty-ass bar like this? In the cold? In the middle of nowhere?'

Ren shrugged. 'I don't know what you're into . . .'

'Who's into that?'

Ren stared back out the window. 'I'm sorry. I didn't mean it like that.' She went quiet, staring at a rising storm. 'What will I do?'

'Is there someone you can call?' said Billy. 'State patrol?'

'No one's going to be out in this weather. Anyway, by the time they make it out here, it will be the middle of the night and the storm will probably have passed. I'd rather stay here until four a.m. . . ' She turned slowly around. 'I mean, if that's OK with you . . .'

'I'm sure whatever's OK with you is OK with everyone. All the time.'

Screw you.

'I didn't mean you have to stay up talking to me until four a.m.,' said Ren. 'You can go ahead to bed. It's not like I'm going to rob the place.'

'I don't know what you'd be like, let loose in a bar.'

'You don't want to know.'

'That sounds interesting.'

'No. Take it from me. It's not.' She turned back to the window. 'Some proper insulation here might be good.' She walked away and took a seat by the fire. 'It's at an annoying level,' she said, pointing to it.

'Its *only* level,' said Billy. 'The boss is tight. The heating's OK, but he doesn't want the fire to ever be turned up.'

'Yeah,' said Ren, stretching her palms toward it. 'God forbid the place ends up looking cozy.'

'Does the princess find anything to her satisfaction?' said Billy.

Ren ignored him.

'I'm going to fix myself a drink,' said Billy. 'Do you want something?'

'I'm not really drinking . . . but, OK. I'll have a vodka Red Bull.'

'Are you worried you might fall asleep?'

Ren smiled. 'Vodka'll do that to you.'

Billy went behind the bar and poured the drinks.

'Cheers.'

'Cheers.'

'So . . .' said Ren.

Billy turned to her, waiting. 'So . . .?' He grabbed the remote control for the television and hit the power button. Nothing happened. He shook out the batteries and tried again. He got up, switched it on and got static. 'Damn,' he said. 'Damn.'

'Yeah, last thing you want to have to do is talk to me,' said Ren.

'It's not that. It's just . . .'

'I'm kidding,' said Ren.

'I don't know what to say to you.'

'Same as what you'd say to anyone else . . .'

'. . . who could put me behind bars for life.'

'Come on. Why would I want to do that?'

'Ask your Atlanta buddies.'

'Oh, come on. Would I be sitting here alone with you if I thought you were . . . you know?'

'It could be all part of your plan.'

'I don't have a plan. I'm just doing my job.'

They sat in silence. 'So . . . how did you end up here?' said Ren.

'It was a long hard climb up the corporate ladder, but I did it. I made it.' He hit his glass off hers.

Ren laughed. 'I don't know what to say to that.'

'OK – let me think – how did I make it here? Do you know that song "God Bless the Broken Road"? Well, think of mine as a broken road, but maybe the devil blessed it.'

'That song's adorable. Was your road that rough?'

'Yes.'

End of discussion. 'But, like, how was it, growing up?' said Ren.

'It was a badly beaten, animal-murdering kind of childhood.'

Ren laughed loud.

'Seriously, though – did my mom send you?' said Billy. 'You're not really the FBI, right? She just wants to make sure I don't blame her for anything.'

'Well, obviously your childhood was just fine.'

'It was. Crazy, but not bad. I saw some weird shit. But . . . I'm all right now.'

She smiled.

'What about you?' said Billy.

'Ooh,' said Ren. 'This is where I lie and say my father worked in an office and my mother was a housewife. Or I tell the truth. Although, maybe you only deserve the pared-back truth, like you've just given me.'

'What? That was all lies. Go with the lies.'

'My father worked in an office and my mother was a housewife.'

'Good for them.' They clinked glasses again. And with the next drink. And the next one . . . all the way to the last one.

'Can I ask?' said Billy. 'Is Ren short for something?'

Ren smiled slowly.

'Ah . . .' said Billy, 'something you don't want to say.'

Ren smiled big. 'Yes.'

'Now I really want to know.'

She paused. 'OK . . . Renegade.'

'What? Are you serious?'

'No.'

He laughed loud. 'I thought your parents might have been Hollywood movie stars or something.'

'No – worse than that on both counts.'

'Yeah? Go ahead.'

'Orenda.'

'Orenda. That's . . . terrible.'

'I know. She's a sacred power . . . it's an Iroquois thing.'

'I thought there might be something like that in you . . . you have a very striking face.'

Shit. 'Thank you.' She moved quickly on. 'The Iroquois believe that if you ignore your dreams, you're in big trouble because your dreams are connected directly to your soul. But also that when you dream you can communicate with the sacred power . . . Orenda.'

Billy paused. 'Mystical . . . but the name still sucks.'

Ren laughed. 'All right, all right . . .'

'Does your family still call you that?'

'Some of them.'

Billy laughed again. 'Yeah, well, I won't. No way.'

'Hey – it's Agent Bryce to you, anyway.'

'Is it?' He made a face.

'I'm joking, you idiot.'

'Can FBI agents call people idiots?'

'We can do whatever we want,' she said, smiling.

He shook his head.

'Right,' said Ren. 'It is four thirty.'

'You can't drive now. Take the prison bunk. And I'll have the . . . booth here.'

'Nah. I'll . . . let's just wait up, eat something, drink coffee, then I'll go on my way in a couple hours. I couldn't sleep here . . . but thanks anyway.'

'OK,' said Billy, reaching out his hand, pulling her to her feet.

'Good grip,' said Ren.

'Yeah. Steady hand. For the drive-bys.'

Ren laughed. 'Stop.' She held his gaze and saw what could be behind it. He hadn't let go of her hand. She looked away. She pulled her hand gently from his and bent down to grab her purse from the floor. 'Right,' she said, 'I've got to –' She stood up. *Do not look at him*. But she did. His eyes. Pale and nervous. *Oh, no. Don't*. She closed her eyes as Billy leaned down to her. He kissed her so slowly and gently she could barely move; he looked like the kind of guy who would slam you up against a wall. She didn't mind that he wasn't that kind of guy.

And she didn't mind that this could be the biggest mistake she had ever made.

33

Ren woke to Billy Waites' arm wrapped around her naked stomach. Her heart flipped. She closed her eyes. *Oh. God.*

The flashback reel kicked in; his face, his mouth, his arms, his hands, edited with all the other parts of his body she never thought she'd see. Or do anything to. It was a great reel. *But WTF?*

Billy woke, groaning, sliding his hand out from under her.

'Good morning,' he said, rolling on to his back. She could hear the smile in his voice.

What have I done?

'The FBI,' said Billy, laughing.

The people who can fire me.

She sat up. 'I'm sorry, Billy. I've got to go . . .'

'Already?'

'Yes.' She looked around the room, trying to pinpoint each item of clothing before she got up.

Hostage training: walk into a room, know immediately where everything is.

'You are not happy this morning,' said Billy.

She turned to look at him. He held her hair out of her eyes.

Don't be nice to me. 'I . . . don't know what to say.'

'That's OK,' said Billy. 'Kind of.'

Ren sat up. *Panties: two o'clock. Jeans: three o'clock. Bra: ten o'clock. Boots: six o'clock. Top . . .*

'Did you see my top?' she said.

'It's behind the bar.'

Oh God. 'I'll get it on the way out.' She stood by the bed. 'Uh . . . thanks.'

'Thanks?' He laughed.

'For putting me up,' said Ren.

'For putting you up to what?'

She gave him a patient face.

'Do I not get a kiss goodbye?' he said.

Jesus Christ. She bent down to kiss him, hovering between his cheek and his forehead. He ignored her and went for her mouth. She stumbled backward.

He laughed.

'I lost my balance,' said Ren.

'Is that what happened last night?'

She tilted her head at him. 'Bye. Thanks. I mean . . .'

She stopped in the bathroom on her way out. She looked in the mirror and saw her hangover face: the skin, paler than her neck, mascara slightly smudged. She spent good money on makeup to withstand a night's drinking and . . . she also saw her mistake face, her eyes slightly haunted and asking that question she could never answer. *What the fuck were you thinking?* She ran her middle finger under each eye and fixed her mascara. She scraped her nails through her hair and stared at her reflection. *What the fuck were you thinking?* She frowned. She smiled. *But WTF?*

She grabbed her top from a pile of upside-down beer glasses and quickly put it on. She walked to the door, unlocked it and pulled it open. The snow was three feet high. She could see her Jeep across the parking lot, settled into a drift. *Shit.* She kept staring as if the snow would part. *Shit.* She went back in to Billy. He was talking quietly into his cellphone. He looked up, slightly confused, then quickly finished his call.

He smiled.

'Do you have a snow shovel?' said Ren.

'Oh yeah. The storm.'

'Yup.'

'Right.' He fell back on the bed. 'Right. Just give me a minute to get my shit together. Is your head hurting this morning? I totally –'

'I'm sorry, but I really need to get to work,' said Ren. 'OK? So just tell me where the fu— snow-plow is and I can do my thing.'

'Wow . . . calm down.'

'One of my least favorite phrases in the world.'

Billy gave her a look she had seen before, usually when her tone had crossed a line. He threw back the covers and sat up. 'Fine.'

'Look, I'm late. That's all.'

She walked back into the bar while he was getting dressed. He came out with the shovel. 'You sit down. Can I get you a coffee?'

Ren shook her head. Her eyes moved to the door. He got the message. And he didn't like it. He went out back and Ren watched from the window as he plowed a path to her Jeep, to the road and back to the door of the bar.

He walked in and unzipped his jacket, throwing it on one of the chairs.

'Well, thanks,' said Ren, standing up, desperate to leave the stale oppression of a bar in the morning. Billy started opening the shutters, his back turned to her, a quick glance over his shoulder for a half-hearted goodbye.

Ren got into the Jeep, took out her phone and dialed Helen's number. She answered as Ren was pulling out of the parking lot.

'Can you talk?' said Ren.

'Five minutes.'

Ren paused. 'I . . . screwed up.'

'OK . . .'

'I . . . slept with a C.I. – a confidential informant. Last night.'

'OK,' said Helen. 'What happened?'

'He works in a bar. I went to see him. We were snowed in. We had a few drinks . . .'

'Are you OK? He didn't, like . . .'

'God, no,' said Ren. 'He's a lovely guy. I mean, he's a criminal, but –'

'He's a criminal.'

'Well, yeah. Obviously. Most C.I.s are. I mean, he's . . . reformed.'

'He told you that?'

'No. But –'

'But . . .?'

'I believe him.'

'Really?'

'No. I guess not. No.' Her voice was shaking. 'OK? Here's how I feel. I am so attracted to him, it's amazing.'

'I have heard you say that before.'

'Really?'

'Yes.'

'Well, I mean it this time.'

Helen said nothing.

'What'll I do?' said Ren.

'How many times have you asked me that?'

'I know, but I'm hoping one day you'll crack . . .'

Helen laughed. 'Look, work out the patterns, Ren. You're an intelligent woman. Why do you put yourself in these situations? What are the factors? Alcohol doesn't help. Stress . . . you know all this.'

'I know, but I still do it anyway. And for the first time, I can say, honestly, that even if I hadn't been drinking, it would have happened. I know there are people who can walk away from this kind of thing . . . but I'm not one of them. I'd love to be, but . . . I never have.'

'But you don't feel good afterwards.'

'I live in the moment.'

'And then you regret the moment. And the moment eats you up, obsesses you. In a really bad way. And then . . .'

'And then nothing, I've too much on now for it to get in the way.'

'Yeah, because "feeling shit" gives a damn about what you have going on in your life.'

'Yeah, well I'm not going to get down about it . . .'

'Are you looking after yourself? Are you eating well? Sleeping?'

'Not really . . . Mom.'

'I'll ignore that. Do me a favor, please. Go to the gym. Go to the health-food store. Get some early nights. Try a routine.'

Ren sighed.

'And stay away from beer,' said Helen.

Ren's shoulders slumped. 'I'll try.'

'Must try harder,' said Helen.

'Story of my life,' said Ren.

When Ren got back to the inn, she went straight to her room and into the shower. And in the tenth minute she stood there, wondering if she had put conditioner in her hair, wondering whether, if she had, she'd rinsed it out, wondering if really hot water ruined your skin, she saw the face of Gary Dettling. In one hour she would be sitting opposite him, discussing the reliability of Billy Waites.

It depends on what you are relying on him for.

34

Gary Dettling was sitting at the edge of his desk with his back to the door, in front of a bunch of very rough-looking Safe Streets guys. He turned around when Ren walked in. He looked rougher than the rest of them.

'What happened to you guys?' said Ren.

'What happened to you?' said Gary.

'Hey, I thought I looked fine,' said Ren.

'You do,' said Gary. 'You look like you had a great night's sleep.'

'No, I didn't, actually.' She looked around the room. 'What?'

'Didn't you get my texts? Didn't you get my calls?' said Gary. 'Didn't you hear your door getting banged on at midnight?'

Ren's heart started hammering.

'Oh no – you didn't,' said Gary. 'Because you were not there.'

'I . . .' *am a bad liar.* 'I . . . had to go see Jean's

one-three-seven. There was a snowstorm. You
might have seen it on the news this morning. It
didn't clear 'til six a.m.'

'You were stuck in a shit-ass bar all night.
Bummer,' said Robbie.

Gary's expression had no empathy.

'Why were you looking for me?' said Ren.

'Well, unfortunately bank robbers have no
consideration that we're – most of us – an hour
and a half away from Denver and it's not too
convenient to be roused from our cozy
Breckenridge beds to go back and investigate the
. . . worst robbery yet, as a matter of fact.'

'Most money?' said Ren.

'Most violent,' said Gary.

'Oh no,' said Ren.

Gary nodded. 'It started about eight p.m. last
night. The manager of the bank was sitting with
his wife watching a movie. One of these goons
shows up at the door in his nice blue and yellow
shirt with a couple Blockbuster DVDs in his hand,
so it looks like they've forgotten something or are
getting some delivery, whatever. When they open
the door, bam – four guys are inside, no masks.
They get the couple into the living room and tie
them up. Without saying one word. So this couple
have no idea what is going on. And get this –
the men really do have some DVDs to show them.
Hardcore porn. Off the charts. And one of the
guys zips open a sports bag. He gets the bank

manager's wife to kneel down and keep her eyes on the television set. Then behind her, so he thinks only the husband can see, he starts taking out every one of the fucked-up toys they're using on the screen in front of them. And the wife's watching all this in the reflection. Meanwhile, another one of these animals is literally jacking off in the corner. Then the first guy gets the remote control and pauses the movie.' He turns to the husband and says:

'Would you like to see this performed live?'

This woman's husband doesn't even say no. Poor bastard just says, "You can do what you like to me. Please do not touch my wife."'

'Oh my God,' said Ren. 'That is horrific.'

'Then the guy with the sports bag leaves the jack-off guy with the toys and the wife – so you can imagine what happened next. And they killed the husband anyway.'

'And the wife?'

'Lived to tell that tale,' said Gary.

'Jesus Christ Almighty,' said Ren. She sat down at her desk. 'Is there any hope of her ID-ing these guys?'

'Their faces reflected in a porn flick . . . not exactly ideal,' said Gary.

'Welcome to Colin Grabien's mirror,' said Ren. 'And what about the bank?'

'They brought the manager to the bank,' said Gary. 'He opened up. At this point they were wearing blank white masks. They got away with a hundred grand.'

Ren nodded.

'We didn't catch it on camera,' said Gary, 'but someone did lose a mask at the scene. It's gone to the lab. There were traces of saliva on it.'

'For what it's worth,' said Colin.

'So we get blank masks,' said Ren. 'And saliva. Like, "We're not giving you a mug shot this time, but we're giving you DNA"?' said Ren. 'Something tells me that DNA is not going to be worth shit.'

Nobody responded.

A chill ran across Ren's shoulders. She shook it away.

'So,' said Gary. 'Billy Waites . . .'

'Billy Waites,' said Ren. 'The Brockton Filly is in an excellent location for through-traffic, so a lot of people stop off there. You've got I 70 to Breck. Then south on Highway 9 past Quandary, then you're through to Alma, Fairplay, then Highway 285 back to Denver – basically the back route. You've got properties on huge tracts of land there . . .' *Everyone is looking at me.*

Gary was frowning. 'And Billy Waites himself?'

'Yes, well, I trust that Jean Transom trusted him, for one,' said Ren. 'So that's what I was saying about the location. He sees a lot. He could be very useful. And, yes, he is a smart guy, as you said, Gary. So he's a good person to have on our side.'

'You think he *is* on our side?' said Colin.

'Absolutely,' said Ren.

Bob Gage stuck his head in the door. 'Ren, you have a visitor. Patrick Transom is in the conference room, he'd like to talk to you.'

Shit. Shit. Shit. Ren glanced at Gary as if he would go talk to Patrick instead. He looked like he hadn't heard any of it.

'OK,' said Ren. 'Thanks, Bob. Could you tell him one minute?'

Patrick Transom was sitting forward on his seat, his hands clasped in front of him on the conference-room table.

'Hello, Mr Transom.' Ren stood up and shook his hand.

'Hello, Agent Bryce.'

'Please call me Ren.'

'OK. And call me Patrick. I just want you to know I'm not someone who would normally just show up like this, so I'm sorry, but I guess I'm feeling at arm's length. I know you don't need family members bearing down on you when you're trying to do your job. But . . . I've left messages and . . . I felt you would be the type of agent who would return them. That's the impression I got from you when I met you.'

I am like that. I – normally – am. 'Thank you, yes. But it's been extremely busy here,' said Ren. 'We have so many agents working on it, the detectives from the Sheriff's Office . . . and every phone call, witness statement and lead is being followed up on. As you can imagine, this is generating even more leads, and on it goes. To be honest, I wanted to make a phone call to you that was – "OK, Mr Transom, we have these solid leads and they are XYZ . . ." As it stands – and I hope this doesn't sound negative – I have not got enough to raise your hopes or mine.' *That, and the fact that I was too busy fucking a C.I. last night.*

Patrick looked crushed. 'Even if I knew that,' he said. 'That would help. I might be able to manage my expectations. I mean, should I give up on you ever finding the body?'

Yes. 'It's not my place to tell people what they should or should not give up on. It's your call. But I will say that I think it's important we all stay positive. Things *are* moving along. But it's a waiting game.' *I can't believe I used that expression.*

'It's hard to wait,' said Patrick. 'I didn't want any of this. The last person I thought I'd be was someone who had to show up at a Sheriff's Office to ask about the investigation into their sister's murder.'

'Well, I'm sorry you had to show up here at all,' said Ren. 'It shouldn't have come to that.

I . . . don't think I got those messages about you calling.' *Shut up.*

His face changed. 'Well, I did leave them,' he said. His voice was tight.

'Because we're in temporary offices at the moment, we can all be quite hard to pin down. There's a lot of coming and going,' said Ren.

Patrick stood up. 'Well, I'm going to leave you to it, Ren,' he said. 'Thank you for taking the time. And . . . I have a good feeling about you. That you're going to find . . . the person who did this.'

Jesus Christ. I deserve this today. 'Thank you,' said Ren. 'I promise I will do everything I can.'

As soon as he left, she ran to the ladies' room and threw up. *I am a loser. I am a terrible human being. I'm not human, in fact.* She washed her face at the sink. As she was drying it with paper towels, the phone beeped.

Hey. Hw r u? Billy.

Ren's heart started pounding. She deleted the text. She brushed her teeth, fixed her face and tried to do as much of it as she could without looking herself in the eye. She ran into Mike in the hallway outside.

'Hey, Ren.'

'Hey, Mike.'

'I was looking into the RUTH folder for you,' he said. 'I couldn't track down who "Ruth" was. There was no corresponding file in Jean's office or on her computer, so it was a dead end. I did talk to the parents of the other children in that file, or the children themselves – some of whom are adults now. Jean hadn't been in contact with any of them any time recently.'

'It's weird that the folder is called RUTH and Ruth is the one girl whose file isn't in the folder.'

Mike shrugged. 'I know.'

That night, Ren sat by the payphone at the inn with a ten-dollar phone card she'd bought at City Market. She barely knew how to use one. She scratched off the number with her nail, dialed a central number, punched in a code, dialed another number. There was a long wait before she was connected.

Billy picked up. 'Hello?'

'Hi, Billy. It's Ren Bryce.'

'Hey. Did you get home OK?' said Billy.

'Yes . . . I got your text.'

'When I didn't hear back . . . I was just wondering if you were OK.'

'I'm fine, but . . .' She ran through the ways to say it, 'you can't text me on my cell . . . unless it's work, unless you have information, need me to come in . . .'

'Oh.'

'I'm sorry. I don't mean to sound –'

'Look, it's fine. Don't worry about it.'

Ren breathed out slowly. 'I'm not going to say

"Can we pretend this didn't happen?" because that wouldn't be very nice. But −'

'− can we pretend this didn't happen?'

'Well, I feel bad. I don't know what to say. I did . . . have a great time.'

'Me too.'

'But . . .'

'So does that mean you don't require my services any more?'

Silence.

'Ren?' He waited. 'Jesus, I meant my services − my work for you guys.'

'Oh God,' said Ren. 'I'm so sorry. I thought you were being an asshole.'

'No.' His voice was firm.

'Sorry.'

'So does this mean you won't be stopping by again?' said Billy.

'No. I *have* to stop by again. I can't *not* stop by. What I'm saying is, it needs to be . . . *I* need to be professional.'

'OK . . .'

'The kids here are going to think I'm nuts,' said Ren. 'I'm clearly not on vacation. In my business suit. Using the payphone . . .'

'They probably think you're tight. That you're going to fill the communal refrigerator with food that is covered in stickers with your name on.'

'I can't find my permanent-ink Sharpie anywhere.'

'I borrowed it to write your name on the label

of the underwear you left behind . . . O-renda. So I can keep track.'

Ren laughed. 'Ugh.'

'I can only joke about it because it's not true,' said Billy.

'Yes. I had my underwear on when I left.'

'I meant it's not true I need to keep track . . . seriously.'

'Really?'

'Really, actually.'

'Well, that's, I guess, good to know.'

'Just in case you were wondering.'

I was. 'I wasn't, don't worry.'

'OK.'

'OK,' said Ren, 'I'd better get to bed.'

'I hope it's more comfortable than last night's.'

'Yeah, me too.' *Even though there was comfort to be found . . . in Billy Waites' arms.*

Ren lay staring. She had drawn the heavy drapes across the bedroom window, blocking the snowy view on to the street. Her heart beat too quickly, her breathing was off. Rushes of heat and nausea swept over her. The clock read one a.m., then two, then three. And as it finally flashed four, every negative sensation sharpened and spiraled and became connected and expanded and hammered at her.

She sat up. She took a drink from the bottle of

water on the night stand. There was a lavender candle beside it. *Do these really work?* She lit it anyway. But the flame was so small, it was swallowed into the dark.

35

Ren woke the next morning at seven and texted Gary.

Cn we meet 2day?

Y. Whn?

7.30?

OK.

Ren liked to have an hour to get ready in the morning. *Not any more.* She left the inn with minimum makeup and wet hair. By seven twenty-five she was in the conference room with a giant coffee and a toasted sesame bagel.

'Hey,' said Gary, walking in. He took the seat beside her. 'What's this all about?'

Ren looked at him and wondered how things would change if her answer was, *I slept with Billy Waites.* She looked at him and said instead, 'The investigation. I'm getting a little anxious . . .'

'OK. Talk to me.'

'Well, I have nothing.'

'I can tell you that's not true, for a start. Everything that could be followed up on, has been. And what we have done is to rule out a hell of a lot already.'

'I'm fine with the ruling out if I've got lots of ruling in going on too,' said Ren. 'I'm like, "What the fuck happened to you, Jean?"'

'Ren – you'll answer that yourself. If you start thinking that you won't, it'll be reflected in your work. Begin every day like it's the first day of the investigation.'

'That's good advice. Thanks.'

'So, give me updates.'

'It seems to be just me getting hunches about people. This guy who drinks at the Brockton Filly – creepy. Caroline Quaintance – lying, even though the animal shelter people had only glowing reports on her; her bosses the same.'

I won't mention Misty.

'Ren, your hunches are usually very good,' said Gary.

I hope so. 'I feel bad because, in a fucked-up way, I wish Jean Transom had had more going on in her life to give us a wider scope. She lived in a tiny little world and I still can't seem to navigate my way around it.'

'Ren, it's not all about you,' said Gary. His voice was kind. 'You're having a day of doubt. So put that aside and turn this all outwards, OK?'

'Ugh. You're right.'

'Go, do it. OK?'
'Thanks, Gary.'

She went to the kitchen to make coffee and eat cookies she didn't like or want. She was alone. She sat at the table and closed her eyes. *I need to separate the part of Billy Waites that is under my skin from the part of Billy Waites that should be under investigation. I need to take a little step back right now – I am too close. And personal.*

She grabbed her coffee, went back to her desk and opened the Mark Wilson file again. Wilson had stayed in the hostel part of The Cheapshot Inn the month before he died. *Why does The Cheapshot Inn sound familiar?* She remembered. *The Welcome Center.*

The Welcome Center had barely opened for the day, but the manager let Ren in. She went quickly to the display she was looking for: the photo montage of Ridge Street through the decades. In one of the photos, a sign swung from the branch of a stooping oak, most of its letters hidden by the leaves: *The Cheapshot Inn.* And in smaller print, *Est. 1962.* Except that it was no longer an inn. Ren knew what someone would find now if they walked through the door – the dark, narrow hallway that led to Dr Charlie Barger.

The manager came over to her. 'Is there anything I can do for you?'

'Yes, there is, as a matter of fact,' said Ren.

She pointed to the photo. 'I was wondering if you could tell me a little bit about The Cheapshot Inn.'

'Charlie Barger's place? Well, it's closed now. He closed it last December.'

Who closes an inn in Breckenridge during peak season?

'And it's been an inn since 1962?' said Ren.

He nodded. 'His father set it up – Emil Barger. He was part of a small group that ended up owning a big part of Breckenridge, but I guess instead of steamrollering his way in, he kind of rode in on a white horse.'

'What do you mean?'

'Well, this would have been in the sixties, when the town was going through a slump. The economy needed these guys – and they knew it. The difference with Barger was that he gave back. He lobbied for affordable housing, he paid his workers well, he took care of people . . .'

'How did he end up owning part of Breckenridge?' said Ren.

'Barger was a 10th Mountain vet. And, like all the others, when he came back from the war, he was looking for something to do. These guys had trained for years before they were sent to Europe, so these were some skilled mountain men. They fought well in the war and, when they came back, a lot of them ended up working at resorts in Colorado in one way or another.'

'When would that have been?'

'Oh, quite a while after the war. We would be talking late fifties when it started to kick in. Developers knew when they were on to a good thing, so they were hiring these 10th Mountain guys left and right.'

'So Emil Barger was hired by developers?'

'Not so much hired – he had family money, so he was right up there with the best of them. He was a developer himself. And, I guess, his own technical advisor. He made some clever choices.'

Ren thought of Salem Swade and how, twenty years later, the mountains welcomed him back from his war. 'I guess it worked out well for Emil Barger,' she said.

'And The Cheapshot Inn was one of the ways he said thank you . . .'

'Ah,' said Ren.

'For most of the year, he got one of the trainee managers from the resorts to take care of it. Then his son, Charlie, took over every time he was back from medical school on vacation.'

'Right.'

'Why the interest in all this?' said the manager.

I get sidetracked. 'I just like the town,' said Ren. She smiled. 'This place is great. You've done a really good job.'

'Thank you. Call back again if there's anything else you need.'

* * *

Ren checked her watch and decided enough time had passed that she could call Helen without waking her up.

'Helen? Hi. It's Ren.'

'Hi. I'm just with someone right now. Can I call you back in two minutes?'

'Like, two minutes or five or ten?' said Ren.

'Two.'

'OK.'

'Are you OK? You sound –'

'No, no. I'm fine,' said Ren. 'I don't want to bother you.'

'You're not. I'll speak to you in a little while.'

Ren breathed out. She looked around the quiet streets of Breckenridge and helped herself to calm down. She stayed, suspended in a silent, baseless panic, until the phone rang.

'How are you doing?' said Helen.

'I'm good, I'm good,' said Ren. 'Well, I'm kind of freaked out. Which is, I guess, why I called.' Her laugh was nervous.

'Why are you freaked out?'

'Well, I just had this thought,' said Ren. 'You know the way I've been spending time with Billy? In the bar . . .'

'Yes.'

Ren's pause stretched for half a minute, time that Helen still didn't break into.

'I know this sounds stupid, OK?' said Ren eventually. 'But I'm like, oh my God, what if they've bugged the bar? What if Billy and I are sitting there or, you know . . . and they're listening in to everything?' Her voice sped up, the sentences rushing out of her, riding a wave of panic. 'I'm screwed. My career's ruined. My life is over. I love my job I –'

'Ren, whoa, whoa. Think about all this logically. What would Billy be under suspicion for?'

'Anything! The murder, drugs, UFAP . . .'

'What is you-fap?'

'Unlawful Flight to Avoid Prosecution.'

'And is Billy on the lam?'

'Well, no . . .'

'And who is the "they" you're referring to when you say "they're listening in"?'

Ren shrugged, then said, 'I don't know. Other agents. Another agency. Maybe one of his former suppliers. Gangs like that, they won't let things go. Those feuds are lifelong. I mean, feud is not even the word. You'd need a new word for what that is. It's a violent –'

'Ren, Ren, slow down, OK? You would know if the bar was being wire-tapped by law enforcement, right? Realistically.'

'Well, yes,' said Ren after another long pause.

'And can we agree it's unlikely any gangs are bugging the bar? Aren't they the type to just show up and blast him away?'

Ren let out a reluctant laugh. 'Yes. I guess so.'

'So why are you working yourself up?' said Helen.

'It's just . . . I guess I'm freaked out. I love my job. There's nothing else I can do. I don't want to screw up. I'm worried I already have. I –'

'Ren, has the case suffered yet because of you?'

'No.'

'Are you going through the tasks you have been given and that you have created using your experience and your observations?'

Ren paused. 'Yes.'

'OK, so why don't you take a little break from beating yourself up? Why not say, "Well done, Ren. Good job."'

'Because, ugh . . .'

'Because it's easier for you to beat yourself up. And it's harder to give yourself a compliment. Try it once in a while.'

'I can't.'

'Well at least let me try it. Let me say, "good job" to you.'

'Thanks.'

'But Billy . . .'

'I know. I know.'

'I'm serious. You know what you need to do.'

Ren sighed. 'Knowing what I need to do and what I want to do and what I'm capable of doing? Well, they're such different things, aren't they?'

36

Ren arrived, drained, at the Sheriff's Office. She didn't want to think any more about how she may have compromised the investigation. She just didn't want to think about the investigation. She knew Billy Waites would jump out at her from every page. Her fear would tie him into every part of Jean's life and implicate him in every part of her death. And now the case she was so desperate to solve could become the one case she would never solve because of her own actions.

Her cellphone rang.

'Hey, Ren. How are you?'

'Oh, hi, Vincent,' said Ren. 'How are you?'

'Fine. You?'

She gave a sad laugh. 'Shit.'

'Yeah, me too.' He paused. 'Any particular reason?'

She sighed. 'Too many to get into.'

'How's the investigation going?'

'Shit too.'

'How cheery are we?'

'I know,' said Ren. 'How's work for you?'

'Not much better . . .'

'We are in high spirits today.'

He laughed. They were quiet for a little while. 'Look . . . I miss you.'

'I miss you too.'

'I was thinking of maybe coming to Breck at the weekend . . .'

'Oh.'

'Once more . . . with feeling.'

'I'm sorry. It's just . . . if you're coming to see *me* . . .'

'That would be part of the plan,' said Vincent.

'I just won't have the time. I'm . . .' *Too busy fucking things up for myself* '. . . working.'

'Not even one evening off?'

'I could do lunch maybe.'

He laughed. 'No alcohol, broad daylight, a set time frame –'

'Stop,' she said. 'It's not like that.'

'Oh, even if it is, I'll take it.'

'I'm glad,' said Ren. 'Text me Saturday morning.'

'You bet.'

Just as she hung up, another call came through.

'Mr Truax, how can I help you?' said Ren.

'I'm helping *you*, Ms Bryce. Your prints are back from the beer bottle.'

'And?'

'*Nada*. No match.'

'And that's supposed to help me how?' said Ren.

'Well, if helping you means ruling out for now that this man is a hardened criminal with a string of violent crimes under his belt, yes.'

'Not that, in fact, he is such a criminal master-mind that he has eluded us for decades to commit some of humanity's vilest atrocities?'

'While you've been fixing your makeup . . .'

'That's crime-fighting in itself.'

Ren walked into Bob's office. 'OK, if you could put your fingers in your ears, say "la la la la la" at the same time, while also listening to my question and answering it, I would be very grateful.'

'La la la la la . . .'

'Where did you all search for Mark Wilson last year?'

'All over town. And out McCullough Gulch Road to the Brockton Filly, around the Filly. We had a hundred volunteers.'

'And no one even found any of Wilson's belongings, nothing?'

'No.'

'Bob, he went missing around the same spot as Jean must have.'

'We don't know that.'

'It's highly likely.'

'Well, all roads lead to the Brockton Filly,' said

Bob. 'Maybe it's not the big shadow of Quandary Peak we should be worried about. Maybe it's the big shadow of Billy Waites. Maybe Waites is the common denominator here. And what better front than being pals with the FBI? A career liar with friends in all the right places.'

Charge the paddles to three hundred.

Bob shrugged. 'It happens,' he said. 'People go missing. They drink too much – the cold, the alcohol, the altitude gets to them, the snow covers them up. It's all nice and tidy.'

'I don't think so,' said Ren.

'Based on what, though? Feelings, nothing more than feelings?'

'I like my feelings.'

'What do you think might have happened?' said Bob.

'*That* is the mystery,' said Ren. 'I guess, you know, the poor guy shows up, he's from out of town –'

'Hey, everyone here's from out of town,' said Bob. 'Nobody is from Breck, as the saying goes. A lot of people *want* to be, they'll tell you they *are* – in an English, Australian, Norwegian accent.'

'My point is, this guy is not expendable,' said Ren. 'And I guess it just feels like someone thought he was.'

'We don't know that he's dead,' said Bob.

'Oh, come on.'

'But please tell me you don't think it's connected to Jean Transom.'

Ren made a face that kept it up for grabs.

'But they are entirely different circumstances. Sounds to me like Mark Wilson was an accident waiting to happen.'

'Sounds to me like he suffered from a disease called alcoholism and that he'd given up all hope.'

'God bless you,' said Bob. 'And save you.' He paused. 'Are you looking for a distraction?'

'Are you nuts?' said Ren. 'Plus,' she checked her watch, 'I have one hour to get to a meeting in Denver. Not going to happen. As if there's not enough for me to do. But you know how something just gets to you . . .'

'Yes. Doesn't mean I know why *this* is getting to *you*.' He started shifting in his seat, dragging his keyboard toward him. 'Are you still here?' he said, glancing back at her.

'Aw, Bob, don't be mean to me,' she said.

37

Robbie Truax stood in the shiny foyer of the Livestock Exchange Building. Four floors up was the Safe Streets office. The elevator that could take him there was open in front of him.

Ren walked in. 'Hello, there. What are you waiting for?'

'No way.' Robbie hopped from left foot to right. 'Not when it opens unbidden. That thing is a freak. It's baiting me.'

'*Unbidden* – I love it,' said Ren. 'What do you think it's going to do to you?'

'Squish me in the doors, take me to a floor with no floor? Slam me down to the bottom of the shaft and spit me out in the haunted basement? You haven't even been there, it's fucked up –'

'You need a night-light . . .' Ren stepped forward. Robbie didn't move.

'Oh, come on,' she said. 'I could hold your hand . . .'

'If my hand is the best you can do . . .'

'You're so scared, grabbing your ass would be a biohazard.'

He paused before he got it. 'Aw, that is gross.'

The elevator doors slid slowly together, paused, shook and finally shut. All the numbers lit up.

'See?' said Robbie, stabbing a finger at it. 'That is not normal. It's got, like, human energy. Look at my arms – I got chills.'

'Are they multiplying?' said Ren.

A voice from behind them sang a few more lines.

They turned around. 'Good afternoon, Clifton,' said Ren. 'Grease lightning.'

'Is he having his elevator thing?' said Cliff. 'Let's try the stairs, scaredy.'

'Go ahead, you guys,' said Ren. 'I'm good with the elevator.'

'The stairs will tighten your ass,' said Robbie. 'I mean, not that it needs –'

'Robbie? Shut up,' said Ren. But she followed them. Upstairs, she headed left into Gary's office. The others went into the bullpen.

'OK, listen up,' said Gary, walking in to them a few minutes later.

'Where's Ren?' said Robbie.

Gary looked at him. 'Jesus, in the ladies' room.'

'Should we wait for her?'

'Yes, we should,' said Gary.

Colin made kissing sounds. Robbie threw him

a look that would never have an impact on him.

Ren stuck her head in the door. 'OK, I'm outta here.'

'What?' said Robbie.

Gary gestured to her to sit down.

Shit.

'I've been going over these bank jobs,' said Gary. 'I've made some calls, spoken with some people, and it looks like these all could have organized crime links.'

'Definitely?' said Robbie.

'I said "looks like".'

'Based on what?' said Cliff.

'Based on the MO,' said Gary.

'Links to who?' said Colin.

'You've all heard of Domenica Val Pando?' said Gary.

They nodded.

'I know the name,' said Robbie.

'Yeah, you're what? Twenty-nine?' said Cliff. 'You're too young.'

Gary took a breath. 'Right, OK. Val Pando was head of one of the most successful organized crime operations in the south. She worked out of a compound in New Mexico. She ran a violent, highly efficient gang that made hundreds of millions in everything – drugs, prostitution, people smuggling, arms dealing –'

'She lectured at universities,' said Ren. 'All across

the US – You and Your Fucked-up Mind: Capitalizing on the Crazy.'

Gary stared at her. She flashed him a smile.

He went on. 'Ten years ago, we put a UCE in there for one year –'

'I still don't know how you pulled that off,' said Colin.

'With great skill,' said Gary.

Ren made a sweeping movement with her arm. 'Why, nothing but the best from the Federal Bureau –'

Gary turned to her, 'Ren, can you put a sock in it? Can we all focus here?'

Ren looked down.

'Anyway,' said Gary, 'the operation was shut down. But there was a time delay going in. The SWAT teams – LA and Albuquerque – panicked, went in unprepared to pull out the agent, who was in fact caught in the middle of a rival gang's assault on the compound. At the very end, it was a mess. The buildings were lit on fire by the rival gang. And Val Pando got away.'

'Wow,' said Robbie. 'Where is she now?'

'Off the radar,' said Gary. 'But her perfume's been left in the air in these latest banks.'

'Really?' said Robbie.

'Not literally,' said Colin.

Robbie nodded. 'I thought that would be pretty amazing . . .'

Gary continued. 'Val Pando is all smoke and

mirrors. One of the world's biggest fashion designers? His entire operation is a front for a multi-million-dollar narcotics operation, and Val Pando's his backer. He loves the hiding in plain sight, the glamour, but he could give two shits if he never sold another dress. His heirs will inherit a drug fortune, not a fashion house. Nice thing to find out when you hit eighteen.'

'My father left me his fishing rod,' said Cliff.

'Yeah, you wish you got some dresses,' said Colin.

'Which designer is it?' said Robbie.

'One of the ones you can't afford to wear,' said Colin.

'Right, OK,' said Gary. 'So, based on her MO, based on talking to some of the players involved at that time, we could be looking at Val Pando. She is an extremely intelligent woman, she plans everything, she only hires people who can understand and implement these plans. She is like one of those organizations that employs over-qualified staff. She has people with Masters degrees, PhDs, side by side with the illegals she brings in from South America.'

Ren could feel Robbie digging a pen into her ribs.

Ow. Shit. She shifted in her seat and refocused on Gary.

'So,' said Gary, 'what she does is plan everything, then get the gang to do something sloppy.

It took a while for us to work this out before, she did it so well. Local police departments would come to us saying a bunch of mouth-breathers had done the job; we'd go back in and realize it was planned right down to the last.'

'Oh yeah, here we go,' said Robbie. 'It's always the PDs' fault.'

'One hundred per cent,' said Gary.

'Woo,' said Ren. 'Young Robbie risks a little joke. Brave.'

Robbie blushed.

'So,' said Gary, 'any of the sloppy shit was done for a reason – any reason except one that would lead them to actually getting caught, obviously. Which leads me to our discarded mask. It's come back from the lab, and the saliva on it? Was traced to a cow.'

'Livestock Building. Cow. Great,' said Ren. 'Did they get a match? Truax, maybe you could look into that . . .'

By midnight, most of the Safe Streets team had been in Gaffney's for six hours. Gary and Cliff had left an hour earlier. Robbie was sitting in a booth between two fifty-something blondes, all three of them laughing hysterically. Ren and Colin were on their only common ground – a sea of alcohol.

'So,' said Colin. 'What sorrows are you drowning tonight?'

Ren looked at him. 'They are innumerable.' She

paused. 'I'm going to use the bathroom . . . not that that will solve anything.' She walked to the door. Her phone beeped as she was about to go down the stairs. She read the text.

Hey. R u around? Billy.

Her heart flipped. She went down to the bathroom and almost turned her phone off and took her battery out. When she got upstairs, she texted back.

N. In Denver.

He texted back.

Me 2. Where?

No. Not again. No way.

38

The Hotel Teatro was the hotel that Ren recommended to anyone she knew who wanted to stay in the city. She had stayed there herself a few times, so she recognized the wallpaper when she woke up. And she recognized the arm again. Billy Waites was just not the kind of guy to sleep on the other side of the bed. He woke up and pulled her closer to him. She groaned.

'Oh no,' said Billy. 'Are you not happy this morning?'

'Billy . . .' She remembered spending most of the previous evening telling him why they couldn't be together.

Billy sang a few lines about regrets.

'Oh my God,' she laughed. 'You look like you can sing.'

'Yeah, no. I cannot sing. But do you want to see some more of my moves?'

She had no answer for that.

'Come here, baby,' he said.

Jesus – baby.

He grabbed her waist, pulling her closer again. He kissed her, then stopped. He looked her straight in the eye. To see would she stop him. She did not.

'Do you feel better now?' he said afterwards.

'Stop.'

'You were angry drunk last night,' said Billy.

'Was I?'

'Yes.'

'Did I say something terrible to you?'

'No,' he said. 'But you just weren't . . . chilled.'

'I had a bad day. And a very long drinking day.'

She got out of bed and went into the shower. She stood under the hot water, sorting through Aveda products, smiling in spite of herself . . . because a bad feeling had sprouted claws inside her and wasn't about to release its grip. *Why had Billy come to Denver?* Her stomach turned. *Coincidence.* But as she reached for the towel, there was the tiniest shake in her hand. She put on the bathrobe and walked back into the bedroom, picking up her clothes as she went. Billy was curled under the covers, looking out the window, his bare back to her. She dressed quickly. He turned around when he heard her grab her purse.

'But I just ordered breakfast,' he said. 'Pancakes, bacon, maple syrup, fruit, coffee . . . eggs, toast, croissants . . .'

'You forgot the nothing.'

'Just covering the bases. I mean, I don't know what you eat for breakfast.'

'Ugh.'

'What?' said Billy.

'Well, you don't know what I eat for breakfast, but you've . . . you know.'

He laughed. 'So what? You feeling cheap?'

'Stop always getting to the point.'

'Stop dancing around shit, Ren. Loosen up. You're not cheap. You're expensive.'

'I'm still going. I'll settle the bill on my way out.'

He frowned. 'No you won't.'

'Yes, I –'

'No.'

'Fine.'

'Thanks.'

'For what?'

'For the . . . hotel.'

Billy laughed again. 'If you ever want another . . . hotel, let me know. I could give you hotels all night long.'

He couldn't see her smiling as she closed the door behind her.

Ren walked quickly through the hotel lobby. The guy at the concierge desk was huge and smiling.

'Good morning, madame.'

'Hi, how are you?' said Ren. *Personally, I am troubled.*

'I am good this morning. Can we give madame a ride anywhere?'

Ooh. Hotel Teatro had a complementary shuttle service. A handsome young man in a black Jeep would take you anywhere you wanted to go.

'Could you give me one moment?' said Ren, walking around the corner where there was a huge open fire. She dialed Robbie's cellphone.

'Truax, are you in the office?'

'Allegedly.'

'Where is my car?'

He laughed. 'Not again. It's right by Gaffney's. You were probably looking at it all night.'

'Shit, yeah. Thanks.'

'Where did you end up?'

Ren paused. 'I gotta go. Thanks.'

'Not fair.'

She walked back into the lobby. 'Could you take me to Gaffney's please?'

'Great spot,' he said.

'Evil,' she said.

Ren's car was exactly where she didn't remember leaving it. She sat inside, reclined the seat a little and blasted the heating. She dialed Helen's number.

'I did it again.'

'Did what?' said Helen.

'Billy.'

Helen paused. 'OK. Tell me what happened.'

'I was here . . . I'm in Denver. So was he, he called, we hooked up. We stayed in a hotel.'

'And how are you feeling this morning?'

'I don't know.' She paused. 'I really like him. I have not been able to stop thinking about him since the last time. But there's something about him I can't describe. I worry. My stomach gets unsettled. I don't know if it's because . . . I don't trust him. Or because I'm falling in love with him.' She slumped back in her chair. 'It sounds ridiculous, I know. I mean, I'm thirty-six years old.'

'So . . . do you think you have a future with him?'

'What? I don't know. Do I have to?'

'I'm just giving you a reality check . . .'

'If I look at it logically, no. I mean, is he going to come with me to the work Christmas party? No. Do I bring him home to my mom? No. Do I do anything other than hole up in a hotel room with him for months on end? No.'

'That's lots of nos.'

'I know.' She glanced at herself in the rear-view mirror. 'Why do I do this?'

'Ren? Only you can answer that.'

Ren brought guilt and a massive headache back to the Sheriff's Office. She drank coffee and water, took Vitamin C and decided ultimately what she needed was some air in her lungs . . . with a stop-off at Charlie Barger's house on the way.

Shannon Barger opened the door a fraction. Direct sunlight did nothing for her; she was a forty-five-year-old mess.

'Hello,' said Ren. 'Is your father in?'

Shannon hung from the door in her low-riding track pants with her bare, bony hip out. Her thin auburn hair was tied with a brown elastic band on top of her head. She opened the door wider without saying a word and walked away.

Weirdo.

Ren knocked on Charlie Barger's door. He took his time to open.

'Hello, I'm Ren Bryce. You helped me with my altitude sickness.' She smiled.

'Oh, yes . . . you're with the FBI. Mike Delaney . . . yes. I remember.'

'You may be able to help me out. I'm doing some research on a case and I came across your house,' she said. 'Actually, I came across the Cheapshot Inn.' She smiled.

Barger looked slightly bewildered. 'Yes,' he said, smiling. 'Come in, let me make us some coffee.'

'That would be great, thank you.'

Barger walked ahead of her down the dark hallway, his footsteps silent in sheepskin slippers. Ren's heels sank into the carpet. She wondered if she was ruining it. But Barger's wool cardigan and jeans, expensive but worn, reminded her everything in the house was fading.

'I saw that photo in the Welcome Center, the people standing outside here,' said Ren. 'The name is great – cheap shot. That's what a lot of young people come here for, right? Spend all their money on ski passes, come off the mountains looking for cheap alcohol.' She smiled.

Barger stood at the kitchen sink, filling the bright red kettle. 'I'm afraid *I've* only got coffee to give you,' he said.

'Well, I'm not a young person, so that's fine.'

He turned around. 'I reckon you're about half my age – which makes you very young to me.'

She laughed. 'I wanted to ask you about this guy –' She placed the photo of Mark Wilson on the table.

'Well, I know who he is. That guy disappeared last year. As a matter of fact, it was only on the news there a little while back.'

'That's him,' said Ren. 'I wanted to know . . . he stayed here for the month that he was in Breckenridge.'

He smiled sadly. 'That's the thing. I've already been through the investigation first time round.'

'Oh, I'm not investigating it. I'm just taking a look at a few things. I had no idea this place used to be an inn.'

'Yes. My father was a . . . generous man. He set this up many years ago. I used to work here on my vacations from college. Then, when he died, it was passed on to me, and when my daughter Shannon got older, she helped take care of it.'

Not very well, obviously.

'Your father sounds like a good man.'

'He was. He was. A champion skier, a 10th Mountain veteran, a developer, a humanitarian.'

A hard act to follow.

39

Ren drove to Main Street and parked across the street from the Gold Pan. She arrived just as Salem Swade was getting up to leave.

'Hey, Salem,' said Ren.

'Hello,' said Salem.

'How do you think Misty would feel about me taking her for a little walk?' said Ren.

Salem glanced down at Misty. 'It might be how *I* feel about you taking Misty for a walk. I doubt she'd have much of a problem. Isn't that right, girl?'

Misty gave him a lazy, loving look. He rubbed her head.

'OK, then,' he said to Ren. 'Where are you going to take her?'

'Well, how about I drop you off at the Filly. I'll take her from there and drop her back to you.'

'You have to take very good care of her. That's all.'

'I can promise you that,' said Ren.

*   *   *

Ren left Salem at the Brockton Filly. Misty sat on the back seat of the Jeep as Ren drove a short distance down the road. She pulled into a rest-stop and parked. When she opened the back door, Misty threw herself at her.

'Hey,' said Ren, 'you can't fool me. I know this is not your first time going for a walk.' She laughed. She secured Misty's leash and they walked for twenty minutes and back again along a winding cycle path that ran in and out of the trees along-side the highway. Few cars and no people passed them by. They got on well. But Salem was very happy to have Misty back.

As Ren was walking, she thought about Caroline Quaintance, Jean Transom's friend from the animal shelter. There was something about her she couldn't put her finger on. Tonight, she decided to put herself through some torture to find out more.

Ren could never get the balance right between the clothes she wore, the outside temperature and the heating in the car. Sub-zero surveillance: compared to the same temperature the evening before, the roads would feel icier, the snow heavier, the seats of the car, harder. And there was something about it all that felt pointless. It is harder to blend into the darkness when your exhaust is pumping white fumes into the air. But at least she *had* heating; half-way down the block

behind her, Todd Austerval was sitting in a car
with none. He was dressed in a massive black
Puffa jacket that made it look as if his airbag had
blown.

Ren circled the block, saw nothing and pulled
back into her original position. She radioed Todd.

'Hey – let's swap cars.'

Silence.

'I'm serious,' said Ren. 'This isn't fair – you
freezing your butt off.'

'Are you for real?' said Todd.

'Yes. I'll walk back to you now.'

'No way,' said Todd. 'I can't let you do that.'

'Is it because I'm such a lady?' said Ren.

Todd snorted.

'Laughing a little too hard,' said Ren. 'Come
on, just let me do this.'

'Look,' said Todd, 'we've been here three hours
and seen nothing. Stay where you are; another
ten minutes and we'll both go.'

'OK. Then we can go track down your mechanic
and kick the crap out of him.'

Todd snorted again. 'Sure, if you want to. But
I'm going home to bed.'

You are so straight. 'Yeah, I wasn't actually
serious?' said Ren.

'It's hard to tell with you,' said Todd.

But Ren had drifted out of Todd's bland world
and was watching headlights approach in her rear-
view mirror. She sank lower in her seat and sat

in silence watching the familiar car as it passed. It circled the block three times.

Todd radioed her. 'Hey, did you see that?'

'That car circling?' said Ren. 'Yeah, I was right up close. He had a map, he was just lost . . . this place has a lot of streets and avenues with similar names.'

'OK – you got a better view.'

'Yep,' said Ren. *A perfect view.*

But was Billy Waites tailing me or Caroline Quaintance?

The Brockton Filly was almost closed, the crowd was thin. Ren had given Billy Waites two hours to get back. She came in, smiled at him across the room and sat up at the bar.

'Hey,' she said.

'Hey,' he said, smiling wide. 'I didn't think you'd ever be coming back to see me.'

She laughed as her heart pounded. 'As if I wouldn't . . .'

'Well, you weren't too keen on my company this morning. And Salem said you did a drive-by to drop him off.'

'Did you get through all that breakfast?'

'I did not,' said Billy. 'You should have seen it – there was enough for ten people. I am not exaggerating. I wrapped it all up in some napkins and brought it back for Salem.'

'Did you check out OK?'

Billy nodded. 'I wasn't thinking about that when I took the food. In fact, I dropped some of my stash.'

'You wouldn't make a great crim—' She almost blushed. 'Oops.'

'I've lost my touch,' said Billy. 'The FBI is messin' with my mojo.'

40

The Brockton Filly quickly emptied. She saw the creepy guy whose prints she had taken. He almost winked at her as he left. *Ugh.* She watched Billy make his way around the bar, closing the shutters. Every time she met him, he was wearing a black T-shirt with a graphic on the front and perfectly sized Diesel jeans.

He looked over his shoulder at her. 'I have three pairs of the same jeans,' he said. 'In case you were wondering.'

Ren laughed. 'Well, what else am I going to be looking at in here?'

'I'm just an object to you . . .'

A subject, actually. 'Yup,' she said.

He kept going and every now and then he would look over and smile. It felt good. She watched him, afraid to rely on what she was feeling right now. He had to know that checking his phone numbers, checking anything out about him now could lead her colleagues directly her way. He had cut off that channel. *Deliberately?* He smiled at her again. If she was to be fair, she had cut off that channel too. But she wasn't feeling fair. She was feeling suspicious. She was sitting with a man linked to a homicide investigation who had been following either her or a young woman who was linked to the homicide victim. *And I am the agent in the middle.*

'Can I fix myself a drink?' said Ren.

'Sure – go ahead,' said Billy. 'I need to bring bottles in from out back.'

By the time she got behind the bar, her heart was beating so hard, it was beginning to turn her stomach. *I can't do this, it's so wrong. If he knew . . .'*

Her hand never shook on the job. She had held a gun steady on people she feared she would have to shoot. She had done terrible things in terrible situations that should have rendered every usable part of her body useless, but it never happened. She did steady better than most. Until tonight. She had crossed over. One sensible-shoed foot was rooted on the professional side. The other was in the personal zone with a trampy stiletto on the chest of a criminal.

Jesus . . . and stop fucking shaking.

She stared down at her hand. It calmed a little. She took a breath and navigated quickly through the unfamiliar menu of Billy Waites' cellphone. Most of the texts were from her, which gave her

an unwanted thrill. As she scrolled down, she realized the Inbox was filled entirely with her texts.

I am the stalker.

The Sent box was different; probably the same
amount of texts to her, but more to numbers and
names she knew she wouldn't recognize anyway.
She started opening them. They were typical
men's texts – direct and written without l8-,
w8-, gr8-style abbreviations. These texts said Y or
N, or had times or . . . Looking for coded messages
seemed ridiculous. With single-letter responses,
the same letters over and over, what was she
going to work out? That yes meant no and no
meant yes? She almost laughed. As she backed
her way out of the menus she had violated, the
phone vibrated in her hand with a text message.
She jumped and almost fucked herself into
dropping it and alerting Billy. He called out from
the back room.

'Shit, Ren? Is my phone out there?'

She half-looked at it, half-tried to put it down
and wholly wanted to press Yes to open the text.
She wanted to find out if Billy was about to bring
in a shipment of coke, arrange a hit, tell his friends
what he did to her, or ask a girl called Cindy to
meet him in a seedy bar. *Is this the seedy bar? And
what are the chances of a sinister text arriving while an
FBI agent is holding his phone? Jesus.*

'I think it's here somewhere,' she shouted back.
'I heard the buzz.'

'You can leave it,' said Billy. 'I'll be out in a minute.'

With a gun to pressed to the back of my neck.

She walked quietly around the front of the bar, leaving the phone where it was. She sat very still, then pretended to look through her bag for a pen. Her heart slowed, but there was a small tremble left in her hand. Billy came up behind her, laid a hand on her shoulder and kissed the top of her head. She reached up and rested her hand on his.

'Hey,' he said.

'Hey.'

He walked over to his phone and checked the message. Ren watched his face. There was no story in it to read.

'Where's your drink?'

'I changed my mind,' she said. 'I need to get back to Breck.'

'What?'

She nodded.

'Oh,' said Billy. 'I was going to fix us something to eat.'

Whoa. Too domestic. 'I can't, I've . . . got to meet up with my bosses.'

'Code for "I can't possibly eat with you because that would be weird."'

And you know all about code . . . And I feel terrible for even thinking that.

She stood up and kissed him briefly on the lips. 'I'll talk to you later.'

'You always say "I'll talk to you later," and you never do.'

She smiled back. 'It's just a saying. You know, like "How are you doing?" or "I love you."'

'What?'

Ren laughed. 'I think Homer said that.'

'Really?'

'Oh, not him – Homer Simpson. Gotta go.'

When Ren finally got away from the Brockton Filly, it was three a.m. A miserable, beautiful, hopeless song played on her iPod to back up her mood. Her hand would never have shook, her heart would not have sped up if Billy Waites had been just who he was and not who he had become. She had been in situations worse than that, she had risked more, but never did she have to ask herself a similar question to the one that was running through her mind right now.

Was I looking for reassurance that Billy Waites was bad . . . or reassurance that he was good?

41

Ren woke with aching shoulders and stiff legs. She took a bath instead of a shower to try to relax her muscles.

Bob had an audience of several detectives when she got to his office.

'I was just telling the guys,' he said, 'there was some late-night action at the hospital. Some guy was dumped out of a car and collapsed in the sliding doors.'

'What was wrong with him?' said Ren.

'The Frisco guys could barely keep a straight face. He said some guy jumped on him, poked him in the neck and the face, did some weird shit to his stomach and his – "privates" is what he called them – and left him in agony. Then bundled him into a car and dumped him at the hospital.'

'Kind of them,' said Ren. 'Where did he say it happened?'

'He didn't. He was understandably reluctant to provide anyone with more information because, of course, there were some outstanding warrants for his arrest.'

'On what charges?'

'Child support.'

'That's it?'

Bob nodded. 'Yup . . .' He turned to her, his expression grave. 'Something smells bad with this guy.'

'Really?'

'No, I mean seriously. We found his truck – he had been transporting manure.'

Ren laughed. 'Ew. Why?'

'Some bullshit reason . . .'

'OK, we could be here all night . . . talking shit.'

The detectives were laughing as they moved past her and went back to their offices.

'Where's this guy now?' said Ren.

'In my little jailhouse,' said Bob.

'What's his name?'

'Erubiel Diaz.'

'Exotic.'

'There was one car driving through the parking lot of the Medical Center around the time Diaz was dropped off,' said Bob.

'What, are you actually following up on this?' said Ren. 'Some dirtbag gets taken off the streets, and you're going to go find the people who did us that favor?'

'The guy hasn't paid his child support – is dirtbag maybe going a little too far?'

Ren paused. 'Um, maybe . . . Did you get the registration?'

'Nope. The driver did quite a cool shimmy around the cameras, by the looks of it. It was like that naked Austin Power thing.'

'Here, let me save you some time on this,' said Ren. 'Could I go talk to him? He may know some of our masked men.'

'Why would you think that?'

'I just would.'

'Knock yourself out,' said Bob. 'He's in a cell right now. You speak Spanish?'

'I have ways of communicating . . .'

Bob led Ren through reception, down a series of hallways and through the steel door into the jail.

'Hey,' said Bob to the female guards behind the desk. 'The reception area,' he said to Ren. 'The inmates need anything sent to their room, they call here: fluffy towels, robes, scented candles . . .'

'Yeah, and today's Champagne-and-Hooker Tuesday,' said one of the guards.

They all laughed.

'Agent Bryce here is going to talk to our new guest, Mr Erubiel Diaz.'

'Enjoy,' said one of the guards.

'They'll whistle and cat-call,' said Bob. 'You know what to do.'

'Get a few phone numbers,' said Ren.

'Nah, just call me, I'll patch you through.'

The Summit County Jail was clean and modern with reinforced glass in all the common areas. In a cell to her right, a brick-shithouse inmate stood freakishly still, his legs slightly spread, his arms folded, his dark eyes dead ahead, his black wavy mullet carefully tended.

'Jesus,' said Ren. 'What's his story?'

'Yeah,' said Bob. 'He hates . . . people.'

A group therapy session was winding down in a glass-walled room on the left. The therapist raised a hand to Bob and nodded.

'We'll wait for these guys to leave,' said Bob. 'I'll bring Diaz to you. You want me to sit in?'

'No, thank you,' said Ren.

'OK. But I'll be right outside, watching through the glass.'

'Don't,' she said. 'I'll be fine.'

Ren eyeballed some of the inmates as they left. She went into the empty room and sat at the table with the glass door to her right. Bob came back with Diaz, then disappeared. He walked to the control booth at the center of the jail, a small hexagonal glass room that looked out over everything.

'Hey,' said Bob to the guy at the controls, 'show me the group therapy room, so I don't have a dead Fed to explain.'

The guy turned to the bank of monitors and flicked a switch. The screen was black. The guy shrugged. 'Hold on. Let me try this.' He hit some more buttons, but the screen didn't come back on.

'Shit,' said Bob. 'Is that busted?'

'Shouldn't be.'

'Shit,' said Bob. He ran back down the steps and along the hallway to the therapy room.

Ren was standing right in front of the glass door with her arms stiffly by her side. Bob jumped. He pulled open the door. She made fava bean and Chianti sounds.

He smiled. 'Phew.' He looked past her.

Diaz was slumped in his chair, his head turned toward the back wall. His left pants leg was wet and there was a small pool under his foot.

Bob glanced at Ren. 'If you've eaten his face . . .'

She looked back at Diaz, then leaned into Bob's ear. 'Much worse than that . . . Just call me Theseus.'

'Who the fuck is Theseus?'

Ren smiled. 'The guy who slayed the Minotaur.'

Bob frowned, then called into the prisoner, 'Diaz, you ready?'

'Get me a towel or something,' said Diaz in Spanish. 'Let me clean myself up.'

'Let him clean himself up first,' said Ren.

'I'll call maintenance.' Bob walked back down

to the control room. 'Hey, you need me to send someone in to look at that camera?' He knew the answer.

'No. It came back just as you got here.'

42

Ren spent an afternoon under the shadow of Mark Wilson. The file was more than just a distraction. She knew it had come her way for a reason. Misty's job the day before had been to clear her hangover and see if she could pick up the scent of a body that may have been overlooked in the search. She succeeded in fifty per cent of her task.

Mike Delaney was dragging file boxes from behind his office door and piling them up behind his desk.

'I think they were hidden better behind the door,' said Ren.

'Ah,' said Mike, 'maybe from people coming *in* to the room. The loser behind the desk had to look at them all day. Until today. I have decided to keep my problems behind me for a little while.'

Ren smiled. 'It could be a self-fulfilling-prophecy thing.'

'I hope so.'

'I was wondering – being the mountain man that you are – would you have a map of the whole area at the base of Quandary Peak and out the road toward Fairplay?'

'Sure,' said Mike. He opened one of the drawers in his desk, checked through a few maps and handed her one.

'Thanks,' said Ren. She went back to her office, opened it out and laid it on the table. It covered a wider area than the previous maps she had been looking at. *Or getting the guys to look at and report back to me on.*

There was a tract of land on the map between the Brockton Filly and Fairplay that had no name or reference number but was marked as private property. Ren went back in to Mike.

'Mike,' she said, 'do you know what this is here? Is it anything?'

He looked where she was pointing. 'It's the old Barger Brewery.'

'Like Charlie Barger Barger?'

'Yup.'

'How does a doctor wind up with a brewery?' said Ren.

'It started out as his father's. Charlie's father, Emil, set up one of the first breweries in town. Have you been to Big Mountain Brewery?'

'Yup.'

'They still sell Lime Beer there. It's a Barger

beer – Emil backward. I'm guessing he was kind of a dork. But the beer is good.'

'Oh, so it's not because it tastes of lime,' said Ren.

'No, but Big Mountain Brewery gets a kick out of confusing the customers.'

'So BMB used to be owned by Emil Barger?'

'Kind of,' said Mike. 'Emil Barger started brewing his own beer in his garage when he retired. This was the late seventies. Anyway, he can't help himself and, within a year, he had bought that place off McCullough Gulch Road. I guess you'd call it a micro-brewery. Two years on, it's huge, it's the Barger Brewery, supplying to a lot of the bars around town, and people are loving it. Emil passes away, leaves the brewery to Charlie who, sadly, runs it into the ground. The brand was bought out and it became Big Mountain Brewery. Charlie got to hang on to the building and land. BMB, as you know, has premises just on the edge of town.'

'Jesus,' said Ren, 'his father's got the Midas touch, Charlie's got the everything-he-touches-turns-to-shit thing. The guy in the Welcome Center told me about the Bargers owning half of Breck. And I'm guessing that's not the case any more.'

'I don't know, Ren . . . I'd rather not . . . Charlie's a friend.'

'I understand that. And I don't want you to betray anything or anyone. But it's in plain sight that his house is run down and his daughter has a touch of the meth face.'

Mike looked at her.

'I'm sorry,' said Ren. 'I shouldn't have said it that way. But there is a sadness about that house.'

A terrible, cloying, sadness.

Mike let out a breath. 'OK – Shannon Barger is a meth addict. And Charlie's in debt. He has been bailing that little bitch – God forgive me – out since she was sixteen years old.'

'Sixteen? How old is she now?'

'Twenty-five.'

'Oh my God, I thought she was, like, over forty.'

He nodded. 'It's very sad. She's been to rehab a dozen times.'

'And he's a doctor,' said Ren. 'That's gotta hurt.'

'And the son of a very successful man, a war hero, an athlete, one of the founding fathers here . . . He owns nothing of what his father built up, and everyone knows it. Apart from the house –'

'That used to be the Cheapshot Inn –'

'Yup, which obviously didn't go too well.'

'No.'

'He told me he's thinking of starting the brewery again,' said Mike. 'Of making money that way.'

'Getting into brewing?' said Ren. 'That will *cost* him money. Why doesn't he just sell the land? That would probably cover his debts. I mean, I don't know how much they are, but . . . none of his idea makes any sense.'

ALEX BARCLAY

'Charlie is far from dumb,' said Mike. 'He is an outstanding doctor, researcher, biochemist . . . His mind is just not big business.'

'Yeah, but you hire in the guys to take care of that,' said Ren.

'He tried that,' said Mike. 'But when the boss is away . . .'

'Well, wouldn't you learn from experience? I mean –'

'Ren – Charlie saved my son's life,' said Mike.

'Oh,' said Ren. 'I'm sorry. I had no idea.'

'I know,' said Mike. 'I just wanted to let you know I'll fight you to the death to defend him.' He was smiling as he said it.

'That's about done it for me,' said Ren, smiling back. 'Is your son doing OK?'

'He is. Thank you. One hundred per cent OK.'

'Saving children's lives versus getting people shitfaced,' said Ren. 'You can't argue with that.'

Even though I would love to keep talking about Charlie Barger, because something is not right with this picture.

Mike looked at her as if he could read her mind.

Ren went back to the inn and sat on the sofa in her room, speeding through the menus in the Gourmet Cabby guide. She went from pizza to salmon to burritos to sushi and back to salmon. When she placed her order, the guy at the other end of the phone said, 'Hey, Ren. Room number nine, right?'

'Hello, yes. Thanks.'

They had all her details. *Grim*. The whole of Breckenridge was going out to party and she was having a thing with Gourmet Cabby. When the food came an hour later, she went downstairs to pick it up. The other guests were drinking wine, watching TV, reading books.

'Hey,' she said.

'What's up?' said one cute snowboarder.

'Not much,' said Ren, hovering, wanting to stay and talk, but finishing with a 'Have a good one' and going back upstairs.

Five hours later, through the window in the darkness, a snowplow moved like a Transformer toward her, mounting inclines, the cab rotating on its tracks, casting golden light across the snow. She couldn't take her eyes off it as it moved past the church and turned back her way. She sat with a stack of notes and a bottle of water on the table in front of her. Two empty boxes of Mike & Ikes were on the floor at her feet. In the window and by her bed, church candles flickered, the flames coming to life a second time in mirrors and glass.

Her eyes started to close, her neck slowly falling toward the pillow at her back. *No, no no. Do. Not. Stop.* She sat up. She had Jean's phone records and bank records in front of her – everything marked with arrows and question marks and Post-Its. Colin Grabien had already been through them;

he had good radar and fresh eyes. Ren had too. And if there was anything new in them, her eyes were blind to it.

She had stacks of witness statements. She had maps. She had photos. She had multicolored pens. She had sketch pads. If she hadn't spent so much time organizing it all, she would have swept the whole lot on to the floor. Instead, without even realizing it was happening, she picked up a coffee mug and pitched it across the room.

'What is important in all this shit?' she shouted.

The mug bounced off the wall in one piece, leaving no mark. She shook her head slowly.

I can't do anything right. Shut up. I can't. Shut up.

43

The next morning, Ren parked outside Caroline Quaintance's house and sat staring down at the photo of Billy Waites and his intense, intelligent – *lying?* – eyes.

He could have any woman he wanted. Why did he pick me? She glanced over at the house. *When maybe tall, athletic twenty-seven-year-olds were his thing.*

She breathed through an irritating stab of jealousy and got out of the car. She jogged across the street to the house and rang the doorbell. Caroline came out, struggling to find an alternative expression for her disappointed face.

'I'm Ren –'

'I know,' said Caroline. 'Come in . . . again.'

'Thanks. I won't take up a lot of your time.'

'That's OK. I'm surprised to see you, that's all. I feel like I'm being involved in something I just don't know much about.'

They went into the kitchen. Ren sat down.
Caroline stood looking at her.

'I know *you're* supposed to be asking the questions,' said Caroline, 'but are you . . . OK? You
look –'

'Yes. I'm fine,' said Ren. 'Why do you ask?'
Ren was training herself to use this question
more. She'd read somewhere that it was the
perfect response to a personal question that you
didn't want to answer. If someone couldn't give
you a good enough reason for asking, you could
bypass revealing something you didn't want to.
My weakness.

'Oh . . . I'm sorry,' said Caroline, 'I just . . .'
Result. 'I'm here to show you a photograph, to
see if you recognize this man.'

'No,' said Caroline immediately.

'Never seen him before?'

'Should I have?'

'Well, no. But . . .'

'No,' said Caroline again. 'Why?'

'I'm just asking around,' said Ren. 'Anyone who
has cropped up in the investigation.' She stood
up. 'Thank you for your time.'

'No problem. But I really can't see why –'

'Look,' said Ren. 'I'm doing my job, OK? It's
for me to know why I'm asking what I'm asking.
And why I'm calling to your door, OK? Is it killing
you to give me five minutes of your time?' She
glanced toward the television, where *Desperate*

Housewives was playing. 'Or are you too busy watching fake people's lives to give a damn about a real person's death?'

At some point, Ren realized, Caroline had taken a step back from her.

'I'm sorry,' said Ren. 'I just . . .' *Stop talking.*

'Really, I do wish I could help,' said Caroline, but I just don't know that guy.'

At least you're not lying this time. I think.

A text came in from Vincent when she got back to her office. She checked the time and sent him back a Yes. She drove down to Main Street and parked outside the Crown. She had been having more success with parking in Breckenridge than Bob had led her to believe.

The Crown was quiet inside, a few couples, a few readers, no one playing board games. Vincent was sitting on the sofa facing her. He stood up, smiling.

'Hey,' he said. They kissed on the cheek.

'Hi,' said Ren. She took off her jacket and hung it on the coat stand beside them. 'It's cold out there.'

'Tonight's going to be worse,' said Vincent. 'Fifteen below.'

'Ugh.'

'Do you have to be anywhere?'

'Inside working, so it could be worse.'

'Crank that heating up.'

'Wow,' said Ren – the waitress arrived with two coffees and a Cinnamonster.

Ren gave him a warm, sad smile. 'Thank you.' She stared at him a little too long.

'What?' he said.

'It's just . . . it's lovely to be known that well. You knew I'd be on time, so you could order. And you knew *what* to order . . .'

'Noo,' said Vincent. 'I just thought it was appropriate ordering you something with "monster" in the title . . .'

Ren laughed. 'Is that better or worse than Ren Noir?'

'Better.'

They sat in silence for a while, then they talked about work.

'You are the only person in the world I can be totally honest with,' said Ren.

'And you are the only person in the world who I can tell straightaway is lying to me.'

Ren frowned.

'Yes, Ren, you *are* honest. Most of what you say to me is the truth. But you are selective in what you say to me.'

Ren opened her mouth and closed it again without speaking.

'When you have looked me in the eye today, it's been nervously,' said Vincent. 'But most of the time, you haven't been able to.'

'That's not true,' said Ren.

'Bing! Lie!' His tone was not unkind.

'Look, stop,' said Ren. 'Come on.'

'Something is making you uncomfortable with me,' said Vincent, 'and because I know that you can't lie – really – I'm not going to ask you what it is. Because I'm not really sure I want to know.'

Ren looked down. *Ugh.* 'I am a loser.'

'Well, I just hope you're a loser who is not doing too much damage to herself.'

Oh, you have no idea.

Ren turned on one light in her suite that night when she got back to the inn. Everyone was flooding her brain without really telling her anything. Checking Billy's phone had resolved nothing. And he could have a hundred other phones. Yet there was something about him she inherently trusted. *But can I trust my trust?*

Later she lay in the dark, filled with hope for the morning. Hope that didn't last. Fear started to dissolve it, like the black, liquid edges of burning plastic. And as she drifted into a world where the worst possible outcomes lived, her mind took her deeper again . . . and the dream came back. This time, it ended with locked door after locked door. This time she didn't make it out alive.

She woke howling, desperately trying to catch her breath. She dragged herself upright to the edge of the bed. Her head felt ice cold inside. She held a hand over her mouth and ran for the bathroom.

She retched, but nothing came up. Her face was red, her eyes streamed. And her heart rate was soaring. She brushed her teeth and put a freezing cloth to her face before she went back to bed. She took her purse with her, shook everything out, couldn't find anything she could take to calm her down. Which made her worse.

I need to sleep. I cannot do this. I cannot do this. I cannot do this alone.

She looked at the clock. It was 1.30 a.m. He would be finishing up about now, he could be here in thirty minutes. She reached for her phone and dialed Billy Waites.

44

Ren had four hours of uninterrupted sleep – the most she'd had in weeks. Billy left her in the shower at eight o'clock. She made it into the office early. The map she had gotten from Mike was on top of her desk. She studied it again. And wondered how Salem would feel if Misty went for another walk.

The Barger Brewery was on an acre of ground a twenty-minute walk from the Brockton Filly. A faded sign lay half-buried in the undergrowth as she pulled off the road. There was barely enough space to park the Jeep. A wide, straight path led under a canopy of trees that had shielded the ground from the snow fall.

Ren had wrapped the leash tight around her gloved hand, but Misty was doing her best to break free. They kept walking, Ren looking left and right along the path. It eventually led to the more open ground that surrounded the brewery. She took a right and they walked a winding path until the brewery was a distant shape behind them.

'I don't want to be negative, here, Misty, but I'm kind of hoping you find nothing,' said Ren, unhooking the leash from Misty's collar. 'You go, girl.'

She watched as Misty ran around in circles as if she was just so happy to be free. Ren walked toward her, laughing. Until she saw Misty sit down. And bark.

That night, Ren went with Bob for a drink in the South Ridge Grill. Mike arrived an hour later.

'Charlie Barger is very upset,' he said. 'He's feeling doubly responsible. Mark Wilson stayed at his inn and his body was found on his land.'

Upset or nervous? 'He really is an unlucky man,' said Ren. 'The inn closes, the brewery name is in the news again for all the wrong reasons.'

'There's no big mystery,' said Bob. 'Wilson was drunk, there was no one in the Brockton Filly to give him a ride to Fairplay – Waites heard him say that's where he was headed that night. Wilson staggers out and walks to the only spot that has space for a car to pull over.'

'Or,' said Mike, 'he's drunk, he sees a sign for a brewery with a name he recognizes, and here he is . . .'

'An alcopopsicle,' said Ren.

Bob laughed.

'I had a look through the window of the brewery earlier,' said Ren. 'It didn't inspire much confidence. I mean, it looks like he's going ahead with the beer thing. The floor was all washed, there were crates stacked up, I saw some nitrogen tanks. But I guess I still don't know why he's –'

Mike stared at her, 'OK, OK.'

Her cellphone rang. *Thank God*. 'Excuse me,' she said, walking into the hallway.

'Hey,' said Gary. 'I heard you found a body.'

'I did,' said Ren.

'Just not the right one.'

'I'm afraid not.'

'Either way, well done,' said Gary.

'Thank you,' said Ren.

'I need you to come see me in Denver.'

'Oh. OK,' said Ren. 'Can I ask why?'

'Twelve o'clock, tomorrow, my office.'

'Sure, no problem.'

What the hell was that about?

It took eighteen hours for Mark Allen Wilson's body to thaw at the Jefferson County Coroner's Office. The following morning, Dr Tolman carried out the autopsy. Nobody expected – or got – any surprises. It was a straightforward case that had got sucked into a high-profile one.

*   *   *

Gary Dettling sat in his office with a stack of files on the desk in front of him.

Ren knocked on the door. 'Can I come in?'

'Yes,' said Gary. He stood up when she walked in and quickly sat down. 'Hey. Good to see you . . .'

'Hey, Gary. You too. I . . .' Ren paused when she saw his face.

'Close the door, please. Sit down.'

She did as he asked. 'Is this about the Mark Wilson thing?'

'No,' said Gary.

'Is this about Jean Transom?' said Ren.

'Yes, it is . . . Ren, sweetheart? You're off the case.'

'What?' said Ren.

'Let's just say you know why and we'll leave it at that,' said Gary.

'What? Are you . . . serious?'

'No, no. Are *you* serious, Ren? Do *not* fuck with me. I acknowledge that you are . . . well, *were*, a team player – you wouldn't be with Safe Streets if you weren't. But, fuck. You know what? I feel like I sent my child off to camp, the prettiest, brightest child I have, thinking she's going to show them all . . . then I get a call to come pick her up because she's . . . Fuck, Ren. Fuck.'

'No one's called you to come –'

'Jesus Christ, no. Because I'm not dumb enough to wait. Daddy doesn't want to be squirming in a seat listening to how he can't control his kids.'

'Loving the metaphor . . .'

'Ren, Ren. Shut the fuck up. You're unbelievable. This is about all of us,' he said, stabbing a
finger toward the other office. 'The fucking fight
to get this place up and running. And off you go,
the syndicated Ren Bryce show, and nearly blow
it all.'

'I don't know –'

Gary held up a hand. 'Don't. Are you listening
to me? Your behavior risked everything – the
squad, the investigation . . . Jesus, Ren, do you
give a shit? *My* ass is on the line . . .' He let out
a breath. 'God knows where yours is.'

'I . . . I . . .'

'I . . . I . . . need you not to say a fucking word,
Ren. Just listen. Here's how it goes: you're
replacing Jean Transom. I mean, you already have
a close working relationship with some of the
people out that way . . . Keep your lies as close to
the truth as possible, right?'

'But how did you –'

'You respect me, right? You never questioned
my appointment to this job, right? That's your
answer. But you learned well. Never ask a question you don't already know the answer to.'

'Can't you just take me back here?'

'No, no. Glenwood Springs can be your new
home for a while. You need to take a little break
from Breckenridge and Denver . . .'

'But –'

'But nada.' He stood up.

Ren stood up. 'Gary, I'm sorry.'

He shook his head. 'Me too.'

She walked toward the door. 'Look, I'd like to know – did Paul Louderback have anything to do with you taking me off this case?'

'Why do you ask?'

She gave him a patient look.

'No, he did not,' said Gary. 'Just you. *You* were to do with me taking you off the case.'

She stared at him. 'I get it.' She walked out and into the bullpen.

'Hey, guys.'

'Baby's back,' said Robbie, flicking a rubber band at her. It hit her shoulder and fell to the floor. She picked it up and fired it back at him. He ducked and slammed his head off his desk lamp. Everyone laughed.

'The best agent in Safe Streets,' said Robbie, pointing to Ren.

The other guys sucked in a breath.

'God bless you,' said Ren.

'What?' said Robbie. 'She is.' He looked at Ren. 'You versus these losers?' The guys all booed.

'And,' said Robbie, 'you're the only person I ever rode shotgun with and didn't fear for my life.'

'Only reason I drive like that,' said Ren, 'is because I don't want you swinging from the hand grip with your ass in my face.'

'Funny,' said one of the others, 'the only reason we drive so bad, Ren, when you're shotgun . . . is for exactly the same reason.'

They all laughed.

Robbie looked around the office. 'Anyway, you guys – I was just being nice. Saying nice things about our baby.'

'I know,' said Ren, leaning down to squeeze his arm. 'I know. Thanks.'

'You coming to lunch?' said Robbie.

She turned around. Gary was putting on his jacket behind her.

'Rain check,' she said.

'Come to lunch,' said Gary.

'I'm sorry,' said Ren. 'I can't.'

She left, jogged down the stairs and out to the Jeep. She pulled her iPod out of the glove box and plugged it in. She started the engine and drove out of the parking lot, heading for I-70. She drove in silence, past her favorite sign warning her not to pick up hitch-hikers because there was a federal penitentiary close by. It usually made her smile. The next familiar sign she passed was the exit for Golden, and something made her take that right.

She pulled into her driveway. It felt so familiar; good, honest, warm, real. She walked in the front door and threw her keys on the table. Her home was reduced to a house; she wasn't living there, Vincent wasn't living there. Yet, as she looked around, their lives leapt from every corner. She knew it would never be the same again. No matter what happened. She waited to cry. But it didn't happen. She waited to feel something normal. But it didn't happen. Instead, she traced an unsentimental path through the house she had loved with the man she had loved. Three months earlier, it had all blown up. And for months beforehand, the wires were being connected, the timer was set. And there was no bomb disposal expert.

She picked up a letter from her bank. *We are writing to inform you that the following checks were presented for payment and the funds were not available in your account* . . . Blah. Blah. Blah. Blah. Blah. She would go online and transfer money from another account. Then wonder where she could get the money to fill that gap.

She heard something that made her chest constrict, the sound of something scraping wood. It was coming from the hall closet. She paused in front of it. They had a mouse once. Vincent had taken care of it. She was tired, distracted, suppressing emotion. And without Vincent to talk her off the ledge, she lacked something solid that was more than the sum of her own resources.

She was about to draw her gun. Instead, she reached for the handle and pulled open the door. A ski fell toward her. She weaved right and ducked. It fell past her on to the pale wooden floor. *Shit.* She stood in front of the closet. She saw the matching ski, a pair of Rollerblades, two squash racquets, boxing gloves and flippers, a basketball, an unopened steamer, three unused rolls of Christmas wrapping paper, a box of greetings cards, a riding helmet. All of them hers. Vincent had paint and tools and timber. Ren had a trail of unfinished business.

45

It was getting dark when Ren got back to the inn. She went in through the front door. A woman wrapped in a towel walked down the hallway toward her. Her husband stood back holding the door to the hot tub open for Ren. She thanked him and went through. A young college guy was sitting in the tub singing opera.

'Wow,' said Ren.

'In a good way?' he said.

'How can someone be that tuneless?' she said, smiling as she walked up the wooden stairs.

'Is that your room up there?'

She nodded. 'Yup.'

'On your own?'

She stopped walking.

'Oh God, I didn't mean it like that,' he said. 'Just – you must be rich. Having a suite.'

Ren laughed out loud. 'Um, no. Definitely not.'

'You must think I'm a freak now.'

'No, I don't. You have a nice night.'

'I will. And sorry again. Don't worry – I'm not going to, like, come up and, like, stalk you or anything.'

She leaned over the railing to him, 'Dude? I'd like to see you fucking try.' She winked.

When she got inside, her smile quickly faded. She walked around, closing all the blinds, switching on lamps, lighting candles. She took a deep breath and called Paul Louderback.

'Paul? Hi, it's me. Can you talk?'

'Sure. Go ahead.'

'What is this about me being TDY'ed to Glenwood?'

He paused. 'Yes. I spoke about it with Gary.'

'What?' said Ren. 'You had something to do with this?'

'We discussed it, yes. I did what I could to get you on the case. And he told me you took care of getting yourself off it.'

'He said that?'

'Yes, so . . . it means I had my chance to assign you to a case I wanted you to head up. But he can override that if it . . . hasn't worked out.'

'Oh,' said Ren. 'And you think it hasn't worked out.'

'No. But I feel that, assigned to Glenwood Springs, you will never be far from the investigation.'

'But not heading it up. How is that going to look?'

'To who?'

'To whoever.' She let out a breath. 'I don't know. It's just . . . I'm sensing somebody out there is pulling strings and I'm the little dancing puppet.'

Paul laughed. 'You? I don't think so. Anyway, if you were a puppet, you'd have scissors stashed in your jeans. No, actually – you'd be Animal. The one on the drums.'

'Hmm, which would I prefer – strings or a hand up my butt?'

Paul laughed.

'But if we were going *Sesame Street*,' said Ren, 'wouldn't I be Oscar? The one in the trash can.'

'Aw.' He laughed.

'This is actually not funny,' said Ren. 'I can't do this. I can't go to Glenwood.'

'And why do you have to?'

'Well, if you're not responsible, then I would say . . . payback.'

'For what?' said Paul.

Ren paused. 'Shenanigans.'

'Riiight. I won't ask. But . . . what did you do?'

'Behavior unbecoming of an agent. How about that?'

'OK. But . . . I will find out.'

'No. You won't.'

'Just for shits and giggles.'

'Jesus, this really is not funny.'

'I'm sorry. But that T in TDY does stand for temporary. And, well, someone had to fill in for Jean.'

'Yeah, maybe someone a little more Glenwood-friendly. And Tiny Gressett-friendly. And Todd, for that matter. They hate me.'

'Poor baby.'

'Shut up.' She shouted.

'Relax.'

'Don't tell me to fucking relax. I'm trying to go along with your lighthearted bullshit because I . . . like you, but I'm totally freaking out here and you're just messing with me.'

'I am taking you seriously, but –'

'It's my career, OK? You're established, I have to –'

'You're established too. What are you talking about? You've been doing this ten years, for Christ's sake. Why would I get you on to the Transom case if I didn't think you were competent?'

'Because . . . I don't know. You feel sorry for me?'

'Don't be an idiot. And don't be so paranoid.'

'Don't call me paranoid. That's not fair.'

'Well, you're acting that way.'

'No, I'm not. I'm afraid I've fucked up my entire career –'

'Well, you haven't, OK? I'm not hearing big bad Ren Bryce whispers around the office. Around anywhere. You need to get some perspective. A good night's sleep, a good meal . . .'

'Now *you* sound like my mom.'

'Me and who?'

'Just Vincent.' She let out a breath. 'I'm just . . . I can't face it all. I'm sick of being tired. I'm sick of running around. I'm not sick of the inn. I love it here. And now I have to leave. And I'll be in a tan motel room.'

'Ask for a pink one.'

She rolled her eyes. 'Jesus, Paul. Look, I gotta go.'

'I'm sorry, two-two-three. I was trying to make you smile.'

'You usually do. Goodnight.' She hung up.

Two-two-three; he hasn't said that in a while.

She lay back on the bed, held the phone over her face and scrolled down to Helen's number. After a minute staring at it, she hit B for Billy.

Ren's makeup had worn off, her nose and her eyes were red when the knock came at the door to the outside stairs.

'Hey,' said Billy. 'What's up? You OK?' Ren shook her head, said nothing, just went back to where she was lying on the sofa. He sat beside her and guided her head gently on to his lap. He stroked her face until it got wet with tears. She sat up eventually and grabbed a handkerchief from the night stand. She looked at him with sad eyes.

'What's up?' he said.

'I have to go,' she said.

'Where? Now?'

'No. I've been . . . transferred. To Glenwood.'

'What? Why?'

Here goes. 'Resources and funding and . . . stuff.'

'The FBI is not short of funds.'

'It's not that. Look, to be honest, I don't know why they're doing this to me. And I'm not happy.'

'Well, that explains the tears then . . .'

Ren tried to smile through them. 'It's not just that, Billy . . .'

'Oh. This is an opportunity for a nice clean break. I was thinking; I mean, Glenwood's only an hour and a half away . . .'

'I'm sorry . . . I don't know what to say.'

'Did they find out about us?'

Yes. 'No.'

'I don't know if I believe you.'

'That's OK. But they don't know. And even if they did, you're OK. Nothing's going to happen to you.'

He let out a long breath. They sat in silence. He dragged her legs on to his lap.

'You have beautiful feet.' He bent down and kissed them.

'Thank you.'

He reached out and slipped a hand under her back and pulled her up to sit on him. He stared into her eyes.

'What do you think you're going to find?' she said.

He shrugged. 'You love having arms wrapped

around you, Ren. But sometimes I get the sense that it doesn't matter whose arms.'

'That's a terrible thing to say.'

'It doesn't matter – as long as whoever owns those arms doesn't care about you too much, right?'

Ren said nothing.

'It's weird . . . you have this look,' said Billy.

'Do I?'

He nodded. 'A faraway look.'

'I don't think so . . . but if I do, it's not because of you.'

'It's kind of aimed through me.'

'I had no idea.'

He shrugged.

'I don't know you very well,' said Ren.

'And you get confused by my game face,' said Billy. 'The one I have on when I'm in the bar. The one I have on when I'm eyeballing the dirtbags that come in and out. The face that makes you wonder.' He tilted his head. 'Am I right? Did you look any deeper? I know you're going, Ren. But what *was* I? I don't get it. What – you were looking for a little danger in your life?'

'Stop,' said Ren. 'Just stop. This isn't fair.'

'You've never known,' said Billy. 'From day one, you have never known how you feel about me, have you? I mean, one part of you does. I've seen that. But what about up here?' He pointed to her head. 'Or here?' He held a hand to her heart. 'Jesus, Ren. If I didn't know better, I'd think I was gay.'

'What?'

'You are the closest to a man of any woman I've ever known. You've been thinking with your dick.'

'Or about yours.' She half-smiled.

'Sweetheart? You've been thinking about more than just my dick, and that's what has you so freaked out.'

Her smile faltered. 'I don't know if –'

'OK, hands up in the audience who hasn't understood that Ren Bryce *doesn't know*?' He threw his arms up in the air. 'How can someone so smart be so out of touch with how she feels? Seriously?'

'But where did you come from?' said Ren. 'You look like a . . . with your tattoos and . . . well . . . then you have this . . .'

Billy laughed out loud. 'Let me help you out – I look like America's Most Wanted.' He smiled sadly. 'And what *my* most wanted is . . . is . . .' He looked away.

Ren's stomach tightened. 'Aw, Billy. Jesus . . .' She frowned. 'I don't deserve this. How can you still be so nice to me?'

'Because I'm hoping that at some point you *will* know. That you'll figure it all out. And that I'll have a shot.'

'But I can't even promise –'

He reached across the table. 'I know. And . . . look, I'll be here . . .' He smiled sadly. 'That's what Billy does. Billy waits.'

46

Ren knew that the best part of her day would be the snowy drive through Glenwood Canyon, one of the most beautiful stretches of highway she had ever traveled. She listened to classical scores from movie soundtracks and the snow fell lightly. When she arrived at Glenwood, Tiny Gressett was there not to welcome her.

'Didn't think it was today you were coming.' He glanced at the desk calendar beside him.

Sure. 'Wow. And that's not even today's date,' said Ren, smiling.

'No. You're right there,' said Gressett. He stared at her and she could see a late-breaking realization. 'That was probably last touched by Jean Transom. There it is. January 12th – the day she left on vacation.'

Ren's smile faded. 'Well, that's very sad.'

'Yes, it is,' said Gressett. 'So, first of all, welcome.'

Gressett turned away and gestured around the

room. 'I know you've been here before, but the bathroom's across the hall. Jean's desk . . . which will be your desk . . . is right here, so you'll be the first person people see when they come in.'

'Let's hope that doesn't affect business,' said Ren, picking up on the look that told her he wasn't quite sure of the wisdom of the placement.

'I'm here,' he said, pointing to a desk almost behind hers, at a right angle and nicely out of sight of any visitors. 'Todd's there. Gun room is there. Coffee machine's there. Bureau computer there. Secret computer there.' He smiled. 'Office supplies – on the shelves right beside you.'

'What are the Crayola for?'

'Kids.'

'You get a lot of them roaming around?'

'Only if they're in on a tour from school, or if they're –'

'Witnesses . . . and need to draw the suspect. Yup, he had *real* skinny arms and legs and a big round head. Circles for eyes . . . No, no other features . . .'

Gressett smiled, but she wasn't sure if he got the joke. Ren suspected they would share lots of strange smiles in the future.

'Let me take you to lunch, your first day,' said Gressett.

Very kind. 'Thank you,' said Ren. 'That would be great. I will have to go back to Breck this afternoon to pick up some things.'

'That's OK,' said Gressett. 'Right – Juicy Lucy's
– the best in Glenwood.'

Ren had eaten there before. At least she agreed
with him on food. She overlooked a lot for food.

Three hours later, she was slumped in a chair
opposite Bob Gage. He was sitting at the edge of
his desk in a boxy gray suit.

'Hello, our little heroine . . . defector,' said Bob.
'Glenwood – what the hell?'

'That tie – what the hell?' said Ren.

'Someone told me it was cool. I can't
remember . . .'

'Maybe because the conversation happened in
1984.'

'Possibly.'

Ren let out a breath. 'I don't want to go,' she
said.

'You will come back to us for a drink or two,'
said Mike.

'You bet,' said Ren. 'But I'm being yanked out
of the middle of something.'

'You are.'

'I know. But it's wrong,' said Ren.

'Why do you think it happened?'

Oh, I wish I didn't have to lie. 'I have no idea.
Resources . . .'

'The Feds? Can't spare one little agent?'

'Hey, I'm indispensable.'

'Glenwood has ground to a standstill?'

'Maybe.'

Ren laughed, hugged them both and left.

The Firelight Inn was quiet, the dining table cleared and re-set for the following day's breakfast. The only person Ren could see was one man sitting on the sofa checking his email. He didn't look up. Ren went to her room and packed everything. Her chest was tight with the familiar sensation of blocked emotion. She remembered someone once telling her, 'Your body knows how to breathe; don't try to control it.' Maybe there was a reason Ren wanted less oxygen going to her brain. Maybe she just wanted it to stop, she just wanted everything to shut down.

She left a check on her bed, left the keys in her bedroom door and said goodbye to the Firelight Inn. It was a beautiful blue and golden day. Seeing everyone on the street made her want to turn right around and stay forever. There were no rules on where she could live. She could commute to Glenwood, she could commute to Denver. But she owed it to Gary Dettling to make the effort in her new position. He was watching her back, he always had, he knew things no one else did and, in his caring intimidation, he reined her in.

She was crying by the time she hit Main Street – for herself, for Jean, for Billy, for Vincent and for a man she had never known but who had died beaten and alone. Through a blur of tears, she saw Salem Swade standing, laughing, outside the Gold Pan. He always got a free breakfast at the Gold Pan. If she could have hugged him goodbye, she would have. She and Salem could be the town crazies together. She looked at him in the rear-view mirror. Right now, a penniless, damaged man with a brokedown cabin for a home looked happier than she did. It warmed her heart that he could mine those nuggets somewhere inside himself.

In the sunlight, something shone in the passenger footwell. Ren looked down and saw the second set of keys to her room. *A sign.* But she kept driving and when she got to the red lights that opened the road to Highway 9, she turned back for one last look.

Breckenridge. Boom and bust.

PART TWO

47

The pretty red pines were dead pines. They broke up the green all across Colorado's forests; millions of acres ruined by mountain pine beetles working their way through to southern Wyoming, a steady assault by a miniature army.

It was ninety degrees with a red-flag wildfire risk across Garfield County. Ren had left Gressett and Todd discussing the price of hay and driven east through Glenwood Canyon under clear skies and beating sun. Next she took a right down a wide dirt track until she reached a gate with a No Trespassing sign. It looked like any old rancher's gate, but it had a sensor that worked with the card she had clipped to her mirror. Ren drove through and carried on a mile further, into a clearing. She jumped out of the Jeep and pulled three black cases from it, laying them on a wooden table set up close by.

The first time Ren had fired a live gun at

Quantico, she thought she would hit the target. She blamed the delusion on her three older brothers who had battered a competitive streak into her from the time she was seven years old.

She walked across the hot dry earth to the target frames and pinned up four, side by side – the standard black outline of a man holding a gun in his right hand. An unarmed man could never be shot – even a paper one. Today he would represent the pervert at Hot Springs who'd taken pictures and exposed himself to a little girl earlier that morning.

Ren had one month to go before her fourth and final weapons proficiency test of the year. She had to follow scores of ninety-four, ninety, and ninety-two on the previous three. Another score over ninety was the only result that would make her happy.

She loaded the MP5 magazines and took out a Heckler and Koch MP5, a ten-millimeter fully automatic submachine gun, custom-made for the FBI. She put on ear protectors and walked up to the twenty-five-yard line. There was something satisfying in watching that red dot hover on her target. Ren blew all four heads full of holes. She fired another round, then replaced the targets with fresh ones – her paper men had lost their inky heads.

She loaded the thirteen-round magazines and took out her Bureau-issued Glock 23. She started at the twenty-five-yard line, shooting prone, kneeling and standing, then moved up to fifteen yards, seven, then three. Again, the heads were blasted.

Her shirt clung to her body in the heat. But it was the first day that week that she hadn't regretted her new shorter hair cut. At least her neck could breathe.

The next case held a Rock River Arms M-4 rifle, her best friend in rural Colorado – deadly close-in or at several hundred yards. She loaded the magazine with two-two-threes: small, thin golden bullets; beautiful and stable until they hit the human body, then rapidly becoming unstable. Two-two-three. She couldn't hold them without thinking: *Paul Louderback.*

Ren went through another course of fire with the M-4, then took the targets down, packed the guns up and put them in the back of the Jeep. Her cellphone beeped with a text message. It was Helen: Are you on your way?

Oh shit. To Denver. Two hours' drive. Ren texted her back: Wrk stuff. So sorry. Cld we meet b4 my meetng 4 5 mins? 2pm.

Y.

Y. I'm so sorry.

OK.

By the time Ren reached Denver, violent winds had been whipped up by storm clouds rolling

in from Central Plains. Hail pounded the car –
deafening and relentless. A Denver afternoon
could move from sunbathing to drowning and
back again in twenty minutes. The previous week,
the skies had dumped enough hail to trap people
in their cars and flood the viaducts.

Helen had been waiting for ten minutes. *Two
hours and ten minutes.* Ren sat holding a coffee,
wondering if she really was in the humor for Helen.

'So, how's work?' she said.

'Ugh,' said Ren.

'Come on,' said Helen. 'I haven't seen you all
summer, you've talked to me only a handful of
times. Have you been quiet . . . or just too busy?'

'Working.'

'OK, working. But what else?'

'Look, I'm fine.'

'How's Glenwood?'

'Well, I'm in the wonderful position of having
a different personality clash with each of my
colleagues. And it's a small office.' *It's Tiny.*

'Hmm.'

'I mean, it's fine. But it's not Safe Streets. In
Glenwood, I just get in there, do my work and leave.'

'Are you seeing Billy?'

'No.'

'Are you OK with that?'

'Not really. But I was afraid it was going to
screw things up for me. And him.'

'Have you met anyone else?'

Ren shook her head. 'No.'

'Have you been going out?'

'Kind of.'

'With who?'

'I've made a few friends, so I'm hanging out with them.'

'New friends?' said Helen.

Ren nodded. 'Some guys, nice guys, I met.'

'OK.'

'Platonic.'

'Think about what has happened to you over the last few months,' said Helen.

'What do you mean? I've solved a lot of Jean's cases, I've worked hard –'

'Can you hear yourself?' said Helen.

'What? OK, I worked. I love my job. Big deal.'

'And what about everything else? It wasn't long ago that you left your boyfriend, you slept with a C.I., you moved locations again . . .'

Ren said nothing. She raised her face to the ceiling and held her breath.

'Part of you thinks you're such a bad person, Ren, that bad things should happen to you, your relationships should be fraught, your decisions should bring pain, you should not be happy . . . I don't know.'

Ren stared out the window, running her finger back and forth under her watch strap.

'It may not be affecting your work now,' said Helen, 'but it will.'

Ren released a heavy, weary breath as she stood up. 'I'm tired, Helen. I'm exhausted. I have too much on. Can't I just have someone to talk to when I need it?'

'Of course,' said Helen.

'Nice shoes, by the way.'

'Thank you.'

'I love shoes,' said Ren, 'But if I hear one more time "Oh, you've big shoes to fill" – meaning Jean Transom's . . .' She paused. 'I've big feet, you know?'

'Well most people have a perception of other people that comes from lots of different things,' said Helen. 'Yes, Jean sounds like she was a talented agent. But so are you. Just because she was – how do I put it? – more . . .'

'Normal . . .'

'Well, whatever you want to say, but I guess more what people would expect an agent to be. From what you've said, she was quiet, soft-spoken, earnest. And you're more . . . out there. Doesn't mean you're any less professional.'

'I know that. The importance of being earnest . . .'

'Look, anyway, why do you care?'

'I actually don't know. Jean wore comfortable shoes. And maybe I don't do comfortable shoes.'

'You don't do comfortable, period. You don't like being comfortable, do you? It's too boring. Your worst nightmare.'

'OK,' said Ren. 'I don't think I can listen to any more wisdom.'

Helen smiled.

'But, thanks,' said Ren.

'OK,' said Helen. 'Look after yourself.'

In the Rocky Mountain Safe Streets office, Gary Dettling stood at the top of the bullpen beside a map of Jefferson and Summit Counties. Red pins surrounded the Denver metropolitan area and green pins stretched west along I-70.

Ren walked in. 'Let me guess – red: places where Colin Grabien has been rejected by women in a bar. Green: places where Colin Grabien has been rejected by women in a bar.'

Colin pointed toward the board. 'Red: places where Ren Bryce has . . .' He paused.

'Not quick enough,' said Ren. 'Thanks for playing.'

'Your hair,' said Robbie. 'What did you do? I loved your long hair.'

'Hate to break it to you,' said Ren. 'But you're not at the forefront of my mind when I'm in the hair salon . . . Actually, neither was getting a good hair cut . . .'

'What *were* you thinking?' said Colin.

'Guys, come on,' said Gary. 'The red pins here represent our random robbers – a mixed bunch of amateurs.'

'So they've all been caught, obviously . . .' said Ren, smiling.

'Our Glenwood visitor appears to be mocking us,' said Cliff. 'Perhaps she feels that, without her, we are nothing.'

Ren nodded.

'And to continue,' said Gary. 'The green pins represent the Val Pando crew. To recap – the first was Arvada, the second here in Denver on Colfax . . .' The rest were off I-70 heading west.' He moved his finger along the map. 'In order of geographical location, east–west: Idaho Springs, Georgetown, Silver Plume, Grand Junction. But as we know, the robberies weren't carried out in that particular order.'

'Because that wouldn't be very smart,' said Ren. 'So – six green pins since this all started back in January.'

'It was bam, bam, bam at the start and now it's slowed,' said Robbie.

'Excuse me for a moment,' said Gary, checking his pager and walking out the door.

'Why are you here?' said Colin.

'Because Gary asked me to be here,' said Ren.

'Secret meetings,' said Robbie.

'Oh, please,' said Ren. 'And it's not exactly secret, is it? Like Colin is *secretly* insecure because his adolescence was *Superbad* . . .'

Colin's eyes went to slits.

'What do you mean, "super bad"?' said Cliff.

'It's a movie,' said Robbie.

'Featuring the hilarious tale of an endless search

by three teenage boys to get laid,' said Ren.
'Endless . . .'

'Yeah, we all know what you were in high
school,' said Colin. 'The –'

'– one who would have sat with you in the
lunch room if she had only known your pain,'
said Ren. 'OK . . . gotta go.'

'Are you coming out with us later?' said Robbie.

'I don't live here any more, remember?' said
Ren.

'We need you, man.'

'I need you guys,' said Ren.

'Come *on*. What did you do?' said Robbie.

'What? To be banished from the kingdom? I ate
a poison apple.'

'You talk a lot of crap,' said Colin.

'I didn't *do* *any*thing,' said Ren. 'Jean had to be
replaced.'

Robbie looked at her. 'Yeah, but by you?'

'Look, I'm tired of talking about it,' said Ren.
'I will be back here. I'm sure. Soon.'

Halfway to Glenwood, Ren wondered if it all fell
apart, could she work as a bus driver for the
Colorado Mountain Express. Each time she met
with Gary, she hoped he would bring out cham-
pagne and cake and tell her she was coming back.
She would drive the two hours from Denver to
Glenwood thinking how great it would be to be
back at her desk firing rubber bands at Robbie or

humiliating Colin Grabien at the firing range. She wanted to see Cliff's sweet face in the morning and get hugs from him when he left in the evening. She sang along to her iPod; her mournful, missing-you playlist.

Gary was teaching her something. But she was getting tired of showing up for class. He still wanted her opinion, he still needed her opinion. *And he gives nothing back.*

Her cellphone rang. She punched the button to answer it. The Jeep swerved a little.

'Mistress Bryce?'

'High Sheriff Gage?' said Ren.

'What shit are you listening to now?' said Bob.

'"I Ain't Missin' You At All",' she sang, turning off the music. She paused. 'And it's not shit. Everyone loves that song.'

'OK, OK,' said Bob. 'Maybe it's just hard to sing . . .'

'I ain't missin' you at all,' she sang again.

'Well, you won't have to for much longer.'

'Why?'

'We found a body on Quandary Peak.'

'Another –'

'No. We found Jean Transom.'

48

When May had come and gone and June had brought snow across Summit County, Ren thought Jean Transom's body would never show. And when the sun blazed in July and still didn't draw the body from the melting snow, Ren figured it had been thrown down a mineshaft – that Misty the dog had located Jean Transom on that snowy slope the night of the avalanche and given someone the chance to bury her again.

'I don't believe it,' said Ren. 'Where?'

'Where we expected,' said Bob. 'Up on Quandary.'

'How do you know it was her?'

'Her clothes, her hair, her watch, her ankle holster – which was empty,' said Bob.

The air-conditioning was on high in the Jeep and the outside temperature was rising.

'Not the best conditions,' said Bob.

'No,' said Ren. 'But at least we've got her.'

'What's your position on the case now?' said Bob.

'Your guess is as good as mine.' She paused. 'Gary Dettling got paged when I was at Safe Streets – was that you?'

'No. I asked Mike to.'

'Well, Gary's been informed and he still let me leave. It's not like he called me in to let me know. I mean, I'm still coming to the scene – Glenwood Springs is the closest RA. Gressett and Todd will be there. Whether I have any more involvement than that, who knows.' She heard beeps on her phone. 'Bob, looks like I'm just about to find out. That's Gary on the other line. See you in a little while.'

'Ren, hey,' said Gary.

'Hey.'

'Jean Transom's body's been found on Quandary.'

'Oh my God. Really?"

'Yes.'

'That's good news, I guess.'

'I know – doesn't feel that way.'

' I'll let Todd and Gressett know.'

'Ren?'

'What?'

'By special request, you're back on the case.'

'Whose special request?' said Ren. 'Paul Louderback?'

'No. Mine.'

'Thank you, Gary. Thanks.'

'See you at Quandary.'

Ren called Gressett. 'Hi, it's Ren. Jean Transom's body's been found . . . on Quandary Peak.'

She could hear his breath catch. 'Sweet Jesus,' he said. His voice cracked.

'I know. I'm heading out right now. See you there.'

'Yes,' said Gressett, trying to find his composure.

'Could you do me a favor?' said Ren. 'I was coming back this afternoon to talk to that little girl from the Hot Springs thing this morning. Would you mind bringing that file over for me?'

'Not a problem.'

Ren drove up Blue Lakes Road past cars and 4x4s full of moved-along hikers. When she reached as far as she could go, she parked and got out, walking past the groups that were hanging back in case they missed any action. She flashed her badge.

'Guys, there's no point in hanging around. Nothing's going to happen for quite a while, and it will be boring when it does – nothing you haven't seen already on *CSI*.'

'Oh, OK,' they said.

'Wow,' said Ren. 'Thank you.' *How did I ever end up in a position of authority?*

She jogged up further and waved at Mike Delaney. 'Hey.'

'Ren,' he said, giving her a hug.

'Well, this is weird.'

'I'm afraid it's a liquid lunch up there.'

'Jesus,' said Ren.

'You got your boots on?' he said, looking down at her feet.

She nodded.

They walked up the first steep incline and through the trees. Ren stopped when the path leveled and the clearing revealed the spectacular view across the valley.

'It's so beautiful up here,' she said, moving off again. 'I don't think I can face seeing Jean . . . like she is.' She paused. 'It'll be hard, I guess.'

'You don't have to –'

Ren smiled patiently.

'It was worth a try,' said Mike. He squeezed her shoulder. 'Come on. Let's just do it.'

Up ahead, one of the young detectives sat on a log with an attractive, fit-looking blonde woman who had just sat up from having her head between her knees. Her skin was the palest gray, her eyes rimmed red. She was in light hiking clothes, with a fleece wrapped around her waist. There were flecks of dried vomit on her sneakers.

The detective stood up. 'This, uh . . . lady found the body,' he said to Ren. He turned to the woman. 'She is the FBI.'

'The entire FBI,' said Ren. She smiled. 'I'm so sorry you had to see that,' she said. 'It can't have been pleasant.'

'I needed to pee . . . that's how I found the body,' said the woman. 'I didn't actually . . . *hit* the body or anything.'

'OK,' said Ren. 'Well, we're going to go ahead up.'

'Good luck with your investigation,' said the woman. She groaned and leaned into the under-growth and threw up.

Ren's cellphone started to ring. It was Paul Louderback.

'Hello?'

'Ren, hi. It's me. I got a call from Gary.'

'Yup – I'm on my way to the scene right now.'

'Oh, OK. I was going to ask you.'

Ren could hear a child screaming in the back-ground.

'I'm sorry,' said Paul. 'I'm in a madhouse. We're packing for . . . Breckenridge.'

'What?'

'Well, this is when we come – same time every year. For the Gold Panning championships. The kids love it. And they always find some gold.' Ren could hear the smile in his voice. 'They just don't realize their daddy has dropped it in their pans when they're not looking.'

'That is so sweet,' said Ren. *There's so much of your life I don't know about.*

'So, yes, the timing's a little strange.'

'Well, if the body was ever going to show, it was going to be around now.'

'True,' said Paul.

'I'll call you when I know more,' said Ren.
'Good luck.'

Ren and Mike followed the snaking path up through the trees. They passed hikers who had been at the summit when the body had been found and who had been rushed down to the bottom.

'"I didn't hit the body" – I liked that,' said Ren.
'I know.'

They hiked for another forty minutes until they came to the bottom of a rich, green space that sloped left off the main trail. They ducked under the crime scene tape and made their way down.

Denis Lasco stood up and waved. 'Anyone got water?'

'Sure,' said Ren, handing him her bottle.

'Hey, Ren,' said Bob. His tanned face was sweaty and blotched red. 'Ladies always carry Kleenex, right?'

'Not this lady,' said Ren. 'You'll have to use your shirt. How've you been?'

'I dropped fourteen pounds,' said Bob, patting his stomach.

'I think I found it,' said Ren, patting her hips.

'Finders keepers,' said Bob. 'Did you find anything else I lost? My self-respect, my dignity?'

Everyone laughed, then hung in silence for a moment.

'Right,' said Ren, 'now that we've gotten through our defensive laughter . . .'

Bob gave a sad smile. 'Wait 'til you see this,' he said, gesturing behind him.

Ren felt rooted, but she was quickly car-crash drawn to the body. 'Whoa . . . ly fuck. That is . . . Jesus Christ.' She held a hand to her mouth, squeezing her nostrils shut at the same time.

'Holy shit,' said Mike, moving up behind her and quickly turning away.

They had lost Jean Transom's body once – nature had swept it away and kept it hidden for months. And they had almost lost it a second time – to the mercy of the sun, the animals and the insects. Ren had seen bodies like this before – split-screens; one half of the body exposed to different elements than the other – one side mummified by a heater, the other turned toward a window open to the cold; a head on a pillow, a body cooking inside an electric blanket.

The left side of Jean Transom's body lay under a fallen tree. The right side, turned away from the splintered trunk, was marbled, bloated and blistering. Her hands and fingers were curled and desiccated. One eyelid had been stripped away by birds, her eyeball pecked out. There was little flesh left on her face – the rest had been eaten, then pared back to the bone by maggots. Her teeth were exposed, her face frozen and grotesque.

Ren looked up at the sky to hold back tears.

She said a silent prayer, then looked down at the body that lay at her feet.

I wish you could have been found perfectly preserved, Jean Transom.

49

Dr Tolman worked with his assistant on Jean Transom's autopsy. Denis Lasco, Ren Bryce, Paul Louderback, Bob Gage and Todd Austerval watched, suited up, masked and wearing booties Ren had brought for everyone.

Ren hadn't eaten for fifteen hours. Her head was spinning and the only thing that was keeping her concentrating on an empty stomach was Jean Transom, her sweet, simple life, her easy-listening CDs, her pastel shirts, her teddy bears . . .

'She has an extensive tattoo,' said Tolman.

'What?' said Ren.

'Look,' he said. They had turned the body over, exposing Jean's back and the jagged, gaping gunshot wound. 'At the base of her back.'

Ren stepped forward, giving herself a better view and another opportunity to retch. What was left of the tattoo was made up of black, heavy-inked shapes – angular and masculine.

'What is it?' said Ren. 'Does it say something?'

'I can't make out what it is,' said Tolman.

'Can you guys?' said Ren.

The others moved closer. No one even took a guess.

Robbie took a photo of the tattoo for Ren.

People who wanted to be noticed got tattoos, people who liked beautiful art on a medium of skin, people who wanted to cover something up, people who had been damaged . . . But Jean Transom with her plain underwear, her neutral clothes, her makeup-free face, didn't seem to fit anywhere in that line-up.

So who was Jean Transom before Special Agent was put before her name?

Patrick Transom was doing his best to fight the weariness of grief and the presence of the FBI in his house again. Ren sat beside him at the kitchen table and showed him a photo of part of the tattoo.

'I was wondering if you could confirm Jean's identity from this,' said Ren.

'What is this?' he said.

'It's part of her tattoo.'

'Jean had a tattoo?'

He shook his head. 'Another thing I didn't know about. When Sheriff Gage came here last night to tell me they had found the body, I . . . It was a shock. I can't keep having these . . . surprises. I know that's not the right word.'

'Well, you're her brother,' said Ren. 'And this tattoo was across her lower back . . .'

'I know,' he said. 'But just that I never knew . . .' He rubbed his hand through his hair. 'I guess all I want now is to feel closer to Jean, and instead I keep feeling further away. Every new thing I hear from you guys makes me feel like she's shrinking into this tiny dot. And it's so terrible, because it's making me feel mad at her. I want to ask her about these things. I want to talk to her. I want her to explain why she hid so much from me. Even if it's just small things. I want to –'

'She didn't hide things from you,' said Ren. 'She was just extremely private.'

'I guess she was kind of like that as a teenager.'

He went over to a cabinet in the corner, pulled out a photo and handed it to Ren. Ren stared at it and looked back at him.

He nodded. 'Yup, that's Jean.'

'Wow,' said Ren.

Who you are to your brothers and sisters is usually who you are at that time, not what you used to be. They watch you through all your changes and know there will always be more. They don't hold you to the past. And they don't always recall it. To Patrick Transom, his sister was a blonde, athletic FBI agent. The black-haired overweight goth was in the photograph was someone he could look back and smile at.

'That's quite a change,' said Ren.

'I know.'

He held the photo Ren had given him. 'I'm . . . afraid to say that this isn't Jean,' he said. 'Because it has to be, right? You wouldn't be here if you had any doubt.'

'I have a second photo,' said Ren, handing it to him.

It was a section of Jean's left shoulder with a birthmark.

He pointed to it. 'You could see it in the summer when she wore sleeveless shirts.'

Ren gave him a gentle smile. 'Thank you.' She took a plastic bag from her pocket. 'I have something else too.' She handed it to him.

He broke down. 'This is Jean's. It's her Brazilian good luck ribbon. You make three wishes, you tie three knots in it, then you leave it on until it falls off naturally. And then all your wishes come true. She had it for over a year, hidden under her watch strap. She couldn't believe it still hung on in. It was driving her nuts.' He stared down at the clean, severed edges. 'I guess you cut it off . . .' He paused. 'I wonder what that means.' He slipped it into the bag and handed it back to Ren. 'The wait for the body is over,' he said. 'And now I have to start all over again and work o it how I feel.'

'Daddy?' They turned as a beautiful little blonde girl walked into the room.

'You must be Amber,' said Ren. And there is something strangely familiar about you.

Amber nodded.

'This is Ren Bryce,' said Patrick. 'She's with the FBI, like Aunt Jean.'

'Oh, hi,' said Amber.

Ren was drawn to the little girl's brown eyes and something in them she couldn't quite define.

'Daddy, could I get some juice, please?'

'Sure, sweetheart, go ahead.' She went to the refrigerator and took out a small carton of apple juice. 'Excuse me, ma'am?' she said.

'Yes?' said Ren.

'I just wanted to tell you that my Aunt Jean wasn't feeling very well the day we went shopping in Breckenridge before she died. We had to go home early . . .'

'Really?' said Ren. 'That's a shame.'

Amber nodded and smiled. 'It was fun and I didn't want to go home early. I was kind of mad . . .' She glanced nervously at her father.

Oh, no. You feel guilty. 'Amber, your Aunt Jean would understand how you could get mad having to go home early from something. Especially because she really wanted to hang out with you all day. That's why she asked you to go shopping. She loved you a lot, I bet.'

Amber smiled. 'OK,' she said. They watched her skip out of the room.

'She is beautiful,' said Ren.

'We're hoping she doesn't know quite how

beautiful yet,' he said, smiling after her. He turned back to Ren. 'I'm sorry – what were we saying?'

'I was about to tell you how well respected and loved by her colleagues your sister was. No one had a bad word to say about Jean. She clearly loved you, your wife and, like I said to Amber, your children. Their photos are all over – you must have seen her refrigerator. So, she had a tattoo on her back you didn't know about,' said Ren. 'That's just ink and needles.' She paused. 'And maybe a few tequilas . . .'

Patrick smiled.

'Nothing at this stage matters,' said Ren, 'except the fact that you were brother and sister, and you loved each other.'

I hope I'm helping.

He reached out. Ren wasn't sure what he wanted. He squeezed her left hand. She could see he was struggling to speak, this sweet, gentle man.

'Thank you,' he said.

50

It was eleven p.m. when Ren reached the Brockton Filly. As she walked across the packed parking lot, she could feel the music throbbing. As she came closer to the building, she saw the sign on the door: *Open Mic night*. And when she opened the door to the bar, she realized that the music was trying to kill the singer.

She pushed through the rowdy crowd – a younger, crazier bunch than the quiet old alcoholics that were sucking the lifeblood out of her the last time. Billy Waites had turned the Filly around. It had customers. Ren took a slot at the bar where no one seemed to be serving. She leaned her elbow on it and turned away, drawn to the little lady on the bar stool with the giant guitar and the intuitive amp. She was winding down.

'Thank God for that.' Billy's voice. Instant impact. Ren turned slowly. But he wasn't talking to her. He was leaning into a blonde two people away from her. *Oh.* Ren faltered. Her heart was letting her down; weighing too much, beating too fast. She had no drink to knock back, nothing to grip to stop her hand from shaking. Billy looked up. They locked eyes. He drew quickly back from the blonde and came toward her.

'Hi.' There was hurt and happiness in his eyes.

'Hi,' said Ren.

'You look good with a tan.' He smiled.

'You too.' She smiled back.

They stared at each other. People were shouting orders at Billy, but he didn't move. People were trying to push Ren away from the bar, but she didn't move.

'So . . .' said Billy.

'This is weird.'

'Yup.'

She looked around the bar. 'I didn't think it would be so –'

Billy laughed. 'You thought the place would have been shut down.'

Ren laughed. 'I didn't mean it like that, asshole. I just thought it would be . . . how it was before.'

He smiled sadly. 'Wouldn't that be great?'

'Get me a beer, mister,' she said. 'And we'll talk when you're finished?'

Billy checked his watch. 'One hour to go. Can you handle it?' He put two fingers in his ears.

Ren laughed. 'Yes, I can.'

She got wired, chatted to random students, bought

them Jagershots, knocked some back with them, danced with a nerd. Every now and then, Billy passed by, caught her eye and smiled.

It was two hours and four rounds of nervous beer-drinking before everyone left and Billy closed up the bar. He sat down on a stool opposite her.

'Is it like that every night?' said Ren.

'Thursday to Sunday – crazy. Or if there's any big thing on, a festival or whatever.'

'That's great,' said Ren.

'New ownership,' said Billy.

'Really?' said Ren. 'What's the boss like?'

'Hot.'

'What?' said Ren.

Billy laughed. 'I'm the new owner.'

Ren laughed out loud. 'No way. Congratulations. Obviously bought with drug money.'

'Obviously.' He smiled.

She gestured to Jo's corner. 'So no more blowjobs for beer?'

'It's full of students,' said Billy. 'They give them out for free.'

Ren laughed. 'So . . .' She tried to avoid his eyes.

'I thought I might see you some time soon,' said Billy.

'You heard about Jean.'

He nodded. 'So is that good or bad for you?'

'Well, here I am, back on the case. So to answer your question – I have no idea.'

He smiled. 'I still can't believe you were ever *off* the case. Why would they do that?'

Ren paused. 'Well . . . I wasn't getting very far, was I?'

'That's not true.'

'I guess I'm getting a second shot,' said Ren.

'You weren't alone in not solving the case,' said Billy. 'You can't take the blame for everything.'

'Yes, I can.'

'You do, but you shouldn't.'

'Thanks,' said Ren. She lowered her head on to the table. 'I want it all to go away.'

'Yes, but you only want it to go away by solving it . . .'

Ren looked up and smiled at him. 'You're right. So . . . go through it all with me – everything from that night.'

'Did anything show up on the body?' said Billy. 'Any new evidence?'

'Probably not . . . the autopsy will tell us more,' said Ren. 'Billy, I need you to give me more. I need you to think more.'

'I'm not a retard.'

'I'm sorry. I didn't realize I was sounding that way. Can you go through again who was here that night?'

'I gave you that list. *Look* at it.'

'Now who's calling who a retard?'

'Don't take your work shit out on me. I've done what I can for you. Including being the invisible fucking man.'

They sat in silence.

'I cannot think of any more people to add to that list, OK?' said Billy. 'They were strangers to me. It's that kind of bar. Of the people you've met? Me, Salem and Jo da Ho.'

'This is driving me nuts,' said Ren. 'Because I know, for certain, that this was Jean Transom's last stop. I just know it.' She shook her head. 'And more than one person is responsible for what happened to her, because they took her car and we don't know where it is. We'll probably never find it. I can't see how all that could have been done otherwise.'

And right now I'm discussing all this with a confidential informant.

51

Ren's phone rang and Denis Lasco's name flashed up on the screen.

'Hello, Ren? I found something when I was going through Jean Transom's pockets. It was in a pocket I missed first time around. You know these ski jackets – they have zips everywhere. It's a photo of a woman. And I know who the woman is, because I was on the case. I'll drop this by your office.'

'Who is the woman?'

'Her name was Ruth Sleight. She was thirty-nine years old, lived in Frisco.'

'Ruth,' said Ren. 'I have a mystery RUTH folder belonging to Jean. In fact, I was just about to add a case to it. What happened to Ruth Sleight?'

'Suicide. June last year. I mean, you can see by the photo that she wasn't in great shape. She'd been an alcoholic half her life.'

'There's too much alcohol everywhere,' said Ren.

'All the better to party with.'

'OK – anything else on this Ruth Sleight?'

'Well, I think I have the reason for her alcoholism. Do you remember the Mayer–Sleight case in the late seventies?'

'Vaguely,' said Ren.

The Mayer–Sleight 'abduction' had been the lead news story on every network in 1979, the headline in every newspaper. Two eleven-year-old girls from Frisco, Jennifer Mayer and Ruth Sleight, disappeared on their way home from dance class, the first day their mothers had allowed them to walk home alone. Both families refused to speak to journalists. The girls showed up . . . three weeks later. The families released a statement saying, *We would like to thank America for the thoughts and prayers that kept us hopeful during such a fearful time. Our beautiful girls have returned to us unharmed and we thank God for this blessing.*

No one mentioned 'abduction'. No one mentioned 'runaways'. The police revealed nothing other than 'happiness and relief' at the outcome, and eventually the story went away.

'So,' said Lasco. 'The media attention at the time, the whispers, the questions, whatever – must have become too much for her. Or something else went on in those three weeks.'

Ren nodded. 'And we can all guess what the answer to that is.'

'I'll drop this by in a little while.'

*   *   *

Ren pulled out the RUTH file again, the thirty-year span of sexual offences against children, all within Summit and Garfield Counties. Ren wondered what more she could get from the latest little girl than what her mother had told her the day it had happened. She had called the Glenwood RA in a state of panic that just seemed to increase as the conversation went on. Ren read back her handwritten notes – she hadn't had time to type them up, she hadn't even had time to write them. Her writing was legible, but still scrawled across the page – real shorthand, mixed with improvised.

The daughter was changing out of her bathing costume, her mother had turned away to attend to her young son, when a man had exposed himself to the little girl and taken pictures of her. He had hair that was neither dark nor light. He was wearing navy blue track pants, a white T-shirt and sneakers. He had a big belly. She described him as 'old', but everyone is old to a seven-year-old. And he was 'missing hair on his head'. Bald, fat and old. *Surprise, surprise.*

Ren read through the file to see was there a similar description from any of the other girls. It looked like Ren wasn't the only one who had to rush through an interview. The page about Ruth Sleight had no case number. Under the heading *WHERE?* was *circles . . . faded . . . dust . . . funny smell . . . bakery?* Under the heading *WHO?* was *musk . . .*

bony hips. Under *WHY?* she had just written *why? why? why?*

Why would Jean be asking why?" *Why what?*

Ren looked at the child's drawing on the page stapled to it – the collection of shapes. Underneath it was adult writing that read: *Love, Ruth XX*.

Ren noticed the back of the first page. There was a phone number scrawled diagonally across it. Something about it looked familiar, a sequence of digits that had once been automatic to her – her only way to reach someone – untraced, a number she associated with laughter and secrecy and risk. It was Paul Louderback's throwaway cellphone number. The man she'd believed when he said he didn't know Jean Transom personally.

Ren jumped when she heard her name being called. She looked up as Denis Lasco walked in the door. He handed her the photo. It was in a Ziploc bag. Ruth Sleight did not look like a well woman. She had qualities you could use to describe a corpse – a red face that was bloated to bursting point, eyes that were swollen and vacant, skin that was almost gray. Her hair was brown, flat and greasy at the roots, red, dried and permed at the ends. She was heavily overweight, dressed in a sleeveless yellow T-shirt and white shorts. She held a cigarette in her hand.

'Yikes,' said Ren. 'Poor woman.'

Lasco nodded.

'Thanks for this,' said Ren. 'It has solved one

mystery for me. Now, if I found Jennifer Mayer, that could help.'

'I hope she has fared better in life than this poor lady.'

Ren pulled out a list of known sex offenders from Summit County and Garfield County. One name hopped out: Malcolm Wardwell. He wasn't bald and fat, but Jean and Amber Transom had been in his store not long before she died. Ren read back through the older files to see if Malcolm Wardwell could have been relevant to any of those descriptions. But then, she didn't know what Malcolm Wardwell might have looked like thirty years ago.

Ren couldn't face supper that night. By five a.m., she was starving and staring blindly into the darkness of her bedroom. Her thoughts were on a loop. *Why did Jean Transom have Paul Louderback's number? Why did he request me on the case? Did he want to steer me? Toward something? Or away from something? What does any of this have to do with Jean's murder? Have I been manipulated for years?*

The theories continued, nauseating and paralysing, until she eventually fell asleep, half an hour before her alarm woke her.

52

Ren sat in her room at the inn. She got up and made coffee. She sat back down. She got up and made her bed. She adjusted the blinds. She laid out files on the sofa. And ultimately, she came back to Paul Louderback's number, scribbled in what was clearly Jean Transom's hand-writing. Her stomach was barely able to keep the coffee down. She sat down and dialed Paul's regular number. And stopped before she had finished. *He will know.* She was about to ask him something strange, but he was the only one who could answer it. *But he will know why I am asking. Or maybe not. Maybe he has no idea Jean Transom had that number. Maybe he really didn't know Jean Transom.*

She dialed his number again. He answered. 'Paul? Hi, it's me.'

'Let me call you back in five minutes.'

Shit. Shit. Shit. I was ready now. I won't be ready when you call back. 'Oh . . . OK. Sure.'

She could feel her momentum draining. She looked at the bright shiny icons on her cellphone screen, moving over them into the menu for Divert All Calls. Her thumb hovered over the Select button. *Jesus – just take his call.* She clutched the phone tight, but let her hand fall down by her side. She stood up and did a tour of the three rooms. She picked up magazines and put them down. She threw clean clothes in the laundry basket. She read the spines on the bookshelf. She squeezed hand-wash on to a paper towel and rubbed it around the sink. *Jesus Christ.*

When the phone rang – twenty minutes later – her heart nearly blew.

'Hi,' he said.

'Hi.'

'How's it going down there?'

'I'm just letting everything go where it takes me. I mean, so far? Finding the body hasn't changed a whole lot. We do have a photo of Ruth Sleight – the young girl from that 1979 Mayer–Sleight case.'

'And how do you think it ties in?'

'I don't know yet.'

'So, that's it?' he said, and she could hear the smile in his voice. 'No one has "suddenly remembered" anything?'

'In a town where Mind Erasers are the shot of choice . . .'

Paul laughed. 'What's in them again?'

'I couldn't tell you.'

'I see.'

'Exactly.'

'So basically no one in Breck ever remembers anything?' said Paul.

'Well, no one under twenty-five. And one person who is thirty-six.'

Paul laughed. 'We need to go out drinking again.'

'Yeah, screw this whole investigation thing.'

They were silent for a few beats. 'Poor Jean Transom,' they both said at the same time.

'Whoa. That was very serious,' said Ren. 'And simultaneous. Time to go. Too much emotion zaps my superpowers.'

'OK. Look, you take care.'

'I will,' said Ren.

'And remember, Superwoman – you can't actually fly.'

'If I ever think I can, I won't go straight to the rooftop/window thing. I'll be smart enough to start on the ground first, see if it works.'

Paul laughed. 'Bill Hicks.'

'An homage, yes.' She paused. 'Shit. One thing. Can you *talk* talk?'

'Sure, go ahead.'

'Did you keep anything I sent you when . . . you know . . . over those six months . . .' said Ren. *When we nearly had an affair.*

He paused. 'Why do you ask?'

'I'm just asking.'

'OK. You gave me one CD. Celine Dion –'

'Shut up.'

'OK. One CD – Dropkick Murphys, which I loved; two DVDs – that Swedish one I had to *read*, thank you very much. And *The Station Agent*. And whatever that book was. And yeah, of course I kept them. I thought they were all great. Apart from the book. Why do you ask? Do you want them back?'

'I guess I was talking about the phone.'

'The piece-of-shit throwaway? Well, it lived up to its name. I threw it away.'

If I ask him when, he will know.

'You didn't write down the texts I sent you or anything before you got rid of it?' said Ren.

'Because I'm not a fourteen-year-old girl, no. I did not. You ain't all that.'

Ren laughed. 'I know they were all just bull-shitty and non-. . . whatever, but . . .'

'But what?'

'Nothing.'

'OK, then.'

'Are your emails, like –'

'If you're going to ask me are my emails secure, I will now think you are crazy. What is your –'

'Nothing! I just . . .'

'What?'

'Nothing. G'bye.'

'You're nuts. You know that. G'bye.'

Ren sat back down and threw the phone on the bed beside her. She only had Paul's word that he had gotten rid of that cellphone. But it had come from the mouth of the same man who'd told her he didn't know Jean Transom. Ren held a hand across her stomach and inhaled deeply. If anyone had asked, she would have said that she trusted Paul Louderback one hundred per cent. She couldn't say that about everyone. And now she was worried that she couldn't even say it about him.

And where does that leave me?

Malcolm Wardwell sat at the edge of his seat in the interview room of the Sheriff's Office. Ren opened the door and closed the distance between them as quickly as possible. She was sitting down before Gressett had closed the door behind him.

'Hello, Mr Wardwell. As you know, I'm Special Agent Ren Bryce, this is Special Agent Gressett from Glenwood Springs. And we're investigating the murder of Jean Transom.'

Wardwell nodded.

She slid the news clipping toward him.

He blinked slowly. 'Why are you showing me this?' His tone was tired, resigned.

'What do you know about Jennifer Mayer and Ruth Sleight?'

'Same as everyone else,' he said. 'The same as everyone else.'

Ren waited.

'Oh, come on,' said Malcolm. 'I turned on my TV set every night for three weeks and saw those beauti— those . . .' He shook his head. 'I can't even call them two beautiful little girls without everyone looking crooked at me. All I know is that they may have been abducted and that they came home. And that they were OK.'

'Do you believe that they were OK?' said Ren.

'No, I don't. Sadly, I don't.'

'Since I last spoke with you,' said Ren, 'I've discovered your name was on a list that Jean Transom had in connection with the case.'

'What?'

Ren nodded.

He paused. 'Can you show me the photo of Jean Transom again?'

'Yes.' Ren handed it to him.

'Like I said, she was in my store,' said Malcolm, 'I do not recall ever seeing her before that. The facts, as far as I'm concerned, is that once – once – I was arrested because of . . . the . . . child porn charges. Not for laying a finger on an actual child. Not for harming a hair on a child's head . . .' Tears welled in his eyes. He swiped them away. 'That arrest was one year before these girls disappeared. And yes, I was brought in after those girls disappeared – by Frisco PD, as I am sure you know. But not by the FBI and not by Jean Transom. Yes, I watched the progress of that case on television, but it was from a rented house my wife and I were staying at in Florida. All of this I proved, and the record is there.'

I have those records, but I wanted to see your face.

53

Wardwell shifted forward in his chair.

'Have you no trust in what the officers working the case believed?' said Malcolm.

'I'm not here to talk about the officers who ran the case, Mr Wardwell.'

He shook his head. 'This is ridiculous.'

'Moving on,' said Ren. 'I'd like to talk to you about the charity work you do for –'

'It's not really charity –'

'Well, it is,' said Ren. 'You give stuff away for free to needy people.'

'Right, but I'm not a formal charity.'

'I know that. I just want to hear how it all works.'

'OK. Well, my son Jason and I get some things together, head up the mountains and bring clothes or food, warm drinks, whatever, to the old guys living up in the cabins or tents around there.'

'When do you do this?' said Ren.

'Maybe once or twice a month. My wife makes the food, so it could be she's made a big batch of chili and has some to spare. Or it could be that it's the end of sale season at the store, so we have some clothes to give away. Or there's a major dip in temperature and we're worried some of those old guys are going to freeze to death up there.'

'There's no regular delivery route . . .'

'No. We don't even deliver to the same people every time.'

'Is it always you and your son?'

'Yes. But we sometimes take some of the kids who work in the stores. Especially the ones I think need to learn to not always just be thinking of themselves.'

Ren pushed a piece of paper and a pen toward him. 'Can you write down the nights you were delivering in January – with whom, to whom and where.'

Wardwell paused. 'That's impossible to do accurately. I can't remember.'

'Try.'

He wrote with thin, light strokes, pausing before he committed each date to paper.

'I'm not going to get all of this right,' he said.

'We'll Xerox you a copy and you can get back to me when you get home and check your diary,' said Ren. 'If you have anything else to add, call me.'

Ren took the page from him when he was finished.

'OK,' she said, scanning the list. 'Where were you Monday night, January fifteenth?'

'At home. My wife can confirm that.'

'OK,' said Ren. 'We'll check that.' She paused. 'OK, let's go back to the child porn . . .'

Wardwell looked away. He started tapping with two fingers of his right hand just above his collar bone. His lips started to move, barely. Ren guessed he was repeating something, but so subtly it was impossible to know what. She stared as his lips kept moving. For almost a minute he said nothing. Then he focused on her as if he'd talked himself into looking her in the eye.

'I do not see what this has to do with anything,' he said. 'A grown woman was found dead, a –'

'I know,' said Ren, 'but you understand you have a record, and therefore you are going to be of interest when a crime is committed in your neck of the woods.' She paused. 'OK, what I have here is that the porn consisted of illustrated magazines, like fifties pin-up pictures where the women are in corsets and suspender belts in the kitchen, smiling gaily. Except these were illustrations of children in regular clothes, doing regular things, like walking to the store. They were cute drawings. But with coded captions: "Little John fights with other boys. He is going to get in so much trouble."' She shook her head. 'There was a phone number on the back for you to call,' said Ren. 'You'd give the illustration number and you'd get a video in the mail that corresponded to it. So if someone found the magazine, it'd look innocent.

'Officers searched your house and not only did you have the magazines, you had the videos – They were labeled Caribou Hunt nineteen-seventy-whatever – you'd get a half-hour of hunting, then it would cut to what you were really hunting for . . .'

'It was thirty years ago,' said Wardwell. 'Yes, I had those magazines, I admitted it almost immediately –'

'Almost. Meaning, when the police arrived at your door, raided your home, found them –'

'I admitted it, yes. I couldn't have admitted it any sooner, could I?'

'No. I guess a *pedophile* doesn't really go around admitting to much, does he? A pedophile only gets the title pedophile when he's caught, right? Y'all don't call each other up, saying, "Hey, pedophile, me and some of the other pedophiles are getting together tonight for a little bowling . . ."'

'Stop. Please,' said Wardwell.

'Aw,' said Ren. She glanced at Gressett; *can you believe this guy?* and turned back to Wardwell. 'I've been here before. You will explain to me how it's normal, you love these kids, they love you, the Romans were at it left and right, society will swing back that way. And I could, for the sake of this interrogation process, pretend that I don't think that that's entirely unreasonable, that maybe you could actually have a point. But I'm really not in the humor. I don't know, but I'm kind of a fan of kids having a childhood.'

'I never laid a finger on one child. It was a couple of magazines,' shouted Wardwell. 'And one video tape –'

'If everyone in the world had one video tape of one child being abused . . .' said Ren. 'And who *knows* what was under your floorboards or up in a cabin somewhere or in a lockbox or in a –'

'You searched everywhere,' he shouted. 'You turned my house upside down. You turned my *life* upside down –'

She leaned into him. 'You pathetic little pricks always blame someone else.'

Gressett stood up. 'Agent Bryce.'

She turned to him, her eyes on fire, then leaned down into his ear and whispered, 'Oh, come on.'

'Agent Bryce.' Gressett slid his chair back a fraction.

When Ren turned back to Malcolm Wardwell, he was nodding.

'What are *you* nodding about?' said Ren.

'I . . . I . . .' He started tapping the side of his thumb with three fingers.

'What,' she shouted, 'is with all the tapping?'

'It calms me down,' said Wardwell.

'Glad someone's calm. And can I say something? How, really, was your life turned upside down?

You got a blink-and-you'd-miss-it sentence, your wife took you back, you still get to run your successful business and you're lucky enough that people come in and out of this town so much that most of them don't even know your secret, and half of those who do are so loyal to your wife that they don't shun you. And the other half just seem to avoid your store, so you lose a few customers; big deal. What about the children you people "love"? Now, there's some destroyed lives for you.' She paused and looked at his eyes. 'Oh, come on, don't you pull that shit on me –'

'Agent Bryce,' said Gressett, standing up. He lowered his voice. 'Please. Can we talk outside a minute?'

Ren took a breath. 'Sure.' She turned to Wardwell. 'We'll be back. You can use your moisture-wicking sleeve to wipe those tears.'

She followed Gressett out the door and closed it softly behind her.

'Are you . . . all right?' said Gressett.

'Me? I could give two shits.'

'Jesus . . . is there something else going on here?'

'What?' said Ren. 'This is a man with a stash of picture-book kiddie porn and fucking caribou hunts with his own special interludes and you think this is *personal*? This is not *personal*, you . . .' She paused. 'If I was a male agent –'

'I wasn't asking you if –'

'What *were* you asking? What does "is there something else going on here?" mean, then? Oh, right . . . is it my time of the month, is that why I'm so angry?'

'Calm down,' said Gressett. His voice was surprisingly gentle. 'Where are you going with all this? I grew up with a single mom and four sisters . . . I was just saying, your anger seems –'

'Do not say out of proportion,' said Ren, taking a step toward him. 'It's . . . these people drive me crazy. If I see one more of them weep in front of me . . .' She paused. 'How appropriate the crocodile tears. Crocodile – the only predator on earth to remain virtually unchanged since the time of the dinosaurs . . .'

Gressett conceded a smile. 'Just don't let your anger cancel out your professionalism. That's all. I could give two hoots about that guy myself. I was just worried that vein on your temple was finally going to blow.'

'Oh no – I need that vein. It hypnotizes people.'

Gressett smiled.

'I know about you and Jean,' said Ren.

'What?'

'I know you were in love with her,' said Ren.

He opened his mouth to deny it, but Ren hoped that the look on her face had only compassion.

'You had such a bad reaction that time to the idea she was gay,' said Ren, 'I thought you were homophobic, but it's been clear since then that you're not – you just didn't want to think you had spent all that time loving her for what you would have seen as no reason and that you may never have found out if she was. Over the past six months I've seen how you are grieving. And that photo you gave me for her file was very touching. You wouldn't come to the autopsy. And then there was me . . . you hated the idea of me taking her place.'

Gressett looked away.

'Even though I had never, even for a second, thought I could,' said Ren.

For a moment, neither of them spoke.

'Did you ever tell her?' said Ren.

'I didn't get the chance.'

54

Bob stuck his head in the door of the office. Robbie and Ren were sitting on Cliff's desk, talking. Gressett was keeping his head down at the computer in the corner.

'Ren, why don't you stop by my office a minute?' said Bob.

'Sure. Now?'

'That would be great.'

They went in and sat down.

'You know I like you, right?' said Bob. His tone was one she had never heard from him before.

'Sure, Bob . . . I like you too.' She smiled.

'Then can you explain to me what the *hell* you were doing with Malcolm Wardwell?'

'I . . . was interrogating him.'

Gary knocked and came in. He threw Ren a look, then turned back to Bob. 'My apologies for all this, Bob.' He sat down.

'Well, when I spoke to an "irate" Mr Wardwell

earlier, it didn't sound quite so much like an interrogation to me as an abusive rant,' said Bob.

'Interesting,' said Ren. 'Irate with you, a pussy with me . . .'

Bob looked at Gary. 'Jesus, aren't you guys trained to get shit out of people in a . . . gentle way? Aren't we the ones supposed to go in all guns blazing?'

'Ren, this really sounded bad,' said Gary. 'It sounded nasty and personal and –'

'It *was* personal,' said Ren, trying to file down the edge in her voice. *Make up something worthy.* 'It is personal to me when a fellow agent is murdered, a woman my age. And I'm leading the case.'

'The man is threatening to sue,' said Bob. He clicked his fingers, 'Like that. I mean, I do not need this right now.' Bob's phone beeped. 'Excuse me,' he said, leaving the room.

Ren turned to Gary. 'I could argue that, say, for example, local businessman, Mr Wardwell had provided money to Sheriff Gage's election campaign, that that would be personal too.'

'Is that a fact?' said Gary.

'"Say, for example" is how I started the sentence.' She said it like a question.

Gary shook his head slowly. 'You sound like my teenage daughter. Who, God forgive me, I would be afraid to bring to the summer picnic she has such an attitude problem. Go take a

break somewhere, Ren. I'll finish this up with
Bob.'

Ren decided to drive into town, park the car and
go for a walk along the Blue River.

Her cellphone rang.

'Hello? Agent Bryce? It's Dr Tolman here.'

'Hello, how are you doing?'

'Good. I'm just calling to say I found something
that may or may not be of interest to you. I did
a little more searching.'

'OK . . .'

'I excise a block of tissue from every organ,
standard practice. This would include the uterus.
If there are problems with a pregnancy –'

'Whoa,' said Ren. 'Jean Transom was pregnant?'

'No, not when she died. But, yes . . . at some
point. And I can confirm that she gave birth.'

'OK,' said Ren. 'Go on.'

'In a problem pregnancy, the placenta can have
an abnormal attachment to the uterine lining. And
that can create problems at delivery and major
blood loss. When I examined her histological slides,
what I found was evidence of retained placental
tissue.'

'How come you didn't see this during the
autopsy? I thought there was some pelvis thing
that would have showed it up.

'Not necessarily,' said Tolman. 'When a woman's
given birth, there's a change in the cervical os –

the opening at the top of the uterus. But you can't always see that. And it's not something you'd pick up routinely. We would only really do a detailed examination if we needed to confirm a recent pregnancy, like if a baby was found abandoned and a woman was found dead nearby . . . you know? We would do a detailed examination if it was relevant to the crime. Do you think it could be relevant this time?'

'I have no idea,' said Ren. 'But thank you for letting me know.'

Ren called Gary Dettling and Bob Gage and told them. She had to leave a message for Paul Louderback.

Patrick Transom's house was in darkness, except for one light glowing somewhere in the back of the house. Ren pulled up outside and jogged up the steps. The night was starless. She was reluctant to ring the doorbell in case it would wake his children. She called him on his cellphone instead. He came out and let her in.

'My apologies for stopping by so late,' she said.

'That's OK,' said Patrick. 'I'm not exactly sleeping these days . . .'

'I know. It must be terrible . . .'

'It is,' said Patrick. 'Can I get you a drink?'

'No, no. I'm fine . . . maybe just a glass of water.'

She sat down on the sofa in the living room

and when he came back, he sat on the chair opposite, creating an awkward distance between them. He seemed to notice, then decide out of nervousness, to ignore it.

'I'm sorry to have to do this,' said Ren, 'but I'm going to have to talk to you about some of Jean's personal details. Again.'

He frowned. '"Personal" as in . . .?'

She paused. 'Well I got some additional information from the pathologist today. And it appears that, Jean, at one point, gave birth.'

He stood up. 'What?'

'Did you have any idea she was ever pregnant?'

'What? Do I look like I had a clue?'

Ren waited.

'I'm sorry,' he said. 'No. I didn't know. I mean, Jean has never had a boyfriend as long as I've known her. When was she supposed to have this baby?'

'It's impossible to say,' said Ren. 'But it is definite that she did. And it couldn't have been in the last fourteen years because she was at the academy or working for the Bureau, so we would have known. And . . . so would you.' She gestured to him. 'You should probably take a seat.'

'Have you found any other evidence that she had a baby? Are there birth records? Did the baby live? Did she put it up for adoption? Jesus.'

'I know. It's extremely difficult in a situation like this to have to come to a family member with this kind of news, but obviously we have to look at every aspect of Jean's life in order to find the person responsible for her death.'

Patrick started shaking his head. 'I'm just in shock about Jean. I . . . is there anything I can do as her family? Is there anywhere I can look or anyone I can ask about this?'

'Did Jean ever hint at anything or give you the impression that there was something she was hiding or –'

He half-laughed. 'You've probably worked out that Jean wasn't stupid. If she wanted to hide something, she'd do a damn good job of it. You folks all seem very good at not betraying any emotion.'

'Well, I hope you can sense the sadness we all feel at her loss.'

'I'm sorry, I didn't mean it like that. It was a compliment. I wasn't talking about –'

'I'm sorry. I just was hoping you didn't think we were all robots.'

'Not at all,' said Patrick. 'I've seen the grief. And it was very touching.'

Breckenridge looked closed by the time Ren drove through. When she got back to the inn, she grabbed a book from the shelf in the living room, something set in a pretty place with a pretty girl and a handsome guy. She went up to the suite, locked herself in and turned on the bedside lamp.

She went to the bathroom, brushed her teeth, changed into pale pink flannel pajamas and got into bed. She lay back with the book on her chest under her hand. She leaned up, opened it and started. Line four talked about a woman with blonde hair. *Jean Transom*. Two paragraphs later, someone's bedroom was painted lavender. *Jean Transom*. By page two, the book was on the night stand and Ren's eyes were dead ahead. Tiny pulses of anxiety struck up all over her body. Her breathing was a mess.

I am a failure. Everyone has been working under me. I have led them all into a dead-end. I cannot take my mind off all this with a book.

She pulled back the covers and got out of bed. She grabbed the coffee pot, turned on the kettle and laid files across the bed while she waited. When her coffee was made, she took her mug and wandered over to the window.

Staring out at the damp, late-evening streets and the solid mountain peaks, she could believe for as long as she stood there that the world was a beautiful place.

55

Ren sat on her bed with a bottle of water beside her. The sun was slowly warming her room. Someone knocked on her door. Quick, relentless knocking – her favorite.

It was the maid. 'Excuse me? Can I clean your room?'

Shit. Ren checked her watch. It was nine a.m. *What?* She had slept twice that night, an hour each time. She looked around the room. There were towels draped on the side of the bath, coffee mugs on every surface, chocolate wrappers, empty and half-empty chip bags, shorts, tops, shoes. *Please clean my room.* Then she looked at the bed and its cute patchwork of crime scene and autopsy photographs.

'No thank you,' said Ren. 'Maybe, if you left a tray for me outside and maybe a cloth and some cleaning supplies . . .' *I would be miserable.*

'Maybe when I finish the rest of the house.'

Ren stood up and escorted herself into the shower. When she was finished and dressed, she went to tidy the pages on the bed. In the back of one of the files was the work photo of Jean Transom. Little Amber Transom had touches of her aunt in her features. Ren pulled out another photo of Jean – the one Gressett had given her. It was a long shot of Jean at a summer party, half-turned to the camera, laughing and holding a red Frisbee by her side. When she smiled, all you could see was dark, straight, long lashes. Ren stopped. *Oh my God*. She grabbed the photo of Amber and the photo of Jean and looked back and forth between them. *Oh my God*.

The drive felt epic. No speed was fast enough. Ren called Gary to let him know what she had discovered and where she was going. If she was taking definitive action on something. Gary needed blocks of complete information – a thoroughly considered theory that explained why she was doing what she was doing. You could theorize with Gary, but if the pieces weren't all in place, you did not act on it until you knew more. It made Ren be a better agent. And it drove her nuts.

She was reeling from a wave of hits about Jean's life. Jean had been murdered and the life she had kept so secret was going to have to be exposed. Ren wished it could be another way.

She pulled up outside the small stuccoed house where Caroline Quaintance lived and walked up the path to the front door.

'Caroline,' said Ren, 'it's Ren Bryce again.'

There was movement behind the stained glass of the door, but no response.

'Please let me in,' said Ren.

Caroline Quaintance opened the door and looked like she was about to try a smile. Ren was looking at her from a new angle. And Caroline knew it.

'I'm guessing you know why I'm here,' said Ren.

'I have no idea,' said Caroline.

'Right, OK,' said Ren. 'Well, I'm going to have to just say it. I know you are Jean Transom's daughter.'

Caroline turned away from Ren, but pushed the door open wider behind her as she walked into the living room. Ren followed her.

'I haven't known long.'

'I'm sorry,' said Ren.

'How did you know?'

'The pathologist discovered Jean had given birth. And when I looked at photos of Jean, when she was relaxed and off-duty, there was something about you and her that connected. Then, when I met her niece, Amber, it was amazing how all three of you have similar expressions.'

'I read that you found her body,' said Caroline.

'I don't know how to feel.' She sat slowly into the corner of the sofa.

Suddenly the young woman started crying with an extraordinary, complex grief. Ren stood rigid, holding her breath, fascinated by the intensity of her emotion.

'I just don't know,' said Caroline eventually. 'She was my mother. It even sounds weird. I didn't know her. But I liked her. We had a connection. But can I say I loved her?' She shrugged. 'Why do I feel I love her, then? I don't get it.'

Ren put a tentative hand on Caroline's arm. 'She was your mother, that's why. She's family. And whatever you feel is what you feel – you can't argue with that.'

'But you read about people in magazines and they have no feelings for their biological family. They feel nothing. Or they hate them. Or they're angry.'

'Everyone reacts differently,' said Ren.

'I'm sorry, but I wish I was more like them now. I wish I felt nothing at all. Because this is way too hard. I've readjusted my whole life to fit Jean into it. And I had the extra pressure of having to hide it, because of her job and well, I don't really know what else. I mean – would you get fired for that? I wouldn't have thought so. And now what do I do?'

'I know how heartbreaking this is,' said Ren, 'but you can feel proud of what you overcame

and for how open you were to having a relationship with her.'

Caroline looked at her. 'Thank you. Thanks.'

'Can I ask?' said Ren. 'What did she tell you
about your father?' *Because whatever it was, it was
bound to be a lie.*

'Just that he was a football god in high school
. . . she was this pretty blonde . . .'

Don't say cheerleader.

'. . . cheerleader,' Caroline finished.

'Did you ever think of tracing him?' said Ren.

Caroline shook her head. 'I thought – well, he
didn't treat her well. And I don't want to meet a
man who treated my mother badly. Based on what
I've heard about him abandoning us, I feel that I
got most of my personality from her, anyway. So
I didn't think I needed to connect any dots, if you
know what I mean.'

Ren nodded.

'Yes . . .' said Caroline.

Jean Transom had told her daughter a trite story
of young, beautiful love, even if it had ended badly.
Everyone wants to be born of two parents who
were in love. It's an easy story to throw out and
an easy one for an abandoned child to swallow.

*The only truth you have about your parents, Caroline
Quaintance, is that your father did treat your mother
badly. A twelve-year-old mother could only ever have
been treated badly.*

*   *   *

Ren pulled into the church car park opposite the Firelight Inn and turned off the engine. She sat still, gripping the wheel. *Jean's body has been found. I have no excuse.* But it was not a negative. She had hope.

From behind her and to the right, she heard angry footsteps, then they stopped. A man's voice rose up over the sound of something or someone slamming against a truck or car.

'What the hell do you think you're doing, going to Mountain Sports?'

'What?'

'Don't "what" me . . . Are you out of your mind?'

'I honestly don't know what you're talking about . . . but you can stop right there.'

A younger voice and an older voice. She recognized the older voice – Malcolm Wardwell.

'Honestly, my ass,' said Malcolm. 'You know damn well what I'm talking about. That's why you want me to stop!'

'This conclusion? You've jumped high and wide.'

'Have I? Really?' said Malcolm. 'Have I? I don't think so . . . you ungrateful . . . piece of shit.'

'Your only son is a piece of shit now?'

Malcolm let rip. 'What the hell have I done to you? You are a spoilt, ungrateful, terrible, terrible child.'

As the anger exploded and she knew they had

been sucked into their own private world, Ren slowly sat up and turned to watch. She saw it was Malcolm Wardwell's son.

'Child?' he said, stepping forward, laughing.

Malcolm slapped him across the face. His son held his cheek, his eyes wounded and angry. 'I asked you for nothing,' he hissed. 'Ever! Stay out of my business, Dad. Like I want to stay out of yours. Funny how I seem to have made a pact with the devil without being there to sign the papers.'

'Oh, you sure did make a pact with the devil . . .' said Malcolm.

'For crying out loud, get me the sackcloth, ashes, let me walk around town ringing a bell, let me –'

'You . . . disgust me.' Malcolm Wardwell's voice was so pained and sincere, his son stopped, mouth open. He looked surprised himself at the tears that flowed. Malcolm Wardwell hesitated, then walked toward him, taking his son in his arms.

56

Mike Delaney sat in his office, leaning back in his chair to close the blinds behind him. Ren knocked on the door.

'Come in, take a seat,' he said.

'Am I interrupting you?'

'Absolutely.' He smiled. 'I will give you two minutes of my precious time.'

'Cool,' said Ren. 'The strangest thing happened last night and I'd just like to see what you think. I was parking my Jeep in the church car park. The one on French Street, opposite the inn. And I heard the Wardwells – Malcolm and his son.'

'Jason.'

'Jason,' said Ren. 'It was creepy. They had this intense argument. Malcolm Wardwell was apoplectic. Which was weird in itself because, when I interviewed him, I thought he was a bit of a pussy. Anyway, Malcolm looked like his head was about to blow, he was so angry. Then the son – this forty-something-year-old guy – starts weeping like a baby, kind of collapses in on himself and the father takes him in his arms. Weird.'

'That is weird,' said Mike. He waited.

'And the argument was just about Jason taking a job in Mountain Sports.'

'That was it?'

'I know,' said Ren. 'So I was thinking, I mean, obviously the stores are in competition, but . . . this argument was a little . . . dramatic.'

'Tensions were high.'

She nodded.

'So what do you want me to do?' said Mike.

'Who owns Mountain Sports?'

'A Norwegian couple. Let me check.' He wheeled his chair to the computer and started typing. After a while, he turned the screen toward her. 'The owners are . . .' He squinted. 'Maria and Sjurd Nordberg –'

'Syurd. The js are like ys,' said Ren.

'Thankjou.'

'It doesn't work the other way round.'

'How do you know shit like that?' said Mike.

'"Norwegian Wood" . . . my boyfriend in college.' She winked.

Mike laughed. 'OK . . . SYURD Nordberg and his wife have had the store nine months.'

'Did we talk to them first time round – in the winter?'

He paused. 'Yes, I think that might have been

me. It's all coming back. Yes – they had nothing much to say. They were too new – new in town, new to the store.'

'I might go say hi today,' said Ren.

'For . . .'

'The holy hell of it.' She smiled. 'Was that two minutes?'

'Yes. Get out.'

Ren stopped by Wardwell's on her way to Mountain Sports. A red-and-yellow banner the length of Wardwell's window read *Twenty-fifth Anniversary Sale: 25% Off*. Ren hovered in front of it. A mother and three blonde identicoiffed daughters bumped past her, confident that high hair, Fake Bake and miniskirts worked well across a forty-year age spread. Ren frowned after them, then walked down the steps into the store.

The sale rails were overloaded and pushed against the wall, leaving space at the center for a stack of cartons. Malcolm Wardwell kneeled beside them with a box cutter, slicing through the brown tape that sealed them. He glanced up at Ren and looked back down again.

'I would like to apologize,' said Ren. 'For that last time.'

Mr Wardwell leaned into the open carton and pulled out a pile of vacuum-packed parkas. He stopped and looked up at her.

'It wasn't professional,' said Ren. She gestured to him. 'Please, don't let me interrupt you.'

'I haven't much help in the mornings,' he said, standing up, flattening the empty carton and leaning it against the window. He kneeled back down and dragged another one toward him. 'It's me versus the slopes for most of the kids who work here.'

Ren watched in silence as Wardwell emptied and folded the next carton.

'So,' she said, 'congratulations on your twenty-five years.'

He nodded. 'Well, it's more like twenty-nine, but I don't include the time it took to set it up. Finding the money, getting around legal stuff. It was a tough time. Jason was on his last vacation before college, we had to readjust our finances. You always have to readjust your finances in this game.'

'What was here before?' said Ren.

'Right before? I'm not sure. Historically? It was a saloon. Full of hurdy girls and rowdy miners.' He smiled. 'It was a shell when we got it; we were able to hang on to the original floor, restore that and some of the other timberwork.' He spoke as if he was telling too much to someone he feared didn't care.

'Really?'

'For whatever use it was. It cost a lot of money and now, because we always need to make so much money, the floors are usually covered in rails and the walls are covered with T-shirts and sweatshirts and jackets . . .'

Ren looked down at the floor. It was mosaic-tiled in pretty shades of gold, green and red. 'Let me help you,' she said, pushing some of the boxes out of the way and opening up the floor. 'That really is beautiful,' she said.

He nodded.

'Where's your son today? said Ren.

'He'll be along.'

'OK.'

He looked up at her.

'I guess I should get going . . .' she said.

'Thanks for stopping by.'

Mountain Sports was between a beauty salon and a jeweler on the mezzanine level of a group of stores. It was open and empty.

'Hello?' said Ren, walking in.

'I'm out back,' shouted Maria. 'If you need any help, let me know.'

Ren walked to the back door and out on to the balcony. 'Maria Nordberg?'

'Yes,' she said, standing up, blowing a stream of smoke away from Ren. She was in her fifties, freckled and blonde with her hair tied up under a faded floral scarf. 'I brave the heat for my cigarette.' She stubbed it out in a pot of sand. From the next-door basement garden, a pre-school teacher stared up as she rubbed sun block on to tiny noses.

Maria rolled her eyes at Ren. 'As if my one cigarette a day . . .' She shook her head.

'Some people . . .' said Ren. She looked out over the Blue River to the mountains where the ski trails wound down smooth and green. The terrace below was filled with people sitting under red umbrellas. 'What a beautiful day.'

'I love it here.'

'Me too. But, sadly, I'm here for work.' She smiled and showed her badge.

Maria smiled back, but it was different.

And then I go and spoil it all . . . 'I'm Ren Bryce with the FBI. I'm looking into the death of Agent Jean Transom.'

'Oh, yes,' said Maria. 'I'm sorry about your colleague. It must have been a relief to find her remains.' Her accent was that happy, sing-song Norwegian that made Ren think of her old boyfriend – he could be saying, 'I'm depressed and I want to kill myself' in Norwegian and it would sound like he was telling you he was in a bath of coke with four supermodels.

'Thank you,' said Ren. 'I know you've already spoken to the Undersheriff about what you saw – or didn't see – back in January, so that's fine, I've re-read that. I was wondering, did you have any other staff members around that time, anyone casual? I don't see anything in the notes. Or anyone that may have seen anything recently. Because the body has been . . . found. And we need to make sure . . .'

'No,' said Maria. 'Back when my husband and I opened this place, we couldn't really afford to hire anyone.'

'Right,' said Ren. 'It's always hard starting out. And how has it been working out for you?'

'Very good, very good. There are so many visitors to Breckenridge. We are very lucky. And we are taking someone new on.'

'I'm sure you can have your pick of college kids around here.'

She smiled. 'We've gone with someone a little more experienced.'

'From here?' said Ren.

'From Wardwell's,' said Maria, with a twinkle in her eye, a sense of validation. 'The son.'

'Ah, he's defecting,' said Ren, smiling.

Maria smiled back. 'Sjurd and I *were* wondering . . .'

'Maybe he just wanted a change of scenery,' said Ren. She looked again through the back door and out over the mountains. 'Beautiful,' she said.

Maria nodded.

'OK,' said Ren. 'I will let you get back to your work. Here's my card. And please do call me if you think of anything.'

57

Ren walked down Main Street under a blazing sun. The mountain breeze struggled to cut through the heat. The sky was cloudless. She went into the quiet cool of the Crown, put in her order and took the sofa. She grabbed one of the Breckenridge tourist maps that were stacked in businesses all over town. She drew a circle over Reign on Main. It was the place where Jean Transom ate her last meal. *Dead woman walking.* Ren remembered Jean's refrigerator, filled with healthy food. And all the snacks in her desk drawer were healthy. The last night she was seen, she ate at five p.m.; too early for Reign on Main to have been a last resort. And if someone who eats healthy wants to have a junk-food blow-out, they'll pick quality junk. At the very least, they'll choose McDonalds. *Does any of this matter?*

Ren wondered if all this thinking, the inability to switch off her brain, was the thing that one day would take her down. Something so terrible would happen that she wouldn't be able to stop thinking about it, and she would implode. *Shut up.* She looked at the map again. On the west side of South Main: Wardwell's. One block north – Mountain Sports. On the east side of South Main, opposite Wardwell's, Reign on Main. She grabbed another map and traced the line from Breckenridge south to the Brockton Filly and Quandary Peak. Jean didn't make or receive any calls on her cellphone from that time, but if she'd had a throwaway phone, this wasn't relevant – she could have made calls, then dumped it or someone else could have dumped it for her.

Ren ate her Cinnamonster in half the time it should have taken her. She used a sticky thumb to dial Mike.

'Hey, it's Ren. Where would I find Salem Swade if, say, I wasn't quite in the humor for hiking up Quandary?'

'Easy,' said Mike. 'Between nine a.m. and eleven a.m. at the Gold Pan. How lazy are you?'

Ren laughed. 'Thanks. Gotta go.' She checked her watch. It was ten a.m.

Salem sat in the Gold Pan reading the *Summit Daily News*. It was in every bar, restaurant, hotel and inn all over the county. He nodded when she walked in.

'Hello . . .' he said.

'Hello, Salem. Remember me? Ren? Nice to see you.'

'My pod is out of juice,' he said. It lay dead beside his plate.

'I can charge it for you,' said Ren, pulling out her laptop.

'Thank you,' he said. With suspicion.

'It's safe with me,' she said, plugging it in.

Salem nodded. 'That's good news. I've a long walk ahead of me.'

'I could give you a ride.'

'No thank you. You going to have breakfast?'

'Just coffee. Mind if I join you?'

'No, ma'am.'

The waiter came by with coffee.

'This place is great,' she said to Salem.

'This place was built the same year they struck gold in the Blue River,' he said. 'Oldest bar around. Never even closed in Prohibition times.'

'Really?' said Ren.

He nodded. They sat in silence for a little while.

'Salem,' said Ren, 'I was wondering if you could do me a favor . . .'

'Maybe. Go ahead.'

'OK,' said Ren. 'If I ask you some questions about some people, can you keep it to yourself?'

'You mean not tell *anyone* you asked me, or not tell *them* you asked me?' said Salem.

'Not tell them *and* not tell anyone,' said Ren.

Salem nodded. 'Not necessarily.' He paused.

'Well, if you asked me to kill them, for example, I'd be obliged to let them *and* your bosses know.' He fixed serious eyes on her. Then broke out in a laugh.

'It's safe to say I have no desire to kill anyone,' said Ren. She smiled. Then noticed Salem's faraway eyes.

Oh shit. 'But I signed up to what I signed up to' said Ren, and, if placed in a situation, I would have no problem using my weapon and taking the necessary action.'

Come back to me. 'I'm sorry,' she said finally.

He turned to her. 'Me too.'

The breakfast arrived with the silence.

'So,' said Salem, when she had finished eating. 'What is this secret question?'

'Thanks,' said Ren. 'OK, I was just wondering who brings you stuff up to the cabin? Is there someone who comes up with, say, food or clothes?' *Like the Wardwells.*

He nodded. 'Sure. The Wardwells from the store down there.'

'Together?'

'Most times.'

'OK. When?'

'Could be any day.'

'Any particular time?'

'Six p.m. Seven.'

'Do they stay long?' said Ren.

''Bout an hour.'

'OK.'

'That's it?'

'That's it. Thank you.'

'Can't see why that's such a big secret.'

'Trust me,' said Ren.

'I would, if you hadn't just stood up and grabbed your computer with my pod hanging out of it.'

'Oops,' said Ren. 'Here you go.' She turned to leave. 'Oh,' she said, 'let me get this –' She took the bill from the table.

He shook his head. 'Mine's free. I get free breakfasts here.'

'Oh. I forgot. I'm sorry.'

He nodded.

'But I doubt I'll be extended the same privilege,' said Ren, smiling.

The waiter was on his way over. 'This is on me.'

Ren looked back and forth between both of them. 'But –'

'No,' he said. 'If Salem has a date, we're going to cover her too.'

'Well, thank you very much,' said Ren. 'Are you sure?'

'You bet.'

'If I'd known I could bring a date here for free . . .' said Salem.

The parking lot of the Brockton Filly was almost deserted. Ren got out of the Jeep, wondering what had happened to all Billy's customers. The new green neon sign looked too bright and shiny for a dead bar. She pushed in the door. Apart from the hum of the air-conditioning, it was like being back in January. There were a few people dotted around, mainly dirty-looking truckers.

Ren went up to the bar. 'Hey,' she said.

Billy's face was stony. 'Hi.'

'What's up?' She looked at him and around the bar.

'Like you don't know . . .'

'Don't know what?'

'I was raided last night for serving alcohol to minors.'

'What?'

'Do you really not know this?'

'No, how the hell *would I*?'

'Well, you're working out of the Sheriff's Office aren't you?'

'Um, yeah, but it's not like my priority is under-age drinking right now, I'm not in there drawing up a hit-list of bars.'

He let out a breath. 'I'm sorry. I'm just pissed off. I'm going to get fined; they rounded up a load of kids and brought them to the Sheriff's Office, so they're going to be really bummed about that and tell everyone. I mean, it's not like it's going to stay quiet for long. But still . . .'

'Oh dear.'

'I'm sorry. I thought you knew.'

'Don't worry about it. I can understand how you might think I know everything . . .'

He smiled.

58

The door to the ladies room burst open and Jo da Ho staggered out.

'Damn you, you son-of-a-bitch,' she shouted, as she fell briefly on her hands, then pushed her weight back up again. The man ran around her and out through the door of the bar.

Billy ran to her. Ren ran too.

'Did he hurt you?' said Billy. 'I will –'

'No,' said Jo. 'But damn him, he broke my damn necklace in two.'

'Oh, your pretty necklace,' said Ren, bending down to pick it off a floor she realized too late was very wet.

'Exactly,' said Jo. 'Thank you.' She held out her hand.

But Ren didn't hand it to her. 'Where did you get this, Jo?'

Jo looked at Ren, then Billy, then down to the necklace.

'Jo?' said Ren. 'This is not a big deal. It's just out of curiosity.'

'I found it in the bathroom,' said Jo. 'A woman dropped it. She'd been in here before and I knew she'd be back, so I kept it for her. But it was pretty, so I wore it. Otherwise I would have just sold it, wouldn't I? My plan all along was to give it back to its rightful owner.'

Good point. 'I know that,' said Ren. She closed her grip on the necklace and put it into her pocket before Billy or Jo could see what she really had in her hand. She took out a photo of Jean Transom that she kept in her wallet. 'Is this the lady who lost it?'

'Exactly,' said Jo. 'Exactly.'

Billy and Ren looked at each other.

'Did you see any pictures of this woman on the news or on the posters around Breckenridge?' said Ren.

'I don't have a television set,' said Jo. 'But I did see a picture something like that, now you mention it. But that woman in the pictures was an FBI agent, it said. The woman who dropped the necklace didn't look like an FBI agent. An FBI agent just wouldn't come into the Filly. So I thought they kind of looked like each other, but it couldn't be the same person.'

Maybe if you had read the poster and seen that the last sighting was here . . .

'That is true,' said Billy.

'Well, Jean was a friend of mine,' said Ren, 'so, if you don't mind, I'm going to hang on to this necklace for her family.'

Jo nodded. 'OK, sure. You do that. I knew I'd only have it for a little while. And I'm sorry I broke it.'

'You didn't break it,' said Ren.

It was designed to come apart. Otherwise you couldn't plug it into a USB port.

Ren turned to Billy. 'I'm just going out to the Jeep for a little while. I'll be back.'

'Sure, no problem. Is everything OK?'

'Absolutely.' She turned to Jo. 'Thank you.'

'A pleasure,' said Jo, sitting down on her corner stool, looking down at her vast, bare cleavage.

Ren grabbed her laptop from the trunk of the Jeep and sat in the front seat. She turned on the heating in the car. She dropped the bottom half of the damp pendant – the cap of the USB flash drive – into the driver's door and held the part with the USB drive against the vents.

What files have you saved on to this?

Ren's fingers started to burn in the hot air. She shook the drive. *Please dry.* After a little while she checked it. There was no way of telling. She plugged it in and a little white disk icon appeared on her screen. Ren clicked on it. There were three files. The first was a Word document called 'listassaults'. The second was a jpg, numbered. The third was just called 'letterforpsych'. The list of names was no surprise to Ren – the young girls, the abuse.

The jpg stalled when she tried to open it. When it did open, it was a small, blurred image taken with a cellphone camera. It looked pixilated – a mess of shapes and colors – but it wasn't. Ren stared at it closely. She had seen it before: in a drawing on the little girls' file in her office, signed Ruth XX. Here in a tiny, badly lit photo. And also at exactly the location the photo had been taken in. Her heart pounded.

I know what this is.

Suddenly, a face appeared at the driver's window.

'Jesus Christ!' She rolled down the window. 'Are you fucking insane?'

'What are you doing out here?' said Billy. 'Are you OK?'

'I'm working,' said Ren, pulling down the laptop screen.

'I was worried, that's all.'

'I'm fine.'

'OK. Jesus. You just ran out –'

'See you inside.'

She opened the last file, 'letterforpsych'. The heading was 'Jennifer Mayer':

Jennifer Mayer sat in the last pew of the condemned church, her eleven-year-old body starved and bruised and torn. Her hazel eyes were vacant, but held more than she ever wanted to know. She slid to the edge, gripped the rail and walked slowly up the aisle, her steps off, her toes pointed; a tiny, broken ballerina. She wore nothing but a flower girl's tight smile as she strew blood-stained petals from a basket that hung on her forearm.

On the altar, in a wreath of fresh lilies, was her last school photograph. She took the three long steps up the soft red carpet to the altar. On a marble plinth in front of her stood a baptismal font with a drying pool of holy water. She reached in and splashed it on to her face, wiping away dirt, revealing wounds she couldn't feel.

In God's safe house, a strange parody of disordered sacraments: baptism, marriage and death, communion with evil and confirmation that she would never be the same again.

She looked into the eyes of all the statues around the church. In an alcove was a portrait of the French saint, St Jean-Marie Vianney. She had learned about him at school. He had found strength in going without food or sleep. He could heal the sick, especially children. Jean. She turned her head to face the huge cross that hung behind the altar. Transom: the horizontal beam on a cross . . . or gallows.

So . . . I can come back to life. Or I can die.

Ren closed the file. It was therapy. A letter to a psychiatrist, written in the third person, to help her get through it. Jean Transom was Jennifer Mayer, the pretty little girl who had been abducted with her friend, Ruth Sleight, and held for three weeks in a place where they should have been discovered.

She called Paul Louderback.

Then she re-read the last line of the letter: "So . . . I can come back to life. Or I can die."

And Jean Marie Transom did both.

59

Salem Swade's cabin was in black mountain darkness, but inside, a muted light glowed. Ren walked around its neat, rotted log walls and boarded-up windows, the beam of her Maglite low on the ground. On the east side, the one remaining window revealed nothing of what lay on the other side. Ren rubbed her forearm across it and got nothing but a sleeve covered in dirt and a spider hanging from her cuff by its silver thread. She paused, sucked in by its manic search for purchase. Holding the flashlight between her teeth, she pinched the thread from her cuff, setting the spider free on the dry earth.

She grabbed the light, then moved around the front of the cabin to the door. She paused, listening to the two voices that were talking inside. She knocked and worked at the rusted doorknob until it gave way. Powdered wood fell from the frame on to the floor.

The smell was pine pot-pourri over locker room, prison, hospital air. Her stomach shifted.

'Hello,' said Salem, raising his hand to wave. He was wearing a red, button-down long-sleeved T-shirt and a pair of light cotton trousers. *A little skinny Santa Claus.*

'Hello, Salem,' said Ren. 'Didn't I tell you I'd come to see you?' She smiled. 'I brought you up . . . some soda.' She lay a cooler box on the floor by the table. A living room/kitchen ran the length of the cabin with two rooms off it to the rear, one with a door, one without. To her right was the kitchen area, to her left was the living area with a rocking chair, a generator, some candles and the rotted stumps of two trees. Across one wall, blocking the window she had tried to look through, were six ceiling-high stacks of the *Summit Daily News*. She closed the door to the fresh air behind her.

Malcolm Wardwell was standing by the stove in the kitchen, heating food. There were some empty plastic containers beside him.

'Hello,' said Ren.

'Hello,' said Malcolm. He turned quickly back to the food. 'Jason,' he called out.

Jason Wardwell came out from the back room.

'This is . . .' said Malcolm, turning to Ren. 'I'm sorry, what was your name again?'

'Ren Bryce. I'm with the FBI.' She reached out a hand to Jason.

'Hi,' said Jason, giving her a firm handshake.

What are you doing here? I thought you and your father had fallen out.

Salem walked her way. 'Everyone wants to feed Salem,' he said. 'People been trying to put meat on these bones since I was a boy.'

'To be fair,' said Jason, 'you know how to put it away. Just where, though, is the thing. That's one of those secrets the ladies would love to know.' He glanced at Ren.

'Hell, yeah,' said Ren. 'The only places I can think to put it are on my big fat hips and my big fat ass.'

'Well . . . I wasn't including you in the ladies,' said Jason.

Ren laughed. *Oh dear – have you ever spoken to a woman before in your life?*

'Back out while you can,' said Salem to Jason. 'Slowly.' He turned to Ren. 'Take a seat,' he said.

'No thank you,' said Ren. She still stood by the door, scanning the room.

Salem wandered away, half talking to himself. 'You don't leave people,' he said. 'You take hits. You take hits for yourself, you take hits for others. You take the bullets. You send 'em back. That's the kind of shit that happens. That's the kind of shit.'

'You're not wrong, buddy,' said Jason. 'Tell us about that time on the river, Salem.'

'You don't need to do that,' said Ren.

Jason glanced at her. 'It's OK, it's a funny story.'

'Goddamn hilarious,' said Salem, slapping a hand on his knee, then leaning on it to stand up, 'Goddamn hilarious, the way they peppered those bullets across that water, crazy, deadly. Like stone-skimming – badam, badam, badam.' He danced around in a circle, then sat back down.

'Look at him dance,' said Jason.

Ren took a deep breath.

'You just chill out, there, Salem,' she said. 'We don't need any entertainment here this evening. You just relax.'

'Can you smell how good this is?' said Jason. 'My mother makes the best –'

He stopped. They all heard a loud noise out the back of the cabin.

'Bears,' shouted Salem, jumping up, grabbing a stick from against the wall and bolting out the door.

'Well, shit,' said Jason, 'let me go get him.'

'Let me go,' said Ren. She didn't give him a chance to argue. She ran around the back and grabbed Salem by the arm.

'Salem, sweetheart, I need you to get out of here, OK? Do you know Billy down at the Filly?'

Salem nodded.

'Just go down to him,' said Ren. 'He will look after you. Don't say anything to anyone about who's up here, OK?'

'But I –'

'Salem? I'm sorry, but you need to get the hell out of here.'

And I am going to hope to fuck that Paul Louderback is on his way.

'Thank you so much, Salem. I owe you.'

She squeezed his hand and ran back around to the front of the house and closed the door. Jason Wardwell looked up.

'Where's Salem?'

'I couldn't find him,' she said. 'But he knows these woods like the back of his hand. And I'm guessing he knows how to handle a bear.' She smiled.

The front door pushed open and swung wide. Salem walked in.

Ren froze. *What are you doing?*

'Misty!' said Salem. 'Misty! Come on, girl. We're going for a little walk.'

Oh shit.

'Where?' said Malcolm. We're about to serve your supper.'

Don't say it. Salem pointed at Ren. 'Robin, here, told me to –'

'Ren,' said Ren, grasping at anything to stop him talking. 'My name is Ren.'

'I knew it was a bird of some description,' said Salem.

'Anyway,' said Ren, 'maybe a walk's not a great idea right now. Like Jason said.'

'I can't keep up,' said Salem. 'You tell me to get the hell down the mountain to the Filly and –'

Ren watched Jason Wardwell's face change. It was instantaneous. But it was Malcolm Wardwell who was holding the gun.

60

It was the worst possible thing to do to Salem Swade. But Malcolm Wardwell knew that. He made a haunted old vet stand with his back to the room while there was a gun somewhere behind him. Someone like Salem needed to face the room and face the door and feel safe. He started shouting; nonsense and swearing and orders and names and places and –

'You – shut up, you crazy son-of-a-bitch, shut up!' said Jason.

Salem stopped. But he was shaking violently, sweat soaking into the thin red fabric.

'Let Salem go,' said Ren. 'Please.'

'Let Ren go,' said Salem.

Oh, God. 'Salem, I'm going to be OK. You don't need to worry about me.'

'Stop talking,' said Malcolm. 'Silence.'

Jason Wardwell was wired, his father eerily still.

'You,' he said, 'can take care of this.'

Jason opened his mouth and closed it.

'At least,' said Ren, 'let Salem stand in front of the mirror.'

'Why would I do that?' said Jason.

So he can see the whole room. 'What harm is it going to do?' said Ren.

Salem started to move sideways toward it. Jason didn't stop him.

'Jason,' said Malcolm, 'put your gun to Salem's temple and shoot him if Agent Bryce here doesn't do what she's told.'

Jason did as he asked.

'Hold your arms up in the air,' said Malcolm.

Ren held her arms up. He reached in and removed her gun from the holster under her arm, his hand brushing off her breast.

Her stomach turned. He bent down to her ankle holster. There was no gun there. He frisked her and found nothing else. He walked over to the battered old sofa and slumped down into it.

What is going on here?

Ren watched Salem. He had started shouting again. And sobbing. If Jason Wardwell, pumped-up and edgy, was going to do something, it would be directed at Salem first, it wouldn't be directed at her. Because, no matter what, she was an agent and Jason Wardwell didn't know yet if he was going to make it through this.

'You need to shut the fuck up,' said Jason to Salem.

'He can't,' said Ren. 'He's afraid.'

'He better get over it,' said Jason. 'Right now.'

Ren saw how Salem had realized he could see her face reflected in the mottled mirror in front of him. He fixed her with beautiful, terrified eyes.

Ren started humming, quietly – a John Prine song, top of the Most Played on Salem's little iPod when she'd charged it. Everyone looked at her. Salem stilled. Ren hummed a little louder, holding him with her eyes.

Jason swung the gun her way, '*What* are you –'

Then there was no more shouting. Only the sound of Ren humming. The others turned to watch Salem, subdued. Jason turned the gun back to him. Ren could see Salem blinking rapidly, his chest heaving. Ren started to sing, '*We lost Davey in the Korean War and I still don't know what for, don't matter any more.*' Her voice was shaking.

'Shut up, you crazy bitch,' said Jason. 'What is wrong with you all?'

'Salem, sweetheart,' said Ren. 'You're going to be OK. Stick with me, OK?'

Tears poured down Salem's face. He started to sob.

Ren kept singing, '*You know that old trees just grow stronger. And old rivers grow wilder every day.*'

'Stop,' said Jason. 'I mean it. Stop.'

Salem was rocking again, his sobs growing

louder and louder.

'Shut up! Shut up!' said Jason, raising the gun, lowering it, running the back of his hand across his forehead. 'Shut up!'

'No,' said Ren. 'No. Let him go, Jason. Let Salem leave. Let him get out.'

'He'll call the Sheriff –'

'Think about it, Jason,' said Ren calmly. 'How can Salem do that? Salem has no way of doing that.'

'She's right,' shouted Salem. 'I don't. I really don't.'

'Stop talking,' said Jason, taking a step toward him.

Salem flinched, throwing his arms up, covering his head. 'No,' he said, over and over.

'Stop,' said Jason. 'Stop.'

Ren started again, singing the rest of the song, her voice steady, but low: '. . . *people just grow lonesome. Waiting for someone to say . . . hello in there . . . hello.*'

Ren stopped as Jason raised the gun again toward Salem. Salem was swaying gently, his eyes closed, his hand across his stomach. Ren wanted to shout at Jason, to tell him Salem was quiet now, to tell him he wasn't a threat, that she would be quiet too. But she knew she would startle Salem and she didn't want him to have to open his eyes to this scene, unless she knew he was going to make it out alive. But in the new silence, Salem opened his eyes and locked on to hers again. Ren smiled at him.

Jason pulled the trigger.

61

Salem was blasted backward, shattering the mirror behind him, a huge hole blown into his sunken chest. Ren had closed her eyes only when she knew Salem could no longer see her. She looked down now on his small, broken frame, slumped against his rocking chair, a plaid blanket half-fallen across his body.

'You fucking bastard,' she roared at Jason. 'You fucking bastard.'

She stepped sideways and took a step forward. She pointed a finger at him. 'Do not say a fucking word, you fucking animal.'

'Do not move,' said Jason, pointing the gun at her.

'I'm not coming near you, you son of a bitch.' She walked with her hands in the air toward Salem, bent down and pulled the rest of the blanket over him. 'I'm trying to give a man some dignity. So, you? *You* stay the fuck away from *me*.'

She had her back to Jason Wardwell as she covered Salem with his coat. With her right hand she reached around to the back of the cooler box, pulled off the gun she had taped there and slipped it into her ankle holster.

She stood back up and turned to face Malcolm Wardwell.

'Jean Transom tracked you down, didn't she? You would remember her as Jennifer Mayer. She came to confront the monster who abducted and abused her and her eleven-year-old friend, Ruth Sleight. She came up to the most remote place she knew she could find you. Somewhere she could talk to you in private. And if anything bad happened, you could be far away from town.'

Ren thought of the image that Ruth Sleight had drawn – the mosaic pattern from the floor of Wardwell's store – the store he had the keys for, the one that had been vacant for years; down the stairs into the darkness, the windows boarded up. The beautiful patterned floor was the only thing Jennifer Mayer could see under the blindfold. And Ruth Sleight was able to back her up. And the smell that came through the vents was from the brewery next door. Jean Transom never drank beer. And never really knew why.

Malcolm's face was gray.

There is something not right here.

Ren thought about the store. She thought of the whole line of stores down Main Street. She thought of the risk of discovery. The argument between Malcolm and Jason Wardwell about Mountain Sports, their bitter words flashing back: *spoilt, ungrateful, terrible, terrible child; stay out of my business, Dad; pact with the devil; sackcloth and ashes*. All because he was going to Mountain Sports. Ren remembered, standing on the balcony, looking out at the beautiful view over the Blue River. And closer still, the day-care center next door.

Oh my God. 'There she was,' said Ren. 'Poor Jean. So close, so close. And she picked the wrong guy.'

Malcolm Wardwell looked at Ren, confused. But he had years of practice in saying nothing. Salem's voice rang in Ren's ears. *You take the hits. You take the hits.*

'When the police came knocking at your door thirty years ago and raided your house,' said Ren, 'and you watched them take away those magazines and videos . . . you were more surprised than they were,' said Ren.

Silence.

'You took the hit, Malcolm, didn't you? You took the hit for your son. In a split second, you made a call. You were forty years old. Jason was sixteen. And maybe . . . maybe Jason was just going through a phase, right? Maybe for him it wasn't a teenage crush on a teacher like everyone else. Maybe if you caught it early enough, his "problem" could be treated and it would all go away. I'm guessing he wasn't on his last vacation before college that summer. My guess is you packed him off to a treatment facility . . . that clearly didn't work.'

Malcolm bowed his head. But still didn't speak.

'And this is how it worked out for you,' said Ren. 'You end up on a freezing mountainside on a January night and you realized that your only son, who you'd laid down your life for, within eight months of him getting out of treatment had abducted two eleven-year-old girls, held them for three weeks in the building you had great plans for, abused them and impregnated one of them . . . And Jean Transom thought it was you. There she was – a strong, bright FBI agent who rarely put a foot wrong, but got tangled in a case so close to her broken heart that she thought it was you.'

'Shut up, shut up.' Jason squeezed his eyes shut briefly, then they were wild and traveling the room, searching for escape.

'There *is* no exit for you,' said Ren.

'I didn't . . .' said Jason. 'Those girls . . . they wanted a ride . . .'

Sweet Jesus. 'And you just gave them a ride.' She nodded.

'Exactly.' Hope sparked in his eyes.

'For three weeks, y'all just drove around in your car,' said Ren, still nodding.

His eyes flashed with anger. 'It's not as if they were behaving like eleven-year-olds anyway . . .'

Ren guessed this was just the beginning of Jason Wardwell's blame plan. DARVO – the sex offender's instant response to accusation – Deny, Attack, and Reverse Victim and Offender.

Ren fell silent. The stench of poor, dead Salem hung in the air with the smell of whatever food had turned black at the bottom of the hot pan. Jason Wardwell's forehead was slick.

Paul Louderback, where are you?

'I had no idea,' said Malcolm, turning to Jason. 'I watched those girls' parents just like every other person in the country. And the screwed-up thing was, I thought I was like them. I thought about how I nearly lost you. I could understand their pain because I thought I nearly lost you. I hoped they were as lucky as I would be, that their little girls would get to come back, that they would get a second chance. I looked at *you*,' he stabbed a finger at Jason, 'and I thought it was all a success story.' He shook his head. 'And you were the one. You were responsible for this agony I was tuning into every day, hoping that, on one of those days, it would be gone, their daughters would be back. And then one day, they did. And we were all told that they were unharmed. And I cried and cried for them and for you, and I thought God is good, God has answered all our prayers.'

'What a fool you were,' said Jason, his tone a rotten collision of rejection and disgust.

'You are a vile, thankless man,' said Ren.

Jason Wardwell's relationship with his father had stalled, aged sixteen, on the day his father made the decision to cover his son's child porn habit. Jason Wardwell lived in a Peter Pan town where people got to play in the snow, say 'dude' and 'super' for as long as they wanted to, because it made them feel good and why shouldn't they? But that didn't cover Jason Wardwell. This paunchy, graying middle-aged man was trying to stay as close as he could to his target market.

'This lady is right.' Malcolm Wardwell was finally having his epiphany, a man too simple and hopeful to have ever pieced together the psychology of his son. 'You are a nasty piece of shit!' was the best he could do. He raised his hands. 'And I love you.'

Broken-down emotions, the plain language of a small-town man who saw no nuances. He looked at 'Jason's problem' and his thought process ran through truth/lie, reveal/hide, break/fix, sick/well. Malcolm Wardwell grew up in a time when parents warned their children in riddles: 'Don't cross the fields with whoever,' 'Don't take a cookie from the man in the white house.'

Ren shook her head. *You poor, sad, old man.* Jason Wardwell's face was almost unbearable to look at, yet drawing her like a magnet to understand what sickness lay behind it.

'I thought you were better,' said Malcolm. 'Until you wanted that job right by the day-care center.'

Jason laughed. 'You thought for twenty-six years I was dead from the waist down?'

You are a sick, sick man.

'What have you *done*?' said Malcolm to his son.

'What have *you* done?' said Jason.

Ren still marveled at the shifting of blame; it was the man at a table on the street corner, playing the shell game, moving the cups to hide the quarter. The quarter will always be there . . . just under whichever cup suits him. And the audience never wins.

'I . . . I didn't do anything . . .' said Malcolm, answering the pathetic question. He turned to Ren. 'Is he right? Is it my fault he did these things?'

'I don't know where to start,' said Ren. 'But it won't be here.'

Fear could come with hope. Fear could be resigned. And fear could be dead if there was no worse consequence to face. Pull back from the screen where all the action is held and it is surrounded by black. Jason Wardwell had reached the edge of the game. Nowhere to go. His eyes were bright with a hopeless fear – a glassy shine that said anything could happen.

62

Jason Wardwell wiped his hand across his brow. He blew sweat from his top lip. Ren's face was burning, her eyes dry. She could hear Malcolm Wardwell struggle for breath.

'At least turn off the stove,' said Ren. 'Please.'

Jason glanced over at it. He looked at his father. 'Go ahead,' said Malcolm.

Jason walked over to the stove, his eyes on Ren. As soon as he turned his body away from her a fraction, she dropped down and pulled the Glock 27 from her ankle holster and aimed it at Jason.

'Drop your weapon,' said Ren.

She watched his gaze flick back toward his father.

'Put your fucking gun down,' she said.

His eyes flicked again to his father, but he put his gun down.

'Kick it over to me,' said Ren.

He did. She bent down and took it. When she
stood up, Malcolm Wardwell stood to her left with
a gun pointed at her.

'That is my gun,' said Ren. 'And I'm afraid I
wasn't kind enough to load it for you before I got
here.'

Malcolm pulled the trigger anyway.

'Clllllick,' said Ren. She jerked her head at
Jason. 'Get over there with your father.'

Jason did as she said. 'You're not going to kill
both of us,' he said.

'Probably not,' said Ren. 'But I could get you
both in the balls.'

Malcolm Wardwell stood, defeated; tired and
old and mistaken. He had spent his life covering
for a son who he didn't even realize had been
showing up at parks and playgrounds and swimming pools, driving around to scout for girls to
make his fantasies real.

Malcolm Wardwell had stood, confronted, on
Quandary Peak – Jean Transom telling him the
last thing he wanted to hear – that his devotion
to his son had not mattered. That he had released
a disturbed and violent child abuser into society,
that from the age of seventeen, Jason Wardwell
had been acting out what he had previously only
ever seen in magazines and on video.

'You hated that Jean Transom had been so
damaged by your son,' said Ren. 'But you hated
her more for thinking that it was you. And you

hated Jason for putting you in that position. And where was he that night? Where was the one person who could have bailed you out when you needed him?'

Malcolm muttered something.

'What?' said Ren.

'He was there,' said Malcolm. 'Behind her. He just stood there, without saying a word. And she wouldn't believe me. She wouldn't believe it wasn't me. He said nothing. He didn't back me up.'

'And there it was,' said Ren. 'You couldn't take one more second of blame. You had lived to protect Jason. And he was happy to let you die to protect him. And it was just too much.'

'It was,' said Malcolm, his voice exhausted from years of lies. 'It was. She wouldn't listen when I told her. I was so terribly confused. On the darkest, coldest night of winter, when I had only gone up to help people: she was there. And I just wanted her to go away.'

The door to the cabin crashed open, shattering the timber frame. Paul Louderback had his gun drawn and moved in quickly opposite Ren. They formed a triangle with Jason Wardwell – both their guns trained on him.

'Malcolm Wardwell killed Jean Transom,' said Ren. 'But it was Jason Wardwell who abducted the girls.'

Paul took two silent steps closer to Jason Wardwell, his face grim resolve.

Something is not right with Paul Louderback.

'So this man in front of me is the man who abducted and raped two eleven-year-old girls,' said Paul.

'One,' said Jason.

'Two,' said Ren. 'Are you out of your mind? Jennifer Mayer and Ruth Sleight. Two.'

'I only wanted the little blonde,' said Jason, as if he was talking about a trip to a nightclub. 'I didn't lay a finger on the other girl, the Ruth girl. I locked her in the fitting room. The only reason she was there was that I saw her with the blonde too late. So I had to take her too. She was an ugly, scrawny thing, covered in freckles, ready for braces – not my type.'

The room was in total silence at the casual defense in his delivery. Paul Louderback lunged for him. He slammed his fist into Jason's face before he had even knocked him to the floor. He gripped him by his neck and used his free hand to quickly impact Jason's eye socket, break his jaw, his nose, loosen his teeth, tear one of his earlobes free.

What the fuck are you doing, Paul?

'You motherfucker,' shouted Paul. He was repeating it over and over, lost in something more than Ren could understand as she watched this handsome man in his fine suit in a shitty cabin, releasing a rage she didn't know he was capable of.

Ren watched, stunned, as Paul Louderback put

into practice everything he had taught her she would never need to do. He had been wrong before. And he was wrong now.

Paul fell on to his back, his breath heaving, his body drenched in sweat. He dragged himself on to his knees, pushing the muzzle of his gun up against Jason Wardwell's temple. Ren knew Paul enough to feel his sense of failure and exposure. He couldn't meet her eyes.

'Nobody move,' said Ren. 'Nobody.' She looked at Paul. 'Give me your gun. Give it to me now.'

Paul reached for the cloth that hung from the back of a chair, wiped his face and threw it on top of Jason Wardwell, who lay curled on the floor, bleeding and moaning.

Ren lowered her voice. 'Paul.'

He handed her the gun.

'But I let them go,' said Jason. 'Those girls were free.'

Paul went rigid. He turned and jumped on Jason again, punching him until Jason blacked out, pounding him until Ren dragged him away.

Malcolm Wardwell stepped forward. 'She told me that night . . . she gave birth to the child. She told me she had a child.'

'She was lying,' said Ren.

63

Bob Gage, Mike Delaney and a team of detectives from the Sheriff's Office were waiting at the trailhead to take the Wardwells into custody.

Ren Bryce and Paul Louderback stood by their Jeeps in the deserted parking lot of the Brockton Filly. There were no lights on in the building.

'See how I parked beside yours?' said Paul.

They both tried to smile.

He unlocked his Jeep. 'Come on,' he said.

'Yes,' she said. 'There is a chill in the air.'

They got in. Ren studied Paul's face as he opened the glove box. He had private-school bone structure. He was a refined kind of handsome. He turned to talk to her and smiled when he saw she was already looking at him. She smiled back.

'In another lifetime . . .' he said.

'Oh, I don't know,' said Ren. 'We were in the situation enough times that we could have done something about it, and we didn't. Like now, for example.'

Paul nodded. 'Maybe you're right.'

'Maybe I am.'

'But you know I care about you so much.'

'Me too.'

'I should have met you when I was in my twenties.'

'Think about that for a second,' said Ren.

'Oh. Yes. OK – we should have met while I was in my thirties and you were in your twenties. You would have loosened me up, we could have done loads of crazy things, we would have had some great photos I could still sneak a look at . . .'

'No – you should have just been a girl,' said Ren. 'That would have been less complicated.'

'Knowing us,' said Paul, 'that probably wouldn't have made a difference.'

'It's weird, but you're one of my best friends, but it's kind of secret. If it wasn't for the fact that we're both in the Bureau, we wouldn't even be at each other's funerals.'

Paul laughed. 'What the –? Only you would say something as screwed up as that –'

'You know what I mean, though. We have this intense friendship that we can't even tell people about. But it's not an affair.'

'Your Safe Streets buddies might think differently.'

'That's *their* problem,' said Ren. 'Projection. We know what we know.'

Paul nodded.

'So . . .' said Ren. 'Jean Transom. Tell me . . .'

Paul let out a breath. 'OK . . .' He paused. 'When Jean was in the academy, I called her in to my office. Her grades were off the charts, but I had some concerns about her . . . psychological well-being. She wouldn't tell me what was going on.' He shrugged. 'I gave her the chance to take care of it on her own. She didn't. I told her she would have to leave the academy. So she had no choice. She told me everything. She was the little girl that for three weeks in 1979 the whole country worried about. Three weeks – it seems weird now. It was like a condensed version of the Elizabeth Smart case.

'What went on during that time was never spoken about outside their families. They had denied there had been any abuse, but it was clear that no one was going to believe that.

'The Mayers were wealthier than the Sleights. They moved to Northern California and changed their names. You know how it works – a Ramsay from Boulder is always going to spark an asso-ciation, a Mayer or a Sleight from Frisco, the same deal. And, of course, Jennifer Mayer was pregnant.'

'I cannot imagine what that must have been like,' said Ren.

'And that is part of the strength people always saw in Jean,' said Paul. 'The source of it was intangible, but it was there.

'So, the Sleights couldn't afford the luxury of moving across the country and changing their entire lives,' said Paul. 'And it wasn't like they were in Witness Protection so the FBI would cover it. Ruth Sleight had to live in Frisco in the same neighborhood she was abducted from, on the same street her friend had left, going to the same school as the kids who whispered about her behind her back.'

'That must have been a nightmare for her.'

Paul nodded. 'Oh, yes. She went completely off the rails. She was an alcoholic by the time she was twenty-two. She was in very bad shape. She had a really tragic existence.

'And about a year ago, Jean Transom was traced by the daughter she had given up for adoption – Caroline Quaintance. And it made her want to get back in touch with Ruth Sleight. They had never spoken since their families had torn them apart. Their parents had always felt that the girls would never get over their trauma if they had to keep seeing each other.

'So, Jean tracks Ruth down – obviously that wasn't difficult: Ruth still lived in Frisco. Jean was devastated when she saw what Ruth had become. She called me that night, terribly distressed. Not only because of that, but because they'd discussed, between themselves, what had happened, for the first time ever. And what was worse was that *Ruth* was devastated at what *Jean* had become. She looked at the kind of future she could have had. She saw the polar opposite of what she was. Two days later, she killed herself. Her suicide note was addressed to Jean. Jean had asked her, the day they met, did she remember the floor of the place they were held. Ruth had said no. But she had – she had drawn a diagram of it when she was a child. And that was her suicide note, signed Ruth XX.

'Oh God,' said Ren. 'That poor woman. And after what Jason Wardwell said tonight, it looks like he didn't sexually abuse her. Do you believe him?'

'I do,' said Paul.

'So Ruth Sleight had to see Jean Transom, apparently solid and successful. And revisit, through this alcoholic haze, the trauma of having to hear her best friend go through what she went through, the guilt of not having been sexually abused herself, the shock of hearing Jean had gotten pregnant, and the guilt at having lied to her about her own abuse . . .' Ren shook her head. 'That woman never stood a chance, did she?'

Paul shook his head. 'I guess not. Which is what made me so mad back there, Ren. I was so fond of Jean and so impressed by her. She had wanted to be an FBI agent from when she was six years old. It had nothing to do with what she had been through at eleven. And then you had Ruth Sleight, destroyed from the moment that sick fuck put her in the trunk of that car.'

'Jean Transom is abducted, completely traumatized, gives birth aged twelve. And *still*, she follows her dream job,' said Ren. 'Even though she knows it will bring her in touch with the kind of fucked-up people she could have spent her life trying to avoid. Jean Transom really was something else.'

'Which is why I put someone on the case who I knew could follow whatever trail Jean had embarked on. I had told her specifically never to pursue this. Ever. But I knew when her body was found that she had. So, Agent Bryce – a shoe analogy for you –'

Ren held up a hand. 'Don't say anything about filling shoes.'

'Let me finish,' said Paul. 'No, you could not fill Jean Transom's shoes. But that is because no one can *ever* fill anyone else's shoes. It's an expression that drives me crazy.'

'Me too,' said Ren. 'That was my point.'

'So,' said Paul. 'I knew you couldn't fill her shoes, but . . . you could follow her footprints in the snow.'

64

The next morning, Ren arrived into an atmosphere in the office she couldn't quite get a handle on: Colin, Cliff and Robbie were sitting around talking and stopped as soon as she walked in.

'Good job,' said Colin, nodding.

'Well done, young lady,' said Cliff.

'You go, girl,' said Robbie.

'Well, thank you very much,' said Ren. She slumped down on the edge of her desk.

'Have you been up all night?' said Robbie.

'I have,' said Ren. 'And I was in Vail by six thirty this morning to deliver Patrick Transom the ultimate good news/bad news scenario. The good news? We found your sister's killer. The bad news? Your whole family lied to you all your life; your family name isn't exactly real and your parents are dead, so you can't even find out any more. Your beloved sister was abducted and raped as an eleven-year-old. Oh – and you have a niece you never knew existed.'

'When you put it like that . . .' said Cliff.

'She probably did,' said Colin.

'Yes,' said Ren, 'at times like that I think "If only I had the tact of Colin Grabien".'

'How did Transom take it?' said Cliff.

'You name it,' said Ren. 'Relief, shock, anger, happiness, sadness . . . a quick burst of all the emotions that he would have to really deal with for the rest of his life. Like a trailer for the big feature.'

'Wow,' said Robbie.

'And,' said Ren, 'he wants to meet Caroline Quaintance. And if she agrees to a meeting, he wants me to be there too. Yikes.'

'Aw, you'd be good at that,' said Robbie.

'I don't know,' said Ren.

'Yeah, you're kind of heartless enough to be neutral,' said Colin.

Cliff and Robbie both turned on him.

'Thank you, guys,' said Ren. 'Now – anyone know why I got a text from our great leader, Gary Dettling, to get my ass in here for nine a.m.?'

'That's what we were talking about when you walked in,' said Robbie. 'There are some interesting people here to see you.'

'What?' said Ren. 'Who?' She studied their faces. No one looked particularly upbeat.

'I fear for you,' said Colin.

Asshole.

'Shut up,' said Robbie.

'Yeah, that's not very helpful,' said Ren.

'She could be getting a Shield of Bravery or something,' said Robbie.

They all laughed.

I have a bad feeling about this. 'Who's here?'

Robbie was about to answer when Bob stuck his head in the door and told her she was needed immediately in the conference room. Facing her, side by side were Special Agent in Charge, Tim Monahan, and Assistant Special Agent in Charge, Jeff Warwick – Gary Dettling's superiors. All the tension in the room was radiating from one point – where Gary Dettling stood.

What are you all doing here?

'Good morning, Agent Bryce,' said Warwick.

'Good morning,' said Ren, taking a seat.

'We've had some interesting developments into the suspected Val Pando robberies . . .'

'OK,' said Ren, nodding.

'And we were curious to know,' said Warwick, 'what exactly is your relationship with Billy Waites?'

Ren stared at the photo of Billy Waites that Warwick had thrown down in front of her. It was Billy's mug shot again, long hair, beard, cold eyes: everything about him that was designed to conceal. But Ren knew what those eyes looked like laughing, what the mouth under that beard could do, what his shaved skin felt like, how his short hair looked shit without gel.

Ren shot a look at Gary. His face said nothing.

'Billy Waites was Jean Transom's one-three-seven,' said Ren. 'He was a source for her around Breckenridge, Frisco, Alma, Fairplay . . . and he was the last person who saw her the night she was killed.'

'This guy ring any alarm bells up until now?' said Monahan.

Ren's heart pounded. 'No. And he's not ringing any alarm bells for me now.'

'Really?' said Monahan.

'Obviously I was wary . . . in the beginning,' said Ren. 'But no . . . I am confident that Billy Waites has turned his life around.'

Monahan raised an eyebrow.

'Why do you ask?' said Ren.

'OK – detectives from the Sheriff's Office here were concerned Waites was serving alcohol to minors in the Brockton Filly. It seems he wasn't paying too much attention to the IDs he was being shown and to what state the kids were in when they were leaving or planning to drive home.

'They raided the place Friday night and, along with rounding up under-age drinkers, they found money in the till from one of the Val Pando robberies.'

'How much?' said Ren.

'Not much,' said Monahan. 'Several hundred dollars.'

'That could have come from anywhere,' said Ren. 'Do you have anything to say he has any connection with Val Pando?'

'Not yet,' said Monahan.

Ren frowned. 'What do you mean?' She glanced at Gary. His eyes were lit with anger.

'I just mean not yet,' said Warwick. 'Mainly because of this –' He lay down another photo.

It was a handsome Hispanic boy, late teens with huge, lost brown eyes.

Sweat was slowly soaking into Ren's shirt. Where the tiny buttons closed at her chest, the fabric trembled. Her face was hot. Her throat felt closed over. Every part of her body seemed to be giving her away. *Everyone needs to stop looking at me.* She uncrossed her legs and leaned slightly forward.

'He is seventeen years old now,' said Monahan.

Ren looked up at them. 'But –'

'When we took in the under-age kids from the Brockton Filly, there were about ten of them. Apparently this guy, who nobody knew, shows up and starts buying them all drinks. He had an extremely professional fake ID. All the kids were rounded up, brought here and searched for drugs,

This guy has no drugs on him, but over a thousand dollars in cash. We ran it through NCIC and it was bait money from the Idaho Springs robbery.

'We're wondering if there is a connection there between him and Billy Waites.'

'No,' said Ren. 'No.'

'Then why did Billy run?'

What? 'What?'

'He ran. Not long after the raid, he was gone,' said Monahan.

The bar was in total darkness . . .

'I just don't believe Billy Waites is involved, I'm sorry.'

'You don't know that,' said Monahan. 'Billy Waites could be one charming motherfucking pig.'

'Yeah, well, charm doesn't cut it with me,' said Ren.

'I'm not talking about a guy chatting you up in a bar,' said Monahan. 'I'm talking about work.'

'So am I,' said Ren, her eyes boring into him.

'I'm talking about the charm of a man who has lied for years, gotten what he wanted for years, evaded law enforcement . . .' said Monahan.

'I would be surprised if he had anything to do with this,' said Ren.

'I bet you would,' said Gary.

Everyone looked at him. Monahan frowned.

'Well, she knows Billy Waites better than any

of us,' said Gary, shrugging. 'And if she says he's reliable, that's good enough for me.'

'Thank you,' said Ren.

'OK,' said Monahan. 'OK. We'll see what comes up. But for now, Mr Waites has the benefit of the doubt. Or at least the benefit of an association with Special Agent Ren Bryce.'

'Now,' said Warwick, 'Agent Bryce. Are you ready to go in and talk to our little friend?

The boy sat in the interview room with his elbows on the table, his hands in fists against his forehead. Ren watched through the small, glass window. Reinforced. *Unlike me.* She breathed in and out, afraid to close her eyes in case she'd see something she didn't want to see. But what she was looking at was hitting her just as hard. *Shut down and you can do this.* It was a physical sensation in her chest, like the sliding shut of prison bars. Her heart was all locked up by the time she was at the other side of the door and it was closed behind her.

The boy looked up. He watched her walk all the way across the room with those lost eyes that had almost broken her before. Ren could see the fight inside him. She sat opposite him. They hung there in silence. Eventually, he looked up at her. Before she had a chance to speak, he did.

'It wasn't always like this,' he said, looking down

at himself as if the clothes he wore were telling her something. 'I used to have someone who looked after me. I was six years old when we met her – in the playground, me and Mama. She was sitting on a bench, crying. She was a pretty lady with a sad story. She told Mama she'd lost a baby and that she liked to come to the playground to be around kids because it made her feel sad and she was hoping that one day it would make her feel happy. It was the only time I saw my mama cry. The only time. Ever. The next week she brought this lady home. She ate with my family, drank with my family and one day? She moved in.

'I was six years old and . . . this lady was, like, magical. She made everything all right for her *bambino*. We lived in this beautiful home, in a secure compound with guards and guns. But hidden in the building at the far corner, there were other things going on that I didn't know about. The men who worked for Mama – her servants, her goons, her guinea pigs? This lady would explain away these creeps. The guy with the twisted spine would walk around with his head tilted sideways, raising his eyes up to you to talk. He scared the shit out of me. Mama would get crazy if she heard me cry out. So this lady – Remy was her name – my Remy would hold me in her arms and rock me and she would say:

There was a crooked man
And he walked a crooked mile . . .

'And it just made it OK for me. It was like a game. Her little rhymes made everything seem like a fairy tale, made these men seem just like characters who had something in them that was good, something we could smile at.

'My father was a monster. He would provoke me like I was an animal. And then he would disappear. For weeks on end. One day Remy was there with me when I had to watch him leave. She said to me:

As I was walking up the stair
I met a man who wasn't there

'And a few days later, I was able to finish it:

He wasn't there again today
I wish, I wish he'd stay away.

'I'll never forget it. And I'll never forget my Remy. You guys don't change your names too much, right? You need to be able to turn your head and respond at the right time, right? Ren. Remy. Ren. Remy.

'So, how are we all doing? You and your fake dead baby. Me and my real gone father. You and your fake name, your fake job, your fake sad, tragic fucking life . . .' He shrugged. 'No wonder the stories you told me were so . . . imaginative.'

Ren got up and left the room. *My little Gavino Bambino Val Pando.*

65

Ren made it down the dark hallway of the prison, then started to run. And run. By the time she got to the Sheriff's Office, her breath was heaving. She made it into the bathroom, locked the door and collapsed on to the floor. Tears streamed down her face, soaking her shirt, wetting the tiles beneath her cheek. She lost control of the terrible, wrenching sobs. She paused to draw breath and could hear someone pounding on the door.

'Ren, open up. Ren, please. You need to open up. Let me in.' It was Gary.

Group One undercover employees are cut off completely from their regular life for as long as it takes them to safely do their job. Each UCE has a contact agent; ten years ago, Gary Dettling was Ren's. Her colleagues then – and now – never knew. Paul Louderback never knew. Only a panel of senior FBI agents in Headquarters knew. Including Jeff Warwick and Tim Monahan.

'Ren, come on,' said Gary. 'Please. This is not good. Please let me in.'

Ren waited, but he didn't go away. She dragged herself to her knees and half crawled to the door. She managed to open it. Gary pushed in and locked it behind him. He knelt down beside her and took her in his arms. She let him.

When she calmed down, he finally spoke.

'Your call, Ren. Can you do this?'

She looked up at him. 'Yes.'

Ren sat again in front of Monahan and Warwick. She was wearing a fresh shirt that Gary had brought for her from the trunk of her Jeep.

'I want to know,' she said, 'how Gavino Val Pando found me. Because I know Billy Waites had nothing to do with it.'

'It was Domenica Val Pando's minions that tracked you down,' said Warwick.

Ren stood up and slammed her fists on the desk and shouted louder than even she expected.

'I brought you Domenica Val Pando,' she said. 'You know the history. And in twenty-four hours, you blew it. And now that bitch . . . Jesus.'

No one spoke.

Ren held Tim Monahan's stare. 'I knew Domenica Val Pando like no other agent could have ever gotten to know her. I know the brand of strip wax her facialist uses on her. I know that, in spite of her cellulite, she wears only g-strings. Her plastic surgeon is French. I know who the real father of her son is. And after one memorable evening, I know what the inside of her fucking mouth tastes like and what her left hand feels like on my right breast – two details that may not have made it into my reports, but by your faces, are clearly working now to illustrate my point.' She flung her arms in the air. 'But what the fuck do I know?'

Monahan glanced down at his notes. 'I will remind you why you needed to be removed for your own safety. Two boys, Enrique Caltano, Paulo Salinas –'

The images returned, the faces swelled by humidity, the ugly, haunting looks. 'Boys?' said Ren. 'Boys? Those *boys* were old enough to rape Domenica Val Pando, to hold me down and make me watch. Old enough to play drinking games to decide who would take me first. Old enough to toss a coin to work out which way. And old enough to be . . . stopped before they got the chance.'

'You certainly stopped them.'

'I certainly did,' said Ren. 'I certainly did not want to be raped. I certainly did not like how the coin fell. And I certainly remember being told when I trained for this job that no criminal was more important than the life of an agent.'

'And you still think you shouldn't have been pulled out?'

'Yes – I still believe that,' said Ren. 'Everyone knows it was a fuck-up. Everyone. Not just me.'

'They didn't need to die,' said Monahan.

'*Two* of them were killed,' said Ren. 'Their buddy, the third guy, who arrived in as it was all over – he let me go. He told me to run. He had a gun, but he still let me go.'

Gary glanced at Monahan and back at Ren.

'We had to pull you out, Ren,' said Monahan. 'We knew your life was in danger. We knew the rival gang was planning the attack on Val Pando's compound.'

'If you had informed me of that, I could have done something, I could have stayed, helped her to –'

'Ren,' said Warwick, 'even with all your skills, the skills that got you handed this assignment at such a young age in the first place, you were still there on the ground with a boot to your head while Domenica Val Pando was being raped. She was looking you in the eye. That is a psychological time bomb. If you stayed, that woman would have bonded with you and you with her so deeply –'

Ren stood up. 'Please, listen to me, all of you. Nobody deserves what happened to Domenica Val Pando that night. Nobody. But bond with her? No. Domenica Val Pando is a vile human being; a trafficker of women, children, drugs and arms, someone who was about to make a move into chem-bio to sell to the highest bidder, a person just . . . absent of anything. You cannot bond with that –'

'In a weakened psychological state –' said Monahan.

'Nobody listened to me!' said Ren. 'You cannot bond with something that is constantly mutating. But if you're really good? You can fake it. But nobody listened. All you need for evil to triumph is that good men don't fucking listen.'

'We were concerned for your safety and your sanity . . .' said Monahan.

'Sanity is bullshit.'

Gary could smile because no one was looking at him.

'I'm serious,' said Ren. 'People prize sanity because of how much they fear *in*sanity. Sanity is like happiness; it comes, it goes, it feels good, it means one thing to me, something else to someone else, but, boy, do we all want it. So bad. It's what keeps people showing up in shrinks' offices every day all over the world. It's like paying a weekly subscription to the Sanity Club. And all that happens there is a lot of talk. Well, screw that. It's all wrapped up in negativity. And losing: lose your grip, lose the plot, lose perspective. Do I seem like a loser to you guys?'

'Calm down, Ren,' said Gary. 'Sit down.'

'The fuck I will.'

'Come on,' said Gary. 'Sit down. No one thinks you're a loser.'

Ren sat down and let her head hang. She ran her fingers through her hair and looked up. 'I'm sorry, OK? I didn't realize I still . . . I'm . . . Bottom line? You really fucked me over. I left Domenica Val Pando, violated by two different men in many different ways, lying with her seven-year-old son in their own waste, both their screams carrying through the trees behind me as I ran. The last thing she saw of me was my sweat-soaked back in my white Donna Karan silk shirt. And because of you, we never saw each other again. To Domenica Val Pando, I had been physically there to kill those guys, but I deserted her emotionally when it mattered most. I was so fucking good, you assholes, that it probably broke her fucking heart.'

Warwick paused. 'Do you recognize this man?' He threw down a color photo on the table, a Latino in his early twenties.

'The third guy,' said Ren. 'The one who let me get away.'

Warwick nodded. 'Mario LaQuestra.'

Warwick threw down another photo; a naked corpse, black, bloated and stripped of any way of identifying gender, race or age. Ren looked up at Warwick.

'Him again,' said Warwick. 'The first photo is from ten years ago, taken around the time of the rape. He was, in fact, twenty-eight years old, but looked younger, like the other boys. Second photo?

Taken one month ago, when his body was found. He had probably been dead six months. He had been tortured. They left a nice snuff movie behind.'

Ren's face was impassive.

'He was an agent, Ren,' said Monahan.

'What?'

'Mario LaQuestra was Agent Maurice Gallardo, worked out of the Nevada office.'

'Jesus Christ,' said Ren.

'He was deep cover with the gang that stormed Val Pando's that night. Like you, he got out of the undercover program shortly afterwards, but he left the Bureau. He was working as an accountant. But they caught up with him.'

Ren could feel her stomach tightening. 'Did he know ten years ago that I was an agent?'

'Yes,' said Warwick. 'He was informed before he went in. That's how he knew to let you go.'

'And . . . he was tortured six months ago . . .' said Ren. 'So they could find out about me.'

'Yes,' said Warwick. 'I'm afraid so.'

66

Ren and Gary walked down the steps of the Sheriff's Office.

'I'm sorry, Gary . . . about Billy Waites,' said Ren.

'Jesus Christ, Ren.' He shook his head. 'He better show up like a shiny new pin. For the first time in a long time, I don't know what to do. I'm in a serious situation here and I don't know what to do. I don't know how far I have to roll with this. Where is Billy Waites? Why did he run? Is he about to go on a rampage? How much does he know? Am I going to be on the witness stand recounting the dumbest fucking conversation I had with you that day in my office when we talked around the whole thing and I sent you to Glenwood? Jesus, Ren. Tell me – what would you do right now? What's your advice?'

'What would *I* do?' said Ren. 'Well, I would be ignored, wouldn't I? My advice would be ignored anyway.'

'What the hell is that supposed to mean?' said Gary.

'Domenica Val Pando!'

'Ren, you're going to have to deal with that. Really deal with it.'

'Deal with it? These psychopaths are after me and I'm supposed to . . .' She shrugged. 'Jesus. I don't know *what* I'm supposed to do.'

'Ren, you're the safest you could be right now,' said Gary.

'I'm going to go with that, Gary, because I'm feeling a little tired. Even though I know it is total and utter bullshit.'

He said nothing.

'I am sorry, though,' said Ren. 'I . . . but I do know Billy is a good person.'

'Do you hear how naïve you sound?'

'Yes, I do hear that. But that doesn't mean that I am actually *being* naïve. I know you're angry at me. And I understand that. But . . . please. Can you trust my judgment?'

'Can *you* trust your judgment?'

'That's not fair.'

'I apologize. But damn you. I'm mad as hell.' He stopped. 'And tell me about Erubiel Diaz,' said Gary. 'The guy shows up in hospital almost debilitated with no marks except for abrasions to the inner thighs and knees. His statement says, "Some guy jumped on me, poked me in the neck and the face, did some weird shit to my stomach and my privates . . ."'

Ren slowed, then stopped. 'Hmm. Offhand? Sounds to me like Erubiel Diaz was loitering in the parking lot of the Brockton Filly with intent. He may have been wearing baggy work-out pants to conceal a Velcro-fastening groin guard. I would guess that an unsporting man like Mr Diaz would be wearing such protection only because he intended to rape a woman – a slight-looking, though deceptively strong brunette – who he expected to instinctively go for his "privates" to fend him off: his genital area would be covered, yet quickly exposed when he needed it to be. Which is why, in fact, the FBI trains us to collapse the knee of an assailant, so his own weight can be used as a weapon against him. Which leads me back to Mr Diaz. I'm guessing he received a downward kick to the left knee, which felled him. I believe his mention of "being poked" is related to pressure point jabs to the neck and face. Ouch. As for the abrasions to his inner thighs, it sounds to me like his groin guard was forcibly removed – to reveal a tiny penis – by either the woman he tried to attack or the "man" he says jumped on him . . .'

Gary rubbed his face. 'Jesus Christ Almighty.'

'The attacker at least drove him to the hospital, while avoiding the security cameras.'

'Lucky for us, Mr Diaz does not want to press charges,' said Gary.

'And who would he press charges against?'

Gary shook his head. 'Jesus Christ, is all I can say.'

They walked on in silence.

'Don't you feel bad when they talk like that, Warwick and Monahan?' said Ren. 'When they think all UCEs get really close to the bad guys? I'm like, shit, I'm not actually getting too tied up with these dirtbags. I couldn't give a shit about them.'

He looked at her like she was nuts. 'And then there's little Gavino Val Pando . . .'

That night, Ren sat on the sofa in her suite, reading the same trash she'd tried to read the last time. There was a knock on the internal door that led down to the hot tub.

Weird. 'Yes?'

'Ren?'

'Yes.' She started to get up.

'It's Billy.'

She walked to the door and opened it.

'Can I come in?'

'Of course you can.'

'I'm sorry. I thought the outside door would be watched.'

'I'm not that important,' she said, smiling.

'Maybe they think I am,' he said. 'I don't know what they think now.'

They sat on opposite ends of the sofa.

They talked their way around all the questions

they wanted to ask each other. They let the same playlist play on a loop – plaintive music, beautiful lyrics. There was a sweet, awkward silence.

'Billy,' said Ren, 'this is terrible and I don't know how to say it . . . but I guess I owe it to you. I know it's not right, but I guess, I've wondered all along if you were . . .'

He waited. 'Say it.'

'Playing me.'

Billy frowned. 'What, like I had other chicks on the –'

'Well, that too, if I'm honest,' said Ren. 'But no – just that maybe you wanted something else from me. An FBI agent to, you know, cover your . . .'

She was not prepared for the hurt in his face.

He turned away, shaking his head slowly. 'But, I've never even . . . why would you think that?'

'I . . .'

'Paranoia,' he answered for her.

'But look at how you came to be what you are . . .' *Oh no.*

'What the hell does that mean?' He stood up.

'Well . . . drugs. Dealing. And wire taps. And codes. I'm sorry, but what do you expect?'

'Shit, I don't know – that someone who fucks me might give a shit. Might, maybe, trust me.'

'*Fucks* you?' said Ren.

'Don't go there,' said Billy. 'Don't get all Little

Miss Shocked, so you can throw this back at me. You can *choose* your reactions, Ren. And your reaction to *fucked* is usually a pretty big smile.' He reached out and held up her chin. 'Look at me. Look. At. Me.'

She raised her head.

'Do you want to know what you really saw hiding behind my eyes? I'll tell you the truth, Ren. If you can handle it.'

'OK. I like the truth.'

He smiled. 'I know that. So here it is. You looked at me and what you saw was . . . fear.' He let out a breath. 'Because I always knew you would go.'

Ren opened her mouth. 'But –'

'I felt like you were on loan to me,' said Billy. 'It was like driving a Maserati on vacation across some exotic country.' He let out a breath. 'But no one can be on vacation forever.'

A tear fell down Ren's cheek.

'I've nothing to lose here,' said Billy. 'So I want you to know that I . . .'

She held her hand to his lips. 'Don't love me, Billy. Please don't. I can't handle it.'

'Hey, neither can I. I'm like those women who write to Jeffrey Dahmer.'

Ren laughed loud. '*How* can you make me laugh? Jesus.'

Billy smiled. 'I *want* you to laugh.'

'Thank you,' said Ren.

'So stop beating yourself up,' he said.

'You are wonderful, Billy. Fuck the drugs, the violence . . .'

He smiled.

'You put up with a lot of shit to be with me,' said Ren.

'I saw *you*. And I love *you*.' He held a hand to her cheek.

'I really wish I didn't associate you with something I shouldn't be doing,' said Ren. 'I wish you never came mixed with guilt and worry and secrets. It breaks my heart. But I can't change that. All I can do is tell you that . . .'

'That . . .'

'I loved you, Billy. As much as I could.' Tears streamed down her face.

'Thank you,' said Billy. 'You've been the best vacation I've ever had.'

'And you've given me the best hotels.'

67

The summer rain in Denver always emptied quickly and heavily from black clouds. Ren ran from the Jeep into the old red-brick building, ten minutes late for her appointment. She was dressed in a pink tracksuit, no makeup.

There was no one at the reception desk. The waiting room was empty, the tables scattered with obscure magazines on crafts and interiors. Ren picked one up – how to liven up denim with prints of the Great Masters. There was a small photo on the cover of a girl with the *Mona Lisa* down the leg of her jeans. *Jesus Christ.*

A grim-faced woman came out from the room behind the desk. Ren had a small flash of irritation. She was replacing the regular receptionist, the one that could make Ren feel better just by her presence.

'Who are you here to see?' said the woman, without bothering to look up. There were two offices off the waiting area – dermatologist and psychiatrist.

Breakouts/breakdowns.

'Dr Helen Wheeler,' said Ren.

'Pardon me?'

'Dr Helen Wheeler.'

The woman finally looked up. 'Oh. Dr Wheeler's gone for the evening.'

'I . . . are you sure? I really need to see her. I . . .' . . . *don't think I will make it through the night.*

The woman gave her a God-bless-the-mentally-ill smile.

Bad sparks flew.

'Hey, Ren,' said Helen, walking into the waiting room.

Ren glanced at the receptionist and back at Helen. 'Hi, Helen. Sorry I'm late.'

Helen led her into the office and closed the door. 'Well . . . finally you make it back in to me.'

'Yes,' said Ren. 'Being forced by Gary Dettling had nothing to do with it . . .'

Helen smiled. 'Well, whatever it takes, I guess. Sit down. How are you holding up?'

Ren didn't speak.

'Do you want to talk about what happened?' said Helen.

'No,' said Ren, drawing out the vowel.

'That's OK,' said Helen.

'Agent in not-talking-about-shooting shocker.'

'Yes,' said Helen. 'I may have come across that before.'

'But you've broken them all down, right? Every time.'

Helen smiled. 'You bet.'

They sat in silence for twenty minutes.

'OK,' said Ren. 'I left Vincent. I left Billy. I was faced with the failure of a massive investigation. A long-dead case, responsible for me almost losing my mind, has come back to haunt me. I miss Vincent. I cannot believe what happened to Jean Transom. I can't believe there are people out there who do that kind of shit. And I can't believe how easy it is for me not to have a flicker of emotion about any of it.' She burst into tears.

Helen let her cry. She handed her a Kleenex. She didn't watch the clock.

'I . . . I'm sorry,' said Ren. 'I . . .'

'Don't be,' said Helen.

'I feel like everything is falling apart.'

'Why do you feel that?'

'Everyone who comes near me is hurt or dies. '

'Ren,' said Helen gently, 'that is not true.'

'It is. I ruin everything. I drag people down.'

Ren cried harder.

'I understand how it could appear that way right now,' said Helen. 'You've been through a lot. And you probably have been running on empty for quite some time.'

Ren nodded.

'You have done a great job, Ren. You set out to solve this case. And you achieved that. And you solved another case that you weren't even assigned to.'

'Yeah, because *that's* professional, getting side-tracked.'

'Ren, everyone gets sidetracked at work. We just don't all end up arresting people as a result.'

Ren laughed. 'I need another Kleenex.'

Helen handed her one. 'You can't keep beating yourself up.'

'Watch me.'

'I don't want to. I want you to get better. Maybe we need to take a look at how you've been.'

Ren stared at the floor. 'No, thank you.'

'Do you think you may have felt your trust slipping away?'

'I'm an FBI agent,' said Ren, deadpan.

Helen smiled, 'Seriously.'

'I'm not paranoid, OK? People *were* out to get me . . .'

'Everyone? Were they? Didn't you express concerns about Paul, Billy, even Vincent at one point . . .'

'But they were all hiding things.'

'They weren't out to get you, though. There was no big conspiracy to wreck your career or your life.'

'Yeah, well, sometimes it didn't feel that way.'

'I understand that.'

'Don't I need to be a little paranoid to do my job?' said Ren.

'Maybe, but in the rest of your life? No. And they're all tied up together. Can you see that?'

'Anyway,' said Ren, 'everyone has two sides. Jean Transom: two people. Malcolm Wardwell: two people. Jason Wardwell, Billy Waites, Paul Louderback . . .'

'I don't know who all those people are, but . . .'

'I'll take myself as I am and –'

'Yes – sometimes you're so happy you'll explode and then . . . the dark side. Can you see how that brings you down?'

'I'm on an even keel right now.'

Helen looked at her.

'I am. Stop. I'm fine.' Tears flowed down her face.

'There's no middle ground for you, Ren. Can you see that?'

'Stop asking me can I see things.'

'Either someone loves you or hates you,' said Helen. 'There's no room for someone just to be annoyed at you. Or to maybe be frustrated. Most people operate somewhere in the middle of the spectrum, not at either end, Ren.'

'Yeah, well, that's why it's called bi-polar . . .' *Shit*.

Helen waited.

'Ren, you know you have a condition . . .'

'Ah,' said Ren, 'that explains why I never get

unconditional love.' She stood up. 'I've got to go. Thank you.'

Helen slid back in her chair and stood up. 'Are you OK?'

'I will be,' said Ren. She pointed at the prescription pad and the pen in Helen's hand. 'I don't want meds right now. But I promise I'll come back if I do. And I give you my permission to call Gary and check in with him. And whatever he says, I'll go along with that.'

Helen paused. 'OK, Ren. I'm going to go with you on this.'

'Thank you. And don't worry – I have a plan.' She smiled. 'Like most lunatics.'

Helen smiled. 'What kind of plan?'

'To meet up with a friend. So I can be the one who takes care of someone for a change.'

68

Ren drove through Clear Creek County and thought of the crooked man ripped apart and discarded in the river. Domenica Val Pando had gone to his family, taken his mother's hands in hers and promised them she would take care of his medical expenses if he came to work for her. And ten years later, he lay, still twisted, on a cold slab.

Did Gavino ever stand a chance? In such a cosseted world, he had no chance to fight what he had been born into. The night the compound was stormed, Ren had watched him from her hiding place in the woods. He was seven years old and his mother had hidden him in the undergrowth so she could be free to leave with 'the man who wasn't there'. Gavino had turned to Ren, his eyes wide, reaching out a shaking hand, the tiny little fingers moving like he was playing the piano. *Oh, God. I want to save you so bad.* Ren had put her finger to her lips and slowly shook her head.

There are too many victims of too many decisions: bring a baby boy into your screwed-up world, lose your business for your meth-addicted daughter, turn your back on your alcoholic son. Domenica Val Pando, Gavino Val Pando; Charlie Barger, Shannon Barger; Diane Wilson, Mark Allen Wilson . . .

Ren's meeting with Warwick and Monahan was like a wound re-opened, a vivid flashback of that final night. And the fire that raged. Ren had seen men in flames that night, fleeing from all the buildings screaming: the same men she used to see shuffling around the compound, blistered and blackened and scarred; all victims of Domenica Val Pando's whims.

Ren was hit with a sudden and violent nausea. She lost the sense of what foot should hit what pedal. Her mind was telling her to brake, to stop everything from moving. But the stronger part had her slam her foot on the accelerator and speed toward Breckenridge.

I always knew there was a bigger picture.

Bob Gage was waiting in reception for her when she arrived in. She didn't stop, just kept moving toward his office. All she managed on the way was:

'Please tell me Mike is not here.'

'No . . . his little boy's ill,' said Bob.

'Oh, no,' said Ren. 'Will he be OK?'

'I think so.'

'What happened to him?'

'Oh, he's the little guy with the health prob-lems. He had some kind of asthma attack last night, Mike brought him to Charlie Barger, but he wasn't home, so they had to go to the hospital. He's OK now, though.'

'I'm afraid Charlie Barger won't be home any time soon,' said Ren.

'What? Why?'

'Charlie Barger was working for Domenica Val Pando. And I'm betting, with the attention Gavino brought down on the operation, Charlie Barger no longer is. Because I'm guessing Domenica Val Pando took care of him and his daughter, Shannon.'

'What?' said Bob.

Ren nodded. 'There is always a bigger picture with Domenica Val Pando. Robberies are not just robberies, drugs are not just drugs, even people are not just people to her. I realized yesterday when I was shouting at my bosses that I knew, from . . . previous research, that Val Pando was moving into chem-bio weapons. And the night her compound was destroyed, the lab work was destroyed and the scientists she had hired were either killed or scared enough to disappear.

'Since she's been gone, 9/11 happened and the

market for chem-bio weapons has shot up – nationally and internationally. And she's logically going for where the money is. And where she can sit back and watch all the chaos.'

Bob was staring at her.

'Charlie Barger wasn't making beer, Bob. He was using the brewery to make hydrogen sulfide. The day we found Mark Wilson's body in the grounds of the brewery, there was a terrible smell in the air like rotten eggs – that's what H_2S smells like. We taped off a reasonable-sized crime scene around the body, but the building was a ways away, so we didn't formally search it. I had a look around, though, and I saw a pallet of nitrogen tanks.

'Anyway, I called Colin Grabien on my way over here to go through Charlie Barger's financial records. I heard what was going out of his account – and I'm thinking, OK, a pallet of nitrogen tanks, the guy is brewing beer, you need nitrogen for that. Then I hear, hold on – another pallet. And another. And another. And soon we realize that Charlie Barger has bought four pallets, each with twenty tanks.'

Bob stayed silent.

'OK,' said Ren, 'no one needs that much nitrogen for brewing. But he could have been draining the nitrogen out and replacing it with H_2S, and there it is – ready to be shipped all over the place with a nice shiny nitrogen label.

'Even our shitty friend, Erubiel Diaz, was involved.

The manure in his truck was being delivered to the brewery. The bacteria that create H_2S are put in a vat – the same kind you brew beer in – manure is added and, when the bacteria feed off it, they release H_2S.'

'I'm sorry to stop you, Ren, but I'm not getting the H_2S thing,' said Bob.

'H_2S is a gas that kills instantly. And it's odorless. In small concentrations, you'll get the smell of rotten eggs, but even then it's probably too late, especially in a non-ventilated space. For most people, their first breath of H_2S is their last.

'All you would need is for a guy to slap on an HVAC uniform, get a couple of tanks labeled nitrogen through a hotel lobby, into a bank, into wherever, and they're good to go. You can direct it through vents into whatever room you want it to go into. It is an instant – mass – killer.

'It is one of the scariest chem-bio weapons out there. It could be rolled out all over the country for a simultaneous attack on cities – whatever Domenica Val Pando or the people she is supplying feel like doing with it.'

'And Charlie Barger is the guy manufacturing it?'

'This is Domenica Val Pando. She went for the best. She researched him and he came up fairly high on the list of people she could use. Because he would also know how to bio-engineer the bacteria to make it all even more powerful.

'Charlie Barger was a desperate man, Bob. She found his strengths – he is a world-renowned bio-chemist – and she exploited his weakness: his financial problems. His father was this huge success whose shadow he has always stood in. Charlie Barger comes back to Breckenridge after a successful career all around the world. And here he is, four hundred and fifty thousand dollars in debt. But a month ago he was five hundred thousand in debt.' She shrugged.

'Jesus,' said Bob.

'I know,' said Ren. 'And we didn't know at the time, but when we found Mark Wilson's body in the grounds, we put a stop to the whole oper-ation by swarming around the brewery. We'll never know, but I'd say Charlie Barger roped Wilson in to working there – he knew he had no money and was in debt. Those vats need to be monitored all the time – it's a delicate process. And maybe Mark Wilson was supposed to be there that afternoon instead of getting shitfaced at the Filly.

'I think it was back in action as recently as two weeks ago, until Gavino Val Pando decides to go flash some stolen cash at the chicks in the Filly. He was blessed with his father's brains. Augusto Val Pando operated on a primal level: eat, fight, fuck. I guess the potential for fucking is what fucked Gavino.'

'What about the brewery?' said Bob.

'A HazMat team is on the way,' said Ren. 'I don't

think Barger got as far as Domenica Val Pando would have liked in the manufacturing, but we can't risk it. As far as the press are concerned, we're shutting down a meth lab. And with Shannon Barger's tragic history, no one's going to question that.'

'Jesus Christ,' said Bob.

'I know,' said Ren. 'Anyway, the team will be in touch with you any minute now. They'll be the ones to go to Barger's house too. So all you need to do is sit tight. And prepare to tell Casey Bonaventure some nice lies.' She stood up.

'Thanks, Ren.'

'My pleasure.'

Ren got into the Jeep and clung to the steering wheel, her head bowed. *Get your shit together.* She pulled out of the parking lot, did a tour of the roundabout and drove to Frisco under a dusky sky.

Gary had once said to her, 'I swear Domenica Val Pando has an island somewhere where she breeds those fucked-up goons.'

Ren disagreed. *She just breaks into your nightmares and takes out the very worst parts – right at the black peak that wakes you up screaming – and she crosses them with an animal that, for a fraction of a second, can convince you he's a man.*

Epilogue

Ren walked the polished steps and shiny hallways up to the third floor of the beige brick building. Denis Lasco was on a call when she arrived in to his office. He put down the phone.

'Hello, Ren.' He was shaking his head, checking his watch. 'You know, you think you are going to have a nice easy evening and now I hear that two bodies have been found in a house in Breckenridge.'

'Ridge Street?' said Ren. 'Older male, younger female, GSW?'

Lasco frowned. 'Yes. Did you flee the scene?' He smiled.

'I guess you could say that. But that's not why I'm here.'

He rolled his chair back and turned it toward her. 'Sit down. I'm surprised to see you here after everything.'

She sat on the edge of his desk. 'Well, I have a favor to ask of you. A couple of favors, actually.'

'Sure, go ahead.'

'You know what you said about those greedy people who show up and take stuff when their relatives die? I was wondering if . . . if I told you a little story, you might like to help me out.'

Ren tied the little white headphones around her rear-view mirror and let the shiny pink iPod shuffle swing in the sunlight; two hundred and fifty songs, a personality preserved in music. She thought of Salem Swade and his eighteen-year-old smile and his perfect uniform and his shaved head and his heavy boots and his blown-apart hopes and his lost friends and his thirteen meds and his free breakfasts and his pale eyes and his skinny shoulders and his big, tortured heart.

She pulled out on to the highway. She was going the wrong way for Glenwood. She pushed her foot down on the accelerator, passing all the cars that wanted to slow her down.

Vincent. Paul. Billy . . . a complex tangle of emotions. Throughout her life, tiny threads had come together, wrapped around each other, twisted, frayed and unraveled. She glanced at herself in the mirror and saw eyes trying to harden. *What is wrong with you?*

Then she felt something at her neck – a warm, gentle comfort. She smiled, reaching her hand back, rubbing the soft, black, furry jaw.

Misty, take it easy. No barking. I'm not dead yet.

Acknowledgments

My first thank you, as always, goes to my agent Darley Anderson and the outstanding team at the Darley Anderson Literary, TV and Film Agency.

He is an editor, a publishing director, a cheer-leader: he is the one and only Wayne Brookes. Love you loads.

Thank you to Amanda Ridout, Lynne Drew, Moira Reilly, Tony Purdue and everyone at HarperCollins for their support and commitment.

Thanks to Anne O'Brien for her razor-sharp copy-editing.

I am, as always, blown away by the experts who take the time to help me with my research, not just for the information given, but also the welcome, the kindness and the hospitality.

Very special thanks go to SSA Phil Niedringhaus – I couldn't have done it without you. And thank you to everyone at the FBI Rocky Mountain Safe Streets Task Force.

Thank you to George Fong, Unit Chief for the Safe Streets and Gang Unit at FBI Headquarters, for making it all possible.

Thank you to Special Agent Rene Vonder Haar for co-ordinating my visit.

Thank you to Special Agent Kenneth Jackson from the Glenwood Springs RA . . . and to his family for their warm welcome.

At the Summit County Sheriff's Office, big thank you to Sheriff John Minor from the capital of Ireland; Undersheriff Derek Woodman; and Captain – Operations, Jaime FitzSimons.

Thank you to Summit County Coroner, Joanne Richardson, aka "the deadchick".

Many thanks to Andy, Niki and Robin Harris from the gorgeous Fireside Inn in Breckenridge. No prizes for guessing the inspiration for the Firelight Inn.

Thank you also to Otto Appenzeller MD., Ph.D.;

Joan M. Brehm, Illinois Search Dogs Inc.; Professor Marie Cassidy; Glen Kraatz, Mission Coordinator, Summit County Rescue Group; Elliott I. Moorhead; Luke Pally, David Siderfin, Silverthorne PD; Phil Walter, Special Agent, FBI (retired).

Thank you to my family who are a constant source of inspiration and guidance. You mean more to me than any acknowledgment can ever say.

For fun and games, friendship and support, thank you to Kefi Chadwick, Damien DB, Maggie Deas, Gerry Fahey, Ian Fahey (awesome), Sue Booth-Forbes, Matthew Higgins, Chris (Rex) Lander and Scott Lander, Ger McDonnell, Leah McDonnell (awesome), Mary Maddison, Aideen and Brendan Mulligan, Joan Murphy, Vanessa O'Loughlin, Anna Philips, Julie and Ronan Sheridan in da house, Maureen and Donal O'Sullivan and family inc. the wonderful Louise.

To Mauser and Little Dick – you rock stars. And mind-erasers.

To everyone at The Copper Kettle – thanks for having me.

Finally, not everyone who helped me can be named. But you know who you are. And you know how much it means . . . seriously.